Amber Witch

R. S. Beck

Prospective Press
Winston-Salem

PROSPECTIVE PRESS LLC
1959 Peace Haven Rd, #246, Winston-Salem, NC 27106 U.S.A.
www.prospectivepress.com

Published in the United States of America by PROSPECTIVE PRESS LLC

TRADEMARK

AMBER WITCH

Cover photography by Paige L. Christie

Cover and interior design by ARTE RAVE

ISBN 978-1-943419-77-7

Second PROSPECTIVE PRESS trade paperback edition

Printed in the United States of America
First printing, September, 2018
Second printing, November, 2018

The text of this book is typeset in Vollkorn
Accent text is typeset in Uncial Antiqua

PUBLISHER'S NOTE

This book is a work of fiction. The people, names, characters, locations, activities, and events portrayed or implied by this book are the product of the author's imagination or are used fictitiously. Any resemblance to actual people, locations, and events is strictly coincidental. No actual witches were harmed in the writing of this novel.

Contents

Dress Rehearsal 1
Uncovered Relative 6
More Questions Than Answers 17
Small Town Surprises 28
It's Just Glass 42
Gran Expectations 49
Invitations 55
Searching for Answers 64
A Forced Invitation 69
The Manor Farm 74
The Gardener's Secret 87
House Arrest 96
Abbey Secrets 106
Cast Off 112
Echoes of Home 118
Kid Gloves 125
Grandma's Treasures 138
In Gran's Words 144
Sleeplessness 151
Gran's Obligation 155
Family Shift 162
Doubles 184
A Woman's Wiles 189
Awkward Conversations 199
Lowered Facades 206
Heated Questions 211
Confounded 214
A Wrong Turn 221
Foul Moods 228
It's All Relative 234
Curious Reprieve 243
Perspective 248
Awkward Questions 251
The Return Call 258
Legal Rights 265
Deadly Secrets 272
The Wrong Foot 277
Finally Some Honesty 282
Feeling Ill 289
Leap of Faith 295
Decisions 302
Blood Debt 306
Biding Time 314
Cheating Fate 320
What If? 327

Dedication

To Linda Jaroszewicz VanNostrand —
the best childhood friends are never forgotten
or far from our hearts

and

In loving memory of my own Edy and Suzy,
two women who taught me everything in life
that was truly important.

Acknowledgements

There are many people I need to thank.

To Becky Secrest, my family away from family, who has given me limitless love, encouragement, countless meals, and her time to not only read this novel once but repeatedly.

Many thanks to my writing partners, Paige L. Christie and Ellen Morrissey. Together we crafted and slashed thousands of words, laughed, and supported each other throughout the writing process. The value of late night conversations, tough love, boundless energy, sometimes tears, and sisterhood cannot be underestimated. Together we are stronger; together we rise.

To Jason T. Graves for his guidance and attention to the smallest details in order to make the best version of this book possible. I especially appreciate your generosity in allowing me to have choices within the process. I have learned much from you.

And finally, my husband, Jerry, who knows how to tiptoe when I am "in" the scene. His selflessness, boundless love, understanding, and sacrifices helped me become who I always needed to be. I love you dearly and look forward to a lifetime of adventures with you.

1

Dress Rehearsal

The dog let loose a stream of urine on the leading man's pant leg, and the stage manager howled in response. Kat choked back laughter as she watched the ensuing chase, dog not done, spraying everywhere.

"Oh my God, if someone doesn't loosen my corset I may pass out!" Kat doubled over in pain. Unable to contain her laughter, she wondered if her ribs could break from the pressure. Kat gulped air, trying to slow the convulsions.

Marcy stood nearby, shaking with anger. Kat watched as Marcy tried to control the shudder that shook her body, arms tight at her sides, hands awkwardly twitching. "I don't know how you can think this is funny?" She said from between clenched teeth.

Kat stared at her for a moment, mute, as she tried to regain her composure. Using the back of her hand to smother a smile, she coughed to clear her throat and tugged at the end of her lace-edged sleeve to stall for time.

"Seriously, Marcy, no worries, it's only dress rehearsal. It'll be fine."

"How can you say that?" Marcy's eyes bulged. "Do you even comprehend how many things have gone wrong—one night before we open? One!" Marcy punctuated with a finger.

Marcy was manic and panicked. Kat knew she would have to say or do something to calm the madly pulsing vein on Marcy's forehead.

"Now, Marcy, isn't it supposed to be good luck if the dress rehearsal is terrible? I know I've heard that before. Yes, that's it! A great dress rehearsal means trouble ahead, but a bad dress rehearsal is lucky." Kat forced a broad smile on her face.

Marcy looked sideways at Kat like she were the village idiot. Kat hadn't seen her this angry since her divorce.

"No." Marcy's disdain was clear as she slowly enunciated each word. "You want a great dress rehearsal—because then that means I get some fucking sleep tonight!"

When Marcy stomped off, Kat exhaled a huge breath she hadn't realized she'd been holding.

"Don't worry about her. She loves the tension." Tara had inched up beside Kat when she hadn't been paying attention. "She just hates that you can laugh at it. She has to create a fiery, ulcerous pit in her stomach to know she's done all she can do. Just stay clear of her for a while, and she'll twist someone else's head off tonight."

"That can't be good for her."

"It's not," Tara continued, while biting into a carrot from the snack bag she always carried. "But that's how she feels important. She needs to yell, panic, and then save the day. I swear she set the dog up to pee just to have something new to stress over. Her mom was high-strung like that, too. You know, like your mom."

"Yeah, don't remind me. Anyway, I'm going home; I am done for the night. My scenes are over, thank God."

"Are you sure? Sure you don't want to check in with 'Her Majesty'?"

"Brian? Hell no! He's more drama than Marcy." Kat tugged on her bodice. "Help me out of this corset, will ya? I'm suffocating. I've had enough. Plus, I have a paper I should work on some more tonight. I am so done."

"Uh oh, don't let Marcy know you care more about college than the play or she'll cast you as the family dog in the next production." Tara laughed.

"How about this—how about they stop casting dogs, and then getting upset when they act like dogs?" Kat squinted one eye while arching the other eyebrow.

"You've got a point there."

Kat tried to shake off the tension as she walked home, but Marcy stayed on her mind. She hoped that in a few days, definitely after opening night, Marcy would look back on this and laugh. Kat couldn't remember the last time Marcy had laughed, probably since before that creepy husband of hers was caught with the babysitter. Kat pulled up the collar of her barn jacket against the chill, night air. She shook out the few remaining hairpins and willed away the headache that was beginning to form. There had been too much noise, chaos, and crowding backstage to fully change out of costume. Relieved of the corset, she took a deep breath. Kat wrapped her arms across her chest to hold in the little bit of warmth the jacket provided. The brisk air whipped about her skirt, baring her legs, and sent prickling sensations of cold up the length of her body. Kat wistfully looked at the jeans she carried over one arm and sighed. She wished she'd taken the time to at least slide them on under her skirt. Thankfully, the short boots were of some comfort.

Kat hurried across the lawn of the town square and down the short landing to get home. The wind nearly pushed her through the doorway. She quickly pulled the door shut, tugging at the latch until she heard the click of the lock engaging. Kat made her way up the narrow stairs to the rooms over the antique shop. She kicked off the boots she'd loosened upon entering and shuffled off in her woolen socks to the kitchen to start a pot of tea.

Pacing to warm herself while she waited for the kettle to whistle, Kat's eyes scanned the apartment. The shop wasn't the only antique shop around here, and it showed. The windows needed replacing, and chipped sills revealed lead paint where the framing had split. The caulking she'd used earlier this week to fill the gaps did little to keep the panes from rattling when the wind tore through town as it did tonight. If she was to stay in these rooms, Kat would have to find the money to replace the windows. But was this what she wanted? Did she want to run an antique store in a po'dunk town for the rest of her life? Kat wished she could know for sure what was the right thing to do.

She shook herself. She couldn't and wouldn't think; she was too tired. Kat put the tea to steep, bringing the mug with her as she went into the other room to fill the tub. Her muscles ached as she twisted and turned, trying to loosen the knots that had settled in her shoulders. As she threw in some almond and oatmeal bath salts her mind wandered, jumping from topic to topic as it usually did when she badly needed sleep. As she drew in a deep whiff, she couldn't help but think in contrast about the actors and their penchant for musky perfumes.

The competing smells on stage were tough to wade through at times, and were only compounded by the heavily brocaded fabrics. Unfortunately, dry cleaning wasn't always possible—especially with the period pieces on loan from the shop. Kat had to sigh when she thought about the dress Sandy Sothersby had recently ruined with a spill of cheap cologne. She'd billed the theatre group, but at a reduced rate out of consideration to their small budget—and not too little consideration that this was a small town and to seem miserly and petty was far more costly to a reputation than the cost of one gown.

Stirring the bath water with one hand, Kat watched the steam further curl her already frizzy hair. She admonished herself that now was not the time to think of finances, the theatre, or life choices. There was enough daylight tomorrow to begin that nightmare. No, tonight she would unwind. Worry about profit margins and overhead could wait for later. Just thinking about the shop and cost statements made her neck re-knot in apprehension. Kat slid a foot into the hot water and sighed in pleasure. She'd been accused before of baking like a lobster in the tub, but Wayne didn't matter—shouldn't have mattered at all. She ignored his opinion then and would continue to do so, with pleasure.

Slowly Kat slid her body beneath the sudsy foam. Stretched almost to full length, submerged up to her chin, she sipped the dark breakfast tea and thought there were few things better in life than a claw-foot tub. Kat told herself to put all those wandering thoughts away to focus on the feeling of the tea warming her throat and the pleasant heat of the water. She closed her eyes, willing the day's cares and all thought to flit away like a steam tendril from the bath.

2

Uncovered Relative

Kat woke with a start—cold, so dreadfully cold. She realized she must have fallen asleep while bathing. Every inch of her body was cramped and achy. Kat shook herself with a start. Looking down she saw half the problem—there was no water left in the tub! Although, she thought, cold water might have been far worse. Reaching back behind herself to the bath-side chair, Kat swatted about in the air for her towel. After a moment or two of no luck, she turned around in the tub.

Kat's eyes widened. This was *not* her bathroom or her tub. Where the hell was she? Frantically, she grabbed the sides of the tub. Her gaze rapidly darting about, she tried to keep up with the startling differences from the room she had closed her eyes in last night. This was a far cry from the humble apartment over the antique shop. Narrow in width but high-ceilinged, this room boasted marble surfaces and ornate trimmings. A cherub held soap aloft in a gilt dish. A low fire burned in a grate at the far side of the room, probably the only thing, she realized, that saved her from freezing to death. Draped over a tufted footstool, not far from where she, too, had placed a chair in proximity to the tub, were what looked like blankets or bath sheets. Kat started to wheeze, recognizing the onset of a panic attack. Squeezing her eyes shut, she fought to control her breathing and hugged her arms to herself. There had to be an explanation, but as she racked her brain, she could think of none.

When she again opened her eyes, Kat slowly panned the room. She stretched to reach one of the cloths from the footstool. Kat tried awkwardly to grasp the end of a bath sheet while not totally removing herself from the tub. The awareness that all that stood between her and this strange place was the now cold, cast-iron tub made her shiver. Kat had barely gripped the edge of a towel when she heard the door behind her open. Yanking with all her might, she hastily draped the cloth over herself.

"Well, that's an elegant entry, if I must say so!"

Kat quickly turned to face the person who spoke. Standing before her was a lovely woman, not particularly tall, with long, dark auburn waves crowning her head. She was in a dress similar to what Kat had been wearing at the play rehearsal—although hers was more formal and made with finer fabrics than the theater dared to finance. The woman was dressed from head to toe in emerald-green velvet; a ribbon, with a single stone centered upon it, encircled her throat. Kat quickly appraised the woman, and realized that the lady, likewise, was doing the same to her. And Kat was, by far, at a disadvantage—tub and towel and all.

Kat's cheeks flared with heat. She clutched the bath towel tightly around herself, trying and failing miserably to wrap herself up to be less...exposed. The skin above her towel flushed pink as her discomfort grew.

The woman laughed, warm and friendly. "How about I help you out of the tub first and then we can wind you better in the bath cloth?"

Kat stared, initially ignoring the offered hand. Her eyes began to dart as she mentally calculated her predicament. She was about to tell the woman that she could do it herself, when the horrid realization that she was too stiff to move overtook her. Kat's left leg began to tingle and twisted into a cramp. Her eyes blinked rapidly in panic and pain. Kat lurched and stretched to rub the offending muscle but found she couldn't reach. She jerked awkwardly, skin that had dried in the empty tub stuck to the side wall of the basin and made an embarrassing sucking sound as it released.

The woman, observing Kat's misgivings and embarrassment, didn't await her permission but extended an arm around Kat's far shoulder while also taking the nearer hand.

"You must surely be stiff—especially with no water. Undoubtedly, you are cramped and chilled to the bone."

In a deft movement, the woman had Kat out of the tub and seated before the fire without her being conscious of having taken a step—and it surely must have been several.

With her back to Kat, the woman worked to bring the fire up to its full strength. She stirred the embers, and fed small twigs from the nearby basket. She spoke while remaining focused on the fire. "I have been waiting for you but never expected to find you in my tub. While embarrassing for you, it will make for a great story someday. Don't you agree?" She looked over her shoulder.

Kat shifted about quickly, trying to better cover herself. At her embarrassed scowl, the woman continued to fidget with the fire. After giving Kat a moment or two to compose herself, the lady rose, dusted the ashes off the hem of her skirts, and faced her.

"So, are you one of Edith's daughters?"

"Excuse me?" Kat leaned in as if to hear her better.

"Edith. She is your mother?"

"I'm sorry. I don't know who you think I am. And honestly, I don't know how I got here. But I can assure you—"

"Edith Morrissey, surely you know the name. You have her eyes and coloring."

Kat's mind reeled. Surely this woman couldn't mean Kat's Gran? While it was true her family had told her that they shared the same eyes and color of hair, she'd never seen her grandmother's hair be anything but thin and white.

"Edith is…my grandmother."

The woman stumbled back and sat upon the adjacent stool, mumbling, "So much time. I had no idea so much time passed." She continued to mutter, forgetting Kat for a moment. "So careless of me. I must regain my focus. I thought Edy kept her secret yet. She'd begged for more time…"

The woman swayed from side to side, as if rocking a child to soothe it. She looked into her lap, wringing her hands, and then shook herself like Kat had seen birds do at the beach to dry their feathers. She abruptly turned and faced Kat.

"Is your grandmother well? Does she still live?"

Kat hesitated a moment. "Um, yeah, she's fine. Driving the nursing home staff a bit crazy with her independence. Always running off somewhere or creating a club or some such."

The woman laughed. "Ah, that is Edy all right. Last time I saw her, she was helping her eldest with the children." She paused, momentarily awkward. "The youngest seemed promising…" Her gaze wandered off then settled on Kat. The silence hung uncomfortably between them for a few moments. "Your name. I am so sorry, dear, I did not ask your name. Please do tell me now." She looked at Kat hopefully.

Kat could see that the woman was trying to be comforting, although it was weird, to say the least.

"Kat. I mean, Kathleen."

The woman's eyes glowed, and her smile widened. "An Irish name. Your grandfather would've liked that, I think."

How? How was this possible? None of this made any sense. Kat rubbed warmth into her limbs as goosebumps assaulted them. She had no idea how long she had sat in cooling water and

then no water whatsoever. She wasn't sure if she was dreaming, but the pain was very real.

The woman continued to speak, making Kat resume her focus. "The year. What year is it?" At Kat's blank stare she demanded, "Don't be daft, girl; what is the year from which you come?"

"2017."

"Really? So much time...and your grandmother lives still. A miracle, surely." The woman appeared pensive, overwhelmed by the number. She muttered more than spoke to Kat.

"Excuse me." Kat cleared her throat to get her attention. "You've been asking the questions, but I have a few of my own... who are you? Where am I? How did I get here?"

The woman released a sigh. "You are quite right. I'm sorry. My name is Helene. I am your grandmother...of sorts—four, or is it five, times removed." She paused, as if watching for a reaction before continuing. "You are here, at my home at Rose Hill Manor, in the county of Berkshire, just south of Northampton, because I called you."

Kat didn't know what to think. She sat, mouth agape, processing what was both ludicrous and unreasonable, and yet this woman, Helene, acted as if it was just another day. She wanted to scream; her body ached, and with nothing on but a towel. Kat, always one to take action, needed to do—something. Storming off was obviously not an option in this case. Yet this was beyond her, beyond all reason and comprehension. She grew frustrated, panicked, scared, and did the one thing she respected least, she cried. Kat gasped for air as tears began to well up in her eyes. She shook herself in anger at her weakness, brusquely wiping and willing the tears away.

"I know it is a lot to take in. Your grandmother was quite distraught her first time around. I thought I'd have to send her directly back in those first few moments but 'tisn't safe." Helene clarified quickly when she saw that Kathleen approved of this option—she was nodding like a bobble-head toy. "But it really isn't safe. You need time to adjust to the time shift and get your head about you." She paused. "How about let's find you some proper clothes, why don't we?"

Helene pulled Kat into the outer dressing room where she bustled about, going through the large wardrobe. "In fact, I may have some of her things left from when she last visited. You look about her size."

She quickly outfitted Kat as there was an abundance of skirts and kirtles stored in the wardrobe that all seemed almost tailored to fit her. Helene seemed to anticipate the question.

"It is odd, isn't it, how similar you are in size to your grandmother? Although I suspect time and aging would make that unrecognizable by now."

"What do you mean?"

"I'm sorry—just chasing a thought. What I meant was that since you are Edith's granddaughter, time has indeed passed—and a lot of it, so that you might not see the resemblance as clearly as I do. It wasn't so long ago that she was here as you are here."

"But how can that be? It must be decades."

"Ah, but time travel is devilish. You can travel to a point, and while time moves on while you are gone, you can return and no time will have passed at all. It's actually rather convenient if you think about it. You can spend some time here with me, and when you choose to go back, it will be as if you never left. It is almost like having two lives where you stretch one out in another reality."

Kat shrugged into the offered bodice, her mind trying to process everything she heard. On one level it made sense, but then when she tried to apply the theory to her life, her life right now, in this place, it was absurd and simply tough to swallow. Kathleen just nodded rather than voice any thoughts.

"Your grandmother had a penchant, I recall—a penchant for reading fortunes." Helene glanced up through a bit of hair that had come undone from her loose chignon. She deftly laced a borrowed boot on Kat's left foot while Kat struggled with the hooks on the right. "You know of her...skills?" Helene asked.

"No." Kat hesitated. "I don't remember her doing that."

"Oh, yes, I forgot, that would be your mother's doing. I believe it was while your mother was in grade school. Some hullaballoo over an irate parent back when your grandmother helped out at a school fundraiser or festival, I think it was. Yes, that was it. You'll have to ask her about it. Hushed up her talents after that. Deirdre was quite unhinged about it. Yes, you'll just have to ask your grandmother to tell you the story."

Helene paused to set down one foot. She relieved Kat of her struggle with the other boot and deftly adjusted the lacings.

"You have to use constant tension to keep the laces taut. When you slow down it causes kinks and bunches, and the hooks don't have the tension they need. Now, how's that?"

"Okay, I guess. Pinches a bit on the left."

"We'll have them stretched, but for tonight it can't be helped. We've got to get you settled in before we deal with better shoe options. I think your foot is a bit wider than Edy's."

Helene hurried about, gathering clothes and draping them over her arm as she quickly moved towards the door.

"Whoa, wait." Now that Kat was dressed, she felt some of her courage come back. "Settled in? I don't think so. I want to go home. None of this makes sense. For all I know this is an elaborate dream, and I'll wake up any moment."

Helene's eyes dimmed. Kat couldn't be sure how she did it, but there was a hardness to her eyes even though her lips were still curled into a smile.

"Oh, I don't think so. You know, deep within you, you know that you are here, with me, and that this is very real. You are fighting it, but you know it to be true. Just as you know that there is something special about your grandmother...just as you know you, too, are destined for more. You are just not ready to accept it yet."

After a moment there was a discernible flicker, and then the ice melted, her eyes brightened, and she was again the genial Helene. Kat wondered if she had imagined the change. But it was gone now. "As for going back, you can and will, but not yet. You are but newly come—it'd be too risky to send you back without having rested fully. Plus, frankly, I went to a lot of trouble to get you here so I'd like for you to stay for a while." Kat shifted uncomfortably, and so Helene quickly followed with, "Not long, just long enough to get your bearings and for us to get to know each other."

Kat made a throat-clearing sound, and then firmly but slowly stated, "I have commitments. I cannot stay. I have a job, a business to run, and opening night at the theater, not to mention the cat, and my friends."

Helene laughed, eyes all warmth again. "I thought you understood. When you go back you will go back to almost the exact minute you left, to the same place. No one will miss you because you won't have been anywhere. No one will notice no matter how long you stay. I must assure you, all will be waiting just as you left it." She cocked an eyebrow, giving Kat the feeling she was being observed under a microscope. "Come now...you don't really have a cat, do you?"

"Um," Kat shifted uncomfortably."Well, um, it actually is the neighbor's cat. He comes in sometimes and I—"

"He'll just have to go home, won't he?" Helene brushed it off.

"Hey, wait a minute. Did you mean that when I go back, I go back—to the bath?"

Helene heartily laughed. "Quite possibly. That could be a bit awkward. You could go back the way you came, or these clothes will be soaked."

Kat scowled at the thought. How ridiculous this all sounded. "Just how long do you suppose I need to 'stay' wherever, whenever we are?"

"I told you where, as to the when, it is late October, 1867. As for how long a visit, I would say it would be at least a week before you are strong enough to travel again, but I suggest two weeks so that we can get to know each other better."

"I feel strong enough now."

"Come, come, would you want to give up the opportunity for a grand adventure? Willing or not, travel such as this is can cause an excessive drain of your vitality, one that could be dangerous. I wouldn't risk it. And again, remember, I did invite you." Helene winked, turned on her heel, and walked out the door.

Kat had no choice but to follow. The hallway was dimly lit with gas sconces, and she couldn't be sure if it was late in the day or just overcast.

"It's late," Helene responded to Kat's unspoken question.

Kat stopped abruptly, staring after Helene's receding back as she continued to speak. "Oh surely, you can accept that I brought you ages before your time, across an ocean, and you are distraught that I could discern so obvious a question? Really girl, don't be so silly and catch up. I need to get you settled so you can get your sleep. You'll be feeling disoriented soon from the travel; your youth has protected you thus far, but if we don't get you settled soon, things will begin to...tip."

As Helene spoke of it, Kat began to feel the floor shift, as if they were walking aboard an ancient ship, bobbing upon the sea. It was quickly followed by the rolling of her stomach and the beginnings of what was sure to be a migraine. When she came to a stop, Helene turned to face Kat, genuine concern in her eyes.

"Oh my, we've pushed too far tonight. Patrice! Patrice! Where are you, girl?"

A chubby blonde emerged from around the bend in the hall.

"Patrice, my cousin has arrived, the one I told you about, but she is feeling ill at the moment. Go down to the larder and bring back some mulled wine and toasted bread with cheese. No meat, just some warmed broth should do. Meet us in the south suite. Hurry."

Patrice scampered off while Helene slipped an arm around Kat's shoulders, helping her move in stride with her own wide steps toward the room at the end of the corridor. She shouldered the heavy door aside and led Kat into a cozy room largely decked in silks. Helene led her to the bedside chair, fairly dumping her into it. Then she coaxed the fire into full attention.

"I hate to have to do this to you as we've just gotten you dressed, but you must get comfortable in case you become ill."

With nimble fingers, Helene soon had Kat down to her shift, with her shoulders swathed in a warm, woolen plaid. Helene kneeled before Kat, rubbed her calves briskly, and thumped upon the soles of her feet.

"We'll get the blood flowing in the limbs, and the nausea will settle."

"How did you know?" Kat had to pause to hold back the bile that built in her throat.

"I'd say that it was obvious, but that would be cruel," Helene brusquely answered. "I'll tell you what, when Patrice gets back, if she ever gets back, you will eat and do as I say, and get a good night's rest, and then I will answer any and all questions you may have in the morning. But first we have to get you through this night. Agreed?"

Kat feebly nodded. The churning inside was both disturbing and growing. She had no choice, no options but to do as she was told and wait for morning. If she made it to morning. Kat didn't doubt that, until this feeling settled, it would be a long night indeed.

Kat woke once that night, groggy but feeling much better, and to the sensation of someone soothing her brow. She glanced through barely opened eyes at Helene, who was backlit by the fire. She rubbed something fragrant upon Kat's forehead and muttered words she couldn't quite make out, or perhaps they weren't even in English. But Kat was too exhausted to care and too cozy to stir, and so she quickly slid back into sleep.

3

More Questions Than Answers

When Kat awoke, feeling fully rested, she stretched her arms wide, arching her back, and drew in a deep breath. The bedding gave off the scent of something pleasant, like fresh laundry after it dried in the sunshine, clean and with a sweet floral scent. A fire crackled in the hearth. On the chair at the far side of the room was draped the clothing she'd worn the night before, but accompanied now by a different pair of short boots. At the bedside was a carafe of water, still cool, and another mug of mulled wine. Kat sat up just enough to sip at the wine; it was lighter than she remembered from last night and more floral in taste. It warmed her as she drank. Tentatively, she sat fully upright and grasped her head at the quick twinge of pain between the eyes.

Kat rubbed the area just above her nose with her thumb and forefinger, and kept her eyes closed. Her forehead wrinkled as she tried to will the headache away. The light dramatically shifted, and Kat looked out from under the hand she'd raised to block the sudden brightness. Patrice stood, framed by the opened drapes, in a flood of sunlight.

"Ugh. Do you have to open them so wide?"

"Miss?"

"The curtains. Give me a break and close them a bit."

"Aye, but the missus said it was past time you rose."

"I'm getting up. Just not all at once." Kat slid her legs over the side of the bed, braced her arms to each side in preparation of a big push to get out of bed, but Patrice rushed to her.

"Missus says you are to be awake but not move too quickly or you'll be sick again. Let's just sit you up in bed, and I'll bring your breakfast to you. Cook's been keeping it warm for you."

"Breakfast in bed? I would have to say I approve of that idea." Kat gratefully slipped back under the covers, tucked and patted the bedding around her legs in anticipation of a breakfast tray. It also gave her a few extra moments to look more closely at her new surroundings.

The room was swathed in silk. Bedding, curtains, chair, and canopy were all in the same rose and silver hues. A canopy bed? Kat had only seen them in museum exhibits. A large window seat filled a bayed out section of the room and a hearth built of marble stood nearby. A gas lamp sat on the chest of drawers closest to the door, and a Persian rug covered most of the floor. All in all, a cheerful room, especially now that the sun was in abundance. But it was also clear that she was far from home. Kat laughed nervously. To her, it looked like a mid-19th century J.C. Penney catalogue page. Kat wondered—and took a closer look—no wall outlets. Her eyes searched the room over. No phone jacks anywhere. No labels on the bedding, rug, or curtains. Could it be she really was in the past?

After she'd eaten, Kat was finally allowed to dress and move about. She paced around the room, impatient for answers and impatient to be gone. She had hoped upon going to bed last night that the whole thing, all of it, was a product of an over-active mind and exhaustion. It simply wasn't possible. Was it?

By the time Helene came to fetch Kat, her nerves were at the breaking point. Patrice returned, following closely on Helene's heels, and set about tidying the room.

Kat didn't wait for privacy but blurted, "I need to know how I got here? How you called me? Why—"

"Let us walk." Helene quickly cut off the question. She turned and left the room, leaving Kat no choice but to follow. "Grab a shawl. It's cold out," she called over her shoulder without slowing her pace.

Kat had to jog to catch up to her long strides.

"You must never, and I repeat never, question me in front of the servants—or indeed anyone. Your arrival shall take no notice other than that I afford you."

"What are you talking about? You promised me answers."

Helene stopped abruptly. "I did, and I will, but in front of a small mind such as Patrice our discussion is quite dangerous. You have read your history books? You do know what they do to witches?"

"Witches?" Kat whispered. It was her turn to be caught off guard.

Helene waved a hand dismissively. "Oh, don't play the ninny. How else did you think you got here?

She started to move on, but Kat just stood there. "Oh, come along. Surely you can move your feet and think at the same time. You'll fairly freeze if you don't move; that shawl isn't much against an English fall day. Plus, after last night, some movement will be good for you."

Kat felt her feet move, as if tugged on strings. She had a moment of panic when she realized it was Helene that drew her forward. Try as she might, she couldn't stop her progress. Kat glared as she followed Helene.

Helene turned a glance over her shoulder. “How else would you deal with a petulant child? Come along.”

Kat felt the tug on her body release and now followed of her own volition. She raced to catch up. When Helene stopped as quickly as she started Kat almost walked into her back.

“Think about it. Hasn’t there been a time when you knew things you shouldn’t know? A time when you felt things or sensed things that no one else noticed?”

“Well, yeah, but doesn’t everyone?”

“No.” Helene resumed her walk but at a steady but comfortable pace now, observing or touching the foliage and plantings as she walked. “You have a gift. A gift that I gave you. And you are here to learn about that gift and hone it. To see what you are ‘made of’ so to speak.”

“I didn’t sign on for any of this.”

“No, you didn’t. But shouldn’t anyone with a talent hone that talent? It’d be a waste otherwise. Don’t you agree?”

Kat couldn’t deny that Helene had a point. But then again how does one respond when someone says she is a witch and you are one as well?

“How did you ‘call me’ to you?”

“Oh, that conversation is for another day,” Helene smugly replied.

“What? No! Not another day, today. You said—”

“I know what I said, and I will. Just not today—not yet. You are in no hurry as you are not fit to travel yet. We’ve time to get to know each other first and then we’ll get around to the details in due course.”

“Oh, you have got to be kidding,” Kat stopped and made evident with her stance that she would not willingly budge.

Helene snorted. “This again.” She continued to walk and stated matter-of-factly, “I would think it would dawn upon you that a woman who is capable of bringing you through time and space is quite capable of keeping you where she wishes and will speak of it when she is ready." Helene paused a moment, as if reflecting on what she said and anticipating how it might be interpreted by Kathleen. She turned, a smile on her face. "I don't mean to be abrupt, but you were being rude. I mean you no harm. I just want to get to know my granddaughter several times removed, and share this gift." She raised her hand as one would to stay a dog. "Now before you say another word, I already told you you'd not be missed. You'll be returned to when you left. You are missing nothing—just taking a 'holiday' as it were, with me. Do try to enjoy this, or it shall be so tedious."

Kat stood, arms crossed, not liking the corner Helene had deftly placed her in but seeing no options. She knew she now stood still because Helene allowed it.

"Oh, stop pouting and enjoy this for what it is. I swear it will be worth your time, and you'll be free to go once you are ready to travel."

"And how long would that be?"

"Usually at least a full week, at the most two. But if you sleep and eat regularly you'll adjust more quickly. You can, of course, stay as long as you'd like, but after a week we'll see how you are feeling and determine what is best."

"But I feel fine now."

"Would you really want to leave now, with only the nausea and none of the answers to all your questions? Would you really rather not stay? Has all curiosity been driven out of you? All sense of adventure?"

Kat scowled at her cynically.

"All right, you think yourself ready to leave? Touch your toes."

Kat looked at her incredulously.

"Go ahead. I'm not making a joke, touch your toes...if you

can."

Kathleen made a sweeping lunge to touch her toes and awoke with her head in Helene's lap. Again she fought the rising bile.

"What happened?"

"You attempted to touch your toes and passed out. You've got a few nasty scrapes from the pathway stones, but I broke some of your fall. Shall we discuss again how you are ready to leave or shall we postpone that for another day?"

Kat nodded. Helene had made her point.

When Kathleen was back on her feet again, Helene insisted that they walk the fullness of the gardens, which were extensive.

"So, um," Kat floundered a moment before blurting out, "what should I call you? Grandma?"

"I would certainly think not! That would be absurd! I have no children as yet, besides it is you who is older than I—although for some reason it doesn't quite show yet." She stopped to peer at Kathleen closely.

Kat felt awkward at how intently she stared and shifted nervously.

"And anyway, I would never consent to be 'Grand-ma' but would be 'Grandmother' when of course it would make logical sense to be so."

Somehow Kat found the surreal conversation hysterical. She focused hard on regulating her blinking so as to not laugh out loud in Helene's face when she was taking this all so seriously. Kat had to admit that by the end of the walk she felt much more herself—her fall earlier all but forgotten. They talked of trivial things, daily life, routines, all to better acquaint Kathleen with her new surroundings. It seemed that there would be a lot she would need to learn.

After their walk, Kathleen milled about the manor as Helene

saw to her duties. Kat soon found herself in the study. It was a book-lover's dream with its dark, wooden shelves and cushioned, high-backed chairs. Row upon row of books filled the shelves, with many of the volumes only accessible by the library ladder. All was completed by a writing desk set into the bay window. Kat sighed at the sight of it. It were as if the pages of a gothic novel had materialized. She couldn't help but touch everything, as if to do so were to confirm that what she saw with her eyes was indeed truly here. Kat tried to imagine for a moment what it must be like to live in this manner, to have a room such as this at her disposal. Would it be like a romantic Brontë novel or would it grow tiresome and tedious?

"A bit of both I am afraid."

"What?" Kat turned about quickly to see Helene perched on the arm of a chair. "I'm sorry. I didn't realize I said that aloud."

"You didn't, but I hear you just the same. Sorry, I didn't mean to intrude. I'll try to refrain next time."

"You can hear my thoughts?"

"Of course not, that would be ridiculous and annoying—not just for you. Too much noise clutter. Lord shield me from the chattering of the servants!" Helene laughed.

"Then how?"

"It's simple really. It's a matter of body language. You can read that as well as a book if you focus enough. I saw you touching the casings and musing, and I could tell the bent of your thoughts as I often think them myself."

Kat wasn't exactly buying Helene's explanation, but she let the topic drop for the moment. Kat wasn't sure if she was ready for the truth just yet. The present was enough to occupy her thoughts.

"Have you lived here long?"

"Not so long as you would think. I have only been married for a few years, so at times I look at these things as a stranger would.

None, nothing in here, truly belongs to me. I married into this, but it has not become part of me yet. I am not sure if it ever will." She looked wistfully about. "Only time will tell." Helene whispered, wringing her hands roughly. When she noticed she did so, she quickly hid them behind herself. Her eyes dimmed, shifting but not alighting on anything in particular. Kat didn't know her well enough to know what to make of it.

They spent the next several minutes in silence—Helene in her thoughts and Kat, awkwardly waiting. Kat moved to the writing desk and looked about at the ink pots, blotter, and stationary. It all seemed so dignified to her, so classy, from another time, another era. For a moment, she forgot that that was exactly where she was. This was no museum exhibit but a home, a fully functioning manor, and she was the guest of the lady of the house. "Guest," was an interesting word as Kat was not a guest on two levels—one being she was Helene's family, apparently, and other being not exactly invited but snatched.

Helene leapt to her feet and, without a word or glance, left the room. Kat had no idea of what had just happened. She waited a moment and then tried to follow. The problem was she had no idea where to go. The little Kat had seen of the estate gave her no bearings other than where she slept and how to get to the gardens and kitchen, so she went back to her room to wait.

And she waited until she had no idea how much time passed. Kat perked up when she heard someone at the door. It was a different servant than brought her a meal earlier. Kat popped out of her seat, brushed her skirts in place, and smiled.

"Hello. I was starting to think I was forgotten. What's your name?"

The maid nodded her head in greeting but didn't respond.

"I'm sorry," Kat leaned in. "I didn't hear your name—"

The maid agitatedly shook her head, avoided eye contact, and said not a word.

Kat followed her progress around the room, leaned in, and tried to peer directly into her face. The girl's eyes widened. She shook her head more vehemently. Her shoulders rose, making it appear as if she shrank into them in defense.

"I only want to—"

But before Kat could get another word out the girl scurried out of the room, tugging the door closed firmly behind her. Kat went to bed late that night, with none of her questions answered and none the wiser as to what had happened to her hostess.

The next day Kat left her room not at all. She was met at each meal time by the same, silent servant who would only shake her head at Kat when she tried to ask a question. So Kat paced, counting steps to pass the time. She began a rhythmic tapping of her hands against her thighs as she marched around the room. At every sound from without, Kat paused, straining to hear any indication that someone was on the way. And each time she was disappointed, her hands began to twitch. She wrestled with containing her alternating fear and anger. Kat scanned the room for a diversion she'd maybe missed. She scowled at the embroidery needle with which she was more successful at pricking the ends of her fingers than staving off the tedium. The charcoal and paper had been amusing, until she realized what she recorded there might have to be explained later. She'd burned the scraps of papers, with unladylike ravings, in the fire to avoid getting herself in further troubles. Kat had no idea what Helene's absence meant. More than ever, she wanted to go home and be rid of all this intrigue. The wait was already bad enough, but now to have the only link she had to this place removed, disturbed her more and more as time passed.

On the eve of the third night, Patrice returned with dinner. Kat was so happy to see a familiar face that she almost cried.

"Patrice, where is Helene? What's happened?"

Patrice shook her head violently in the negative and made motions of silence. The terror built in Kat's chest as she feared the worst. Could Helene be gone? Would she be stranded here? Her heart beat wildly in her chest. She felt sure anyone could hear it.

Kat's fears were soon assuaged as Helene swept into the room. Her eyes looked agitated as they canvassed the room.

"Helene!"

She quickly placed a hand over Kat's mouth and whispered horsely, "No."

Helene grabbed a cloth bag and took Kat by the arm. She swiftly pulled her down the hall and by a back corridor Kat had not known existed until Helene revealed it by moving back a tapestry. Silently they made their way down the dimly lit and narrow passage, sometimes winding left to right and other times down. With a slide of a bolt and a tap on a panel Kat found herself in the side garden, disoriented save for the fountain and stars.

Helene turned Kathleen to face her. "I'm sorry, but we haven't time. You need to get back today while you can."

A question perched, ached to be asked, but Helene stopped Kat by hastily adding. "No time for that; no time for anything. If you want to get home, now is the time. We will meet again, soon as I get this settled. I promise."

Helene drew Kathleen closer to her, hugged her tight, and barely mouthed, "My hope." She thrust the small cloth bag in her hand, pulled her under the huge willow that draped over the edge of the fountain, and drew Kat in to its center.

"I can't send you back the way you came. I can't be sure, but you may have to walk a bit to get back to your starting point. But I know the stars are right, so you'll be close. I'm sorry."

With that Helene began to whirl Kathleen about, spinning

her until she started to feel lightheaded. Kat sensed rather than saw a fog or mist envelope her until she no longer was being spun by Helene but of her own volition. Words could be heard as Kat spun. Whether without or within her head, they became clear.

> "Send the wind, send the light
> Bring what's mine, through this night
> Take her hold, bear her tight
> Bring her back, to her right.
> Compass hold, compass bright
> Waver not, guide my sight
> As you will, so mote it be.
> Hasten all, hasten three."

The air about Kat seemed to brighten with iridescent pops of color that enveloped her. And then suddenly all went dark and silent.

4

Small Town Surprises

Kat landed in the neighbor's shrubbery with a grunt and a string of profanity that would make a sailor blush. Her legs draped over each side of a flowering bush in a most unladylike manner, but if Helene were right about being returned at the same time Kat had departed, then it was quite late, and she had little risk of being noticed. Kat clambered out as best she could. Branches were strewn in her hair and tore at the clothes she wore, tangled in the skirt's folds. With a tug and a small leap Kat was out of the bush and cursing again, this time at a twisted ankle. The laced boots, less flexible than her usual Converse, had caught on something on her landing. But late or not, Kat knew she was pressing her luck with the neighbors waking up and noticing her so she quickly hustled around the side of the building to the antique shop's side entrance.

Key? Damn it! She had no key. She berated herself, "Why didn't I listen when people said hide a key near my door?" It had seemed foolish to her as it defeated the purpose of locking the door in the first place, and now she regretted her caution.

Pacing back and forth, Kat winced each time she stepped with her twisted ankle. Between the cold and the warning twinges of nausea, she knew she had to get inside quickly. Kat did the only she could think to do. Picking up a rock, she broke the door's side panel out, reached her arm through the opening, and let herself in. She couldn't help wondering why she locked the door at all if it was so easy to break in anyway? But she couldn't worry about that now. Kat made her way up the stairs to her apartment. Thankfully, she hadn't locked that door. She slid the deadbolt into place as the shop was already compromised. It would be just her luck to be robbed on the night she already broke in. It seemed her life was always destined to be full of irony. Kat wasn't taking any chances. Tonight had already been too weird.

Kat needed to just reach her bed so she could collapse. But as she made her way across the room, curiosity got the better of her. She had to know! Kat limped to the bathroom, working her way slowly towards the tub. Kat leaned on to the fixtures to help alleviate the weight on her ankle, which was now throbbing. She dipped her fingers in to the tub. "Well I'll be damned!" she blurted; the water was still warm.

Kat woke up the next morning to Tara pounding on her apartment door.

"Come on! Wake up and open up!"

Kat muttered curses into the pillow. The pounding continued.

"Come on! You're scaring me. I saw the broken panel. Are you okay?"

Kat lurched upright. "All right, all right, I am coming." Kat slid from under the covers. Forgotten, the bad ankle hit the floor first. "Mother-fucking-toad-lover!" Kat had no idea where that one came from—just moved in the moment she guessed. She shuffled over to the door, using the furniture along the way to help her avoid putting pressure on the injured joint.

Kat struggled with the bolt a bit as she was still half asleep and disoriented; waves of nausea swept over her. "Oh sure," she muttered to herself, "you go back the moment you left. You forgot about the recovery time, Grandma!"

Tara almost fell into the room when the door swung open. "Well, it's about time. Do you know how late it is? You're supposed to be over at the theater at eleven, and here you are still! Oh my God!" She paused and looked Kat over. "You look like crap!"

"Uh...thanks." Kat turned to slowly make her way back to the bed.

"Marcy is going to have a seizure with you sick on opening night."

Kat attempted to make a pithy and vulgar retort but instead succeeded in vomiting last night's—or was it last century's?—dinner all over the floor.

"Ewww! Geez." Tara skipped around the mess and helped Kat back into bed. "And what are you wearing? Did you get that out of the prop closet?"

She looked down. In her exhaustion last night Kat had fallen into bed still fully clothed. "Nope, it's my...grandmother's." Kat began to laugh hysterically like that was the funniest thing on the earth.

Tara felt her forehead. "Did you go out last night with Wayne and get hammered?"

"Wayne's an asshole."

"Beside the point, we all know that. Did you?"

"No, took a bath." New fits of laughter threatened to take over.

"Yeah. Sure. Look, I understand a booty call as well as the next woman, but you are truly a hot mess today. Let's get you out of that get up and back in bed."

Thankfully, Tara stopped her incessant questioning. As much as Kat wanted to scream at her to stop talking because her head ached, pounded, and throbbed, she knew better. She needed her. As much as Kat hated to admit it, she did. Thankfully Tara shifted from talking to humming. Kat sighed a breath of relief as she sank into the covers. She stripped down to only her shift. It looked like a nightgown, she figured, so why not?

"Okay, honey, no more grief from me. Do you want some tea after I clean this mess up?"

Kat grunted in response, rolled onto her belly, and slid back to sleep.

She heard later that opening night was a success. Marcy cut Kat's part out entirely. She guessed they didn't need her after all. Knowing Marcy all these years, Kat concluded it was just as well. If an understudy had screwed up her lines, Marcy still would have blamed Kat. This way Marcy would hate her for far less time.

The shop didn't open for the next three days. And with the added interest of the broken window, the small town gossip was churning. Kat slept through it mostly, blissfully unaware of much. Tara stopped by from time to time to make sure she ate something. On the fourth day the gossip must have grown to a fever pitch because her insurance agent called.

"Hello, Kathleen, I heard you had a bit of trouble out there."

"No, ma'am."

"Now, Kathleen, there really isn't a reason to be coy with me. That is what you pay insurance for, dear. Now tell me about your troubles."

Kat stifled a groan. "No, really, I'm fine."

"You do understand how insurance works? And since this is your first claim your premiums won't be going up. Is that what you are worried about?"

"Mrs. Stevens—"

"Agnes, dear. I've known you since you were a baby. How is your grandmother?"

"Agnes," Kat took a deep breath. "there is nothing to report."

"But your window, dear. Everyone's talking about it. And then the shop was closed for three days. Really. It's not your fault. It happens even in these small towns."

"I broke the window."

"Why in heaven's name would you break your own window? That makes no sense."

"Well, I did, Agnes. I didn't have my key. It was late and cold, so I broke the window. Nothing to worry about. Just me being careless."

Kat could hear her sigh and mutter on the other end of the line. She was probably passing the info on to someone else. Small towns!

"Were you," she paused, "were you drinking, dear? Too much at the Egg's Nest Pub was it? I heard Wayne is in town."

Kat wanted to scream. Was her past love life in the newspaper? She decided the easiest way off the phone was by a harmless lie. "Yeah, that was it. I was in the pub and forgot my keys."

But Agnes just wouldn't let it drop. "I hear Wayne is looking mighty fine with a new job, fancy car, and even brought a girl with him." She prodded, most likely looking for new gossip as the break-in theory hit a dead end.

Kat hung up the phone. She knew she'd pay for it later—probably for quite some while, but she knew Agnes wasn't going to be satisfied until she had her juicy story. Well, she could just make it up in her own head. Kat had too much to do around the shop to make up for the lost time and revenue to worry about that.

To top off her already annoying day, Marcy dropped by late afternoon. Kat was on the back screen porch, airing out the dress she came back in from Helene's. Careful not to leave it out in full sunlight, even on these shorter fall days, Kat was using a fabric brush to tidy it up a bit and admiring the trim work.

"So I've found you at last. Whoa, that's nice. Where'd you find that? I know every piece in the theater's 'Barn' closet so I know it's not one of ours."

"No, it's mine."

"Yours? Then why didn't you wear it for the show?"

"Well, actually I just got it...from my grandmother." Well, at least that part was mostly true, just not exactly which grandmother.

"Really?" Kat could see Marcy's interest perk up. "I thought you got all of the antiques when she moved into the assisted living facility."

Since she'd already started this path Kat saw no reason to abandon it. "Oh, she still has a few things stored away, this and that."

"Really?" Marcy was practically salivating and doing a poor job trying to hide it from her. "Do you know where she is storing them? I would love to borrow or even perhaps buy a piece or two if she'd consider selling."

"Nope, sorry. You know how stubborn she is. I only borrowed this one for a bit and then it's going back."

"Back? Were you going to use this to try to get me to let you into the next production? Because, you know, you really left us in the lurch for the last show. I'm not sure I could overlook that, but this dress is quite authentic." She fingered the fabric.

Kat's temper was starting to boil, and she slapped her hand away. "Oh, for goodness sakes, Marcy, everything isn't about you. This dress isn't for any show. In fact, this dress is none of your business. Honestly, you act like I set out to sabotage the show." Kat didn't stop at Marcy's gap-mouthed expression. "As a matter of fact, I also happen to know that the show managed just fine without me as you cut my part out altogether. I was sick. I have nothing to apologize for!"

"Well, we managed because I had given you a pity part. It never was that important. Just didn't want to leave you out in the cold!" Marcy turned to storm out, paused, and turned part way to look over her shoulder. "But I'll not make that mistake again!" The slammed door that followed was too clichéd, even for Marcy, but then she always had loved theatrics.

Kat worried less about Marcy getting over her snit than about Mrs. Stevens. She was sure she was due for an awkward phone call from her mother later to top off her already stellar day. She sighed, plopped into the papasan chair on the deck, wishing she had brought a hard cider out on the porch with her, or maybe something stronger. She could feel the headache she thought she'd finally put at bay edging back.

She wallowed about a quarter of an hour until she decided that sitting there was doing no one any favors, especially herself. She grabbed her barn coat, pulled on the hikers she always left at the back door, and headed across the small square to the Corner Pantry. Kat knew she needed to eat something to keep this headache from blooming further, but unfortunately what she had in the house to eat was...questionable. She'd have to eventually shop and clean out the science experiment growing at the back of her fridge.

Kat had intended to get a bagel and a schmear or a buttered hard roll but the pastrami's decadence seemed to be calling her name. She skipped the reuben—wasn't about to risk that much grease, and went for a simple turkey on a hard roll with some hoop cheese and mustard. She grabbed a six of Moosehead at the last moment, laughing to herself as she knew this would undoubtedly add to her tainted reputation this week. As she stood in line at the register waiting to pay, Kat saw the raised eyebrows. Oh no, she was not going down with a pathetic story! Kat grabbed a handful of condoms, a box of beef jerky, and a mini headlight flashlight. She actually heard a gasp from the old lady who volunteered at the library. Kat laughed out loud as she walked down the front steps with her purchases. That should at least guarantee her story got interesting!

Kat kept busy and spent the next few days taking inventory, rotating the stock to anticipate and highlight the seasonal offerings. Antiques were often overlooked this time of year in favor of something flashy with batteries, but she knew that ultimately people wanted comfort and a sense of home for the holidays. Especially in the cold, dreary northeast, it was the little touches that conveyed comfort. Each year, she'd dress the storefront with a specific family scenario in mind, going with the story she created in her mind. Kat would imagine who would come to dinner, how many children, family tastes and interests, a color scheme, and of course all the trimmings that made it look plausible. She even included a very realistic, stuffed dog that Tara had thought looked creepy but had been the final touch on many a room over the years. Ironically, Fang, the next door neighbor's cat, loved to come visit and snuggle with the big, yellow dog adding to the illusion. Sometimes, Kat would get so taken with the scene that she'd created that she wished it was her sitting room, that those settings were for her large family that would be coming to dinner. And then as the pieces would sell, bit by bit, rather than be comforted by the profit, she'd be saddened by the loss.

She stood back in the street to admire this year's window. Kat had stuck to white, silver, and teal-blue lights to create a winter wonderland, complete with foil stars that hung from the rafters. Tiny feathered and sequined fairies, which she'd bought last year on a whim at a craft fair, appeared to whisk about the room, thanks to clear fishing line. Crystal candlesticks of cobalt blue gleamed. Kat mixed rustic with elegant, simple with ornate—the table settings with mismatched pieces but in complementary blues, grays, silvers, and white. The handmade napkins with fanciful monogramming that she bought from a local craftswoman finished the table with that personal flair that took it from "storefront" to home. Woolen whites draped the lounge chair, finished off with blue-gray slippers that were purposefully placed to look as if they had been casually cast off. Kat added a mounted white barn owl that she'd found at an estate sale and perched him on a chunk of pale driftwood that she had found mucking about on the river front. It was cool, casual, sophisticated, and fantasy-filled. She loved it. Kat assumed she'd pushed back thoughts of her recent trip to the past in order to get caught up in the here and now, but the theme of magic emerged nonetheless.

Her mother had advised Kat to stick with the warm reds, deep greens, and gold from all her traditional childhood Christmases. And while Kat appreciated tradition, this year she needed something more ethereal. More arctic. More...whimsical. She stood back with her hands in her back pockets, rocked on her heels, and whistled. If she must say so herself, it looked wonderful. Kat suddenly hoped it wouldn't sell too quickly. Inspiration struck, and she ran back inside, not to get the jacket that she'd forgotten twice now but to grab her Canon. She really did need to keep a catalogue of all the windows she created, that way she could keep the illusion with her always.

Kat was just framing her last shot when Wayne pulled up to the entrance. "Damn it!" she muttered under her breath. He'd taken her off guard. He always was a sneaky, little bastard. Kat almost backed into the hood of his very sleek, very new, very red sports car.

"Hey, watch it, Red."

She turned around quickly. *Shit. Shit. Shit!* she chanted in her head. She did not need Wayne to add to an already stellar week. Kat gave him a quick nod and pasted on her polite "company" smile.

"Hey," was all the greeting Kat would muster. Wayne was past history as far as she was concerned, but ever since they broke up last year it seemed people had been plotting their reunion. *I mean really, get over the break up already people—it wasn't yours!* They took Kat not dating to mean she was pining over lost love rather than what it was—disinterest. There simply hadn't been the time nor the temptation to date. All the same people, all the same conversations, nothing new, why even bother? She certainly hadn't missed Wayne—well, after that first month. He had done both too much—cheated on her—and too little—never remembered a special day or made a romantic gesture. Nope, she hadn't looked back in almost a year, and here he was on her stoop.

He stood quietly, staring at the window for a moment. "It looks good. Not what I would've expected, but good."

"Okay, uh, thanks."

Wayne shrugged off the less than warm welcome. "So what's new?" he asked, turning to eye Kat. She could feel him analyzing her face. *For what? A reaction? Wrinkles? Oh, who knew?* She'd stopped trying to figure Wayne out when she sent him on a one-way hike out of her life.

"Nothing's new; it's an antique store." Kat laughed at her own joke.

He didn't seem to think it particularly witty and made that face, that face of derision she so loathed.

"So what brings you here?"

"Town or the store?"

"The store." Kat didn't care why he was in town, just why was he bothering her.

"Oh, um," sounding a bit disappointed that she hadn't asked about his plans. "I need a gift for Shayla. She likes old things. She's an old-fashioned, southern girl. Mainly likes jewelry, and thought that since I was in town and she was out shopping with my mother that I might stop in. We usually shop together, so since I had this break, thought I'd get a head start on the holiday shopping."

Well, so some things do change. "Uh, sure. Just go on in and let me finish up out here. The jewelry is mostly in the case except for the costume and replica stuff."

"Oh, I won't be buying any replicas." Wayne smirked as he clomped up the stairs and into the shop.

No, Wayne would blow a wad of money in here just to show Kat his devotion to his new girl. And that was good for the bottom line. Maybe, Kat thought, she could get him to make up the money she'd lost by being ill earlier this week. God, she hoped he wanted to impress her big! Kat took her final photos of the display and headed in, trying not to look too pleased at the thought of a sale. Wayne wouldn't buy anything unless it looked expensive. She was going to make him pay through the nose!

Forty-five minutes later Wayne was no closer to making his decision than when they'd started. Kat's impatience wore down her greed as she tried to think of ways to get him to buy something and leave already.

"Nope, not sure. It has to be special, really special, for my Shayla. Do you have anything else?"

Wayne wandered about poking into the smaller display cases, handling some delicate and truly valuable glass.

"Just what you see." To keep busy, Kat grabbed a bottle of wood polish and started to wipe down the front of a Davenport door panel.

"Well, you could be more helpful."

Kat dropped the cleaning rag and turned. "Seriously, Wayne, I have shown you everything in the shop that I have in jewelry. Unless you can come up with another category, or perhaps I could interest you in that glass you are handling...and by the way, be careful with that or you bought it."

Wayne clumsily put down the crystal egg. Thankfully it didn't roll far, and Kat was able to get it back on its stand with no harm done.

"How about a vintage, beaded purse. They are hand done so they are one of a kind."

"One of a kind, like my Shayla."

Kat stifled a snotty retort. "Yes, exactly."

She led him to a hall tree at the back of the shop. It was staged, much like the front window, to look as if the family had just returned and carelessly draped the wraps, hats, and bags as they entered. A bright display of beaded bags imported from the Ukraine stood next to it. Kat couldn't watch as his bulky hands handled the delicate work. She reassured herself that it would be fine; he'd find what he needed and leave. The more he looked, the sooner it would be over.

"Hey, what is this?"

Wayne pulled out a small parcel, tied with string, that Kat didn't initially recognize. And when she did, her heart stopped beating. Kat grabbed it from his hand. Lord knew what was in that package! It was the one that Helene had thrust in her hands that night as she left her time so hastily from under the willow.

"Hey!"

"Sorry, nope, this is personal. Shouldn't be in the shop at all."

"Well, okay. Um, I guess I'll take that dark, purple bag and that egg thing."

Kat couldn't wrap up his parcels quickly enough; she needed to get him out of the shop so she could see what it was Helene had sent her home with. She couldn't believe she'd forgotten all about it. In her distraction, Kat didn't even register the size of that sale until days later. Kat couldn't work quickly enough as she closed shop. She didn't want to risk being disturbed while handling her mystery package. And based on her last experience with Helene, it could well be dangerous. She tucked the parcel in the lower, register drawer and set about buttoning up the shop.

She decided to leave the front window lights flickering, might as well start a buzz about the holidays. Sure, Christmas was more than a month away, but these days if you didn't advertise early you missed out on significant sales. Armed with Christmas Club checks in October, the frenzy began earlier and earlier each year. Her own mother could attest to this as she was out on her second shopping spree thus far. Kat had caved to the pressure to ready the shop early, and, honestly, she was glad she had as now she could focus on other things.

Taking the stairs two at a time, Kat pushed through her apartment door, remembering to shoulder it shut with a shove and slide the deadbolt. Today the door seemed excessively resistant, having warped ages ago, but in her eagerness to get to her task she mustered the energy to give it that final shove without wasting much effort or time.

Kat moved to sit at the farmhouse work table that served as her desk and office area. She thought about taking off her shoes and thought better of it, remembering the last trip to "Grandma's." She sure as hell didn't want to repeat that indecorous meeting. Pulling the work lamp towards herself, she hovered over the package. Inside the bag, drawn closed with a golden silk cord, was an oilcloth package tied with twine. Kat deftly but tentatively removed the cording and pulled the package open, lifting one side up to let the contents tumble onto the tabletop. Out slid a piece of parchment paper and a pendant.

She looked closely, analyzing it. Kat had never seen one such as this. The pendant held a deep, golden-orange amber, tapered to be smaller at the top and wider at the base. Flecks of gold and ribbons of deepest red threaded through the stone. It was encased in pale gold, wrapping its sides but leaving the stone so it could rest directly against the skin. Small markings were etched on the edges within the gold framing, but in spite of her jewelers' lens and magnifying glass, she could not identify what they meant. A thin chain of gold thread through the small opening at the top of the pendant. Kat held the pendant in her hand and sensed a weight far more than its sum should have accounted for.

And then it dawned on her. "Holy cow!" Kat's head snapped up in realization. There in her right hand rested the pendant. Its soft golden hue matched the ring she wore on the same hand. How had Kat spent so many moments without making the connection was beyond her. She dropped the pendant onto the table to look at the ring she had worn since her 18th birthday when Gran—Grandma Edy—had given it to her as a graduation gift. She slid the ring off to look at it objectively, side by side with the pendant. There were no matching markings around the edge, but the amber was the clue. Ambers, she knew, came in a variety of hues and density of "golden fire." To find matching ambers meant you had found those of the same origin or source. Being a composite, amber is influenced from its source. Kat had no doubt in her mind that these two pieces were one and the same.

Kat sat pondering this when she abruptly realized she had totally neglected the accompanying parchment. Pushing the pendant aside, she carefully bent back the folds of the heavy paper. Kat couldn't be sure if her caution were warranted, but after countlessly handling aged papers and archives, she knew sometimes pages could look solid one moment and disintegrate the next, turning into a papery ash. The page bent back slowly as if it had indeed traveled through ages to come to rest here, but there was still strength in the threads that comprised it.

In a fine, delicate hand was just one line of script:

For all the birthdays I have so far missed, to celebrate your 29th. -H.

5

It's Just Glass

It was definitely time to visit Gran.

Kat resisted the urge to try the pendant on. Instead she quickly wrapped the whole lot up in reverse order, tied the package again in the twine, and went to the wall safe to lock the contents away. Kat realized she had been trying to deal with whatever it was that happened to her that night by working too much and so hard, that thought, real thought, wasn't possible. This package was verifiable proof that she hadn't imagined any of it. It happened. It could not be denied, and the time to think on what it meant could no longer be delayed.

Always a practical sort, Kat rolled her head from side to side to loosen her neck muscles, and then sat at her desk to make a list of things she needed to talk to Gran about. She felt she must be methodical—if not for Gran's sake then at least to organize her own thoughts. Kat only broke from the task briefly when she stopped to heat up a bowl of soup and tear a hunk of questionably-aged bread to make the meal more filling. *Note to self, go grocery shopping.* Oddly enough the more questions she listed, the more she had. It seemed endless. But eventually exhaustion took over, and she went to bed.

Kat couldn't get away to make the trip to visit Gran the next day no matter how much she wanted to. Her mother called, as expected, over Mrs. Stevens and Kat's rudeness in hanging up on her. After the obligatory "I will apologize" for about the hundredth time, that topic was finally abandoned but followed with the news that her mother, too, had heard that Wayne was in town and was that the reason for her mood? An hour later, Kat could claim only the return of her headache as to what was gained by that phone call.

She jumped into the shower, already miles behind where she expected to be that day, "old school" James Brown wailing on the CD player, when she heard urgent pounding on the shop door. It couldn't be that late in the morning, could it?

Literally sliding out of the shower, she barely saved herself from a fall. She toweled off in record time, tugged on sweatpants, sports bra, and a college hoodie as the banging continued. Kat made her way barefooted down the stairs and across the shop, muttering to herself that someone had better be dead.

As she got closer to the door Kat could see Wayne's mother with who must be his new girlfriend in tow. *Shit, shit, shit!* She absentmindedly pushed wet hair out of her eyes as she unlocked the shop door.

"Hello, Mrs. Gilman. What's wrong?"

"Wrong? Why ever would you think that there was something wrong, dear?"

"Well, you were banging as if to wake the dead."

Mrs. Gilman chuckled. "Oh no, no, nothing like that. Just need to get my 'shop on' and we," nodding to the girl to her left, "know Wayne was here yesterday and didn't want him to have an advantage over us. Isn't that so, Shayla?" She smiled widely at the girl, patting her arm as she spoke.

Shayla cocked an eye in response and smiled like the cat who found the cream as she pointedly looked Kat over from head to toe. Obviously seeing nothing to worry about in her department, she smiled a broad, smug grin.

"That's right, Mom," Kat noted the emphasis on 'Mom.' "Just trying to get some shopping in before we head back to the city. Mom seems to think you have some quaint things I might like," she paused, "but I doubt it as I suspect our tastes are not the same. But I said I would be a sport and give you, your shop, a look-see. Your window is...cute." She brushed past Kat, purse held high in her bent elbow.

As Kat stepped back she glanced at the grandfather clock and noted that it was a full fifteen minutes earlier than the posted store hours to open. She shook her head and wondered about the self-esteem of a woman that needed to resort to such schoolyard tricks. *Ah well.* Kat didn't really care anyway. Wayne was ages ago, and what this girl thought didn't matter to her.

"Um, Mrs. Gilman, I am going to leave the two of you to it for a few minutes so I can finish getting dressed. I know you know your way around the shop."

Kat didn't wait for an answer but headed back up the stairs. She could hear mention of her name between them but really couldn't care less to try to hear more. Ten minutes later, she was back downstairs, dressed in smart, black jeans, a teal cable-knit sweater that highlighted her now dried pale auburn curls, and just a hint of make up in fall shades that did the same. Her black high tops had custom art in a Day of the Dead motif. Seemed appropriate for the mood she was in.

She found the two of them, still the only customers this early in the morning "ooh'ing" and "ah'ing" over Kat's Italian glass. She had to admit they had good taste. It had cost her a small fortune to import it, but it seemed a risk worth making, especially when you saw the glass in direct light. Kat had seen some of the work firsthand ages ago when she toured Europe on a school trip and had never forgotten the magic of the craftsmanship. Her mother had thought it a ridiculous extravagance—and not at all in line with an antique store. Kat's Gran, too, hadn't thought it meshed with the general theme of the store, but had liked the glass. She'd already sold a third of the stock, making well more than the original outlay for the whole lot. Kat decided to see if she could add a bit to the profit margin with these two. If they wanted to impress her, she'd let them.

"Hello again. Sorry to keep you waiting. Have you found anything I can help you with?"

At the sound of Kat's voice, Shayla's hand quickly dropped from the piece she had just been caressing with obvious admiration. She pursed her lips and turned up her nose to affect indifference.

Mrs. Gilman stepped in. "Kathleen, dear, I forgot to introduce you to Wayne's girl, Shayla."

"Pleased to meet you," Kat smiled, but she didn't extend a hand as she could predict it wouldn't be accepted, or worse yet, she'd have the limp-hand tango.

Shayla nodded in response, then looked back at the glass. "This is pretty. Wasn't expecting this in an antique shop."

Kat decided to give Shayla a break as she looked so uncomfortable now that Kat was properly dressed and not the plain Jane she initially thought her to be. "Well, trying to expand and experiment to see what people want. Just because most of the stuff in here is old doesn't mean the things can't change. I, myself, like the contrast of old and new. Respect the old but embrace it in a new way." She smiled but faced a cold stare. Kat could see Shayla was just going to make it a point to hate her no matter what she said or did. *That's fine. Her problem, not mine.*

Shayla turned back to the glass, barely acknowledging that Kat had spoken. "Are these prices marked what you expect to get for them? Seems mighty dear for glass that probably just came out of a warehouse in China."

Oh, was she really going to try to play it that way? Small, petty woman. "Afraid so. Had it imported from Italy. Very expensive to do so. I met the artist years ago so I know what talent it takes to get the glass to form such a dance of art and light within each piece." Kat held one up to grab the sunlight to catch its full effect.

Shayla couldn't help but gasp. Kat knew she had her. She placed it back on the shelf, rearranging its tag as if she knew there would be no purchase today. "I do sometimes cut a small deal if a patron buys several pieces, but as this is too expensive for you, let's head back up front where I do have some nice replica tea sets you might appreciate." Kat turned and headed back up the aisle toward the front displays of old-time candy and reproduction tin toys that were largely set out for tourists that wanted a souvenir rather than an antique. She listened for their following steps but heard none.

Kat busied herself refolding embroidered linens to best highlight the detail in the stitching. She couldn't help hum to herself as she already knew the outcome. Shayla came up the aisle balancing three glass pieces with Mrs. Gilman following with a large centerpiece, all of the hand-blown and cut Italian glass. They placed all on the polished, circa 1810 barn plank counter, Shayla's face triumphant.

"I assume you do take American Express."

"Of course," Kat nodded professionally, keeping her inward smile in check. "Would you like these wrapped as gifts?"

At her quick moment of panic, Kat followed with, "Of course that is included in the price, and I'll take ten percent off to cover the tax as you are buying so many wonderful pieces. You have excellent taste." She thought of adding that she would've kept these for herself if she could've afforded them, but Kat thought she'd be sure to go to Hell with that much duplicity.

Shayla seemed relieved and agreed to all. Kat almost felt sorry for her and the impact on her card, but she was hell-bent on impressing her, so she let her think she did. All in all, Shayla's purchase cemented in Kat's mind that this Italian glass was a gold mine, and she would need to reorder soon.

Kat tried not to look as if she was rushing as she wrapped each piece with care in a craft paper box, loaded with raffia shreds in festive forest green and deep reds and then tied all in a neutral raffia bow with a cinnamon stick and sprig of clear-dipped, frosted holly. She really couldn't complain; it was barely noon, and she had made more on this sale than she usually did in a week. Kat chuckled to herself. If she had known breaking up with Wayne was going to be this profitable she would've done it ages ago! Maybe he'd break up with this one, get another jealous and petty girlfriend, and she could come and "humble" Kat as well. She was still chuckling at that thought as she locked up the register so she could run over to the Corner Pantry to grab a lunch to go. She dashed out the door, making a mental note that she'd have to reorganize the display as so much was missing from it. She definitely would have to get to Gran's another day.

The shop picked up considerably after lunch. Apparently the window display was drawing them in in droves. Amazing what a little whimsy and color can do to a traditional store. Kat was already plotting new ideas for her next window. One woman even jokingly, or at least Kat took to be so, asked Kat to come home with her and do the same in her house. Of course she declined but sold her a trunk full of items and even sketched out a design plan based on what the woman said her parlor looked like. She tipped Kat twenty dollars for the help. She hated to take the money, but the woman had insisted, she was so happy.

Later that night, once Kat was finally back upstairs in her

rooms, she sat again under her work lamp and unwrapped the pendant. She turned it back and forth, watching how the light animated the deep amber color and sent sparks within the red strands. Kat didn't know what bothered her more, that the pendant obviously belonged to a set with the ring she already owned or that it came from Helene. But then again, that was the same thing, wasn't it?

Kat took her ring off. She hadn't removed it in ages so it was resistant at first. She wanted to analyze it like she had the pendant. Nothing seemed remarkable, not that Kat knew what she was looking for. She laid the ring down to reach for her cup of English breakfast tea that was rapidly cooling. When Kat glanced back she noticed a change in the ring's stone. She had inadvertently placed the ring so it touched the pendant. Now the threads of red that were suspended in the pendant were evident in the ring. Was it a play of the light, one reflecting the other? Kat lifted the ring back up to analyze it and what she thought she saw was gone. She must have imagined it, or they must've reflected off of each other. Kat decided it was either that or she just had an active imagination. She slid the ring on her finger, wrapped the pendant back up as it came, and returned it to the safe.

God, Kat thought, *I could use a soak in the tub*. However, after her last escapade, she was afraid to—afraid to relax that much, afraid to let her mind wander. Afraid. No one saw her leave. No one saw Kat return. Other than the pendant and dress, she had no proof of what happened. Who could she tell? Who could she trust? Kat resolved to keep the shop closed tomorrow to see Gran.

Kat shook herself and decided to take charge, and now. She filled the tub. She'd be damned if she was going to be afraid of a porcelain tub. But, to be sure she didn't drop off asleep, Kat cranked the Rolling Stones on the stereo. Granted she didn't soak as long as she would've prior, but she did sing along to the tunes and faced her fears head on—that at least was a small victory.

6

Gran Expectations

The drive to the nursing home was pleasant and winding. Most of the trees hadn't lost their leaves yet as there hadn't been any strong rain or early snow to hasten them along. Kat couldn't remember just taking a day off, without being sick, in ages. Sure this was the normal day for the shop to be closed, but any business owner could tell you that while the shop may be closed, there was always work to be done. But, thanks to Shayla's bout of pride, she didn't have to worry about meeting sales numbers for the month.

Kat drove with windows partially opened although it really was a crisp, cool day. She always loved the smell of autumn, the wood fires, the damp soil. And if she was being a bit romantic, so what?

Gravel crunched as Kat pulled her truck into the lot. Mondays were always quiet at the home, a fact she appreciated. Kat's mom would've visited Gran all afternoon after church yesterday. That and having a standing hair appointment on Mondays, set and brush out, meant Kat had a lessened chance of running into her. Kat thought that was the key to survival in a small town—learn the routines of the inhabitants and then avoid those you'd rather not see. Then it hit her—that was what Mrs. Stevens had done to her! She knew Kat's schedule and used it to keep her off kilter by arriving way too early. Nope, she was not sorry that she gave her a ten percent discount. Kat had planned a twenty percent cut for hagglers, and she still would've made a killing. Not that she was feeling any guilt on their accounts, but it was nice knowing that she was right.

Gran looked to be in high spirits when Kat was shown into her rooms. In her window sat a potted, golden mum in full bloom. Kat mentally kicked herself for not bringing her anything. She should've smuggled in some of those chocolate-covered cherries she loved. Kat made a mental note to do so next time. Gran wasn't supposed to have them with her diabetes and all, but at 96, she and Kat both agreed she should damn well have whatever she wanted.

"Carol!" She called out to Kat.

Oh no. It was going to one of those days. "No Gran, it's me, Kat. Aunt Carol is in Florida with the boys."

"That's what I said. Kathleen. I think you are hearing things, kiddo. You might want to get your ears checked."

That was her gran—full of beans, thank God.

They spent the better part of the morning with Gran introducing Kat to everyone she knew. Then she got wrangled into a game of Rummy-O, followed by UpWords. Kat was relieved when they were able finally to break away; those seniors were wearing her out. It was as if they all had an internal clock and were racing against it—which maybe they truly were.

Gran wanted to sit out in the garden for whatever sun there was left from midday as it would soon turn colder. They sat clear of any shade, pulling their jackets closer. Kat tucked her hands in her pockets.

How could she bring up the topic of Helene? It seemed more and more absurd as the days passed. What had really happened? Aside from the necklace, what was real?

They sat in companionable silence for a while. Kat leaned her head back to soak in the sun. With no wind today, it actually did feel good. She closed her eyes, felt the sun's glow through her closed eyelids, and enjoyed the moment, just being, when Gran spoke.

"Frank says we ought to have pork chops for dinner. What do you think, Carol?"

Kat sighed, and opened her eyes to face her. Gran looked at her so intently, believing Kat to be who she thought she was.

"I don't know. What did we have for dinner last night?"

"Oh, how could you forget? It was spaghetti and meatballs at Noella's Cafe. Donny wanted it after the little league game. He was so hungry." She smiled at the memory.

Kat's uncle Donny was long dead of pancreatic cancer. And Noella's Cafe was an urban legend, it closed before she was born. No restaurant lived up to the tales of their sauce. Kat feared she'd lost her opportunity to talk to Gran, to ask the unthinkable. When she drifted away like this it could be moments or days. Kat didn't know what she should wish for—her to stay in the now, or perhaps she was happier in the past. Kat just knew that when Gran slipped away like this she felt lonelier than ever.

Gran tugged at Kat's sleeve. "Can we ride the Ferris wheel, Mama? I promise to be good."

Kat tried not to cry when this happened. But it broke her heart that the smartest woman she knew was reduced to this. It just wasn't fair.

"Not today, Gran. It's too cold. Let's get you inside and warm you up."

Gran said not a word but stood to walk back with Kat, sliding her hand into Kat's. They got back to her suite without another

word passing between them until they sat in her tiny, sitting room.

"Do you want some tea, honey? I could ask the nurses." Gran was back. "They will even bring some cookies for Teddy."

Or maybe not. Kat sighed and said she could do as she liked; she cared not either way.

"Well, that is no attitude. At some point you will have to choose. And choose wisely. Don't let her make the choice for you."

Kat's ears picked up at this turn of conversation.

Gran continued, "Not so pretty."

"Gran, who's not so pretty?"

"Teddy doesn't like the smile. Smile's all wrong. Not happy."

Smile all wrong? When have I heard that before? Something tugged at Kat's memory.

"I told her no, but she said she must. You must. The glow..."

"Gran, what are you talking about?"

Kat watched her grandmother wag her head slowly back and forth, as if dragging the weight of it through molasses. Her shoulders hunched inwards as she crossed her hands over her chest, clenching and unclenching them.

"Your gift. My gift..." she muttered.

With a firm but gentle hand to each side of her grandmother's face, Kat was able to stop her movement temporarily. Kat leaned in, peered directly in her eyes, "Gran? Gran, it's Kat. What can you tell me about Helene?"

Gran snapped her head back, eyes wide, and began to shake her head wildly back and forth. "No, no, no! I don't want to go. Don't want to. Too far. Too scary."

"Gran, it's me, Kat." Kat tried to calm her grandmother, taking her hands in her own, trying but failing to pull her into a hug. "Gran, tell me about Helene. I need to know what you know about Helene."

With a sigh, Gran's movement stopped. She slumped where she sat, spent. "I want to go home. Take me home, Kathleen." She stopped and looked deeply into Kat's eyes, "I'm just so tired. I can't... I can't tonight."

For a brief moment Kat knew Gran was back with her. "Gran, what do you need?"

But then Gran gave no response, just looked at Kat, appraising her. Kat swore she saw something flicker in her eyes and go out.

"Where's Donny? He never visits. He needs to see his mother."

It was gut-wrenching to visit Gran. After Kat got her settled in and her caregivers had taken over, she drove home slowly, not enjoying the ride back at all. Thoughts swam in her head. Gran had moments of lucidity, but what was true and what was manufactured, Kat was incapable of sorting out. If Gran had traveled back in time to Helene, she'd not learn of it from her. Kat was alone again, and that was scary.

Kat went back to work the next day with a heavy heart, unable to keep Gran off her mind. While she was so saddened by Gran's confusion, Kat also replayed her words in her mind, played them over and over again as she felt sure there were nuggets of truth in there. The question was, what were they?

She didn't have too long to mull it over when the door jangled with the first customer of the day. It was Suzy, Kat's best friend's mother and Gran's old neighbor. They had been friends for ages although Suzy was more her mother's age than Gran's. Somehow the hip Suzy and the salt-of-the-earth and homespun Gran got along; it made no sense to anyone other than the two of them. Suzy was known to bake a "special" brownie or two, and her herbal lemonade always had a way of making the day far sunnier than it had a right to. But overall she was harmless. As a kid, Kat loved to sit in her garden and watch her work with her shears. She'd lovingly trim the garden beds, never out of efficiency but out of love. Her garden was not a chore but a way of life, a way to nurture, and filled with hope. Kat always loved how the merging scents of rosemary and mint would waft along the air with the twinkle of the wind chimes Suzy'd created out of found silverware she'd bent this way and that. Mixed in with natural stones and hard clay beads, it was avant-garde then, but Kat bet she could sell a ton of them now. People were into "re-purposing" now.

"Hello, Suzy. What brings you into town? Ready to make a rich woman out of me and sell me some of your handmade chimes?"

"In your dreams, kid. They are made out of heart and soul, and you can't sell a soul. At least not cheaply." She winked at Kat.

Nope, time hadn't aged Suzy a bit. "But I will get around to finishing one for you—but not to sell, for you. To help you remember."

Kat knew just what she meant. Those days on her back deck were the purest days of summer fun and trust. The last night she spent on that deck was with Suzy's daughter and her best friend. Until the accident...but Kat couldn't think on that now. Between Gran yesterday and Helene, she didn't think she had the strength to think back to what if. *What if Sky and I had gone off to California like we had planned?*

Suzy snapped her fingers in Kat's face. "Where'd you go, girl?"

"Oh, sorry, got a lot on my mind."

"I know. That's why I am here."

"Excuse me?"

"Your Gran called first thing this morning. Wanted me to come and set some things straight with you. Said it was urgent."

Knowing Gran, and her current state, it could be anything.

"She wants me to ask if Helene called you...back."

7

Invitations

The arrival of an early morning mini-bus group of tourists was the only thing that stopped Kat from grabbing Suzy by the arm and dragging her upstairs. It was torture for her watching the ladies fuss and prattle over this or that. Normally she loved listening to the thought processes and debate of her shoppers, partially because she genuinely cared about people, but also because it gave Kat insight in to how to better set up her shop and market her wares. But today she felt an inner scream welling in her head.

Suzy watched her over the top of her glasses from a willow-branch rocker close to the front of the shop. She rocked and smiled knowingly. Sometimes, over the years, Kat thought that Suzy could read her thoughts; she had always known what Sky and Kat were up to—almost before they knew. Today, Kat knew Suzy truly did see right through her as she rushed the ladies through some handmade, lace linens she'd imported from Ireland as they, frankly, went well with everything. Thankfully, the driver announced the group needed to head out in the next ten minutes so decisions were made hastily. After Kat rang up the last customer and locked the door behind her, turning the 'Out to Lunch' sign around, Suzy laughed heartily.

"I don't think your momma would be pleased with your manners this morning. You fairly wrestled that one woman through those quilts like they were on fire. Can't be good for business."

Kat scowled at her, mockingly. "Ah, come on, Suz." She never let them use the more formal Mrs. Carleson even when they were kids. "You know they were just wasting time—theirs and mine. Those tours are about 'thrifty ways for senior travel' more than anything else. I swear they come in just to have something to chat about."

"Now that is kind of rude for someone with a grandmother who could be on such a tour herself."

Suzy always knew how to be the best person in every situation. Kat had often wished she could be more like her, none so much as today. She felt justly ashamed.

"So," Suzy said, lightening the mood, "are we going out to eat as the sign says or did you have something else in mind?"

"Could you handle grilled cheese and homemade, split-pea soup upstairs? I have something to show you."

"Depends. Whose pea soup?" Suzy's eyes narrowed as she laughed.

"My mother's. You'll live."

"Why, yes, thank you. That woman sure can cook."

"You know I can cook, too."

"Heating and cooking are two very different things."

"No really, I've learned how to cook."

"Well then, invite me to dinner sometime, and I'll bring the cannolis."

"You're on. Shall we go?" Kat motioned to the stairs.

They weren't far into the apartment when Suzy stopped, lowered her glasses further down her nose. She'd spotted the outfit Helene sent Kat home in hanging on the outside of the wardrobe.

She stood silently for a minute, fingering the fabric and inspecting the interfacing and stitchings.

"Nice dress, good stitch work, but then again I recognize the work. Have one similar at home." She turned to face Kat.

Her mouth hung open a moment, stunned. "You?" was all Kat sputtered.

"Oh, goodness no. One of your gran's. She knew that your grandfather would want her to sell it, being so old and all. She never would or could find a way to explain it. Could you?"

"No, I suppose not. So then Gran was…?" Kat's shoulders relaxed. She let loose a deep breath.

"Yes, I expect you each had quite a similar experience with Helene. So, after a time, she passed it along to me for safekeeping…although she was slow to tell me the truth of it all. Let's get lunch on, and we can talk as we grill those sandwiches."

Lunch was put together in short order. Kat had just flipped the second sandwich to brown when Suzy added, "You should fit in the other dress just fine. Maybe let the hem down a bit as you're taller."

Kat turned to face her. "Oh, I don't know about that…I mean I am curious and all, but I got so sick coming and going, I don't think I could stomach it—literally, or even think about it just yet. Not that I have a choice at all, I know. And that's what has been wearing on me these last few weeks."

"I know, honey. Your gran was the same. No, that's not true. She told me she had been sick, but she was also scared shitless. Definitely not like you in that manner. You, you have the courage to face the opportunity and see what there is to see. You're not shut off to possibility like she was even at such a young age. Come to think of it, I think that may be why Helene waited so long to call to you. Let you grow up a bit, determine first the woman you are to be, before she showed you another possibility. Hmm, I will have to think on that some more."

Suzy paused, contemplative. "But I think I could help you with the other matter, the sickness." She smiled brightly. "I have some herbs I could bundle for you, taken with hot cider and honey, that should set you to rights when need be."

"Oh, really?" Kat cocked an eyebrow.

"Yes, wise ass. And, come to think about it, one of my brownies after would help, too."

Kat laughed. "Oh, I bet they would. I'll have to remember that."

"Sure you're not a preacher or a school teacher?"

"Far from it. I just don't want to ingest marijuana."

"There are more herbs than just marijuana, girl. Such a narrow mind, tsk, tsk. The secret to my brownies is coconut oil, cinnamon, and ground oats. Good for stomach balance."

"After how I felt after, I would take Drano if it would help. No offense to your brownies."

"Really, you felt that sick? Okay, when I go home tonight I will fix you up a jar, and a batch of brownies," Suzy paused as Kat made a face, and then continued, "that you could freeze for emergency use only. Fair enough?"

"Oh, there's no rush."

"Really? Did she make an appointment with you? Set a date?"

"Uh, no."

"Then she could just come and get you next minute, couldn't she?"

Kat was silent as she let that thought sink in. Suzy was right. Last time Helene reached her in the tub; Kat could be nipped out in a moment. It was horrifying to think on.

"But first things first, let's get some food in us and then I'll tell you your gran's story as I know it, and then you can tell me yours. We'll figure this out. Don't you worry."

Apparently Gran had been "invited" while asleep and awoke in a strange bed. She'd been terrified the whole time, cried most of the time away. But then again she had only been twelve at the time. A fully grown woman by Depression Era standards but far from it in the twenty-first century. Gran hadn't learned that much about Helene as she refused to leave her room and had her meals brought to her there as well. When she returned home, to her own time, she told her story to her parents and siblings but no one believed her. They all insisted that she had been dreaming, and wouldn't even consider the clothing she had returned with as anything more than a terrible attempt at a joke. So Gran had bundled the whole lot in some linens and placed it in the bottom of her hope chest, hoping that she, too, could forget the whole thing.

"Why did she keep the dress if it upset her so?"

"It was proof that she hadn't imagined it all."

Kat could fully understand that. If she had returned with nothing to show for it, would she believe it herself? How often had Kat felt the dress's folds and thought of her experience there...then. Kat slowly filled Suzy in on what had transpired, with as much detail as she could recall, and only stopped when Suzy asked questions to clarify. Encouraged by her attention, Kat gained a feeling of relief in that she could indeed tell her tale to someone and have it believed.

"Oh my God! I forgot to show you something!" Kat rushed off to gather the packet that Helene had given her. She quickly brought the bundle and laid it before Suzy on the small, kitchen table.

"She sent this back with you?" Suzy asked incredulously.

"Yes, and she seemed to believe it quite urgent that I have it."

Suzy handled the bundle carefully. She barely touched the letter and pendant with her hands, just moved them about as minimally as possible. When Kat asked about her trepidation, she matter-of-factly responded, "Your great, great, many greats grandmother was or is a witch. I think we can confirm that. These items were meant for you. I shouldn't interfere. Who knows what chaos I could inadvertently cause. These things may be charmed."

Kat hadn't thought of that, and it disturbed her to think on it now.

Suzy saw her distress and jumped in, "I'm sure it is nothing for you to worry over. But there may be magic here. You've her blood. We've no idea what would happen if someone else uses this."

It made sense on one level but scared Kat as well.

"This pendant…I know this pendant. Reminds me of something."

Kat held out the hand upon which she was wearing the ring. "Maybe this?"

Suzy tucked her glasses on top of her head, pulled Kat's hand closer, squinted over her ring, and then again at the pendant.

"Similar, yes." She paused, remembering. "This was your grandmother's ring? Edy's?"

"Yes, she gave it to me for my graduation present. Said there was no sense waiting to die to give it to me."

"Yes, I remember that…but there was something else to it. I am trying to remember. She wore it on her hand for the longest time and then—didn't. Said it made your grandfather jealous. He wouldn't believe that she hadn't gotten it from a beau, but she would never tell him where she had gotten it. Come to think of it, I don't recall knowing where she had gotten that ring either. Curious. Now this pendant is similar enough to be part of a set but different, too." She paused to poke at its side with the rubber end of a pencil she'd plucked from the jar on the table. "These markings, these I recognize. It's Ogham."

"What?"

"Ogham. Ancient Celtic writing…or was it before the Celts? Not sure, but it is old. Maybe we could get it translated at some point. Hmmm." She looked and pondered, making humming noise as she did so. Kat didn't say a word lest she break her concentration.

After a few moments Suzy stopped. "The pendant's stone is deeper somehow than the ring. More red in it. It looks almost alive with the movement of the thread of red."

Kat had thought so, too. It was interesting that she noted the same.

"Makes me wonder if the ring was Helene's, too."

"But how?"

"I think that may be easier than explaining those little trips you and Edy, I mean your gran, took."

"But if I have the ring, and now the pendant, what would be the purpose? Why would she want me to have these?"

"I don't know, honey. Only person who could help would really be Edy. Was there anything she said to you that made sense?"

"Only a little. She kept...shifting, talking about Donny and things long past. She kept losing reality. She did say she had been scared. Wait! She said the ring was her gift! Maybe it was given to her like the pendant was given to me! And she said something else, something about a glow."

Suzy slid the ring onto the pencil and held it up more closely to the light. The ring glowed like amber expectedly does. Suzy raised an eyebrow and nodded for Kat to hold the pendant up to the light as well. The amber held similar properties, but the red thread pulsed and swayed in the light as if it were beating to the thump of a heartbeat.

Kat dropped it to the floor and pointed. "What the hell is that?"

"I think that that would be a piece of magic tied up in a pretty pendant. And also all the more reason to get the damn thing translated." They both stood just looking at it a moment before she added, "Have you told anyone else about this?"

"Who would I tell?"

Suzy looked at Kat with that motherly, I-can-see-through-your-lies-young-lady look that always made her and Sky squirm as kids.

"Seriously, who could I tell—that would believe me?"

"Kathleen…?"

"No one, honest." Kat gave a huge sigh. "I tried to get some info out of Gran since Helene mentioned her, but I told her nothing. Never got a chance to. I might be too late for that conversation…"

Suzy gave Kat a quick squeeze.

"Might be for the best." Suzy relaxed. "Good. Let's keep it that way. Could be dangerous for them, anyone you would tell, or dangerous for you. I don't know. Got your gran in a tizzy this morning just thinking about it."

Kat bent to pick up the pendant. It felt heavier. The red was stagnant; maybe it was the heat of the lamp that made it swim so. She placed it next to the ring. It had to have been cut of the same source. Together, it was unmistakable.

"Have you worn it yet?"

"No, it's tempting, but I was afraid to."

"Well, kiddo, we can wait and see what she'll do next and wait in fear, or you could try the thing on and see what's to be. Your call. I am here for you either way."

Both Gran and Suzy called Kat kiddo. She couldn't remember who had started it, but it stuck. And with the shared endearment, Kat felt that Suzy was more than just herself but speaking for Gran as well.

Kat thought it over but a moment. She realized that sometimes you had to take a leap to see where you'd land. She slid the delicate, gold chain over her head to let the pendant rest on her chest. The red thread pulsed and surged again.

"Shall we go for the whole enchilada?" Suzy asked, holding out the ring.

She slid on the ring, and as Kat did so noticed that both the pendant and ring began to warm against her skin. The red pulsed now madly in the pendant, and then the ring began to glow. Kat quickly tossed both pieces off. The glow waned to nothingness, and the stone no longer pulsed. They were as dull as any paste jewelry in a costume shop.

Kat sat gulping air, trying to slow her panic.

"Well, I guess you have your answer. And I think we know what your gran meant about the glow. I would say that that was your calling card, some sort of invitation. Now you've just got to decide what your answer will be."

Kat didn't like it, not one little bit. Did she have a choice? She would have to find out. And Kat would start by having the damn thing translated.

8

Searching for Answers

The next day's visit to the local library wasn't much help—nor the Internet. Type in Ogham and all you got were Celtic jewelry sites and alphabet charts. The trouble was that with the alphabet chart it only worked if you were translating into Ogham from English. Added to that, some of the markings were only partial, so Kat couldn't be sure where one word ended and one began as the piece had worn down over time. It was far above her linguistic skills.

Looking up Helene's name in ancestry searches proved futile as well. It seemed she was untraceable…at least here in the states. Undoubtedly there were records, somewhere…church baptism or marriage certificate near the village she lived in. Kat quickly gave up as her existence wasn't the issue, and it was unlikely her "talents" had been recorded.

After more than a week of researching any chance she got, Kat decided it wasn't going to be a mystery solved in a conventional way. It was time to do something about all this waiting. She and Suzy met a few times. And true to her word Suzy made up a batch of her special, herbal tea guaranteed to help with the after effects of travel. She even made up a travel version to keep on her person. Kat kept it on her at all times. She just felt better having it.

Kat went back to visit Gran and still heard nothing lucid enough to be of any help. She just kept chanting, "Glow, glow, glow," with no clear meaning. Kat already knew that when you held the ring or pendant together they glowed. But what did that really mean? It was frustrating for both of them. Kat knew Gran was trying to get her to understand, but she couldn't find the words. And the more Gran tried, the worse it got. It was breaking Kat's heart. She knew she was in there, somewhere. The nurses told Kat there still could be good days, but she didn't trust them; they probably used platitudes with everyone.

Suzy and Kat spent considerable time together that week. Kat had forgotten what a fun person Suzy was and how much she'd missed her. After Sky's accident, it was hard facing her sorrow as it magnified her own. They'd both been broken, but Kat simply could not find comfort at her best friend's house. Kat knew she reminded Suzy of what she'd lost, and Suzy reminded Kat so much of Sky that it was haunting. But time, Kat agreed, does heal after a fashion, and they were able to put their heads together to come up with a plan.

Suzy decided they should stop waiting and try to make a "call" of their own to Helene. Suzy would help Kat compose a "psychic entreaty" and then stay at her home waiting for Kat should she be "picked up." It was crazy, Kat knew. But what else could they do? Kat hated waiting—for anything. Helene had said that Kat would be returned to the moment she left, and aside from the terrible aim of the last trip, this was mostly true, so she knew Suzy would not have long to wait for a report. The question was, could, or rather should, they call upon a witch? And did they really want to? How would Helene hear them? Neither Suzy nor

Kat had the faintest idea whether what they plotted was even possible, but it sure felt better than waiting around.

They decided the second Tuesday in November was the wisest to make their attempt. Plus, on a practical side, if Kat needed a few days off it wasn't during the holiday rush. They settled on a date; November 14th was going to be a cool, clear night. Suzy recalled as a kid that on cool, clear nights with no wind, when one played "Hide-and-Seek," voices carried further. She thought that would help their plan succeed. Kat didn't have the heart to tell her she thought that that was rubbish, but since Kat had no other thoughts or ideas on the matter, she figured, *what-the-hell, couldn't hurt*. Neither one of them had any idea what they were doing.

So late on a Tuesday night they prepared. Kat slipped back into the gown Helene had sent her home in, careful to stash Suzy's herbs within her bodice. She slipped the pendant over her head. Suzy and Kat sat on the carpet, facing each other as they attempted to call upon Helene. Suzy thought a nice fire would add to the mood but as Kat had modern heat and had replaced the gas stove with a pellet one, it couldn't be helped. So instead Suzy insisted she bring up one of the larger pieces of crystal Kat kept in the shop for them to focus their thoughts. "Centering," she called it.

Now that they were about to try this, really try, Kat felt foolish. Between the dress, the crystal, and Suzy's "spell," Kat felt sure she was losing her mind by going along with this plan. Maybe it was a one time trip, and she was just getting herself upset over nothing.

Suzy had researched and found some such spell on-line and reworded it to try to create the right tone for what they wanted to do. Kat had always believed in the saying about "nothing ventured..." but she felt sillier and sillier as they said the words together:

"Oh, spirit, guide my feet,
To the someone I must meet,
Light my way, which way to go,
Fire, wind, earth, sky,
Take to wings, guide my eye,
As I will, so may it be."

Kat squeezed closed her eyes in anticipation. When nothing happened, she slowly opened one eye, and squinted up at Suzy.

"Well?"

"Well, what?" Kat decided to tease. "Didn't you see me leave? And I'm back already. Whew!"

"You're a damn brat." Suzy cuffed her on her left ear.

Kat wanted to cry, not because she hit her, but because it reminded her of all the times she had before but no longer did, since Sky...

Suzy must've realized it, too, as she teared up a bit. "Sorry, kiddo."

"Naw, that was awesome. And I deserved it, too. Reminds me of home." Kat smiled, and then Suzy did, too. By the time they had hugged a handful of times and squeezed out a few tears, all their years of tip-toe-ing around each other faded away.

"That was a damn, stupid spell."

Kat nodded heartily, laughing. "Can't argue with that." She started to remove the pendant and then got to thinking...what was it that Helene said? Kat held the pendant in her hand as she thought back to that last night with Helene.

What if she could say her words in reverse? Or at least try some of it? If she could just remember... As Kat stared deeply into the stone, it began to pulse and glow, and the words came, both similar and different to the ones she had heard before:

"Bring the wind, bring the light,
Bring me to what's mine by right,

Compass hold, compass bright,
Waver not, guide my flight,
Hasten all, hasten three,
Bring me back, I take to thee
As you will, so mote it be."

Kat continued to stare into the pendant's stone, stared as though sucked into its core, the red thread weaving and surging. She heard wind and felt rushing air while all around her grew hazy like she was suspended in a heavy fog.

And then a voice seemed to echo from the stone.

9

A Forced Invitation

"You would call upon me?"

It was unmistakably Helene, with her lofty vowels and arrogant tone.

"Yes. It's my turn to ask questions."

"And you seek the answers willingly, Kathleen?"

"Yes, willingly."

"Then you are quite welcome."

Kat saw all go dark for a moment and the familiar swirl of color and light. It felt like she was being dropped into a tunnel, tossed like laundry in a dryer. Kat tried to relax as much as that was possible, taking slow, measured breaths. Maybe, she thought, if she didn't fight it this time the nausea wouldn't be as bad. And, on the plus side, she wasn't going to arrive in the nude, fresh from a bath. That had to be a huge improvement.

When Kat *arrived* she was startled. She was nowhere near the manor, but rather in a field near a large, sprawling, farm house in the shape of an L, in full daylight, not nighttime as she had left. As Kat looked wildly about, trying to get her bearings, Helene stepped out of the farm house and into the light.

She was dressed more simply than before but Helene's regal bearing was still evident. Her only flourish was a wine-colored cape.

"A brave one you are, seeking me out this time. How wonderful. How unlike your predecessors. A grand improvement." Helene swept towards Kathleen.

It seemed warmer here this time, and brighter. There were subtle changes about her face as well. It was fuller, with a sunnier glow.

Kat looked about, disoriented. "Where are we?"

"Don't you mean when and where are we?" Helene snickered at her own joke. "In your time, about four months since you were here last. It's spring here although this past winter only recently gave way. We're at the farm house, the manor farm. I am here regaining my strength after a strained and tiresome winter."

Helene moved away from the house, walking towards the field, newly sprouted. She held one hand at the base of her arched back. That's when Kat realized Helene was clearly pregnant.

Noticing Kat's glance, Helene laughed. "Yes, things have changed a wee bit. I've several months to go yet, but I am most decidedly swell." She patted her barely distended belly lovingly.

Kat had no idea what to say so she conceded to the most obvious, "Congratulations."

Helene smiled and nodded. "It is a blessing, and a mighty welcome one." She paused, eyed Kat from head to toe. "As are you. But what shall I do with you?"

"Teach me." Kat wasn't sure where that came from, but once uttered, she knew it to be true. "Teach me what this is. Why? How? I need to know." Her hands flailed at her sides awkwardly as she sought for the words to explain how much she wanted this.

"You may need to know, but are you ready to learn?" Helene cocked one eyebrow, a move Kat recognized as she herself often did it. "Ah, but there is a small problem. Last time, I called to you. This time I am not prepared to have you as a guest."

Kat shifted uncomfortably.

"You are not to give it undue worry; you are quite welcome. However, I have not prepared my husband or the household that a guest would be arriving. Hence, I diverted you here." Helene's hands spanned side to side. "If you could but spend a day or three here, I can make preparations at home so they would know to expect you. No one can or will know of our little secret. You shall be my younger cousin returning to visit on your way through to Hertfordshire. That should serve. I shall scurry about and set things in motion. Not to fret, my dear, you'll be quite comfortable here. I shall provide you with garments and all you should need before I can send for you at the big house."

Kat wasn't sure how to interpret this. She found it ironic that Helene had called her out of her home, out of her tub, and she was supposed to just "go with it," but now she was left to wait in another place—for days.

Helene must have seen Kathleen's confusion because she touched her on the forearm and drew Kat's gaze within her own.

"Please, I know it is confusing, and I am happy to see you. But things after last time became quite...complicated." Helene gave Kat a knowing glare. "I had to rush you off because of some of those developments. I will explain what I can at a later time, but for now, I am expected at the manor house. And it is there I can set things in motion to better receive you." She paused, her stare uncomfortably direct and unwavering. "Please be patient. I do this for your and my protection."

"Helene?" Kat ventured as Helene turned to lead her into the farmhouse to introduce Kat to her hosts. "Helene," she began again, "I have someone waiting for me. How long...?"

Helene smiled broadly. "That's the joy of time travel, no one on the other side need wait. She will only know a moment's loss of you, no more."

"How did you know it was a 'she'?"

Helene laughed. "Come along. I will teach you all this and more someday. Let's get you settled first. How are you feeling?"

"A bit queasy but not as bad as last time. A friend concoct—"

"Ah, a home witch! How wonderful! Those are the best to keep near." Helene clapped her hands.

"No, no, she's not a witch, she's just a friend who—"

"Call it what you will, but there are all sorts of magic and all levels of witches." Helene abruptly got quiet at the appearance of someone just outside the farmhouse door but then leaned in conspiratorially. "We have this and so many other things to discuss—but not here. Later. I will be back for you as soon as I can, a day at most."

Kat must've had a panicked look because Helene quickly continued, "Do not dismay, all will be made clear. Plus, you have my pendant. You already reached me across time and space. Wear it always and you are never far. And by the way, I will want a full explanation on just what you did that got you here. Hush. Later."

Helene gave Kat's hand a quick, hard squeeze before she led her to be introduced to the head housekeeper. In a low voice, Helene explained that the farm had kept boarders or visitors several times in the past as the main house would require, so the housekeeper would think nothing of the impromptu guest.

"Mrs. Brown, I'd like you to take special care of my guest here, Miss Kathleen...Evans. She will be joining the manor house as soon as it may be arranged and just needs temporary lodgings. I will send for a few of her things as she would need for a day or three." Helene casually winked at Kat. "Oh, and she is to be a special guest only, not a hand. I have other plans for her."

"Yes, ma'am. In which room do you desire her to be housed?"

"Put her in my rooms for when I am in residence as she is a distant," she again winked, "relative. I want every comfort that is desired fulfilled. Just send young Travis to me with word if you need supplies or want for anything."

"Understood," Mrs. Brown gave a quick head bob.

Helene turned to explain, "Mrs. Brown came with Alastair up from London to help him set up house. She's been quite indispensable."

Mrs. Brown preened under her praise. Kat suspected that Helene had no doubt added this bit of flattery to soften any inconvenience she might be. It appeared Helene was a smart business woman, too.

Helene soon set off to the manor, which was less than a half hour's ride away in the hansom carriage that had been sent to fetch her.

While on one level Kat understood that she needed to wait, not knowing what caused the turmoil previously left her nervous. She realized part of her discomfort was in again being left helpless. Sure, she had taken the initiative and summoned herself back, but what did that serve? Kat still had no better idea than the last time as to what she was dealing with and no power to do anything about it either way. It was a precarious situation, and she didn't like the tug of unanswered questions and feelings of doubt. As Kat waved goodbye she couldn't help but wonder if she'd made a terrible mistake. God, she hoped not.

Kat stood there in the drive a few extra minutes, hesitant to move, unsure of her surroundings, and doubting everything after the carriage drove from view. She held her shoulders with crossed arms—not to ward off any chill but rather her misgivings. Kat took a deep breath, jutted out her chin, and headed up the few steps.

10

The Manor Farm

Mrs. Brown, upon hearing that Kathleen was to have Helene's rooms, seemed to view her in a reverential light. She was not merely a boarder but someone of consequence. Kat had to admit she enjoyed the welcome.

The first thing Mrs. Brown did was take Kat to Helene's rooms, bustling about and setting them to rights although Kat saw nothing out of place. By comparison to the manor, the rooms were quite simple, and maybe that knowledge concerned her. Gone were the velvets and satins, instead were the cottons, woolens, and even leather. However, Mrs. Brown need not have worried as Kat found the rooms all the more pleasing because of it. Here was a place she could relax in rather than feel like she was always waiting in state for the queen. The windows were smaller out of practicality, but through them she could see woods to the one side and the newly groomed furrows to the other.

Mrs. Brown opened the windows wide to freshen the room, and the smell of lilacs wafted up from below. While the air was yet brisk, it nonetheless infused everything with the fresh scent. Mrs. Brown pointed out proudly the indoor toilet down the hall, a pull cord, should Kathleen desire anything, and a chest at the foot of the bed that held extra linens and pillows, should she need them.

"We might not be in the great city anymore, but I run a proper English home." Mrs. Brown then left Kat to her devices for the time being while she prepared tea.

Kat sat in the deep, horsehair chair and tugged off her boots, stretched out her legs before tucking them under herself. She scanned her new surroundings. At first glance it looked like the room was taken straight out of a romance novel—with its wide, wooden-plank flooring partially covered in woolen rugs. There were a couple of seating areas—the one Kat sat in beneath the window, and a pair of high-backed chairs facing the fieldstone hearth. A massive chest butted up to the foot of the bed. The bed itself had posts of carved wood in a Celtic knot pattern that was covered with Irish linens and wools. Quite taken by the room, Kat realized if she staged this same room in the 21st century it would probably sell for a mint. She made a mental note to recreate it later at home. She might even try to sketch it while she was here.

Stretching as she rose, Kat wandered and touched everything. She knew little to nothing, and she wanted to learn the secrets of her host, Helene. In one windowsill, Kat found a tiny, blown-glass bottle filled with Lily of the Valley flowers. On the hearth, a sharpened quill and sealing wax sat without the benefit of ink or paper. Kathleen poked and peeked in every crevice and corner, and found partially done snatches of embroidery, an errant shoe, and a basket of sewing notions.

She grew tired and bored, and wondered if tea would ever come. She wished she could've brought her watch for there was no way for her to measure the time. The room seemed to have anything she could need—save a clock. As the sky began to gray over, she became chilled and went back to the chest, hoping to find a throw. Kat was reluctant to close the window just yet. The deliciously, large chair called to her, and she was dying to curl up in it. Kat tugged and pulled at a coverlet. She knew she could've removed a blanket from the bed, but Kat, in a sentimental bent, didn't want to mess the coverings and destroy the lovely picture they presented.

The blanket appeared to be caught or tangled. Kat wrestled with the piles of linens, trying to remove any impeding weight. When she finally yanked the blanket free, Kat fell to the floor with a thump. But that wasn't the only noise she heard. It sounded like she had released a latch or catch when she finally drew the blanket clear. Curiosity piqued, Kat decided to unload the entire chest. She laid layer after layer of linens aside, trying to carefully stack, in order, the contents so that she could reassemble it back later—Mrs. Brown none the wiser. After reaching a layer of bolt cloth and removing it, she finally saw the bottom. Curious. What could've made that clicking sound? Kat thought she must have either imagined it or the sound had carried from elsewhere. She couldn't see anything else to blame it on. Then a moment of inspiration hit. Kat felt along the base of the chest, the boards within, and all about the trim work for a latch, a catch, or secret drawer. Her fingers nimbly scrambled about seeking the combination that would reveal…who knew what?

After several minutes of frustrated exertion Kat stopped and laughed at herself. She had obviously seen far too many Hollywood movies! Seriously, what did she think she'd find? Between old *Raiders of the Lost Ark* movies and the conspiracy novels, Kat had let her imagination run wild. Wasn't it enough that she was several generations back in time with an ancestral witch? "Pull it together, Kat," she muttered to herself.

Kat had just replaced everything except the coverlet back in to the chest when Mrs. Brown returned to announce tea.

"Would you be wanting tea in your rooms or would you care to join the household and a boarder downstairs?"

Kat quickly agreed to have tea below. She had fully explored her room, so any change would be an improvement. Kat was ready to climb the walls with boredom. As she motioned to let Mrs. Brown walk ahead, Kat feigned a need to tighten her shoe laces so she could remove Suzy's herbal remedy from her bodice. The last dose was wearing off, and she knew she'd need to add some to her tea or the nausea would threaten to take over. Not knowing what Mrs. Brown would think on this, and remembering Helene's admonition towards caution, Kat decided that her little remedy would remain her secret.

Mrs. Brown was busy enough that Kat's caution was nearly unwarranted. The woman briskly went about serving and orchestrating the kitchen help. The tea consisted of watercress and cucumber sandwiches cut on the diagonal, hunks of hearty, brown breads, and clay pots of honey and butter. Scones stood cooling on the sideboard, the smells tantalized and teased. Like a woman at her last meal, Kat absorbed it all and stored it into memory.

However, even Kat had her limits and finally excused herself. Mrs. Brown, upon seeing her fatigue, had a kitchen maid escort Kathleen to her rooms. The girl carried a large hamper with her. Apparently Helene had hastened to send a few "of her belongings" with a young stable hand who had been on his way to the farm. The maid that led Kat back to her rooms was small but strong, like a young boy. The girl refused all of Kat's offers of assistance—whether that was due to pride or Mrs. Brown's insistence, Kat could not know. The maid placed the basket on the foot of the bed and began to unpack "Kathleen's" things. Helene had sent three day dresses, several undergarments that looked rather complicated, a sleeping gown, and a wrap. Assorted woolens, a secondary pair of shoes, and a set of hair brushes rounded out the set. Kathleen thanked the girl and quickly sent her on her way. Kat pleaded the need for rest due to her long journey.

Once the door closed, Kat looked over the clothing options more closely. She slipped on the wrap, drawn by its deep, green color. As she tied it about herself for warmth, she felt something out of place. Tucked within the folds was a parchment. Kat hastened to open it and read the contents.

Small delay. Two to three days. Will handle situation. You are not forgotten.
H~

Kat really couldn't say she was surprised; Helene had warned her that she might need to stay put. Kat felt about in the other clothing and found nothing more until she reached into the right boot. There she found a small bag of coins and a bundle of herbs much like what Suzy had constructed and another note.

I find this helps if the other will not.
H~

Well, okay then. *I guess I'll be just fine.* Kat kept that thought in her head as she curled up in the chair for a nap.

It was several hours later when Mrs. Brown came by lamplight to rouse her. Mrs. Brown explained that Kathleen had slept through supper even though attempts had been made by Maeve, the kitchen girl, to wake her. She only now disturbed her, Mrs. Brown continued, as she worried Kathleen would be stiff if she continued to sleep twisted up so in the chair.

"Would you like help getting ready for bed now or could you eat a bite of something beforehand?"

Kat could indeed eat. For some reason she'd awakened famished. Mrs. Brown had a plate ready at hand, a joint of meat dressed in acorns and some wild mushrooms, a hunk of bread from earlier, and a thick slice of cheese. All was followed with a heated mug of mulled wine. Kat ate quickly as she again struggled to fight off sleep. She soon realized she would lose the battle as the wine worked to ease her aches. Kat climbed into bed and to the best night's rest she had literally in ages.

The following morning Kat awoke feeling refreshed and fully herself. She would need to remember to thank Suzy for that when she got back. Kat threw back the blankets and stepped across to the window in attempt to guess what the time was. The house was surrounded in a fine mist and rain, making all look dark and shadowed. Kat gathered the woolen shawl from the foot of the bed and made her way downstairs as best she could in the dim light. She rapped her knee on the edge of a hall table and muffled her curses. Kat hadn't paid enough attention last night and had no idea where to get a candle or oil lamp. She vowed she wouldn't make that mistake again.

Several of what Kat was sure would undoubtedly be bruises later, she neared the kitchen as she wound her way down the back hall. She was led by the voices and the general kitchen clatter. Kat hesitated a moment as her stomach began to rumble. She wasn't sure how to proceed. Was she supposed to lie abed and wait to be fed? Kat had no idea the protocol of both the home nor the time. Just thinking about it made her nerves twitch. The magnitude of what she'd done, not once but twice, began to make her anxious. *Just what have I gotten myself in to?* Her head began to ache just thinking about it.

Kat suddenly worried about all the possibilities of what could happen this time around when the door opened and was brisk-

ly exited by a young girl carrying a surprisingly large bundle of wood for her size. The girl nodded as she brushed past, calling back over her shoulder, "The lady is awake, Mrs. Brown."

Mrs. Brown popped her head out the kitchen door, "Ah, so you are, Miss. Are you be needing anything?"

Kathleen awkwardly stammered, "I didn't know whether I should wait upstairs or come down, but I wondered about breakfast and the hour."

"Well, you must be fair starving to come down as you have! 'Tis early though, can't be more than half past six or quarter till. I had thought you'd sleep a bit longer, or I'd have had a tray up to you. My mistake. I see you are an early riser. I'll be sure to note it for as long as you stay. But let's get you upstairs and dressed before any of the men or hands catch sight of you."

As Mrs. Brown looked her over, Kat could see where she'd erred based on her reaction. Kat felt Mrs. Brown measure her appearance and couldn't help but squirm. She was sure that Mrs. Brown could clearly see her blush as she was fair to begin with.

"I'll send the girl up to dress you once she's done with setting up the hearths. Would you like breakfast in the main room or your own rooms?" Mrs. Brown paused, waiting for instruction.

Kat had no idea what was expected of her, what was proper, what Helene would think best. She took a moment to think; she stalled by gathering and adjusting the wrap that covered her. "I think in my rooms would be best, if that is not too inconvenient." Kat thought that was the safest reply. Alone in her rooms she knew she would be the furthest from observation.

Mrs. Brown nodded and smiled in approval, "Just so, seems fit. The lady does the same when she's here. Very good, Miss."

"If it's not too much trouble."

"Far from it, Miss. You see the kitchen on this farm is the busiest in the morning with all the comings and goings. It is actually a kindness not to have to set out the table in the main." When Kat moved to interrupt, Mrs. Brown anticipated her thoughts and quickly stated, "And the kitchen is no place for a lady or guest." She smiled, softened by Kathleen's consideration, "I thank you for asking. You'll quickly get the rhythm of the place. When I get a break, I'll come up and sit with you for a bit and let you know the general running of the house so's you can not be troubled."

Kat said thank you, sincerely, and hastened upstairs. What had she been thinking? By their standards she might as well have come downstairs naked! This was not her family home where she could wander into the kitchen and grab a bite out of the fridge! How could she have been so stupid and careless? As a working farm there were untold numbers of servants and workers. Kat raced up the stairs, taking them two at a time. She hoped that she could get back to her rooms without being noticed by anyone else.

Once behind the closed door of Helene's rooms Kat cursed herself. She must get smarter about these things! Kat sat heavily in the chair before the hearth. *Damn it, Helene, I need you back. I haven't a clue about how to behave, what to say—anything*. Kat pulled out the pendant and stared at the stone. She brought it close to her mouth, breathed heavily on it to make a haze, and rubbed it clear. Nothing happened. Kat whispered Helene's name into the stone, nothing still.

"Well, this is useless," Kat said with a groan. She absentmindedly poked about the banked fire with a stick in an attempt to increase the glow. There were a few pops and sparks as the exposed bits flared up to meet the air but not much else. She tried to think of any movie she had ever watched, any book she had ever read, or any painting that remotely was close to this time. And now she laughed at herself. Hadn't she just been in a play set in approximately the same time period? Kat realized she simply would have to behave as the others did.

Kat didn't know why this distressed her so, other than a premonition of danger if she did not figure out how to blend in—

and quickly. She couldn't help but remember Helene's face the last time they fled her home in haste. Something, or someone, had troubled Helene. Something had made it impossible for Kat to stay. She needed to be more observant in the future. If only Helene were here to guide her in what she should do. Perhaps, she thought optimistically, she would not have so long to wait.

The girl, Maeve, arrived soon after carrying a large tray with both hands and a bag slung across her body. She placed the tray on the table by the hearth before she spoke.

"Would you like to dress first, Miss, or break your fast?"

"I think dress would be best. It is very chilly this morning. Is it always this cool this time of the year?"

"No, Miss, and the fog's a bit thick, too. I'll get the fire to rights first if you don't mind."

Kathleen nodded to the logic in that and went over to see what smelled so good. There were huge sausages swimming in some sort of gravy, dark bread, a small pot of honey, a few pats of butter, cream, a pot of tea, and looking under a lid, she found a bowl of coarse-cut oatmeal. She couldn't have asked for a better meal on such a miserable morning.

Within moments the girl had the fire in its full glory again, and Maeve turned her attention to dressing Kathleen. Without bothering to ask her opinion in the matter, Maeve sorted through the garments sent over by Helene to find a suitable choice for the day. She chose a simple, flannel plaid and a fresh cotton underdress in shades of soft grays and muted blues. Maeve found tall woolens in navy that slid far up Kathleen's thigh. Before Kat knew it the girl had laced her bodice with the nimble speed of a practiced hand, kindly pulling the stays in a way that allowed both support and breathing. Kat couldn't help but compare this to the discomfort of the theatre costume. Obviously the dress consultant had gotten the grooming habits incorrect as she felt encased rather than strangled.

"If Miss would like to eat now whiles it's still hot, I could sort the room and then dress your hair."

Kat heartily agreed as in the few minutes it took to dress, the smells of the sausages were killing her with anticipation. Kathleen couldn't know how a lady ate, nor how much of the breakfast she was anticipated to eat, but she couldn't worry about it. Kat had always had a hearty appetite. The sausages were like none she had had before, more grainy and leaner than she was used to but good nonetheless. Kat silently wished for sugar in her oatmeal but made do with the honey and butter. Maeve raised an eyebrow at that, but Kat ignored her—she wasn't going to eat it plain. The girl could think what she would. Kat was from "away," and at "away," this was how they ate oatmeal. Kat laid waste to most of the tray while Maeve tidied the room, made the bed, and folded the blanket she had left in a pile over the side of the arm chair. When she saw Kathleen was finished eating, she went through her bag and brought out brushes and an assortment of hair combs, pins, and ribbons.

Maeve brushed through Kathleen's tousled curls, pushing and pulling, testing to see which was the way of it before she could decide what best to do with her hair.

"Well, Miss, I think a twist in the back might do so's we could leave out a few curls about your face. With the rain and mist, there's no hope of keeping it smooth anyway."

"As you will," Kat said, conceding. She let Maeve do what she would, appreciating the attention to her hair in whatever form it took. At least with the girl doing it, she knew it would be appropriate.

Maeve held up the small glass she had removed from her bag. Kat saw she'd done a fine job, far better than she would have with far more modern appliances. As she moved to leave, gathering her things up and shoving them back in her bag, Kat thought she'd ask her a few questions.

"How long have you worked here, Maeve?"

The girl seemed startled and surprised that Kathleen wanted to talk to her. "My whole life, Miss. I was born on this land."

"Um, yes, but how long have you worked here?"

"I don't know the difference, Miss. Always worked here so long as I could carry or fetch."

Kat decided to change tack. "I might decide to walk later but do not know what there is nearby. Is there somewhere you'd suggest for me to walk to and explore?"

Maeve seemed relieved that the conversation moved from her to something less personal.

"Aye, Miss. There's a lovely garden just to the left side of the house if you've a mind towards some flowers and herbs. We grow the cutting blooms for the main house here. There's a greenhouse behind that that will have some new seedlings rooting."

"What about towards the woods? Is there anything there of interest?"

"Miss?"

Kat decided on a quick lie as her eyes glanced upon a charcoal pencil and parchment on the table at the window furthest. "I like to sketch things in nature sometimes."

The girl seemed to visibly relax, "Ah, like the lady of the house, to be sure." She beamed. "She drew my dog this last year. 'Twas a very near likeness."

"Yes, well," Kat pushed the idea, "I like to walk about and find new things to inspire me. Anything about that might make a good subject?"

"Well," Maeve paused and thought. "Not so far in is an old graveyard but that would be gruesome to draw. But beside it you'll find the old abbey ruins. The one turret is mostly intact although I'd warn you not to try the stairs. Mrs. Brown would hide me if anything happened to you, especially since you are a special guest of the lady and kin. But I have always thought the abbey romantic somehow, especially the bits covered by ivy."

Kat didn't want to keep the girl any longer as she would bet the girl had a full day's chores ahead. "Thank you, Maeve, I'm sure it's lovely."

"Oh, but Miss, don't go through the woods alone and in this mist. You wouldn't want to get lost. Many a person has gotten turned around in there. If you decide to walk that way, let the kitchen know, and they'll send a lad with you."

"Oh, I wouldn't want to be a bother..."

"No bother, Miss. The lady walks there often enough, and the hounds always need a walk. One direction is the same as the other to them to be sure."

Kat thanked her again, and Maeve took her cue to leave. Kat had already learned more about Helene than she had thought to without even trying. She rummaged in the wardrobe for a cape and found a woolen cloak that should wick away the light rain that continued to fall. It seemed Helene and Kat did have several things in common—she would always choose the woods over fields given the choice. However, Kat hoped to avoid having a pack of dogs and a farm boy in tow. She wanted the time to think and to explore her surroundings.

Maeve must have gone directly to Mrs. Brown and told her Kathleen's intention to take a walk as she hadn't made it to the bottom of the stairs when Mrs. Brown met her.

"Miss Kathleen, if you've a minute?"

"Yes, Mrs. Brown, how can I help you?"

"Might I have a word with you in the front room?" She turned before Kat could utter a response, making her thoughts on the matter a moot point. When she caught up with her, Mrs. Brown motioned to the chair nearest. "Please."

Kathleen sat and waited for her to do the same.

"Maeve tells me you've a mind to a morning walk. And I can see you are ready to do so, promptly."

“Yes, I thought I’d look about the grounds a bit, to get acquainted.”

“Yes, yes, that’s a fine thought, but I must urge you not to wander past the gardens without a guide.”

“I’m sure that I’d be fine. I won’t go far, just stretching my legs a bit.”

“Yes, dear, I am sure that that is all you intend, but you see I am under strict orders from her ladyship that you must be cared for, and as you are not from around here, I’m to take extra special care. Those were her words.”

“I see,” Kat did indeed begin to see, but she wasn’t sure if she was being paranoid in thinking perhaps that she wasn’t quite as free here as she thought.

“It would be no trouble at all to send a lad with you if it is the woods you be wanting.” Mrs. Brown looked at Kathleen expectantly.

“No, that won’t be necessary.” Kat quickly lied for the second time that morning. “Because of the rain, I was thinking of just exploring the greenhouse. Maeve said there are some new seedlings. I’ve no mind to get soaked after she spent so much time making my hair look so lovely.” Kat smiled broadly, hoping she looked sincere.

Mrs. Brown heaved a sigh of relief. “Ah well, that’s fine then. You could always see the woods another day when the weather’s clearer.” As she rose to take her leave Mrs. Brown continued, “Lunch is midday. The lady likes to take it in the front parlor as the sun’s best there this time of year. You should be back in plenty of time.”

Kathleen gave her a quick nod, smile still on her face as she hastened to slip out the door.

11

The Gardener's Secret

Once outside, Kathleen wandered the gardens at the side of the house for a while before continuing on to the greenhouse. It hadn't been her goal for the morning, but perhaps it was wisest to stay close, Kat thought. Helene could come back this morning, ready to whisk her away. Plus, the weather encouraged her hesitancy as the mist seemed to grow instead of wane.

Kat pulled the hood of her cloak closer, enjoying the warmth and the privacy it afforded her. It was too early in the season to see more than just the beginnings of growth in the garden beds, but the patterns someone had created out of the bed formation made the paths wind and twist in a charming way. She was sure it would be lovely when fully fleshed out with plants. Kat recognized many of the plantings with the help of the names on each bed's marker. Otherwise it would be difficult to recognize one plant from the other in their infant state. Kat let her mind wander and imagined what would be here. She knew a master gardener must've been the cause of this. It reminded her of a long ago trip to the countryside and the English gardens she had seen in full bloom. There would be several layers of growth, heights, colors, and textures when it all filled in. Kat doubted once summer was in full swing there would be a bare or bland section to be found.

There was something about the thought of so much planning and consideration to something as germane as a garden that made Kat sigh at the elegance and dignity of such an endeavor. In her day, most gardens were a tedious row of one type of bloom or practical but inornate, food stuffs. Only in modern day corporate gardening did one see fullness and pattern. But even there it was dictated by practicality and volume, beds filled with one or two hardy plantings rather than the variety present here. This garden was truly a representation of a different time and values.

In such a sentimental mood Kathleen entered the greenhouse. She stopped to shake and knock the droplets of water off her cloak. She knew that wool deflected water only until a certain point. Once saturated, she would be soaked through much like a wet dog would. Kat stood stomping her boots until finally tossing back her hood, but when she did she noticed something or someone scurry off to her left. She twisted and turned quickly to catch a glimpse. She saw a wizened and hunched old man in shirtsleeves, woolen vest, and coarse trousers ending in very practical boots.

"Oh, hello. I'm sorry," Kat began to apologize. "I didn't see you."

The man turned with a *harrumph*, moving more quickly than Kat imagined possible towards the other side of the greenhouse.

Kat followed him, calling, "Excuse me, sir."

He continued on, either ignorant to the advance she was making or purposely ignoring her. Kat couldn't tell which. But with her longer legs and youth she soon caught up with him. Kat tapped him on his still fleeing shoulder in effort to detain him and make contact.

"Excuse me, sir. Is this your garden?"

He stopped abruptly. "Persistent, aren't you?" He said, evidently not pleased at Kat's intrusion.

"Pardon? I was told I could walk in the gardens."

"Yes, yes, I am sure. But next time knock at the door before you disturb us in here. Bringing your wet and muck from outside." He tsked, tsked Kat.

"I am so sorry," she stammered. "I assure you that I hadn't meant—"

"Yes, yes, well, you are here now. You can look about all you want, just don't touch anything. Anything! Do you hear me?"

"Yes, sir, I do. I used to garden back home with my grandmother..."

He gave a quick glare and turned to walk away, leaving Kathleen in mid-sentence, making it quite clear he was done discussing anything with her. Kat stood, watching him go. Seldom had she encountered such rudeness. He made his way to the door at the far side which now dawned on her must be the gardener's cottage attached to the greenhouse that she had noticed upon arrival at the farm. He stopped with the door partially open and called back over his shoulder.

"I would stay put if I was you, young lady, and not leave the house at all. Curiosity killed the cat, you know. It's best if you stayed put. I promise you, you'd wish you did." He trudged through his door without a backward glance, letting the door slam behind him.

Kat stopped, transfixed. She was stunned not by his words but by what she saw just as his door was about to close. Kat had, most clearly and distinctly, seen a swath of sunshine cut through the very room he entered. She quickly looked to both sides of her through the exposed greenhouse glass and still heard the patter of persistent rain and saw nothing but thick fog. But there, most clearly, there had been sunlight!

"Well, who cares what that troll thinks of me. I have to know the truth!" Kat grumbled under her breath.

Kat eased his door open, leaned in, pausing only to let her eyes adjust, and sought in the recesses of the long hallway before her for any sign of the gardener. He was nowhere in sight, but from the banging and thumping she heard, she knew he must be in a room to the far side of the corridor. Kat stepped fully into his home, pulled the door quietly shut behind her, and used the stray beam of light to lead herself further down the hall. She moved slowly, wary lest she make a noise or disturb something that would give her away. The noises and bumblings about in the far room reassured her she was safe so far.

The sunbeam grew stronger as Kat drew closer to it, and she was drawn like the proverbial moth to a flame. The light came from a partially closed shade in a front room. Kat bent to peer beneath it and saw what she knew to be true—it was a glorious, sunny spring day outside. Kat didn't care if he heard her anymore. She went across the room to the nearest door and stepped out into full sunshine. The brightness hurt, and she quickly threw a hand up to create some shade. She walked out past the far side of the cottage and looked back on the greenhouse, gardens, and farmhouse. Kat saw all was swathed in a blanket of fog, much like when one bundles oneself with a blanket when chilled. The entire lot was encapsulated in a bubble of rain and mist that had a discernible start and end. Looking past the house towards the woods she saw sheets of rain that grew denser the further you looked into the forest.

It appeared that Helene, like the old man, wanted Kat to stay put. She pulled her cloak about herself as if chilled. She couldn't help but wonder why would Helene be so intent on her staying in the farmhouse? And what kind of power must she have that she could create and maintain this from afar? It was mind-boggling to think about, so instead, Kat focused on the immediate mystery at hand. She was willing to bet money that the rain did not last far into the woods either. And she was determined to find out!

12

The Abbey

Making a point to try to stay clear of the line of sight of any windows and sticking to the shrubbery, Kat moved as quickly as she could across the grounds to circle over toward the woods. It troubled her that despite her caution she couldn't know if anyone looking out could see her. When she glanced back over at the farmhouse all she could see was mist and rain. Kat hoped that that obscured view was true of each window. It pained her that it seemed forever before she would reach the edge of the forest. Her heart raced. She could feel her pulse quicken as beads of sweat formed along her brow.

Once inside the tree line, Kat had no clear plan other than to try to find the abbey that Maeve spoke of. Her eyes strained, sought, and adjusted to the dappled light. She finally caught a fleeting glance of an abbey spire or turret. Instinct told her to choose her direction based on where she could see it was raining the hardest. That must be what Helene wanted hidden, and therefore, that was what Kat was most curious of. She might regret it, but Kat figured why not, *nothing ventured* as she dove into the thicket.

The rain grew stronger, and the fog thickened with each step she took, but Kat did not let it deter her from her goal. She tried to keep to a general direction as much as the undergrowth would allow. When she felt she was turned about, having lost her way, she always moved to where the rain was strongest. Kat quickly learned to hold out a hand to test the pressure of the drops and then moved toward the worst. It wasn't scientific, but it seemed logical. After about a half hour she could see through the mist to the outline of the ruins of the abbey. It seemed almost ghostly, the softened image of an ancient, Medieval abbey, as removed from the world as Avalon. Kat pushed onward, now a clear target in sight. However, the more she walked the farther it seemed to get. She chalked it up to more of Helene's mischief. No matter how hard she tried to move forward, she simply could not get there.

The abbey seemed to recede with every step she made so that Kat felt she was interminably on a treadmill to nowhere. Kat began to run, heedless of the brambles that tore at her skirts and tugged at her legs. The faster she ran, the more her target receded. The wind blew, pummeled Kat's body, and tugged her back. Rain lashed at her face, pelleting her with drops of water set on blinding her progress. The harder she pushed, the more intently the forces of nature pushed her back.

Frustrated and angry, fueled by her time alone and days with no answers, Kat struggled to control her emotions. Kat took a deep breath and simply stopped. This was obviously some game that Helene had created. She closed her eyes to imagine the abbey as she first saw its outline, recounted her steps in her mind. Kat ran back through the scene as though it was in instant replay on a DVD player and mentally applied her movements to where she should have been had her steps moved her forward. She visualized forward movement toward the abbey and opened her eyes. Kat had successfully brought herself to the base of the abbey wall and defeated the spell! She found that within the shadow of the abbey there was no rain but rather glorious sunshine. Kat shook out her cloak, much like a matador must encourage a bull, relieved at both the end of her search and as the recipient of the warming sunlight. The rain had soaked both the cloak and Kat thoroughly. But she was relieved that in this warmth, she should be back to rights shortly.

The abbey ruins were a stunning display of a moment set back in time. Overgrown and dilapidated, it nonetheless harkened back to a time when the church was the center of social order. It was really little more than a shell, with many sections tumbled and overgrown by bracken and brambles. Early spring flowers, violets and crocus, budded unbidden in unusual spots. But a few walls soared, the arches outlining previous grandeur and glory. The tower Kathleen had been warned of was missing a span of stairs that must have measured at least ten feet off the ground. Why Maeve would think that anyone would think to attempt the climb, she'd no idea. The remaining stairs wound in a circular manner, and past the first few, it could not be known if they continued or not as they were obscured by shadows and wall. Kat would think anyone would be terrified that the tower itself would topple as there seemed to be little supporting it as the one wall was completely gone and the others in ruins.

Kat made her way down the one full wall and pushed through a heavy door to enter the main chapel area. Most of it was now exposed to the open air, the roof long gone and the back corner entirely missing, with large saplings growing where pews once stood. A large portion of the alter still stood, as it was mainly just a large, hewn boulder shaped into a table. Though largely moss-covered, its sheer size alone led Kat to believe this was an eminent and revered church seat. She tried to imagine worshipping here with the hinted size of the main chapel and the soaring reaches. It inspired thoughts of the churches she had seen in paintings of Europe. Had the forest grown at its feet? It was truly hard to say as it all looked timeless. Kat reclined against the alter, closed her eyes to lean back and best enjoy the sun.

Why the secrecy? Why the elaborate plan to keep Kat, or anyone, from this place? Or was it just she who needed to stay away? And if so, to what end? The more she thought about it the less she could relax. Kat dusted off the bracken that had attached to her skirts. She was mostly dry now—for the time being. She grimaced at the thought of making her way back to the farmhouse and back through the frigid rain. She resigned herself that there was no hope for it. She had more questions than answers. When Kat remembered the graveyard that Maeve had mentioned she figured she might as well take a look before she headed back.

Kat made her way along the back side of the chapel. It really wasn't as large as she initially thought, just tall—its height created the image of grandeur. Sure enough, at the back side, in a fenced in area outlined with a fieldstone wall lay a quaint graveyard. All was a bit neglected and overgrown, but nonetheless the site looked to have been a cheery place to be laid to rest. From this vantage point, as it was set on a sloping hill, Kat could see past the forest to the fields and lands beyond. Far in the distance, she could even see the bend of a river and what must be a hamlet or village.

The cemetery's enclosing wall was on level with Kat's bottom ribs and thus too tall to merely slip over. She worked her way around its perimeter to find the entry. She had not gotten within a dozen feet of the gate when she heard growling. Two, huge mastiffs came running towards her, teeth bared, dripping saliva, and quickly closing the distance between Kat and themselves. Kat's heart pounded in her chest, and she felt sure that anyone within earshot could have heard it. She sucked in a deep breath, trying to slow her pulse from the racing that was making her light-headed. So Kat did the only thing she could think to do—she turned and fled the way she had come.

Kat's nerves reverberated with tension as she figured the odds and didn't like her conclusions. She quickly left the clearing and raced back into the woods, to the break in the brambles from which she had so recently come. Kat braced herself as she assumed that she would be met with the same resistance of wind and rain as met her coming. Instead, the farther Kat got away from the abbey, the easier and more clear the way. It was as if the winds parted from her and blew at her back, hastening her movements away. Soon the sound of the dogs receded in the distance. Apparently they had quickly given up the hunt. Kat could not fathom what would discourage their pursuit so quickly but was glad of the lucky break.

13

House Arrest

Before Kat knew it she was at the back of the farmhouse. It only seemed moments since she'd left the forest and the abbey, and yet she must've covered close to a half mile in but a step. She quickly slid through the door and dashed up the stairs to her room.

There, sitting by the hearth, was Mrs. Brown who had just laid out lunch.

Kat strained to catch her breath. She held a hand to her chest, and focused on slowing her breathing.

"I'd heard you had a nice walk and thought you'd be ready for a hot lunch and some tea," Mrs. Brown smiled.

Kat couldn't put her finger on it, but it seemed the smile didn't reach her eyes. She felt trapped, like she was caught with her hand in the proverbial honey jar. Kat's mind raced, but her pulse slowed, and her stomach demanded. She couldn't shake the feeling that she had escaped one situation only to be trapped by another.

"Here, let me help you out of your cloak, dear."

Kat stood silently as Mrs. Brown moved to remove the woolen from her shoulders, stopping only to pick out a few twigs out of her hair as well. She tucked and sorted Kat's hair a bit, smoothing what ends would obey.

When Kat still said nothing, Mrs. Brown continued, "Did you have a nice walk?" She smiled knowingly, wide and slowly, like a cat who had tasted cream.

Kat nodded, still not trusting herself to say a word.

"Well, walking's tiresome business if done properly. Come, sit by the fire and warm up some. There's a hearty lamb stew, fresh rolls to be had, and cider or tea if you've half a mind to have some."

Kathleen allowed herself to be led into the other chair with the table set at her elbow.

"How about I talk while you eat? We'll save time that way."

While she was initially hungry, Kat started to lose her appetite in her wariness, full of questions about all she'd seen and done. These thoughts swam in her mind as Mrs. Brown chattered away about this and that—largely the running of the manor farm and schedules of plantings. She would occasionally nudge Kathleen to take a bit of this or that, but, by the end of lunch, Kat wouldn't be able to make an account of anything she had eaten or in what quantity. Kat wanted to scream. How could she stay focused on the here and now? And she couldn't shake the feeling of resentment that rippled towards her from every word Mrs. Brown spoke.

They'd hit a lull when Mrs. Brown stopped her monologue on the feeding of a large farming staff. She just sat and stared at Kathleen, waiting for her to acknowledge and attend to her.

"So about your adventure today," Mrs. Brown paused. "I don't know exactly where you had gotten to other than it was not just the greenhouse." She cleared her throat as she casually removed the plausible white lie Kathleen had prepared. "Although you did upset Mr. Fitzwilliam by entering the greenhouse without a 'by your leave,' but I explained to him that you were not from here and would announce yourself next time rather than just barge in and disturb his thoughts."

Kat began to apologize, but she waved her off.

"'Tis no matter. He thinks it is his greenhouse instead of the lady's. He'll forget about it soon enough. Just be sure to inquire about his Royal Lady roses and all will be forgiven. They're his special pets, you know."

Kat wondered just how much more Mrs. Brown knew about her day, but she hinted not a word about her leaving through the gardener's cottage. Maybe Mr. Fitzwilliam didn't know Kat had entered, not just his greenhouse, but his private residence as well.

"So what was it you were looking for in your wanderings?" Mrs. Brown brought Kat back out of her thoughts.

"Excuse me?" Kat asked to be sure she had heard correctly and to stall for time.

"For what were you looking? You were out such a very long time for just a walk." Mrs. Brown continued to stare at her as Kat mentally squirmed.

"I...I wasn't looking for anything. Not really, just exploring about the house and grounds a bit."

"Well, that makes no sense to me at all," Mrs. Brown countered. "You did hear the missus say you were to stay put?"

Kat nodded, wary of where this was going.

"And you do recall that she put me in charge of keeping you safe?"

She again nodded, unsure of what could be said to appease the woman.

"Well then, if you stick by your story that you weren't looking *for* anything then it shouldn't be hard for you to follow instructions and stay put. I'd hate to disappoint my lady by losing her kin when I'd made my point clear. And I think we both know that the missus is something special." Mrs. Brown paused and made a point of getting the full attention of Kathleen's gaze before she continued. "She has a far reach, that one. I'd not want to risk her ire. And frankly, I'd not appreciate angering her when I am doing my duty by you. I'd consider it a kindness, in all fairness, if you thought of someone other than yourself and stayed put until she has a mind to move you."

The warnings were clear. The threat barely glossed over. Kat told her she appreciated her concern and that she was tired and would take a nap now if it would not inconvenience Mrs. Brown. Her points made, she left Kathleen to her own devices. Kat knew that neither one of them had fooled the other, but at least their positions were clear. Kat welcomed the alone time to think on this and all she had seen thus far. While she hadn't really intended to nap, she did fall asleep in the big chair, her last thoughts being that she had been foolish to come.

For the next two days Kat stayed put. She asked Maeve to get her something with which to keep her hands busy, and Kat soon had threads with which to embroider. Embroidery had the unpleasant side effect of making the day drag on. That, and the eyestrain in the dim light, made her foul-tempered and reticent. The rain continued in full force, and wind bashed against the shuttered windows with a violence that was almost comical. Kat wondered if it was indeed a rainy day or was there something Helene truly did not want her to see so badly that the weather turned sentry.

She was in such a foul mood when Mrs. Brown hurried into the front parlor to inform Kathleen that a message had been sent from the manor house that Helene would be coming for tea this very day. At this point Kat wasn't sure if she should be excited or wary. After the events of the past few days, including the veiled threat from Mrs. Brown, Kat didn't know what to think other than she wanted to go home. She had had enough. Whether she was being reasonable or not, Kat didn't care. Being left here, in the farm house, with nothing to do but measure the hours was driving her mad. She had a life in the 21st century, and Kat was ready to return to it and forget this all happened.

When Helene arrived looking chipper and healthy, she was met with a scowl. While Kat was relieved to see her, she was also resentful that she was so dependent on her. Kat hadn't been dependent on anyone in many years, and it was a feeling she would just as soon not feel ever again.

Kat could tell at a glance that Helene could sense her mood, but Helene did not falter or waver in attitude as she addressed Mrs. Brown with smiles and cheer. Kathleen mentally tried to send her jabs of her mood which she soon learned Helene felt. When Mrs. Brown paused in her mindless banter to turn away to talk to a farm hand who'd run in and interrupted, Helene gave Kat a quick glare and a silent warning to hold her temper tantrum at bay. Kat returned the glare boldly, a move that was met with momentary surprise and a bit of amusement. But Helene quickly, almost imperceptibly, composed herself again, meeting Mrs. Brown's smiles with her own.

When Mrs. Brown finally scurried away on some errand, Helene stood motionless for a moment as if gathering her thoughts. When she turned to face Kathleen she could now see the weariness that Helene worked so hard to conceal. There were dark circles under her eyes, giving them a hollowed out look, and fine lines could be seen around the edges. She moved slowly to a chair and sat, hands placed in her lap as if waiting.

How long they sat like that, in facing chairs, silent, Kat couldn't begin to guess, but it seemed interminable. Helene canvased her face, reading it for clues. It was disconcerting to be observed so, and so boldly. Kat felt like she was in a petri dish—prodded and squinted at as if to determine her origin.

When Mrs. Brown returned with the tea and biscuits, they still had not said a word to each other. Kat watched Helene transform before her eyes. She sat taller, color rose in her face, and the wrinkle lines faded. Her voice was animated as she asked about the most mundane facets of Mrs. Brown's day, which pleased Mrs. Brown to no end. She was lightheartedly charming. But Kat had seen the other Helene. Which was the real one and which the act? She pondered this as she watched their interactions.

Kat started to see the strain wear on Helene around the corners of her eyes. The cheer was an act, and it was time to stop. Helene tactfully shifted.

"Mrs. Brown, I cannot in good conscience keep a woman of your obvious demand about this farm manor a moment longer. How they do without you for a minute, I cannot fathom. I will not detain you further. My apologies for demanding so much of your precious time."

Mrs. Brown could not refute her as all was in her favor. Kat was impressed as it was delicately done. Mrs. Brown took her leave after but a moment or two of fluttering about the tea table.

Helene heaved a huge sigh when she left, the exhaustion clearly written upon her face, etched in the eyes and furrowed brow.

"She means well, and is a kind woman, but she wears a person out. She would deem it an insult to leave me be in silence rather than the reprieve it truly would be."

Kat still said not a word.

Helene looked at Kat, waited for a response. Upon finding none she continued, "I know you're upset and probably tired of waiting for me, but there are things at play which I cannot discuss with you just yet and certainly not here. No one is ever truly alone here." She cast a knowing glance towards the kitchen.

"So, then, what's the plan?"

"Plan?"

"Yes, plan. What do you plan to do with me? What is the next step? What have you arranged?" Kat pushed boldly.

"Well, you see, it's not quite that simple—"

"Send me back. I want to go home."

"You don't understand. You see—"

"What I see is that you are stalling. I see that I might sit here and be bored to death while I wait. I see that you could yank me out of my home, and I must attend to you, but when I come calling I must 'understand.' I also know that I have a life—elsewhere, and I want to be returned to it, now. If you've no time for me now there is no point waiting here." As Helene shifted to speak Kat barreled on, "I am done waiting and couldn't care less what the excuse is."

"Well, I underestimated your patience, or should I say lack thereof? Things do not move as quickly in this time as you've noticed."

"Funny, you have a sense of humor." Kat knew she was being beyond rude at this point, but she'd had it. She was frustrated, confused, and irritated that she'd learned little more than when she had come before. After the adventure she had the other day, she felt more trapped than anything. The rain was interminable—except when Helene arrived. Kat raised an eyebrow and glared. "Uh, Helene. Tell me about the rain."

"Well, you see, being an island, England is a milder clime you know. We are prone to moisture at all times of the year," she began.

"No, *this* rain."

"But it's not raining, dear." Helene smiled innocently.

"You know full well what I mean. We're constantly in a rain bubble here. Only here."

Kat saw something flash in her eyes but couldn't be sure what it was or what it meant, but it made her nervous nevertheless.

"You are observant. Interesting. Very interesting." Helene paused to stretch. "It's a simple enchantment to keep you safe."

"Safe or indoors?"

"Safely indoors."

"Safe from what?"

"Largely yourself, Kathleen. Can't have you wandering about, being noticed, and so obviously out of place until I can be with you. 'Tis a simple thing really and truly for your protection."

Kat rose to pace the floor. "I'll tell you what, I'll make a deal. You send me back to where and when I came from, and I'll come back to visit when you have time for me."

"How very considerate of you but not altogether possible at the moment."

Kat had no idea that she would be rejected. It felt like a slap in her face while done with such politeness and poise. She was both angry and terrified at the same time.

"Why?" was all Kat managed to get out.

"Use your brain, dear. Right now, at this place, you are here to visit me. It would seem ludicrous that you only stayed here and didn't come over to the manor house. Why, how would it look? It'd cause eyebrows to wag and tongues to flap. No, this cannot be done from here at this moment. I would ask you only wait a day or so, and I will send for you."

"One day."

That had done it; now Kat had her ire. "You dare dictate to me!"

"Just giving out what I am getting. I will go crazy if I stay here any longer."

Helene saw Kat meant what she said, and softened. "All right, I will send a coach for you the morning of the day after tomorrow. And I will terminate the rain for now, so long as you don't get into any mischief. Stay to the grounds and do not speak to anyone unless necessary. The less you say, the less risk to all of us."

Kat nodded. She had no words. She hadn't thought about the risk. Hadn't considered it. All Kat knew was the feeling that she was trapped. Helene seemed to realize by Kat's awkward movements that she hadn't thought it through so she softened.

"I am sorry. I should have explained things better. Honestly, we've had no time at all really to get to know each other. I will send for you. I promise, day after tomorrow. Just give me a bit more time to arrange things. Yes?"

Helene was being reasonable in a ridiculous situation. Kat would have to wait.

Kat busied herself all through the next day. She readied herself and her belongings to leave, carefully packing the small trunk Mrs. Brown returned to Kathleen. With Mrs. Brown's help it was short work. Kat believed she would leave at any moment, partially because Mrs. Brown believed it to be so. But when midday the next day came and no coach, and then dinner that eve, and no coach, Kat was at a loss.

On the third day, Mrs. Brown herself set out the breakfast dishes and began to unpack Kathleen's things and return them to the wardrobe.

"Have you heard from Helene?" Kat didn't know what to make of this behavior.

"No, why do you ask?"

"Because you are unpacking!"

"Oh, this. Well, seems silly to let your things wrinkle when they could be hung out so nicely."

"She said to be ready," Kat persisted.

"Yes, dear, but she didn't come."

"What do you know? What has changed?"

"Oh, same as you dear. Something must've come up or she's been delayed. She'll get around to sending word when she will be by again, you can be sure."

"So what am I to do?" Kathleen said in complaint.

"I would hope you'd find something useful to do with your time," Mrs. Brown said, snipping as she turned to leave the room. Apparently she was none too pleased with this delay either, Kat realized.

Kat sat on the edge of the bed and wondered whether to cry or rage when she wanted to do both. This waiting was interminable. Frustrated but determined, she threw a light cloak over her shoulders and headed out.

14

Abbey Secrets

Kat had almost gotten to the back door when Mrs. Brown detained her.

"Where are you going, might I ask?"

"Out."

"Out where, dear?"

"Just out." Kat brushed past her and headed towards the woods. She was determined to find what it was that Helene was hiding out there. She had waited for answers, and now Kat would find them for herself. Maybe it was the key to Helene or the key to going home, but either way it was action, and that was far better than the waiting.

Mrs. Brown ran up behind Kathleen and, panting, the older woman said, "You mustn't go into the woods."

Kat stopped and spun around to talk to her.

"Why?"

"You just can't."

Disgusted, Kat turned away and continued as she was briskly determined in her path.

Mrs. Brown grabbed her by the arm to stop Kathleen. "The lady will not like it. 'Tis forbidden."

"Well, that's just too bad. If she had come back like she said she would I wouldn't be here to disobey her."

"You know not what you say, lass."

Kat stopped then, and she shook with rage. "Fine. Then explain to me what I should know!"

"I cannot."

"Well, then, there you go. I'm off."

Mrs. Brown called after Kathleen, but Kat ignored her. She cried out warnings of Helene's displeasure, but it was all the same, nothing remotely new to make Kat want to stay. She almost paused when Mrs. Brown verged on verbal tactics that were indicative of fear—hers.

As soon as Kat entered the woods, the rain and wind started again as if she had crossed a trigger. It made her think of those Hope Diamond movies with the laser beam security system. Kat refused to let the rain bother her, just pulled up her hood and plowed on. The wind and rain doubled the further she got, but this was old news to her. Kat knew what to expect and feared it not. She chuckled at the feeble attempt to keep her in line. She was still so angry at the frustrating conversation with Mrs. Brown that Kat welcomed the challenge. She plunged forward, her head down like a bull as step-by-step the forces of nature battled her.

When Kat got to the point once again where the harder she walked the farther the abbey seemed, she stopped, and imagined herself at the side door. She slowed her breathing, ignoring the tree branches that swayed to scratch at her face. Kat casually brushed aside the leaves and debris that blew into her hood and upon her closed eyes. She focused deeper, kept her concentration on the details of the door, the hinges, the ironwork, the strappings as she remembered them. Kat reached forward with one hand as if to touch and feel the wood she imagined to be there...and met wood.

This time without spanning the distance with her feet, no matter what the visual illusion, Kat had physically covered the span of an acre or more with a thought. She truly stood before the door of the dilapidated abbey. Kat made a mental note to herself to try to get here another time from a farther distance. Perhaps truly for the first time, Kat realized that as Helene's descendant she was not helpless but had some of her power, yet untapped and untrained. It startled her to think of what she'd accomplished with only thoughts. Kat would have to think on this further, figure out what it all meant, but that would have to wait.

The rain and wind stopped within the circle of cleared ground closest to the abbey. Kat reached out to the door before her, pushed it open. It creaked upon its hinges. All was as she remembered it last. Kat moved along the remaining walls, squinting into the images that were etched on each. Most dulled by dust and worn by time but others were eerily, vibrantly crisp, as if newly commissioned. Routine images of biblical scenes dotted the walls, the remaining sconces embossed with the symbolic carvings. Fragments of glass remained in the window panels that still stood.

Kat made her way back to the alter. She wanted to explore a bit more than last time. How had this stayed so intact and undisturbed when all was in decay? She moved forward in the chapel, admiring the arches, wishing she could have seen the church in its glory and intact. The dais held the alter. The alter stone seemed timeless. Smooth and unworn by time, Kat could find nothing remarkable nor telling. As she felt about the alter, she looked for an engraving, anything that would help identify the abbey. The alter felt warm to the touch, disquietingly warm. Could there be a hot spring beneath the stone?

In an attempt to learn the truth, Kat looked behind the alter to what remained of a door to a sacristy. It appeared largely collapsed from the outside, but she wondered, if she could get the door ajar, maybe she would spy the edge of a spring? Kat had been to the city of Bath years ago on a college trip and knew that such things existed. Maybe here too?

The door held fast. Kat looked closely after waging a tug fest with no progress. The keyhole in the door showed a broken lock. There was no latch to speak of to lift. She peered into the hole and saw only darkness. Kat was about to give up when she had a perverse thought—what if? What if it was like the abbey itself? What if she imagined opening the door—if her focus held, could she open it? Realistically Kat had seen and done some remarkable things this week. Why not give it a try? Plus, since no one was here to see her fail… "Nothing ventured, nothing gained."

Handle held in one hand, Kat closed her eyes and imagined the key mechanism turning, the lock shifting open, the door swinging wide. She felt, rather than saw the lock release. When she looked to see what she knew to be true, Kat drew the door freely open, revealing a full-sized sacristy. It was resplendent, as if the abbot himself had just left, robes draped over a chair, chalice on a small table, the communion wafers in a dish. Kat was stunned. How was this possible? Did she dream this? She moved about the small room in wonder while she kept one eye on the door as she always had a fear of being in locked places. It seemed an ordinary room, unremarkable except that it looked untouched from the last use as if it was just yesterday. And then she realized the true marvel.

Kat darted out of the sacristy to look to where it stood within the chapel. In the main hall it appeared collapsed, not much more than a partial door remained, yet inside the room, it was full sized and unblemished. Helene? Had Helene attempted to hide this? And if she did, why? Or was someone or something else to be blamed for this anomaly? That was a scarier thought still.

Combing the chapel to see if there was anything else she might have missed, Kat noticed nothing else out of place. She returned the door to its locked position and heard an audible catch as it closed. She made a mental note to puzzle on that one for a while. Plus, it might be handy to have a hidden room should she have need of one for any reason.

Back outside, Kathleen walked closely around the perimeter of the abbey. She glanced back at the woods and saw the rain and wind rage, forming a circle. It seemed to pulse and tug, as though trying to get to her but couldn't, held back by an invisible guard-rail. She was thinking about this when she came across the destroyed tower. Its last several feet of stairs were destroyed, part of its castellated wall missing, the top looked a ruin. Or was it?

Kat stood at the bottom where the first step should be...and stepped. The step, though invisible, was indeed there! Another ruse. She stepped back down and gathered up a handful of sand and small stones from the base of the abbey. These she strew at where the stairs should be, and saw the bits of debris quickly outline the missing steps. She collected more sand and some dirt from around the plantings, casting these over the stairs as she climbed them. The stairs spiraled to the top. Not one step was missing, worn, but not missing. When Kat reached the platform at the top, she could see for miles. She saw the farm just beyond the woods in a large clearing. The fields beyond that could be seen as well, and farther still, Kat could see the top of what must be the manor house as it was far larger than any building she could see in any direction. She compared the direction of the building to the farmhouse and determined that she had indeed found the manor house. Kat tried to fathom the distance, noting landmarks along the way, a gnarled tree not far from the farm house, the bend of the road, a stand of populars, and determined that if she set out early enough she should easily be able to walk that in a morning and be at the manor before anyone was the wiser. Kat looked at the ringed forest and the likewise encircling rainstorm. It was comical to see it like this. It seemed petty and spiteful when she could see the parameters of her cage.

After taking a look from each vantage point Kat made her way down the stairs. Already the gentle winds had displaced most of the soil and stones she had used to mark the path. She kicked the rest loose, one step at a time, as she descended. It might be best if she let it stay her secret for now.

Now ready to head back to the farmhouse, Kat's mood was diffused with the excitement over her findings when she remembered the graveyard. What untold knowledge could she find there today? Bolstered by her newfound talents, she made her way back around the abbey and was about to open the gate when she heard a familiar growling. Kat turned to face a pair of charging hounds. This time she didn't hesitate. She ran—again. Her lungs cried with the strain, but Kat knew now, that as before, once inside the tree line she'd be safe.

Stopping just inside the forest, Kat doubled over and clutched her knees as she caught her breath. As her heart slowed to a normal pace she gathered her thoughts. There must be something very important here that needed such protection. Kat couldn't help the nagging suspicion that there was more than Helene tied to this. It was too convenient and far too easy to think that there was only one witch. Was this her sole doing? Or was she judging Helene too harshly as she knew of no one else to blame? Kat hoped, sincerely hoped, that when she found out the secret of this place that Helene was not the cause. Because if she were, then Kathleen needed to be very afraid.

15

Cast Off

Mrs. Brown let it be known that she was none too happy with Kathleen for "traipsing off" into the woods. Kat didn't care anymore what Mrs. Brown thought and made that clear by not stopping to listen to her rant. Instead Kat brushed past her as she made her way to her rooms.

Kat had just changed into drier clothing and was toweling her hair when there was a knock on the door. It was Maeve with a message for her. Mrs. Brown decreed that she was to sup in her room tonight. She was being sent to her room for supper! Kat laughed outright while Maeve looked on in horror. The girl must have heard an earful in Kat's place. She pitied the girl. She truly did, but she wasn't done being angry at the situation.

So Kathleen ate alone that night and was relieved to do so. She needed to sort her thoughts and plan what to do next. That was indeed the difficult question. Without an answer forthcoming, she resigned herself to go to bed. Kat curled up under the bedcovers and tried to count the number of days she had already spent here. It disturbed her to find it wasn't easy to do as each day had blended into the next with the interminable boredom. She simply couldn't be positive of the exact day count. Kat decided then and there that she either went to the manor house tomorrow or she went home. How to manage either was the problem. Kat fell asleep not having come to any conclusions.

It was actually due to Mrs. Brown's meddling that the problem was solved. Apparently, distraught over Kathleen's actions yesterday, Mrs. Brown had sent a boy with a message to Helene that Kathleen had defied instructions, fled into the woods, and that she was simply unmanageable. It resulted in a coach at the farmhouse barely after daybreak carrying a none-too-pleased Helene. She didn't even get out of the carriage to fetch Kathleen but rather sent Patrice in to gather her and the small trunk. Kat knew it would be wisest to be contrite when again in Helene's presence, but she didn't care. Oddly enough, Kat didn't fear Helene, although she suspected Helene had powers she could barely fathom. Helene was family—and family gets upset with each other, she rationalized. Kat blamed her behavior on Helene's.

"If I had been acknowledged and claimed as promised, I wouldn't need to explore. I've been here far too long to still be waiting for answers...to anything."

Helene didn't respond when Kathleen thus accused her, but instead, far worse, she looked at her in disgust and then turned away to look out the window the entirety of the trip. Only then did Kat began to question herself and feel badly.

Some time later when the carriage approached the manor it did not go around the front as Kat had expected but to the back entrance where she assumed the household deliveries were made. Patrice jumped out and gathered the small trunk without a backward glance or a word to Kathleen. No doubt she took her ladyship's lead.

"Patrice, put the chest in my second wardrobe, after which, help in the kitchens as we're having guests tonight."

That sounded promising, Kat thought as she smiled, sat fully upright, and sorted her skirts so as to not trip on her way out of the carriage.

"No," Helene clearly and succinctly stopped Kathleen's progress. "You do not get out here. We've one more stop."

Kat looked at her, startled. Helene said not one more word nor acknowledged her at all as she gazed once again out the window. They left the manor and rode the better part of a half hour when the carriage stopped. Helene motioned Kathleen to follow her out of the carriage. They were at the edge of town, in front of the dressmaker's shop. Kat followed her without question. It became abundantly clear from Helene's backward glare that that was what was expected of her.

After Helene made a brief greeting to the shopkeep, they walked through the front showroom to the rooms at the back, and then into a dressing room.

"I have enough clothing," Kathleen said.

"Agreed," Helene curtly answered. "It is for something else that you desire that we are here."

Helene stepped into the spacious dressing closet and closed the door behind them. She turned to face Kathleen, resignation and disappointment appearing on her face. Helene held her lips in a tight line and her eyes again appeared hollowed out by the dark circles beneath them.

"When you can be patient I will welcome you back. For now, it is time for you to go home."

Helene gave Kathleen a firm hug, whispering something she could not make out. Her voice felt like the buzzing of a small bee in Kat's ear, verbal but incomprehensible all the same. When Helene pushed Kat from an arm's length, she felt herself released and the dizzying sensation of falling.

Kat landed with a thud on her sofa, one leg draped over the side arm. Suzy's eyes, wide in surprise, met her.

Suzy laughed. "Well, that was a hell of an entrance!"

"Yeah, well, Helene wasn't so thrilled with me lately so she was a bit careless. How long was I gone?"

"Ah, about six minutes."

"Seriously?" Kat scratched her head in confusion. "It's been days. More than a week on my end."

"Are you sure?"

"Definitely, that's part of what the trouble was between us. She put me at the manor's farm house and then left me there for days."

"What were you doing then?"

"Nothing really, until I decided to explore."

Suzy cackled. "Oh no, fill me in."

When Kat started to sway and look green, Suzy jumped up to get her some water and an oatmeal cookie—one of hers.

"By the way, how did the herbs work?"

"Like a charm."

"Good, I'll whip you up another 'travel' packet to keep with you, just in case."

"Oh, I don't know that I'll be going back anytime soon. She's really pissed."

"Gobble that cookie up. This must be a good story, and I can't wait to hear it."

Sometime later Kat finished her tale and a sliced turkey sandwich. She'd gulped her food down in huge, man-sized bites.

"Or maybe it was your eating habits that got you in trouble?" Suzy cocked a wicked smile.

Kat belched in response.

"Nice, real nice. There's my little lady."

Suzy silently sat, thinking through all Kat had told her. Kat was still mulling it over herself when Suzy said, "She's terrified."

"What are you talking about?"

"Okay, let's look at this from her angle. You show up virtually unannounced, and she hides you. She hides you at the farm. She hides you by rain and fog, and she hides the abbey with a storm. True, there might be a bit of a liar in there as well, but Helene's the one who is scared."

"Okay, how do you explain that she dumps me in a dressing room and essentially tosses me here."

"Same thing. For some reason she couldn't take you home yet. By taking you into the store her coach driver only knew that you were dropped off at the store. The shopkeep probably won't even notice you went in but didn't leave. No one ever notices the servants of a great person. I would say that the people at her home have no idea of her powers, or, they disapprove. And when a woman with the type of power she has needs to hide you—that's fear. You, and your antics, gave her an excuse to send you home. But overall, I think it best you don't go knocking on her door but let her come to you." Suzy shook her head side to side. "Nope, I don't like it one bit. I am very glad you're back."

Suzy paused and looked thoughtful for a moment. "Makes me wonder if your gran was really the timid type or perhaps she saw something that made her afraid."

Kat hated that she couldn't count on Gran answering that question, not with any reliability. She couldn't even be sure Gran would know who she was from day to day.

She must've seen something in Kat's face because Suzy quickly changed the subject. "Well, it's just as well that you're back because we've tons to do."

"Huh? What are you talking about?"

"A week and a day after tomorrow is Thanksgiving."

"Ah, man." Kat scrubbed her hand over her face. "Can't I just skip it this year?"

"Nope, kiddo, your mom will be counting on you to be there. Your sister will be back in town, too."

"Great, that's all I need, dinner with Candace. Timmy?"

"Don't know, honey. No one has heard from him in a while."

"That's because Timmy probably planned ahead." Kat sighed. "So it's time for the yearly inquisition."

"This year will be better."

"How? Seriously, you know my mom. She'll grill me in front of the whole family about what am I doing with my life, who am I dating, blah, blah, blah. Sheesh."

"Nope, this year will be better because you are taking a date—me!"

Suzy gave Kat hope that she might survive this year with only minor scars.

16

Echoes of Home

The next day, Kat fussed about the shop, arranged displays, dusted. She felt like she'd been away for ages. For her, she had, but for the shop, there really wasn't much to be done as she'd not neglected it. The problem was that it meant Kat had plenty of time to think and worry. So when a shipment that she'd purchased weeks ago from an estate sale was delivered, Kat was thrilled to be distracted.

Kat pulled back the packing material and unwrapped the shipping cloth that was wound around the first item she reached—a small, china-faced, rag doll. She generally didn't go in for dolls as sometimes they can be really creepy, but Kat had purchased this one specifically for the seasonal display. She knew that people tended to get nostalgic for simpler times when the holidays drew near. As she glanced at its bow-shaped, cherry lips, she could imagine it in a child's rocker by the fireplace. Kat would need to see if Doreen, her Irish lace connection, had any doll clothes or embroidery she could sell with it as a set. She'd have to remember to talk to her soon.

Next she pulled out a pair of cloisonné hair combs and felt a small jolt of energy. An image passed through Kat's mind of a woman standing in front of a long mirror, pulling back her long, honey tresses. For a moment it was as if she were looking out of the woman's eyes, staring at herself in the mirror. When muscular arms came around her...um, the woman's waist...Kat saw a soft smile play upon her lips.

Kat dropped the combs on the countertop, panting to compose herself. *What the hell just happened?* Kat had never seen the woman before. She racked her brain to recall meeting her when she was in Helene's time and couldn't recall anyone even remotely like the woman she had seen in the reflection. And to be honest, Helene had made sure that she didn't meet many. Kat picked up the combs again, tentatively, and again saw the woman as if in a mirror in her mind. This time she was seated before a dressing table, gilt fobs in her ears with an ornate bodice covered in lace. Kat got the sense of an elegant evening out and an overwhelming feeling of contentment. She placed the combs gently on the counter and reached for the next item, an antique man's shaving kit. Kat handled all with nothing unusual noted. The rest of the lot were assorted lapel pins, brooches, and one strand of nearly perfect, tiny pearls. None of these items caused any emotion or reaction. It was solely the combs.

As she worked, Kat continued to think on it. What could it mean? What changed? And why, for God's sake, now? It was the last thing she needed. She had previously researched every item she'd purchased and already logged into her book what price would be appropriate. She'd checked each item, save the combs, for defects. Satisfied by all, Kat tagged and marked each for sale. The doll was tucked into the holiday scene she had created in the front window. Kat was confident she'd have a home by the week's end. The other pieces were strategically placed, on velvets that would best highlight each, in the glass-fronted jewelry case. The combs, however, she wrapped in a bit of cloth and took them to the wall safe to lock them away. She wanted more time with them before she determined what was to be done.

Thanksgiving came and went without incident. Candace had just gotten engaged, so the focus was on her and wedding plans. Anytime it looked like Kat was about to get ambushed, Suzy came up with a diversion. Gran was doing well and likewise enjoyed Suzy's company.

At the end of the evening Kat walked Suzy out to her car, carrying the box of assorted dishes she had brought, now emptied, to her trunk.

"Thanks for running interference tonight."

"Not a problem, kiddo. Had nothing better to do anyway, and the food was good."

Suddenly, as realization hit, she felt horrible. After Sky died, Kat had avoided Suzy—because Suzy always meant Sky, and home, and it was too painful to face. It had never dawned on her that Suzy was alone, totally alone. She never thought...

Suzy must've seen some "tell" on Kat's face, some clue as to what she was thinking. "Think nothing of it, girl. I could've gone to Jersey to see my brother and his idiot wife, but I'd rather not. And it was nice having an excuse not to cook a big meal again."

"So, you're not alone?"

"Kitty Kat, you are only truly alone when you can't stand your own company. And I like me just fine." Suzy winked while adjusting her brightly colored, gypsy shawl about her. She was about to get in her car when Kat stopped her.

"Suzy, something else happened."

Concern jumped in her eyes. "What? What did Helene do?"

"No, no, nothing like that...or at least nothing to do with her. Something weird happened with me yesterday. It was..." Kat didn't know how to begin.

"You okay?" She patted Kat's cheek.

"Yeah. Yes, fine. It's just I have something to show you at the shop. Then maybe I can explain what happened."

"Okay, kiddo, I'll see you in the morning. Nine okay?"

"Sure, great." Kat breathed a sigh of relief.

"Get some sleep and I'll see you in the morning." Suzy turned as she was getting in to the car, "Oh, and do me a favor, get out of here soon. They'll run out of wedding plans and start on you if you don't hustle."

Kat laughed. "You bet."

Suzy showed up right on time. Kat had just opened shop and was waiting for the pot of coffee to finish brewing. She stopped to peer in the window.

"Doll's new. Creepy and sweet at the same time."

"I agree." Kat laughed.

"So what's up, kiddo? What happened?"

"I'll have to show you. Just give me a minute. They're in the safe."

"Well, go on then. I'll get us both some coffee while you get whatever it is."

When she returned, Kat saw that alongside the coffee were some cranberry-orange scones on a platter with small plates set out.

"Hey, were'd you get the scones?" She grabbed one gratefully.

"Baked them, of course."

Kat had forgotten Suzy baked. They'd baked together often, Sky always coming up with some exotic recipe to try. She'd forgotten so much by trying to forget Sky.

Suzy placed a hand over hers and patted. "It's okay. I miss her, too. It's really okay to remember. You know, it's also a way to keep her with you. It was unbearable at first, but now I find it kind of soothing, remembering her, the good times. I figure as long as I remember, a part of her is here. I think she'd like that."

Tears welled in Kat's eyes, and she tried to brush them away with her sleeve. "I tried to push her away. I couldn't, just couldn't..."

"I know, honey. You loved her like she was your twin. And she was. You needed time to heal. But you do know that when you love someone, really love someone, they change you, shape you, become part of how you think and who you are. So she's in there," she tapped Kat's forehead, "in how you think, and what you value. Just as you were part of her. You made each other better, stronger. Don't be afraid to hold on to that."

"I've just been so lost...I didn't have any of my own dreams, not really. We had them together. We were going to get an apartment, she was going to go to school, and I was going to work while I figured my shit out. And then she had that damned car accident..."

"Her body wasn't the only thing broken. I know. A lot of things came crashing down that day, a lot of futures shifted." Suzy's eyes took a far off look before they returned. "Come on, girl. Eat before your scone gets cold. I do mean fresh baked." She winked, and the matter was closed.

They sipped coffee companionably for a while until they were interrupted by a few Black Friday shoppers hoping to get a deal here as well. Because Kat was now in such a good mood, she gave them an extra ten percent off an English tea set that honestly was a pain in her rear as it had sat in the shop so long and always seemed to need dusting. She packed the set up as quickly as she could without appearing rude, tying the whole lot in seasonal raffia and a cinnamon stick.

"Well that was a nice bit of business. The wrapping was a nice touch. People will remember the small touches like that and come back to shop again. I think you have a knack for this. More than your grandmother or grandfather, that's for sure. To them it was all profit."

"That's it!" Kat said. "The small touches. That's what I wanted to talk to you about." She'd forgotten about the combs momentarily for the lure of warm scones and then the brief shopping rush. Kat told Suzy about the shipment and the items in the box she'd received yesterday. She didn't say anything about the combs. Kat just handed them still wrapped in cloth to her.

Suzy took them out carefully, turning them this way and that. "Lovely, truly lovely. Too bad women don't wear this kind of stuff any more. Combs came back in style for a while back in the '60s and '70s, but it was mostly the hippy thing, not fancy stuff like this. Are they worth a lot?" She looked up at Kat.

"No, not particularly. I bought them thinking someone might want to frame them, you know, matted to show off the embedded gemstones. Would look nice in a girl's bedroom or by a bathroom vanity."

"Well, see, that's a fine idea. Your grandparents would never think to do something like that."

"But there was something else. You know how you said we carry those we love inside?"

Suzy didn't interrupt, just waited.

"Well," Kat paused, "when I got these unwrapped, I could feel her."

"Her? Who?"

"I don't really know, but the combs were hers. I could see her like she was me looking in a mirror, and feel..." Kat waved her hands about, searching for the right words to explain it.

"Interesting." Suzy again looked at each comb, turning them over this way and that. "Just these, nothing else in the shipment?"

Kat shook her head no.

"Well then, these must have been treasured, and she associated them with an emotion. Interesting that this would happen now." Suzy grew reflectively quiet.

"*What* happens now?"

"Well, I've heard of this before. You had what's called an empathic reaction. You sensed the history of the piece. Happens to some people, rare gift. It's just unusual that you've got it, at least for these pieces, when you've been handling antiques for years now. Could be a blessing or a nuisance. Not sure which."

"But it's just these combs."

"Did you handle other things in the shop?"

"Of course."

"No new reactions?"

"No, I was just dusting."

"Okay, humor me, let's test this out. Let's go through some of your honest-to-God antiques—not the 'faux-tiques' you use to set the stage, and see if you don't react to some of this other stuff."

They worked their way through the store, randomly touching things that had been owned by people, not just warehoused. Several items that Kat had handled numerous times before now gave her an empathic reaction. Many not pleasant at all. It was disturbing and exhausting. After the last piece, a toy wagon that made Kat cringe in fear with the sound of lashings in her ear, she had to stop.

"That," Kat said, pointing, "is going in the burn barrel. I'm not selling that to anyone." She shuddered.

"Yup, kiddo, you've got the gift."

"But why now?" Kat asked, convinced it was a curse rather than a blessing.

"I've heard magic breeds magic. Could be your exposure to Helene released or magnified what you already had. You are kin. And you told me how you moved through the rain curtain in the forest with a thought. I think, like it or not, in finding Helene, you are finding yourself."

17

Kid Gloves

She thought a lot about those words over the next few days as Kat tried to decipher what exactly that would mean for her. She made a point to get to the campus library after the weekly night class she took, to do some research. The toughest thing was Kat didn't know what to research exactly. Did she research time travel? Empaths? Witchcraft?

After wandering the stacks for a while, Kat decided to start with 'witchcraft' as that was the one variable that was common with them all. Most of the college references noted the history of witch burnings, false accusations, and general Wiccan philosophy. None of this was particularly helpful. Kat didn't know why she was hesitant to ask the college librarian for help in the search. He surely got many such requests, but it seemed awkward nonetheless. Kat eventually gave up her search to think of other angles to pursue. She was spinning her wheels, making no progress whatsoever.

It wasn't until Kat was doing some casual Christmas shopping at the local B&N, a task she hated more and more each year as her family never seemed pleased with their gifts, when she wandered down the New Age aisle. Kat perused shelves with titles of: *The Inner Wiccan*, *Healing Stones*, *Know Your Chakras* and the like, when she stumbled across volumes of spell books. Granted many of the covers looked like a Hollywood production and a fairy had a baby, books with sparkly glitter and swirls of bright colors, but some of the others seemed more serious, if not academic. It never crossed her mind to look in a mainstream bookstore for answers.

Grabbing a stack of the most promising titles, Kat headed into the attached coffee shop to grab a cappuccino and peruse, a trick she learned when she briefly was a full time psych major several years back. Two hours, three coffees, and a scone later, Tara found Kat buried in her stack of books. She had taken over a four-seater table as it wasn't busy, spread the books wide, and was comparing everything from assorted spells to folklore. She had discovered that they were surprisingly similar.

"So this is where you've been hiding."

Kat was so immersed in her reading that it didn't register at first that Tara was talking to her. "Huh, what?"

"Kat, what's up? No one's seen you in ages."

"Oh, um, been busy, shop, end of the semester at school, research. You know, usual stuff."

Tara dumped her shopping bags on top of Kat's books, forcing her to look up and break her concentration.

"Yeah, sure, this stuff is research for Econ 171? Try again."

Kat hated to be interrupted, especially since she was on a roll, and she hated Tara's tone even more, so she decided to take a stand. "Actually, yes, I'm comparing the marketing of similar topics in assorted media to identify the strategy and visual cues to entice purchasers of luxury publishing."

"These are all about witchcraft." Tara looked skeptical.

"Exactly. We were assigned a topic that is not in a 'need' market to research so that we could compare different companies' handling and marketing. Apples to apples." Kat pointed to assorted titles, "See how this one uses bright colors to entice while this one uses provocative wording. This one uses 'expert' contributors, and this one handles 'everyday' magic." She held the book out game-show-model style to make her point.

"Um, okay. Cool, I guess. But anyway, seriously, what have you been up to?"

"Holiday season, obligatory Mom visits, finals coming up. Same old thing."

"Well, you look different."

"What so you mean, different?"

"I don't know, older, distant."

"I feel older." Kat paused, seeing actual concern in Tara. She hadn't thought about her friends in ages. She'd been engrossed in the Helene mysteries, and the new sensitivity at work made each day a strain. Kat vowed to herself to make it right soon. She put on the warmest smile she could muster, pushing her sense of urgency aside, ignoring her desire to get back to her reading. "Fill me in on what's new with you."

Later Kat ended up buying a few of the books. She wanted to run some of the ideas they sparked past Suzy to see what she thought.

Suzy popped in to the antique shop the next morning just as Kat was about to sign for some new merchandise. What used to be so exciting for her, to handle things from a time past, now terrified her. She simply didn't want to know what now came unbidden. Suzy found Kat just standing there, looking at but not opening her latest shipment.

"Hey kiddo, I got something for you."

Kat welcomed the break and couldn't move quickly enough

to the other side of the counter where she stood. Suzy handed her a bag. Inside were assorted gloves.

"Um, thank you, I think."

Suzy gave her a glare. "Think about it, dumb ass. You're having trouble. Let's see if any of this will help. Try these on first." She broke open a box of surgical gloves and handed Kat a pair. "Personally, I am hoping these work as they'd probably be the most comfortable...and no laundering involved." She eyed Kat over her readers.

"Yeah, yeah, cheap shot. I've gotten better at doing my wash. Sheesh."

Kat held the gloves in her hand, turned them over, unconvinced this was going to be a viable solution.

"Okay, humor me. You've got nothing to lose by trying."

She couldn't argue with that logic, so slid them on. "Now what?"

"How about you unload this new box?"

Slowly Kat unpacked and gloriously felt nothing, no twinge of the past, for good or bad.

Pleased, Suzy handed her an object that she had had a strong, and pleasant, reaction to previously—nothing now.

"There, see. Sometimes the easiest solution is the solution."

"Okay, yeah, but I can't work all the time in gloves. People will notice."

"So what? And why not? Tell them it's for some archival, museum 'preserve the artifact,' body oils, some such bull shit. Hell, it might help the sales seeing as you are handling truly delicate, antique stuff." Suzy winked.

"Nice one." Kat laughed. "Talk about spin-doctoring."

"Well, at least now you have a way to cope. I'm worried about you, kiddo. You're thinner, and your smile got lost somewhere in the mix."

Kat sighed and pulled up a seat. "I know. The worst part is I don't know how to fix it. It's like Helene got inside my head, like a migraine, and I can't shake it. Totally botched a paper for class. I can't focus on anything but her and this," she held her hands before her helplessly, "and everything in between. I don't know what to do about any of it."

"We'll figure it out, one step at a time. I'll come over tonight, bring dinner, and we'll get started."

Knowing that action, any action, was going to be taken helped Kat get through the rest of the day. And the thought of dinner, whatever that might be, but not the usual can of soup she'd been living on lately, sparked her appetite, too.

Homemade chicken pot pie and a tossed salad were the perfect end to Kat's day, especially when the day turned colder, adding bits of ice to the current drizzle. She had worried that the weather would keep Suzy away and told her so.

Suzy shrugged it off. "Brought a sleeping bag and a change of clothes just in case—in case it got worse, or in case you invited me to stay. But either way we are going to make a late night of it and come up with some sort of answer or plan. It's Saturday so you can sleep late."

Unable to argue with that logic Kat insisted Suzy bring in that change of clothes to stay, but she wouldn't hear of the sleeping bag. Suzy was to get the bed in her room, and Kat would be perfectly comfortable on the sofa, especially since it pulled out.

"Since I'm older and achier, I accept."

That's part of what Kat loved about Suzy—there wouldn't be any bull shit, faux polite back and forth banter over who slept where. She'd always been a straight shooter, and Kat needed that more than ever in her life.

Suzy, too, had been scouring the shelves, looking for answers. She'd gone to the church archives, the local library, and The Archivist, a dusty bookshop about an hour away that boasted first editions, trying to find answers, leads, anything that would help Kat.

After dinner, they sat on the area rug in front of the low coffee table with books spread wide, Kat's flashier offerings and Suzy's older tombs, debating and comparing ideas. Suzy'd also brought along a box of petit fours she'd received from a nephew, so they munched and casually flipped pages, debating the viability of assorted topics as they came across them.

Kat left her poring over one book to pour some more tea. Like her, Suzy favored caffeinated tea before bed. She would laugh and say it helped her stay alert in her dreams. But the truth was they were fading fast as it was already well after one AM. Kat figured anything, even a little caffeine boost, couldn't hurt.

"Where is the necklace Helene gave you?" Suzy called to the kitchen.

"In the safe. Why?"

"Bring it. I've an idea."

Kat brought both the necklace and the mugs of tea, which were ignored for a time while they puzzled over the amber.

Suzy gathered the pendant in the palm of her hand and closely peered. The deeper red thread within was stagnant but vivid as she held it beneath the small, work light she had on her side table.

"What did Helene say when she gave this to you?"

"Nothing."

"Did she say anything about it the last time you were in her time?"

"Just that it suited me. And to keep it with me always."

"Then why is it in the safe?"

"Other than I don't trust her, and that she's never explained a damn thing, I'd say because I don't want to be told what to do."

"Hmmm. Come, sit by me and take this in your hand so I can see it there."

Suzy slid the pendant into Kat's hand when she came to sit near her. As they watched, it became clear that the amber changed properties when in her hand. The deep, red pockets shifted and contorted like dancing oil in a lava lamp. Suzy lifted the pendant out of Kat's hand by the chain, and the stone became dormant again. She again released it, letting it fall in her hand, and the red thread resumed dancing.

"Okay, I think I have something here. Put that down somewhere and come closer and see what I've been reading."

While Kat was nervous to see what Suzy had found, she was also relived that maybe at last they had something to build upon.

"Here, listen to this—'Blood stones or candles were sometimes used to connect one member in the family to another. One relative would take a malleable material, such as wax, gold, or even amber as the holding vessel. The practicing witch would take drops of his blood to blend in the molten mass. It is believed that the blood would not dissipate but remain as clearly identifiable drops. Cast with a seeking or similar spell, the blood would call one unto the other. This practice was considered part of the Dark Arts and feared by those who knew of the practice. Witch to witch, it is rumored to create a blood connection that magnifies the power of the individual witch as it is doubled by one of his or her own blood. The use of blood in general is also seen as a form of pagan worship as there is a "blood sacrifice" in its construction. No proof exists of any Blood Stones, but is only passed down by folklore and journaled accounts of extremist witch hunters.' How do you like that?"

Kat blew out a breath. "I don't know...seems creepy, Morticia Adams creepy." She had seen many forms of amber before, with assorted fossilized bits floating within, but never had she seen the bits move about freely. Kat looked into the ring she always wore. It, too, had red flecks within, but it had never shifted in any way. She held it closer to the light, and as it got nearer to the pendant, the flecks began to swim about within the amber.

"Suz, look!"

"Well, I'll be damned. How did we miss that little trick before? Let's try something else. Place the pendant on a pulse point, your wrist, side of your neck, or crook of your elbow."

Kat placed it on the inside of her wrist so they both could observe the result.

"Fascinating. It really gets them jumping, doesn't it?"

The red droplets seemed to hop in place to the beat of a pulse. It was both amazing and scary as hell. Kat tossed both pieces away. They landed in the cushioned chair, flickered, and then quieted.

"It says here," Suzy continued, pointing to two books alternately, " 'that sometimes an object can be used to focus or channel an idea or thought.' A focal point. Now as to why the damn thing dances like that, I don't know, but these books all say the same thing in a different way, that you could use it as a connection, a way to call to one another. Bet it had more to do with getting you back to Helene than any words said."

Kat was silent a moment, taking it all in, weighing the magnitude of what they now knew. "Then that might be how she called me to her in the first place? How she found me?"

"Makes sense. You already had the ring."

"But Gran gave me that ring as a high school graduation present. Not Helene grandma, but Gran grandma."

"I know, dear."

"Do you think she knew?" It hurt to think it, but Kat had to say it out loud.

"I don't know what she knew, kiddo. She came back pretty messed up. Confused. Babbling. They talked of putting her away for a while until she stopped talking about it. No one believed her, myself included at first, I'm ashamed to say. Course I heard about it years later, back when you were probably just a toddler, and I was busy with my Sky. I barely had enough time to spare with that little one as I was working so much, so I sure didn't pay your Gran enough attention. She was already getting up in years by then...not that that's an excuse. I'm right ashamed now. Imagine, to be so frightened and have no one that believed you, must've been terrifying. I guess I wasn't a very good friend back then." Suzy stared off in the distance. It was as if she were viewing the scene unfold before her once again. Shaking herself, she refocused. "I am probably the age she was then when she told me about this mess. I wished I'd paid more attention. A lot of things I wished I did."

Suzy paused, deep in thoughts of regret as well as their current problem. "I would think your Gran thought she was giving you something old, passed down in the family."

"But Helene said that when I arrived she had seen Gran just four months earlier."

"Really? That's interesting...hmm." Suzy shuffled through pages trying to grab onto an elusive thread of an idea. "Might have to dig on that another time. A good idea might be to create a timeline of what we do know to see if we can make rhyme or reason of it."

Kat didn't really see the point, but as they had nothing else, she figured it couldn't hurt. Their timeline didn't take long to create as they only knew of a few visits, Kat's and Gran's. On the bottom of the timeline they put the date in real time, above the line they listed Helene's date, as closely as they could approximate it. No clear pattern yet appeared so they put it aside to consider at a another time.

"Wait a minute!" Kat hopped up to pace. Sometimes she did her best thinking that way. "If I already had the ring, what is the purpose of giving me the pendant as well? Wouldn't one be enough?"

"Well, she did 'bring you' back with just the ring. Maybe the pendant makes a stronger connection?"

"I read once, back when Wayne and I were dating and it looked like it might get serious—"

"The asshole," Suzy said.

"Yes, anyway, I read that the wedding ring goes on the left hand because it is thought that the vein in the left hand goes right to the heart. I'd always worn Gran's ring on my right hand. What would happen if I put the ring on my left hand and wore the pendant over my heart?"

"Wouldn't you be afraid that it might call to Helene or make a connection where she could call you more easily?"

"Yes, and no. I want answers. I need them. And unless Gran was to become suddenly lucid and explain herself, Helene is all we have."

"Well then, if you're going to try this, I'd suggest you change into something more timely. If it takes you back you'll not arrive a fool, like—"

"Yeah, yeah, don't remind me."

"And," Suzy continued, "if nothing happens all it cost you is a few minutes of changing. Oh! Let's get a bundle of herbs for you, too." Suzy scurried into the front room to dig in her bags.

Suzy came back with the small bundle of herbs, but Kat did not come back changed. She'd had second thoughts.

"Well that should cause a stir." Suzy remarked, looking at her Hello Kitty pajama pants and SUNY sweatshirt.

"I think I'd better wait."

"Okay, what are you thinking?"

"Well, when I was there she was pretty intense. You said maybe scared, even. I want the answers, but don't think I am going to get them if I am not 'invited.' I really don't want to sit around hidden again. I thought I'd go mad. Other than sneaking out to the abbey a couple of times, it was frustratingly boring. Plus, who knows, if I tick her off she could keep me there or ban me forever."

"Hmm, good points all. So what do you want to do?"

"Let's do that 'calling to' that you read about. Let's see if that works first."

"Okay, well like last time when you actually sent yourself there, there seems to be a need for a focal point. I suggest you use the pendant as it's the larger piece."

Kat placed both pieces of jewelry on the coffee table, side by side. "So do we say anything special?"

"There's nothing in any of these books that says what to do definitively."

They shuffled through *Modern Spells*, *Daily Spells*, and *The Country Witch* and found general spells that looked largely to be stolen from bad '80s movies.

"These are useless."

"Well of course they are. If they knew anything about witchcraft would they sell it for twenty-five bucks? I would think that any witch worth her salt would keep something that important a secret. These folks are all just guessing, hoping, romanticizing, or preying on gullible readers."

"Gee, thanks." Kat slumped.

"Oh, don't go all sensitive on me now; you know what I mean."

"Okay, so what do we do?"

"I vote you keep it simple, something like what you did when you managed your way back to her."

Kat had to rack her brain to think back as that had been a spontaneous recitation. "I honestly can't remember what I said. It just kind of happened."

"Well, I would think that would be the best way to go here as well—especially since it worked for you. Let's be honest, you must have some magical talent or you wouldn't have been able to succeed in breaking through that weather-forcefield thing at the abbey."

"I'm going to try to focus first on what I remember of her, try to recall all the details of her face. I don't know why I know that is the right thing to do, but it is." Kat picked up the pendant, held it in her hand, and turned it so it drew the most light from the table lamp.

Suzy nodded and watched her concentrate. It was odd, but just having her there made Kat feel less silly for trying. Kat tuned out everything but the light playing off the amber. She narrowed her gaze until it was the only thing she saw. Kat slowly, by degrees, shut down her periphery sight until, the stone, and only it, was her focus. She tried to peer into the amber's depth, hoping to see Helene's face. She began by recalling small details, her hair, long, auburn waves cascading around an oval face. Kat tried to remember the exact color of her eyes, brown with orange and gold flecks, like honey and amber. That was it, just like the amber! She focused on this mental image of Helene's eyes and then expanded her view so it could encompass her whole face. Kat saw worry lines around the eyes, fine lines at the sides of her mouth. Her skin was waxy, pale, gaunt. It startled her to see Helene thus, especially when she realized this wasn't the Helene she remembered but a different version. Kat saw her eyes flicker and shift, and then stare into hers, surprised. Helene smiled slowly and nodded. It was her! Not just Kat remembering her—but her!

Kat dropped the pendant as it had suddenly gotten warm to the touch, breaking the contact. She blinked several times, shaking herself free of the image.

Suzy sat beside her looking stunned.

"What?" She asked. "Something wrong?"

Suzy pointed at the ring that still rested on the table. It very clearly glowed as did the pendant on the rug. Then slowly both dimmed and flickered out.

"Wow."

"Yeah, I'd say so. I didn't hear you say anything."

"I didn't, not even in my head. I just focused really hard, but I know that I saw her. And not her that I remember, her now, this moment. She felt me looking for her, and...she smiled." Kat paused, searching for the words, "It's weird. I have no proof per se, but I know we connected. She saw me looking at her, for her."

"Holy crap!"

"Yeah. And I thought we needed words..."

"Maybe that's why they make all that crap up in the books, the rhyming poems and flourishes, so you feel like you are doing something. Maybe the reality is that the power comes from within." Suzy nodded, convincing herself.

"I don't know. Sounds like something out of *The Wizard of Oz* with the whole, 'Oh, Dorothy, you had the power all the time'."

"Well, you just proved it's true."

"Or we got lucky."

Suzy poked at the ring with the butt of a pen. "Nope, I think you had some help here, too. Don't forget that."

"It got warm."

"What did?"

"The pendant. Not burn-you-hot but living hot."

"Not trying to scare you, kiddo, but I don't know that I like that. You do what you think best, but I think I'd rest better if you put the whole lot in the safe until we can research some more. This is getting weirder and weirder—and normally I am okay with weird. But not with you. I'm not risking you."

Kat gave Suzy a hug. "It'll be okay. I came back each time."

"I just wish we knew more. I keep thinking there is something we missed. Some resource we haven't tapped."

"I could go and see Gran. Been meaning to anyway."

"Sure, sure, but we can't count on her these days. If only we knew more about what happened to her then. There might be something we can use, to protect you."

"I don't think I am in danger. We're family. What I need to learn is what is in me and how to control it, and even if I want it."

"Well, we are definitely not going to figure this out tonight. I am too exhausted and befuddled to untangle this, kiddo. Let's get some sleep and start in on this in the morning when we are fresh."

18

Grandma's Treasures

Suzy got settled for the night, and Kat made up the sofa for herself, but she couldn't sleep. She trolled through late night TV and landed on a classic comedy / horror film, *Abbott and Costello Meet Frankenstein and Dracula*. She thought it would help get her mind off of things, but eerily, it made her thoughts circle, and circle back, over the events of the night and her current worries. All the classic Hollywood schtick: heavy drapes, the lurking monster, candelabras, capes, made her wonder what did she really know about witches and witchcraft?

Kat decided to make a list. Some people counted sheep, but she made Excel sheets to wind down. She made three columns: what she knew of the history of witches, what she knew from Hollywood about witches, and what she knew first hand—bound to be the shortest of the lists, but one had to start somewhere. Kat listed several movie titles and noticed a ridiculous number of clichéd scenes. Or were they truths so they became cliché? Who knew? She listed every witch trial, literary references to witches, and even references in Bugs Bunny cartoons. Once she started, it poured out of her. Lists begot lists it seemed.

When Kat shifted to what she knew firsthand, the content came more slowly. She was missing something. Suzy was trying to help, but to be honest, she knew even less than Kat did about the situation. Suzy kept her grounded, kept her fed, and helped her stay sane, but Kat knew she would ultimately have to help herself. Suzy couldn't protect her from that.

Kat began to list what she knew about Gran's "episode" with Helene. Details were scant. But she did have the ring. The ring! What was it she said about the ring? Kat remembered now... when she was little she had found Gran's ring box. It was dark, red leather with gold embossing on the lid with a tiny, gold clasp. It was a perfect, little, treasure box. But when Kat opened it, it was empty. She remembered asking Gran about the box. She had said that it belonged to a special ring, and that when Kat was older, she would tell her the story. Gran had given her that empty box ages ago but never told her the story. If her ring, Gran's amber ring, was the ring from this box Kat still cherished, who did Gran tell the story to? Did she plan to ever tell her? With Gran's wavering mind, Kat feared she was too late to learn the truth of it now.

These mysteries kept Kat awake for hours. She was chasing metaphorical rabbits with no clear end in sight, but she didn't know what else to do. This was beyond surreal. Now that Kat was showing signs of some of her own power, wouldn't it be dangerous for her to not understand what it was and how it worked? Well, she certainly wasn't getting anywhere this way. Kat hopped up, decided to go into the attic's eave to find Gran's trunk. Gran used to let her play in the eave as a kid. She would let Kat try on her fox stole with which she would costume herself along with Gran's paste beads and pearls. Gran had a parasol in there, too, she remembered. There were also pictures of family that were long gone before she was born. Maybe, just maybe, there was something in there that could help. A clue...anything.

Once inside, Kat moved the junk piled up against the trunk. As she pushed the chest open, she couldn't help but admire the wood and thick, metal strappings. The lock had been broken for as long as she could remember so all Kat needed was one big shove to throw the lid back.

Gran had done what she called a "pre-funeral" before she went into the assisted-living apartment. She said she wasn't going to wait until she was dead to sort her affairs, and as she couldn't take all her things with her, she needed to see that they went to whomever she wanted herself. Mom had balked at the idea, saying it was morbid, and the aunts were fit to be tied. Gran told Kat they probably wanted the pleasure of squabbling after she passed so they could do what they "thought best" rather than abide by her wishes. She was on to them. But Gran, being the independent woman that Kat loved, knew better, and settled the items in question with whomever she chose. She figured she'd silenced them for once and for all. There would be no "misunderstanding" or "misinterpretation" of her last wishes because she was making them now. The pearls, the genuine set, went to Sadie, Grandma's long-time friend and shop hand. Kat had thought that Aunt Maureen was going to lose her mind over that one.

But when it came down to it, Gran really didn't have anything much of value other than the antiques in the shop. She hadn't had much personal property at all. The aunts had descended on the shop and ransacked it, looking for hidden treasure. One even tried pulling up floorboards in the corner where it looked uneven and badly repaired. They'd found nothing more than a few glass beads and a silvered magnifying glass that had little value, nothing more. Of course nothing was put back in its place so it took Kat ages to get the shop back to rights. The valuable stock had been sold and divided among the sisters even though the contents of the shop had been left to Kat. She didn't fight it—seemed simplest that way. Plus, Kat knew if she appeased them now they'd stay away, and it worked. Now there would be no doubt that when Gran does pass, what was in the shop was hers because she'd bought and paid for it. They'd had their "inheritance"; they'd have no more from Kat. One aunt had made motions of taking the trunk she now held to use as a coffee table in her family room, but Mom stood up for Kat that time. It was the one item Gran insisted, had been adamant in fact, that was Kat's and Kat's alone. After the aunts had rifled through it and recognized nothing of worth, they let Kat be with her memories of attic tea parties with Gran.

Kat went through the trunk now, methodically. If there was something, anything, that could help she didn't want to miss it. She found a small stack of Gran's journals—she'd have to sift through those later. She pulled out layers of parchment paper. There were a few of Gran's favorite books. The moth-eaten stole was tucked in tissue paper. Someone's baby shoes were in another bundle of tissue. A bit of Irish lace was wrapped in a velvet cloth. Kat didn't remember ever seeing that before, which was curious. There were Grandpa's medals from the war in a cigar box, left only by the aunts as the metal was merely tin and no one had liked him when he was alive so the sentiment was wasted on them. There was an elaborately embroidered tablecloth with a riot of colored flowers dancing over it; some of the colors so misplaced as this was from the time when Great Grandma, Gran's mother, had started to go blind. Kat held the cloth close to her, inhaling the mothball smell but recalling Great Grandma. She'd only been saved this table cloth as the others had snapped up the "valuable" ones. Hers had flower petals of green and stems of pink and orange as Great Grandma had been mostly working from touch memory rather than sight at this point. But she didn't care—it still reminded Kat of her. She remembered her sitting in the waning evening sun, alone, keeping her hands busy for to do otherwise was a sin.

She had just reached the bottom of the trunk when Suzy found Kat in the eave. "So this is where you'd gotten off to. Did you get any sleep at all?"

Kat shook her head, no. "I tried. Honestly, I did, but I kept thinking that I was missing something, a key. Gran was there. Maybe she left a hint of what to expect. I don't know. It seems silly now that I say it out loud, but I just keep wishing we weren't so in the dark."

Suzy patted her head.

"I feel so… inept. Bumbling. And this is far too important to botch."

"So, what'd you find?" Suzy asked, peering over her shoulder.

"Nothing much. All the same stuff that has always been in here. Well," remembering, "except for this bit of Irish lace."

"That is curious. I don't remember your grandmother getting to Ireland although she always talked of going there someday. That's where you got your name, you know. Kathleen was as Irish a name as you could get. Your grandfather loved Ireland, especially the County Clare and went on about it to anyone that'd listen."

Kat had known the story, but it felt good to hear it retold nonetheless.

"Did you check the bottom of the trunk?"

"What?"

"Turn it over girl. Might be something on the bottom. I used to tape my marijuana to the bottom of my hope chest," Suzy giggled.

Together they lifted and turned the trunk on its side. Nothing there.

"Ah well, 'no stone unturned' sort of thing you know."

They started to reload the trunk when they heard a loud crack.

"Oh, man!" Kat panicked. "This is not what I need! Please don't be broken!"

"Wait, wait, wait!" Suzy enthusiastically thumped on Kat's shoulder. "Get the stuff back out."

Suzy fairly pushed Kat aside in her eagerness. "I've seen this in spy movie. I wonder..?" She pushed at the bottom of the chest in what looked like assorted pressure points. The cracking sound repeated and was followed by a definitively audible click. The bottom of the chest lifted as if on a hinge.

There, beneath the false bottom, was taped an envelope clearly labeled in Gran's fine script, "*For Kathleen.*" Both of them stared at the packet, transfixed. Was this really happening?

Since Kat didn't seem to be capable of making a move, Suzy used her fingernails to carefully pry the tape holding the envelope from the bottom of the inside of the trunk. She handed the packet to Kat to open.

The aged glue came loose easily, and Kat peeled the flap open and found within it pages that had been torn out of a journal. She remembered asking Gran about the missing section in her journal. Gran used to read pages from it to her as if they were only stories—stories of when she was a kid and growing up. The stories were indeed old as they spanned from about the age of twelve to twenty or so. Gran had told her that she had spilled ink and soaked the pages so the pages had to be torn out to save the rest. Now, as Kat held the missing pages in her hand, she knew the truth.

19

In Gran's Words

Kat carefully unfolded the yellowed pages, fearful that they would blow apart like the paper she'd seen exposed to air on an archeological dig she once watched on television. Tucked within the packet was a page that was significantly whiter, a letter to Kat. It began:

> My darling Kathleen,
> I'm sorry. I'm sorry I didn't have the opportunity to talk to you about what I've been dying to for years. There never seemed to be the right time. Plus, how could I get you to believe what I would tell you when no one else did? I guess I was being selfish. I didn't want to see the same look on your face as I saw on my parents' faces or the look on your mother's. So I hid this, hoping you might not need to know the truth but fearing all the while that Helene would come for you.
> You asked me once about the ring box. I told you

that it had an important story, and it does. But when you'd asked you were much too young to hear of it. You see, I, like you, inherited a ring. Gaudy, terrible thing it was. Much bigger than the one you were given. I've thought often over the years that if it hadn't been so hideous my older sister would've kept the ring for herself. That ring is now long gone, lost 'between' trips. Anyway, I made Helene promise not to try to reach you until you were much older. So far she has honored my request. I didn't know how to handle the new knowledge I had; I was terrified. I'd been taught that magic was a sign of the devil and to be feared. So I, being a good girl, went immediately to tell to my parents what happened, and I nearly lost my life because of it. When I wouldn't change my tale no matter how they beat and threatened me, they locked me away. They put me away for years, bringing only priests to visit. Kathleen, I hope you understand that I was just a child, and my perspective was of a child's. I didn't fully understand what I was part of, the gift it could be, nor the hatred people have of things they fear. And so I learned to be silent, to hide, to conceal, and to wait. Eventually they allowed me to come home, and the matter was not mentioned again. That was until your mother turned sixteen. I told Deirdre my tale then, and she cried. She called me a liar, and ran from our home to your great grandparents. I had thought she was old enough to learn the truth. I'd seen little sparks in her for witchcraft, but she suppressed it, hid it.

I had modeled that well— hiding. Well, she told my parents, and I almost lost her to the state. I had to have tests, examinations, the ministry was called in again, and I learned to shut it all down, changed my story, and lied. In the end it was blamed on a vitamin deficiency.

Anyway, I've gotten long-winded. I am sorry for that as the enclosed journal pages of what happened, as I remembered it best, should suffice. Just please know I did what I thought was best for you each and every time I lied to you. I only hope that if she has called you already that you forgive me; she gave me no choice in the matter. We are what we are, Kathleen. I think we spend far too much time trying to be something else rather than embracing our true selves. You are far smarter and braver than I ever could hope to be. I hope you use your talents as you see fit. There is strength in you—a power evident since you were a small child. Dearest Kathleen, I never really owned anything that was truly my own, but this was my legacy to you. I always loved you best.

I hope you can forgive me, Gran

When Kat finished the letter she just sat there, staring at the words while no longer seeing them.

Suzy finally broke the silence, "Wow, just wow."

"Yeah, right? I am kind of scared to read the journal but also excited. How does one begin to open a new chapter? What new family surprise will I find out now?"

Suzy shrugged and nimbly hopped back up onto her feet. "But we are not doing it on an empty stomach. Come on, bring the pages with you. It's too damp and chilly in here. I'll make a snack and," anticipating Kat's objections, "you can read the journal aloud. Deal?"

It was hard to argue with that logic. Kat settled in to read while Suzy put together English muffins topped with tomato and muenster cheese. Looking at the pages Kat noticed that they were written in the tighter fist of a child, so sometimes the reading was slow as she tried to make out the words.

November 12, 1924

I am allowed my journal and ink back but know I will have to hide it or risk being punished again. I don't understand why they keep asking me the same questions over and over. The answers won't change, can't change, because they are true. Aren't they?

I thought father was going to kill me. He shook so as he yelled, his face all purply. He'd whipped me so long and hard that I passed out. And I know I am his favorite. He cried; my father actually cried while he hit me saying he loved me. But if he loved me how could he beat me so long and so mercilessly?

I had proof. My hair was longer when I returned that first time, just about an inch. But they said it was trickery in the styling. The dress I wore was obviously from another time, but they'd insisted that I'd found it in the attic and that I was playing a charade on them. I had the jewelry, too, but dared not give it to them; she'd know and then she'd be angry, too. I'd rather have the lashes.

On second thought I'd better rip these pages out. They'll be sure to check on me later. I hate being so afraid all the time.

Dec. 9, 1924

I was packed off to another Christian school. This time I

know I am to be away for months. I think they think it will be a punishment for me, but I feel safe here.

It's an austere place. They took almost everything I had away for safekeeping, locked it in a box, and stowed it on a shelf behind a bolted door with an iron cage. They made a point of showing me this. I was only allowed to keep a doll although they say I'm too old for dolls at twelve..

No one beats me here.

We spend a lot of the daytime in quiet contemplation and prayers. I'm happy to do this. Feels safe. Feels right. What Helene is surely can't be holy; this I know, no matter how kind she was to me. The nuns have told me that magic is sent by the devil himself to lead us astray. I don't know why the devil would want me.

She was good to me, even when I didn't deserve it. I cried a lot and complained all the time. Once she shook me, but it wasn't anything my parents hadn't done although it made me feel like my teeth were rattling in my head. It was my own fault; she'd been nothing but kind.

March 19, 1925

I've been here for months now, but I no longer feel as safe as I used to. They keep pressuring me to give these thoughts away to God. I love God; I do. But how can I say a lie to God? He'd know.

They said I am a good girl; I could be a nun. I might like that. But they say that what I saw and did was a lie. I know I made a spark with my hands; I know I did. I felt the heat, and I still have the burn mark on my finger tip. They say I had a bad dream, and that the scar is from the drip from a lit candle. I know that isn't true. I know it. I'm so tired. I can't tell what day it is anymore. I don't know what is real anymore. If

I say now it was all a lie, they say I have to not just say it but believe it, too. They don't tell me how to believe. How can I lie and say I didn't do what I did? They don't know, but I sometimes still do it, even without her.

The letter that followed was obviously written by a much older woman; Kat didn't need a date to clarify that. She recognized some of the style from the others.

April 27, 1947 - I hadn't expected to see Helene again—especially after she'd ruined my childhood so thoroughly. I was older and angrier this time, and I told her so. I'd spent years in treatment or locked away at various Christian schools trying to "release the demon" I possessed. I'd finally given in and confessed it was a game, and that lie alone set me free as long as I was consistent and private in my shame. It became clear I must protect the family from the truth no matter what it cost me.
But this time it wasn't me Helene'd wanted. She wanted my girl, my Deirdre. But Deirdre had not the gift, not really, and it shamed her hearing from the family about my past. There were some in the community that still avoided me and would not let their girls socialize with mine. Deirdre had enough hurt from this as it was.
So instead she kept me through the better part of the summer and none were the wiser. When I was to be returned I had had my hair cut and simpler clothes ready to return in, what to them, would be but hours. I was loath to risk all again. Howard was such a good man, and he'd tak-

en enough grief over what they all said of me. He was a saint to marry me in spite of it all. The fact that it was true didn't help because I'd renounced those truths for the freedom of a simple life, a life at all. I'd even forgotten what I'd dreamed of becoming when I was a girl, but I know I dreamed of something other than what I became.

But this time I was ready for her. I'd been dabbling in the arts when I could, and I showed Helene what I'd accomplished while I was away and on my own. She seemed pleased that I had developed so far without her guidance, but next to her it was true that I was but a small talent. And she was thoughtful after all; she offered to take what skill I had away. I didn't think long on that. I paid so dearly for it over the years, the jeers, the exclusions, the pointing at and whispers to this day at the A&P and at parent meetings. Deirdre could never have a sleepover because of me, the penalty of a small town. No, I would keep what little power I had as proof that I wasn't insane. I did travel through time. I did see what I saw. I had not imagined this. I was not insane, although many said I was. No, this bit would be my secret, and now, after all these years, it made me feel safer, as if I had a choice.

20

Sleeplessness

Kat sat cross-legged on the sofa, sipping her Lady Grey. At some point Suzy must've covered her with Gran's throw that Kat always kept on the arm of the sofa. She pulled it closer about her shoulders, not so much for warmth but for comfort.

It was a lot to mull over. Kat was grateful that Suzy was giving her the space to simply think. So many others would've bombarded her with questions, not that she had the answer to any of them. It was a natural reaction to want to talk it over—really more like just vocalizing thoughts to process them more than for clarity. But not yet. She needed time to think, not talk.

Suzy must've left sometime ago; an hour had passed since Kat noticed she was gone. She couldn't even remember if Suzy'd said anything before she left. Kat was tired and wasn't sure she could recall her own name right now.

Kat was snapped back into reality when she heard a key in the door. It only took a glance to see that it was Suzy, back with a couple of bags.

"Hey, kiddo."

"Where'd you go? How long were you gone?"

"Wasn't sure you'd notice. You were...somewhere else. How you doing?"

"Tired, just tired. I can't think."

"Well, I've got a few solutions to that. You could eat what I brought you and perk up, or, eat what I brought you, ruminate over it, or, finally get to bed. That late night snack must've worn through you by now. "

"Food? Yeah, I could eat. Bed? I am not sure I could sleep, but I know I need to."

"Let's just eat and then you decide after, okay?"

Suzy had gotten the good bagels and cream cheese from Deising's and Greek omelets and fruit from the nearby diner—complete with double sides of thick bacon and large, dark coffees. Kat thought she could cry from the sheer joy of it.

They sat on the floor on the living room rug to eat at the coffee table. Kat ate and stretched, feeling the blood fill her brain with every sip of coffee and bite of bacon. Tara always complained that she could eat pounds of it and never gain weight—her true super power.

After they'd eaten Suzy asked, "Well, what's it going to be, kiddo? Do we try to sort through this now or bed first? You haven't slept at all. "

"I know I should sleep, but I can't. It all keeps swimming around in my head. Let's talk some of it through and then maybe it'll settle in my head so I can sleep. That okay?"

"Of course. How do you want to start?"

"I'm not sure."

"Got a legal pad?"

"Huh?"

"Legal pad. It's what us old farts use to sort ideas."

Kat laughed. "Well then I guess I am an old fart, too. I buy them in bundles."

Suzy raised an eyebrow at her over her reading glasses.

"I deal with antiques, must've rubbed off."

"Watch it, kid," Suzy poked her in the gut.

Kat stretched out her arms, rolling her head on her shoulders to work out the kinks. She got the legal pads and the smooth roller gel pens she loved—helped her ideas flow, literally.

"How about we make lists of what we know now for sure and then we can sort through what questions we have left."

It seemed as good a plan as any, and at least they each could jump in and start doing—something. They wrote steadily for about a quarter of an hour, not speaking, each focused on her own thoughts.

Kat focused on what she knew of Gran from the journals first, and then what she knew of her now. The questions column seemed to grow with no end in sight. When she exhausted all ideas and questions, Kat looked up to see Suzy watching her.

She glanced at Suzy's list—it was significantly shorter than hers.

"Hey, slacker. What gives?"

"I realized something." Suzy began.

Kat waited for Suzy to continue on her own rather than interrupt her.

"It all boils down to fear."

"What do you mean?"

"Everything she did or didn't do was based on fear. Even the parts of the journal where it got jumbled and difficult to follow, we can blame fear. I realized that until we find out what Edy feared, we can't know for sure what we are dealing with."

"But isn't magic, the thought of it, time travel, and her parents enough motivation for fear?"

"Normally, yes, but I think there was something she wasn't saying. Plus, think on it, she hid this all, for you, for this time, for you to find. If everyone involved knew all as she claimed, then why would she need to hide these pages? What was the danger? She already almost destroyed her life in discussing it."

Exasperated, Kat sighed. It seemed she kept circling back to dead ends. "Well, then I guess the next step is to visit Gran."

"Don't be discouraged, kiddo. She has some good days. She's been fighting it. She's a smart woman. At least let her try to help you."

"I'm grateful for what she risked already with the journal pages and letter. I can't imagine what it must have felt to be her, then. If I didn't have someone to talk to about this, I think I would've gone mad."

"Oh, stop looking at me all sappy, hang-dog like. You were already mad." Suzy gave her a playful shove.

"Nice, real nice. I was trying to have a moment." Kat excessively batted her eyes.

"Ah, there's the wise-ass I know and love. Now shut up, get in a hot shower, and plaster on a layer of make up. You look terrible."

"You mean we are going now to talk to her? Today?"

"Have a good reason why not? Are you going to bed, finally?"

"Nope, you're right on both accounts. I guess today is as good as any other day."

"Oh, and pack up the pendant and the ring. Might help jog her memory."

21

Gran's Obligation

They found Gran happily engaged in a game of Backgammon in the morning room. But upon seeing Kat she lit up and quickly excused herself from the game.

"What? You get a visitor and now I'm chopped liver?" Gran's friend called out after her.

"No, dummy, you always were chopped liver!" She laughed. "This is my granddaughter. I'll play you later."

"Yeah, sure, I'm not going anywhere."

Gran beamed. "Well, what a wonderful surprise!" She gave them each a tight squeeze. "Come, sit down, and tell me all about you and what you've been up to."

"Edy, is there somewhere more private we can talk?"

Gran looked Suzy in the eye, and saw the import in her glance. She quickly turned to Kat. "You okay? In any trouble, Kathleen?"

Kat was relieved to hear her say her name. She shook her head although tears came to her eyes.

"Tell me the truth, Kitty Kat. What has you tearing up? Is it some boy?"

"No, Gran, I'm just so happy to see you," Kat truthfully replied. And she was. She just couldn't tell her she was relieved Gran was herself, lucid. It'd hurt her feelings.

Gran looked back at Suzy. At a pointed head nod from her, Gran's focused glance now shifted to look at Kat's hand that held the ring box.

"Ah," Gran blinked. "So she's come for you. I'd hoped she'd forgotten about the whole lot of us," she sighed. "Let's go for a walk. Prying ears here."

It was too cold to walk outside, but the senior center had many sitting rooms, studies, and tea tables scattered throughout. They headed up to the small library alcove that boasted a wall of local history books on one wall and an atrium wall of glass.

They sat with the sun on their backs reflecting off the light dusting of snow that had fallen that morning, creating a reassuring warmth.

Once alone, Kat felt Gran's open stare taking in all the details of her face. "Okay, spill it. What happened? Are you okay?"

"No, Gran, we're here to talk about you first. I need to know what you know."

Gran sighed, shifting in her seat uncomfortably. "You found the letter, the journal pages?"

Kat nodded.

"Well, that's it. What more could there be?"

"Tell me about the ring, Gran, the ring you gave me. Where did it come from?"

Gran looked away for a moment, then at Suzy, and finally back at Kat. "I didn't want to give it to you at all. She'd come to me, begged, entreated, and then demanded I pass the ring on. I couldn't get her voice to stop." Gran sat up straighter, "but I held out, fought it until you were older, eighteen. I'd hoped she'd forget about you, us, but it's now clear she didn't. But at least you weren't a little girl like I was."

Gran reached out to touch the box that held the ring. She slowly opened it. Her thumb stroked over the stone and a momentary spark of color could be seen. She quickly closed the lid and pushed the box back to Kat.

"But I couldn't deny who I was nor who you are. We are of her—her blood, her legacy. I understood it and yet didn't want it. I didn't want to be 'special.' Special only got me beatings, years of doctors and beatings. And then when I married..." Her eyes drifted off, following a thought.

"Gran?"

"No, I will not speak ill about your grandfather." Gran shook herself, as if shaking away a chill. "Anyway, she'd offered me a gift, and when I refused, she tried with your mother, and now you, to share it. It is for you to choose or reject. But either way, it is in your blood."

"Wait. Mom was...called?" Kat sought for a word that would make sense.

"Well, yes and no. The stone turned gray."

"Gran, what are you talking about?"

"Well, apparently, what we are is passed down from generation to generation, like hair or eye color. But when your mom was old enough to see what was what, I gave her that ring. No matter how we tried, it didn't seem to fit right, too small or too big. Well, she wore it on her finger anyway, and curled her hand up to keep the ring on when it was too large, and the stone turned gray. It was like it died on her hand. She got scared and dropped the ring and ran. When I picked it back up it looked the way it does now."

"You said something about the 'glow.' What did you mean by that?"

"Ah, yes. When it glows she is focusing on you. It might call to you or call you 'out,' you know, to the other place."

Kat looked at Suzy. She nodded. "Makes sense. Show her the other."

Kat pulled the pendent out of its velvet case. It glowed and pulsed brilliantly—more so, the closer it got to the ring.

"Oh, my." Gran exclaimed. "Is that...?" She paused. "Well of course it must be, but how?"

"She gave it to me."

Kat quickly gave her an overview of how she came to have the pendant.

Gran thought for a few minutes, none of them talking. "She must've seen something in you that makes you extra special, you know. What can you do?"

"Not much really, except now I feel things that I shouldn't."

Gran didn't seem surprised at all. "Being with her magnifies the gift or awakens it. I know. I came back and had all this extra energy. Started noticing weird things I could do. Minor tricks really but new to me."

"I heard you read cards."

Gran laughed outright. "No, they think I can read cards—parlor trick really. I read faces. That'll tell you more than any damn card any day. Had my fun with it, too, until your mother... well, to be fair she was embarrassed, so I stopped. Made your grandfather uncomfortable. Did you know your great-granddad was a preacher?"

"No, I didn't."

"Well, that's a tale for another day anyway. So, you having problems 'feeling'?"

"Yeah, the antiques—"

Gran continued Kat's thought herself. "Leave a residue of emotion if the person who owned it had some passion towards it. Very common. It was always there, you just are more sensitive because you've gotten closer to who you really are. You're a witch, not a trained one yet, but one by birth, so that means there are latent talents in you. Wear cotton gloves."

"Excuse me?"

"Wear cotton gloves when you get new shipments. Your granddad thought I was overly fastidious. I told him it was to protect the antiques from body oils. Then, when you're alone you can deal with each item in private. But," Gran warned, "if I were you, I'd keep the damn gloves on. When you go back to look you will see a lot of things you might not want to see or know."

"Yeah, there was this wagon I had to burn."

"Just remember you are in a business to make money. You can't change the past, but you can feel it. And that feeling will depress you. So wear the gloves."

Gran must've seen something in Kat's face because she quickly continued. "It's a lucky thing, too. You'll be able to tell the true worth of an item, know if it's real without spending hours researching." She laughed, "Although that's how I'd get my alone time. I'd tell your granddad I was researching the shipment. That was always good for a few hours of peace."

"Okay, but why? Why does she call us back? Do you know?"

"I'm not sure. I think it is to pass on the family wisdom, spells, training. Not quite sure. I wish I had been braver. I wish I were young nowadays. People are okay with the New Age stuff. Hell, they have shops all over the place. I'd be hip rather than something to be exorcised." Gran looked sad and distant for a moment but then almost visibly shook herself out of her thoughts. "The truth of the matter is, I was afraid. Maybe I should've stayed with her and never come back. I think on that sometimes. When you are sitting on my end of life's journey you look back and realize it is such a small life. So easy to slip past and have no impact, no meaning. I wish I had been brave enough to try. To learn. To see what I could've been. It was my chance to be more, and I squandered it."

"Oh, Gran, you are not small. Sometimes I think you are too much!" They both laughed and then Kat hugged her tight. "So, you think I should go for it?"

"Well, why not? You don't want to let that antique shop tie you down. I was afraid that might happen."

"No, I do love it, and I think I am good at it. I just wonder—"

"There! That's it! You wonder. So go and find out. You won't miss anything here, literally. So you've nothing to lose. Go and be brave and come back and tell me all about it."

"Gran, is there," Kat started tentatively,"is there anything I could do for you...here?"

"I doubt that, honey. Magic doesn't work like that. And I think the kind that can might not be the kind you want to dabble in. I'm aging. It's all a course of nature."

"But, sometimes..."

"Sometimes I am not quite there?" Gran finished her thought.

"Um, well, yeah."

"Okay, so sometimes I am not at my best. I forget things and names, but I am not always as bad as I seem. It takes courage to get old, but it's better than the alternative."

"Gran?"

She laughed. "Okay, it's no secret your mom is a pain in my ass, and my sisters are even worse. Plus, it is amazing what you learn about people when they think you've lost your mind." She laughed harder.

"Gran! That's horrible! How could you?"

"I said not ALL of the time. Sometimes I have hard days. And that's okay. It's better than not having them at all."

"But when I visited you last..."

"Tell you what, we'll come up with a code word. If I'm playing possum, use the word, and I'll let you know. If it's my bad day, you'll know. Fair enough?"

"What's the code word?"

"How about 'Helene'? No one else knows her."

"Fine. But I will hold you to it. Damn it, Gran, you are so bad sometimes."

She giggled like a girl. "It's my revenge for always coloring in the lines when I wanted to run and scream and forget all their names by choice. Don't do the same. Find your own way."

"Gran, is there anything I need to know about Helene that I don't know? I had a weird feeling she was hiding something."

"She probably was—she's a woman. We either bend, break, or hide who we are. That's our lot in life. I wouldn't be surprised if she has a man like mine was. Go. Ask. Find out. I don't know any more as I wasn't there that long to learn. I was too 'chicken shit' as you say, to open my eyes to the gift she was offering. Don't you do the same."

When it came time to say goodbye, Kat held on, taking in her smell and vowing to come back soon and often.

22

Family Shift

The ride back to town was a quiet one. Suzy and Kathleen were both deep in their own thoughts. Kat had so many mixed emotions. She was angry at Gran for exacerbating the dementia issue by choosing to disconnect at will. But she also felt saddened that Gran felt the need to do so, that the others made her want to disappear.

And then there was Helene. Apparently, Gran felt she needed to take what was offered. She saw it as an adventure, an escape. But Kat didn't need to escape. She didn't want to...or did she? Kat both loved the shop and felt held back by it, that was true. She'd been unlucky in love, and school didn't feel that important right now. Taking one class at a time made college feel interminable.

Kat clicked the car radio off to signal to Suzy that she was ready to talk.

"I think I am ready to go back. As soon as she'll have me," she said before Suzy could ask.

"I kind of always thought that was what you'd do. You're no quitter. And certainly no runner. When did you have in mind?"

"We've only got a few weeks until Christmas. I have to focus on the shop. We both know that if I leave now I'll be returned almost as soon as I left. But where will my mind be then? Certainly not on the shop and all I have to do to get through these last weeks. I've been thinking that the day after Christmas day would be best. The shop would be closed for a week anyway. All the relatives will go back to under whatever rock they crawled out from, and I can come back to peace. And I might need it."

"So what do you need to get ready—other than my herbs?"

"I think that I need to know what to expect. Not of magic—I doubt we can really research that as what we've found as sources are questionable at best. Nope, I think I need to learn how people acted: spoke, behaved, ate, dressed, and such so I won't cause trouble once I am there. There is some danger there—from whom or what I have no idea, but Helene did make it clear that what we are needs to be kept a secret."

"I agree. And I'll help with the research."

Kat scoured the local library, finally abandoning it for the college library when she ran out of resources. She looked everywhere, followed any lead, studied habits, common English phrases, outdated vocabulary, and etiquette. It was dry stuff but enlightening. Kat now began to see what she must have seemed to be by Mrs. Brown and the others—a careless, selfish, crude invader. She watched movie after movie set in the time period, but now that she'd studied, she realized other than table settings and clothing, some of it they had gotten laughably wrong.

Once Kat had done what she could in the now, she began to wonder if she could truly blend in enough to be able to stay and learn? Kat realized the more she researched that this wasn't like research for a class, but something she truly cared about. Something she wanted. She didn't want Gran's regrets, and if truth be told, Kat had been wondering what she was doing with her life. Was it passing her by? Was she hiding in Gran's shop, licking her wounds from a failed relationship? In her college classes Kat realized that she was already treading water with no clear direction. She had been playing at life, joining the play at Marcy's insistence rather than any real desire of her own to do so. She'd been adrift, and it needed to stop. Where magic came to play in all of this, Kat didn't know. But if it was indeed in her, didn't she owe it to herself to see all that there was?

Before long, the holiday dinners were eaten, gifts exchanged, duties to family and friends completed. It was time. Kat had made all the correct responses, niceties, and overtures as the season required. Since she was determined to be away right after Christmas, in her mind she ached to be done with it all already and so only went through the motions. But no one seemed to notice as she said all the right things, did all the expected actions, and fulfilled every obligation. Kat couldn't help thinking that if she could convince those here, who knew her best, that she fit in, wouldn't it be easier in Helene's time where no one expected anything of her? She certainly hoped so.

After Helene's anger during her last visit, Kat knew she couldn't risk her ire again and be welcomed back. Even now, after all this time, she couldn't be sure that she could or would be allowed to do so. As the season wore on, that thought nagged. Kat pushed those ideas aside because she couldn't risk dwelling on them or she'd never get what she needed to do done. But now it was the morning of the day after Christmas. Family had returned to their own homes, and Kat sat nervously sipping coffee in her Giants sweatpants and a baggy, flannel shirt.

Kat found herself at a loss as to how best begin. She didn't have long to wallow in her thoughts before Suzy arrived bearing bags.

"I thought this was how I'd find you."

"Did we plan on meeting this morning? I'm sorry. I forgot."

"No, we didn't make plans, but today is the day, isn't it? I knew you wouldn't be sleeping in, especially after the last few days. I think you smiled at everything your mother said. How she didn't see your heart wasn't in it is beyond me. I almost fell over when I heard some of the inane conversations, and you just smiling and nodding like a dutiful daughter and niece."

"Was it that obvious?"

"No, honey. People see what they want to see at all times. There's none the wiser. All this training and studying is paying off. I think if you kept it up, you'd never have a fight with your mother again."

"Yeah…no. Eventually I'd have to do something she wanted me to do, and that would be it."

"True, true. Anyway, enough on that silly lot. I brought you a few things. After all that rich holiday food I figured you'd need to be set to rights before we send you on your 'magical mystery tour' of the past—nausea, you know." She winked.

Kat groaned. She'd forgotten about that lovely side effect.

"None's to worry. I've got the ticket right here—steel cut oatmeal. It'll make anyone's stomach as solid as a tin drum."

"Yum," Kat said sarcastically.

"Oh, shut up. You'll like it just fine, and you'll eat it just the same if you don't."

"Well, good morning to you! What has you in a snit?"

"Gee, I don't know? A girl as dear to me as if she was my own is going to leave today for I don't know how long, to dabble in stuff she doesn't really understand yet, and I'm supposed to act like I'm not sad."

"I thought you agreed that this is what I should do?"

"I do, and it is, but it doesn't stop me from worrying."

Kat stood to give her a sideways hug. "Remember, I may be

gone for a while, but for you it won't be long at all. I'll be back soon on your end."

"You'd better, or I'll go crazy with the waiting."

"Nah, I'll be back before you know it."

"Just promise me that you'll remember who you are—truly are inside, no matter what you learn while there. And don't forget to come home."

"I won't. I promise." But Suzy had planted some doubt in her mind. Would Kat forget? She really didn't have much here aside from Suzy. Would she want to stay away? Kat shook her head as if shaking out the thought. She had her, Gran, her shop, friends.

"I brought you this, just in case." It was a miniature, a locket, like the painted ones in the shop but instead, in the inside was a picture of Kat and Sky when they were kids, faces smooshed side by side in wide grins.

She started to tear up so Suzy quickly continued, "It's not meant for tears but for remembrance. The two of you brought out the best in each other. It'll bring you home."

Kat could only trust herself to nod.

After everything was checked and double checked, the 'away on holiday' window sign in the shop window, they sat down to begin.

"So where do we start?"

"Well," Suzy tapped a finger to her lips as she thought. "You were able to do it before so I would start there but..." She paused to eye Kat up and down.

"What?"

"Nope, it will not do. Let's get you gussied up in case you are able to shift quickly." She pulled from a rolled bag a dress. "Thought you'd be wanting something 'new' to wear." She laughed at the irony. "This was your Gran's. She wore this back from...you know, Helene's, so I knew it'd work."

She was right. Kat had to be ready in case they succeeded

immediately. She went into the back room and returned fully decked from head to toe in period wear, excepting her bra and underwear. She just couldn't make that transition yet, and she hoped Suzy didn't notice.

"Don't the 'girls' seem a bit perky for the date you'll be traveling to?" Suzy cocked an eye.

"Ah man, I just can't. Not yet. I know I'll have to wear what they wear there, but I need to go with one good bra, please."

Suzy laughed. "If you are careful no one will notice. But be sure to take care. I saw those *Back to the Future* movies. You know how that works out."

It was Kat's turn to laugh. "I seriously doubt that a modern bra will cause an alternate timeline. I don't think it really works like that."

"I certainly hope not. Anyway, let's get to business. I'd just as soon send you on your way so you can be coming back just as quickly."

Suzy pinned the miniature into Kat's sash at her waist, hiding it in the folds of fabric and then did the same with a packet of herbs to help with the nausea.

"Do you have words to say?"

"I don't know that the words are that important. I thought I'd try to focus on the ring and pendant."

Suzy nodded and handed her the jewels.

Kat slid the ring on her right ring finger and the pendant's chain over her head. She felt them both heat against her body and a faintly perceptible glow began to flicker within.

Suzy's eyes went wide, and she just pointed, mute.

"I know," Kat whispered. "Plus, they are getting warm." She placed her hand over the pendant and could feel a slight pulse. It was both disconcerting and exciting. "Helene? Are you there?"

The ring brightened and pulsed in time with the pendant. The red bits formed ribbons and moved in time with the pulse.

"With the power within me and thee, I call unto thou. Heed my plea." Kat didn't know where the words came from, but they came unsolicited.

Kat heard a low hum, and then words started to form in her head. But they didn't belong to her. It was Helene. She quickly threw a wink at Suzy who gave her hand a squeeze. Kat closed her eyes, focusing on the voice within while still feeling the support of Suzy's hand. She couldn't make out the individual words, but they were there nonetheless. It sounded Gaelic or perhaps something older than that, Kat couldn't tell. Slowly the words chanted and grew stronger in her head until she could only focus on that. Kat felt herself slipping away, out of Suzy's grasp, unconscious of the floor beneath her feet, even the air around her. Just nothingness and Helene's voice. Her voice soothed as it beckoned, lured, and led. With a rush of air she then felt acutely aware of each limb stretching and flexing.

When Kat opened her eyes it was to the latter 1800s once again. They stood in a bed chamber. Helene was dressed in robes of soft cream and palest yellow, her hair unbound as if for bed. There was a cheery fire behind her, sending sparks of light into her dark, auburn hair. She smiled broadly and held out her arms to Kat, who could see that Helene was big with child.

Kat laughed in nervous relief and hugged Helene as tightly as the protruding belly would allow.

"Welcome, Kathleen. I am glad to have you come back."

"I am glad to be here. I wasn't sure I'd be welcome after last time."

"We both have had time to think on it, and I believe we both did wrong. 'Tis no matter, though. You are here now, and there is much to say. But for the moment, you must rest. We'll get you changed out of that dress and into a shift." She nodded approvingly at the gown Kat wore as it was one she had provided Gran. "Let's get you settled and in bed. The hour is late here. We can talk in the morning."

"Will I need to go back to the farmhouse?" Kat tentatively asked. She feared that most but knew it might be necessary as it once had been.

"No need for that now. You've chosen an easy time for me to receive visitors. Alastair is away at the moment, as is much of the household. So we'll be at each other's disposal for a time. It'll give us opportunity to prepare a story for you as well. If you're to stay, I will have to explain who you are, and as this is my first child," she rubbed her belly affectionately, "I doubt that great, great, great, great granddaughter will be the appropriate title, and for 'cousin' to suffice we'll need more detail to be believed. But we'll sort this all out in the morning. Let's get you off to bed."

Helene led Kat to a room not far from her own. It was smaller than the last but cheerful with its fire in the hearth and Scottish plaids. She called on no servants this first night, for which Kat was deeply grateful, but instead helped her into a simple shift of cotton and soft, Irish lace. Helene raised an eyebrow at her undergarments but said not a word. All Kat could do was shrug and blush. She drank the offered tea with Suzy's herbs added liberally to it, and was almost instantly asleep.

23

Lessons

The next day Kat awoke to a bright, cheerful morning of early sun through the window panes. Patrice was busying herself at the hearth, stoking the coals, encouraging them to spark and take in the new wood she'd added. There was a table set in front of the window with what she could see was a full breakfast for two complete with rashers of ham and coddled eggs.

Helene swept in as Kat still lounged in the bed, luxuriating in the lack of nausea.

"You certainly look hale and hearty this morning."

"I feel awesome!" Kat stretched, twisting the kinks out of her neck and shoulders."And I am starved."

Helene laughed. "Maybe I should've asked your Suzy to mix me some herbs when I was having all the morning discomfort with this little one." She smiled and patted her belly.

Kat stepped over to the table to delve into the warm bread, heedless of her bare feet and bedclothes.

Helene laughed again. "We'll forgive your lack of decorum this morning as you've just arrived, but in the future you shall wear a robe and slippers even while you sup in your own room. I trust the room pleases you?"

She looked around, taking it all in for the first time, for much had been in shadows when Kat had arrived last night. Aside from the tartan of deep and muted greens on the bed, the room was decked in cream tones and soft greens, like the green of new moss on a stone. The heavy drapes were of the darkest green and edged in tan. The hearth rug was an array of jewel colors woven together upon which a deep, low bench was set before the fire. Oil lamps sat on either side of the plump bed and a wardrobe stood with carved images in a vining, leaf pattern.

"It's perfect."

"Good. It's yours for as long as you'd like to stay. It used to be my brother-in-law's room hence the deep, manly colors. But after getting to know you better I thought the strength in the room might suit your personality rather than a frilly, lady's quarter. No offense meant."

"None taken." Kat looked around at the lace at the bed's footings, under the lamps, and fringing the pillow cases and felt no lack of a woman's touch in the room. As far as she was concerned it was perfectly balanced and suited her to a tee. Kat was optimistic that they were off to a good start.

"And your brother-in-law? Will he be returning anytime soon?"

"He's been gone for ages. No one has seen him in months. I wouldn't worry about him needing his room. Not that it much matters in a house this size." Helene sighed. "It's largely empty most of the year. I could breed a dozen children and still have room left over." Helene looked sad for but a moment as she stroked her extended belly. "Anyway, I've been thinking of a solution to our problem," she said, quickly changing tack. "Nursemaid. You shall be the daughter of a distant cousin that is here to help with the baby." She smiled broadly. "What do you think?"

"Um, I don't know much about babies, but I am willing to try. Would I have to...?" Kat awkwardly sought for the words.

"No, of course not. I have enough maids and servants for quite anything I could want. You won't have to do anything other than keep me company. They tell me that women get weak and peevish when the time nears and prone to tears after. We'll use those expectations to closet ourselves up in my study and rooms. Patrice and a new girl I got from the village should be able to take care of the actual necessities."

Helene paused to look Kathleen over closely, scrutinizing. "You'll have to wear your hair done up as it is a bit short by the day's standards."

Kat pulled at her shoulder-length hair, awkwardly.

"It's a good thing you have an older name. Kathleen will suit and will not need be changed. But we'll affect a surname in good time that will be plausible. The rest you'll learn as quickly as you may."

"You used 'Evans' at the manor farm."

"So I did. I am absent-minded these days. It would be best we continued with it to be safe. 'Tis generic enough to suffice."

"Okay, when do we start?"

"Today, as soon as you can be readied. I'd like to take you around the manor while I am still unrestricted in my movements. When Alastair returns, I will like as not be confined to my rooms. I'd like to get you acquainted with all long before he returns."

"Okay, let me just finish this bite, and I'll get ready." Kat wolfed down the honey-slathered roll and made move to rise.

"No, no, no. This isn't right." Helene paused, looked about. "Patrice, you may leave us be for a while. Please see to the kitchens. Let them know my cousin has arrived and that I'm feeling capon for lunch and soup of hearty broth with cream. Please let the cook know."

Patrice rose, curtsied, and left.

"Before she returns, let me clarify. Patrice is privy to some, not all of my—our secrets. Leave her to me. However, I must warn you to not augment her knowledge. Let's not give her power over us. Trust no one." She pointedly held Kat's gaze.

After a moment Helene lightened her tone after seeing Kat tense. "Alastair is quite taken with me right now as I bear the heir to his fortune. The cook's on orders to see to my every whim while he is gone—and I intend to use that privilege." She stopped, and looked startled as if remembering. "I never did ask, are you betrothed? Engaged?"

Kat snorted to choke back a laugh. "No, I think not."

Helene ignored her sarcasm with only a raised eyebrow to acknowledge her rude answer. "Then you wouldn't know how it is to be married, obligated, and indebted as I do." Her voice faded; her eyes took on a far off, wistful look before snapping back to full sharpness. Kathleen shifted uncomfortably under the piercing gaze. "You'll find that when Alastair is home I am...somewhat restricted. But do not worry, I will explain all so you'll know what to expect—all the procedures and protocols and the like. You'll also find it convenient that you are here for the birth as most men, especially particularly strong men, avoid the birthing room like the plague. Once I am set up for my confinement, we shall have all the time in the world together—me, mostly getting fatter by the day. And after," she paused and a monstrous shadow passed over her eyes, but in a blink was gone, "we shall be left to our own devices for several weeks. And as it is a girl, we should be left to tend her as we wish."

"You know already that she...?

Helene looked at Kathleen as if from under a cap, her eyes lifting under her brow.

"Oh, of course you would know. Sorry."

"Witchcraft does have its benefits. Although Alastair is none the wiser. Best leave that news till it must be told. He should get over it soon enough as we've time to make more children, and one is bound to be a boy." She shook herself as if to chase off a sudden chill and then smiled warmly.

Kat decided to ignore the gesture. She didn't know if Helene realized she had done it, and if not, Kat was not about to reveal Helene's "tells" to her. She just stored the thought away to reflect on later when she would be alone and could figure out what it meant.

"Enough of what will be, let's get on with today. I've a mind to show you about the house so you can learn your way about the manor. It's best to get you acclimated while we can as he's an astute man. The sooner you get into the routine of the manor the sooner you'll be invisible to scrutiny. And that is best for both of us."

In the full light of day, the manor wasn't as overwhelming as Kat first thought. Unaccompanied by nausea and the initial shock of time travel, she could keep her wits about her as they methodically made their way through the house. Helene graciously started with what Kathleen knew of the building, Helene's room and accompanying garderobe, Kat's room within the same wing, and slowly circled outwards. Helene helped her retrace her steps as often as needed to keep mental track of the house and the rooms within and their relation to one another. Compared to the last visit, Helene seemed endlessly patient as she moved room by room, expanding Kat's knowledge of the place and its layout. When asked was it necessary that she learn each of the many guest rooms, closets, and privies, Helene was adamant that she was to know where she was at all times as a precaution—a precaution to what Helene never said, but was insistent that she learn it all thoroughly nonetheless.

Kat found the house smaller than she first recalled. It boasted twelve guest rooms, a linen and basic laundry prep room on each of the three levels above ground with the main laundry below.

There were several rooms with adjacent sitting rooms, some with an attached maid's quarters. She explained there was one such a room attached to her own. But since Patrice was her lady's maid, Kat would need not lose her room when the baby came. She was near enough being just a few doors down the hallway. Kat was not quite sure why she felt so relieved at that idea, but she did. There were several lovely rooms but none suited her as much as the one she inhabited. Not manly exactly, but sturdier furnishings and the deep colors made the room both cozy and strong at the same time.

The house sprawled in three main wings with servants' quarters both above and below the family rooms. The ground floor was mainly composed of assorted receiving rooms, parlors, and formal dining. The second floor boasted a walnut-encased library with books from floor to ceiling, several writing tables, and lounge chairs in comfortable groupings sprinkled about the room. A game room was adjacent, with chess and backgammon boards set up and ready to play at a few of the tables set about the room. Alastair's den, smoking room, and private chambers were locked, but all else was open to view. Helene didn't seem to think it odd to be locked out of her husband's rooms so Kathleen didn't ask about it but merely stored that fact away to look at later as well. Helene's rooms were across the hall from his, his double doors mirroring her own.

They spent the morning exploring the house, stopping only to have a cup of morning tea in the front solar while Helene attended to a few bits of household business. The afternoon they spent walking the grounds. It was late summer here, but fall had taken root early. The grounds were largely wet, soaked from recent rains, and mud caked everything.

Helene led the way across the side lawn to a gardening cottage. It housed the normal gardening tools, starter pots sat in the window sills, and empty pots cluttered the floor. Helene moved with purpose to the back of the cottage to tiered benches filled with assorted potted moss, sacks of seed, and a stack of folded burlap. She took a quick look about, and with the flick of a wrist, caused a door to appear where there had been none. It was as if some of the items on the shelves faded from view, as if they'd never been there but the door always had been. Unremarkable save for its appearance, the door blended into its surrounding with peeling, chipped, white paint, and earthen smudges.

"Let's hurry," Helene said over her shoulder as she moved to open the door.

Kathleen didn't question but followed, curiosity overtaking any hesitancy. The door opened up into a room about half the size of the gardener's shed. No outside light showed and no window was evident. Yet all was swathed in a low glow of greenish blue. Helene raised her arms in a fluid movement and with them brought a heightened light. Her arms reached together above her head. She clapped her hands lightly creating a focal glow at the center of the room that radiated, bathing the small room in a swath of soft light, and illuminating the small crystals, that until now had been unnoticed, that strung about the room. The ceiling was indiscernible, but now Kat could make out her surroundings.

At the far side of the room was a small hearth. With a snap, Helene set the bricks of peat to a low burn, taking the chill out of the room. Helene removed her wrap and motioned Kathleen to do the same. There were hooks on the one side wall upon which she hung their outer garments. Clusters of herbs hung tied with string from beams, and small jars and bottles filled the remaining walls' recesses. A farmhouse table filled the center of the room, a low shelf beneath housed assorted bowls, mortars, pestles, and several items yet unknown to Kat. Helene motioned to her to take one of the stools that stood next to the table and seated herself on the other.

"Like your friend, Suzy, I have a talent for herbals."

Kat nodded only, taking in all she could.

"It's good to have a private place to work." Helene moved around the small space.

Kat again nodded, mentally cataloging it all as if she were in the storeroom at the antique shop. Helene waited, watching her.

When she saw Kathleen's thoughts and attention again returned to her she spoke. "Good. It's good that you take it all in as I need you to learn as much as you can as quickly as you can. I know not how much time I have." She rubbed her belly fondly. "I can see some things but not all. Some things are best left as a mystery."

"It's a lovely room, but how can you hide all this from outsiders?"

"Well, for one, it's not really here." At Kathleen's puzzled look she continued, "I mean it is here as we are obviously somewhere, or rather somewhen. This room used to be a silkworm hutch. It was dismantled decades ago as it was deemed unsightly." She continued as Kathleen's unasked question was obvious. "When you crossed the threshold we went back to when it still stood so we are unable to be detected from the outside as there is no here in the now."

"Then how do you explain where you are when you've been away for what would probably be hours?"

"Same way you do when you return from here—I've learned how to stall time. When I enter the garden house it is but moments when I exit, so none are the wiser. The only catch is to enter when the gardener is away and not expected back. Also, I can't always count on being able to get here, especially in my current state. Alastair likes to keep me near so that he can watch over me and the babe. But not to worry, I have another such room much closer than you think that I will show you another time. But I wanted to take advantage of the time we have now to show you this one as it is my treasured retreat." Helene sighed, and for just a moment Kat could see just how tired she had grown of late.

Helene bustled about making a pot of something in the hearth. Kat couldn't place the smell.

"Mulled wine. It's what I always used to drink after time travel, always seemed to set me to rights. It thickens and warms the blood." With a flick of her wrist she converted a simple planter pot into a proper tea cup and saucer. With another quick motion the cup filled before she handed it to Kat to sample.

"Wow, will you show me how to do that?"

"Quite simple actually, but that is for another time."

Kat took a sip and felt its warmth course through her body. Looking over her cup she could see the color rise in Helene's cheeks, visibly fleshing her cheeks out in a robust manner. Kat hadn't realized how thin she was until then.

"Should you be doing so much?"

"Nonsense. It's the 'not' doing that wears on me. When I live day to day doing 'normal' things it drains me. It's as if air were denied me to not be openly who I am. This, all this," she spread her arms wide, "this is who I am and what I need to feel whole."

She wiped a stray bit of dust off the work table, a momentary pensive look on her face. "I don't know when I will be able to get back here after the baby comes. I doubt I'll have much time to myself, let alone to just think. At least I have the other room being set up, that should help." She pasted on a weak smile.

"Hey, don't forget you have me to help—at least for a while. We could always take the baby for a walk in the garden, or I could while you get some time away. You did say it would look to be but a moment?"

"Why, yes, I did!" Helene perked up. "But why would I be in the garden house when I have the baby?"

"Well," Kat paused to think, "Gran likes to grow lilies. Perhaps you could create some sort of pet project that you could be 'checking on' its progress so to speak. Would that do?"

"You're a genius! Alastair always wanted a more traditional wife. I could develop some plantings for the main house. It is considered quite proper for a lady to do so. But how did you think of it?"

"Lifetime TV for Women."

"What, pray tell, is that?"

"Nevermind," Kat said and chuckled. "Something not invented yet." At Helene's raised eyebrow, she followed with, "Trust me, you are not missing anything."

Helene busied herself with setting up a stone bowl, pestle, and a few small but very sharp looking knives to either side of the bowl. With a motion she brought the fire brighter, but it threw no extra heat, keeping the room comfortable. Kat recognized some of the items she pulled from the shelves: thyme, marjoram, and thistle but much of the other plants and clippings were a mystery to her. Kat made a mental note to herself to remedy this lack when she returned to her own time. Perhaps a book on Herbology from the B&N would suffice or a trip to the library for sure.

"Here," Helene pulled from a satchel a small, plain, leather-bound journal tied with a bit of cording. "Keep this with you at all times." She pulled out another such notebook, weatherworn and well-handled, embossed with roses. She opened to a page marked by a bit of ribbon. On the page Kat saw drawings of the very articles she'd gathered on the worktable. Each plant was drawn in remarkable likeness, labeled in Latin, and surrounded by other wording that she did not recognize.

"The wording? I can't read any of it, though I recognize some of the Latin."

"And ancient Gaelic."

"Gaelic?" Kat squinted over the lettering as if proximity would bring clarity.

"Of course. Learning it has gone out of favor over the years, but my grandmother insisted I learn. You do recall you are part Irish?"

Kat nodded, feeling a bit like a dunce.

"Well, I don't know about your 'Lifetime TV,' but it is quite common for a lady to carry a small notebook to keep track of her daily tasks and obligations, visitations, correspondences, and the like." Helene pulled out a second, identical notebook from her pocket hidden in the folds of her skirt.

"Two?"

"But of course. A husband is master of all in his reach. Should he request to see my notebook I must oblige, and it certainly would not do to give him that," gesturing to the one that lay open on the workbench.

"Then he doesn't approve?"

"He doesn't know about…my talents. 'Doesn't approve' would be an understatement. I am not sure what he'd do, but I know it would not be pleasant." Again Kat saw the involuntary, quick shudder.

"Surely a woman of such talents would be an asset?"

"No!" Helene snapped, eyes fiery. "He must never know what I am, who WE are. Never. Swear to it!"

"I swear. But honestly, I am not so sure that I want to meet him at all if I must fear his knowing why I came."

"Oh tush, you've nothing to worry about. He'll not take notice of you at all. He never notices the serving class unless he wants to bed them."

She paused and looked Kathleen over closely. "Hmm. You are a bit old for his tastes but otherwise quite desirable. I could just…"

"Whoa! What are you talking about?"

"Oh, no worries, I'll just put a distortion spell on you so that in his presence he shall both see you and not."

Kat couldn't help herself but backed up a few steps.

"Ah, we are a vain one aren't we?" Helene laughed. "It shall be slight, just a bit of mottled skin perhaps over this one cheek and a slightly lower, left eye." She tapped Kathleen's cheek and then smiled, pleased with the effect. "He is a demanding master and such small things would put you below notice. You've nothing to fear now."

Kat felt about her face but could feel nothing amiss.

"It's a trick, not reality. Nothing amiss. Only he shall see what I want him to see, nothing more. I think you'll thank me for it when you meet him."

Kat nodded, understanding, yet also appalled that it should be necessary.

"So he…cheats often?"

Helene drew herself up to her full height. "You are so naïve to the ways of the world. Men of power do not 'cheat,' they claim it as their due. And it is tolerated for what else can a woman do? She could be cast off with nothing to gain from the marriage. Marriage may be something else in your day, but I assure you in mine that other considerations are in play than love when these joinings are made. If the woman is bright, as I am, there is much that can be gained and leveraged in marriage. Should you stay, you'll see the same and find that a husband's wandering gaze can be a blessing and a relief."

Kat shook her head, and shuddered to think that she could ever be content to live in this manner. She would never think to stay, not that she'd ever considered it before.

"But enough on that." Helene clapped her hands quickly, breaking the tension. "We've work to do if you are to learn some of the basics today. I can bend time but only so far. We've much to do to begin."

Helene spent the last part of the morning and several hours of the afternoon teaching Kathleen basic healing combinations for headaches, menstrual cramps, chest pains, and simple poultices. Kat had several pages of her journal filled with her terrible scrawl. As she flipped pages, squinting at the text, she doubted if anyone could read her thoughts as sometimes even Kat couldn't recognize what she had written days later.

"Remember, you are beneath his notice. No one will ask to see your book."

Kat hated that Helene read her so well. It was disconcerting.

"So you read minds?"

Helene put her cutting instruments down, dusting her hands off on her skirts. "Truly? Is that what you surmise? You are not that hard to read. Your face reveals all your thoughts. You really must work on that." She paused, seeing the insult. "It's not your fault. You live in a different day when perhaps such games need not be played. We'll work on this together. Here, try this." She pasted on what Kat knew now to be a fake smile as it did not reach her eyes. Her eyes looked vacant, removed, but her overall appearance was pleasant.

Kat laughed heartily. "Yeah, I will try that sometime when I've a mirror to practice in."

"It's not a laughing matter. 'Tis a skill that will be necessary at times, you will find. Mark my words."

Realizing that Helene was quite serious removed the smirk from Kat's face. "Understood."

"Good. Now it's time to pack up and head back for lunch. By my measure we've worked well past lunch. The true hour does not move here as it does on the outside. I am ravenous, and you must be, too." She quickly moved about straightening, sorting, and replacing items.

"But we haven't done any magic yet."

Helene stopped mid-stride. "Is that what you think? I am an Elemental. I work within the laws of nature and bend them to my will. This," she waved her hands over the various packets and concoctions of healing that they worked on, "is the most basic form of magic. Simple, yes, but a necessary step before we proceed further. You must master each element before moving to the next, no matter how much you desire to hasten forward. To do so could cause you to miss a step with a catastrophic result. Patience, Kathleen. A witch is both born and made. And the making takes time."

24

doubles

Helene and Kat didn't go back to the gardener's cottage for several days but were instead wrapped up in the minutia of running a large household. And apparently this wasn't the only house managed by the estate. Alastair was in residence at the city townhouse, and yet Helene managed the ordering and supplying of it, the manor, and much of the farmstead as well. All things domestic were referred to her. Some tasks she delegated to others, but she still maintained all of the accounts and oversaw the comings and goings of deliveries, service workers, and purchasing of supplies. When asked, Helene said Alastair could've hired people to take over, and he would do so once she became a mother and her free hours restricted, but she admitted to liking knowing what was going on around her.

Kat tried to follow Helene's logic but was stymied at the sheer quantity of work one woman oversaw and directed. She suspected that it was more than curiosity that kept her involved but rather a form of control in a world of marginal, female input.

Helene informed Kat that Alastair had sent word that he was

to arrive in six days and to stay for an indeterminate amount of time. And while it would be unlikely that he'd stay during Helene's confinement, he could oversee everything from afar with the help of the advisors he'd be bringing to stay at the manor in her absence from public view. Helene seemed unfazed about this development as she had anticipated the move. Regardless of when Alastair's men stepped in, she would not fear an audit or any issues as she kept meticulous books.

What Kat worried about was that Helene looked a bit peaked about the face and shoulders as the weight of the growing babe drained her.

"You're doing too much. Let me help."

"You are helping. You've been blending in beautifully this time around. You've quite picked up the rhythm of things here." Helene smiled.

Kat didn't want to insult her by saying that the routine was just that—routine. Once she learned which fork went with what, the rest was easy. The laundry was a challenge, but as that was a task delegated elsewhere, Kat didn't need to bother with it much. Her primary task was to assist Helene and keep her company, which kept Kat removed from much of the prying eyes of the staff.

With the somewhat true story of Kathleen being a distant relative of a cousin Helene hadn't seen in ages, and being of similar coloring, the story was quickly accepted as truth. If Helene sensed someone unduly watching or questioning, she'd simply ask about Kathleen's mother and grandmother. Kat would respond with tales converted to the mode of the day. Biologically they were similar in age, Kat a few years her senior, but she looked much younger, probably due to the availability of fresh foods year round in her day and all those vitamin supplements. To compensate, Helene told them Kathleen was a full ten years younger than she, and to Kat's surprise that was taken as a matter of course. Helene explained that at her true age Kat would have to be mentally incapable to marry to be thus long unwed, regardless of what prospects were offered.

And if Kat ever romanticized the late 19th century, she now repented of it. For all their simplicity, the days were terribly long, filled with hours-long tasks that could be done in a matter of minutes in the modern world. Kat had seldom ironed clothes previously, instead tossing items in the dryer with a damp cloth to remove most of the offending wrinkles, but in Helene's day the mere heating of the iron was a task all in itself. Sometimes Kat held back an inner scream at the seemingly endless items that needed attending to, and a glance from Helene told her she knew of Kat's frustration. Kat remembered that this was part of the deal. She needed to blend in to Helene's world so that they could afford the time to work on what she came for—to find out more of what she could accomplish with the gift she was given.

They finally finished for the day and were sitting in chairs placed in front of Helene's bedroom hearth, sipping mulled wine after the evening meal. Helene felt particularly drained today and requested dinner served in her rooms. And, as her requests were always modest, although she was afforded the freedom to demand more, the cook and serving girl were only too happy to agree. The staff was especially pleased when they learned Kathleen would join her; the dining room need not be decked out in its normal manner, thus alleviating, rather than adding to, their work for the evening.

It had been a particularly cold day—wild winds mixed in with the rain, causing any to venture out of doors to be quickly soaked. They'd been out earlier for Helene's routine walk about the waning gardens as it was deemed healthy for both the mother and child, but now she looked chilled to the bone and haggard.

"Tomorrow we will focus on what we need done."

"Helene, you look worn out. Perhaps you need a day in bed."

"Exactly. My time for confinement will start soon, and with Alastair arriving any day, we've no time to waste." Helene pushed at the arms of the chair to rise. Kat jumped up to help and tried to stay her movements.

"Don't be silly." Helene shook her off. "I can still move about my rooms. I'm not going far. And you'll want to see what I've arranged for us." Helene moved through her room to the anteroom that contained her gowns and trunks. Going to the right side wall, she pulled aside the cloaks and mantles that hung there to reveal the wall. She smiled a slow, languorous, feline smile and traced with her fingernail the outline of a door, and it appeared. Kat didn't need to be told to follow her through to see what lay beyond.

This room was outfitted similarly to the garden cottage with a small hearth and work table. Bottles and herbs sat on rough shelves here and there. Suspended from the rafters were domes of glass that flickered with what looked like fairy lights from within. Helene waved a hand to increase the glow so Kat could take it all in. The room bent around the corner, and therein lay a chair with a small trunk at its foot. Next to the chair stood a cradle fully decked and awaiting its occupant.

Kat raised her eyes in question. "How did you arrange all of this? I've been with you the whole time."

"Have you, now?"

Aside from brief meetings with the land agents, merchants, and the field manager, they had been seldom parted. Then it dawned on Kat that Helene had been using her talents to stretch time.

"That's why you are so worn! You've been living a double day haven't you?"

"Sometimes more than that as well," Helene said and sighed. "You catch on quickly, and that's good as I'll need your wits about you as my body may betray me."

Kat led Helene back to her chair in front of the hearth. When she glanced back, no trace could be seen of the door nor that the closet had been disturbed in any way.

"Okay, this has to stop. There are still too many secrets between us, and if I am to help you, you must let me in."

"Agreed."

It startled Kat with how quickly she agreed. She realized this concession must have been due to her truly being exhausted.

"I just wanted to show you that I have not forgotten our deal. I agreed to teach you what I could in the time you give me. My opportunity for freely getting about will end momentarily. You'll see I'll soon have so much free time on my hands I'd go mad if I hadn't had this escape prepared for us. Plus, I've another surprise. You have one such cupboard to the side of your room as well, though not so big or so well-equipped—in case."

"In case of what?"

Helene ignored this question and continued. "And there is a way to travel from one to the other without being exposed to outside eyes."

"I don't understand why any of this is necessary."

Kat didn't know how she felt about having a side room attached to her own that she hadn't detected. That Helene knew Kat still had trust issues was obvious, so she tried to take it all in the spirit she deemed Helene intended. Kat had learned quite a bit in the weeks she already spent with Helene, but she dreaded the arrival of her husband. Kat wasn't sure how he would impact life as she knew it. But all these precautions gave her a clue, and she didn't like where they pointed.

25

A Woman's Wiles

They didn't have long to wait as Alastair arrived two days earlier than anticipated. Apparently, he liked to arrive early on occasion so as to see what was really going on in his absence. He found them in the great library. Helene was working on some needlework for the baby's room, while Kathleen read some verses of poetry aloud. Helene had suggested it as she insisted the cadence of old poetry served the witch in creating spells.

Kat looked up, startled by his entrance. But when she glanced at Helene she saw a flicker of a smug smile. Kat realized she had staged them to be found thus. Helene was the picture of motherly serenity—her gown was arranged to show her in the best light, in the deep plum that she had told Kat he favored against her complexion, with her midriff prominently propped up against a pillow at her side. Alastair, being a man, saw only what he wished to see—what Helene had created through her guile.

"Ah, there's my beloved." His voice boomed.

Helene feigned surprise and made movements to rise. He hurried over to her, staying her, and knelt at her feet.

"Nay, love, stay as you are. You are the very picture of beauty, and I'll not have you upset the babe." He leaned in and placed a chaste kiss on her cheek.

"Oh, Alastair, you spoil me so," Helene said.

"And I mean to spoil the mother of my son." Alastair pulled from inside his breast pocket a golden locket with emeralds embedded in the casing. He opened the locket to reveal a miniature portrait of himself, smiling widely. "This is so I can always watch over you and be close to your heart, my love."

Kat perceived rather than saw Helene flinch ever-so-slightly at the word "son." Outwardly, she saw only a woman happy to see her husband. Perhaps, Kat, like Helene, was learning to read people.

"Oh, this is too much. Your presence is all I need, dear." But as Helene opened her arms to receive him in an embrace, Alastair noticed Kat.

"And who is this we have here?"

"This is Kathleen," Helene said simply as introduction. "She's daughter to a distant cousin. I believe you remember Sarah. You met her at the wedding." She ad libbed.

"But dear, there were so many in attendance. I couldn't tell you rightly who was whom."

Kat knew Helene was counting on that.

"Well, Kathleen has come to help out with my impending confinement and birth, as you so directed me to look to taking extra care and caution. I did as you bid and hope you will be pleased. However, I did tell her mother that her staying would be at your discretion and only with your approval." Helene lowered her lashes demurely, but Kat caught the quick wink unnoticed by her husband.

"Well, then good. I am so pleased you did as I asked. But let me have a look at the girl."

Helene motioned Kathleen to step forward. Kat felt like she

would shake out of her boots, but she did as she was told. She sincerely hoped Helene knew what she was doing. Alastair peered into her face, scrutinizing her appearance. Kat saw his slight wince of disapproval at the cheek Helene had marred with her magic and breathed an inward sigh of relief.

"I see you share a similar coloring overall but naught else." Kat could tell as his gaze shifted away that Helene was right—she was dismissed as un-noteworthy.

At a glance from Helene, Kat left the library, taking her book with her to return to her rooms to think on what she had learned. Kat couldn't help the sinking feeling that she hadn't really avoided danger, but she couldn't put her finger on it.

Time alone with Helene wasn't really possible over the next couple of days, and while it frustrated her, Kat understood the necessity of it. She found Alastair to be attentive, devoted, and charming in all his dealings with Helene. She couldn't seem to reconcile the man she'd anticipated with the man before her but soon chalked it up to Helene's pregnancy nerves. What new mother didn't fear disappointing her husband?

Kat spent some of her alone time in her room seeking the mystery door Helene hinted at. She racked her brain going over what she knew already: the room could be behind furniture as Helene had already proven she could move that at will with the flick of a hand. So what were the limitations? Kat decided to eliminate the wall with windows encased in it—even that most certainly would be against all logic, both natural and supernatural. She found she now spent time looking into doorways, at doorway frames, measuring depth mentally. Could there be a room hidden within these very walls? Based on the architectural flourishes of the time period and their penchant for alcoves, nooks, and cupboards, it made perfect sense that there would be wasted space between the walls. Perhaps Helene had merely found a way to access what already was there?

Helene found Kat sitting cross-legged on the floor contemplating an expanse of wall beneath a portrait of a hunting scene, dogs, horses, a hedge, and that lot.

"Well you certainly won't find it that way." She cheerily entered the room.

Kat hopped to her feet. "I can't see how I can find it at all—if it even is here," Kat countered.

"Oh, it's here all right, but you're going about it all wrong. First you have to use some logic."

Kat felt insulted but kept her mouth shut. She knew if she piped off at Helene she'd be less likely to teach her.

"Now think about what I told you. Your room will access mine. Which direction would that be?"

"Why, that wall, of course, the one behind the bed."

"Yes, exactly. However, if we need haste and secrecy that headboard would be a bit cumbersome to get past as well as possibly noisy."

At Kat's blank look, Helene continued. "Which side of the bed would seem most logical?"

"The left."

"Yes. Just brush back the bed curtain to the left and look."

"But I see nothing, just the pattern of the wallpaper."

"That's because you are not looking at it right. Close your eyes and focus. Imagine the door, how it would open, in or out, its width, height. Think."

Kat did as she bid but felt self-conscious as she knew Helene was watching her, scrutinizing her efforts. Kat pushed down her pride and drew more within herself and focused. Helene kept repeating the same words over and over again, "Focus and think," droning until Kat was able to completely ignore her, like white noise.

She felt the door shift open rather than heard it. Kat opened her eyes and saw to be so that which she imagined was. Helene motioned for Kat to enter.

It was not much more than a passthrough or passageway with recesses and nooks stocked with supplies of crystals, crude pottery, and yet more herbs. It was dark, gloomy, and narrow. Kat felt her way through initially until she heard the door behind her gently snick into place. Kat couldn't help a few moments of panic. Her heart raced, and she held her breath. But once the door firmly closed, Helene snapped her fingers and glass orbs overhead, previously unnoticed, glowed with a soft blue-green light. Kat followed the passage as it twisted and turned, wove and jogged for an interminable time until it stopped at a plaster and lath wall. A dead end.

Kat turned to Helene, a question hanging unsaid on her lips. But before she could say a word, Helene reached past her, and placed her fingertips to either side of Kat. Kathleen could see the golden outline of an illuminated door form.

"Try now."

Kat pushed on the side that seemed most obvious to have a knob based on its orientation, and the door easily gave way, swinging into the room. They were once again in Helene's secret room off of her bed chamber.

Kat had barely gotten her bearings when Helene said. "We've found what you'd been looking for, now let's head back out."

Kat moved toward the door on the other side of the workroom, but Helene quickly stopped her with a hand on her forearm.

"Not that way. It wouldn't do for me to go into your room and come out in mine. Would take the secret away or at least cause questions. When using such means one must remember to be smart. We must go out the way we came."

Now Kat truly felt stupid. But of course that must be the way of it! Why hadn't she thought of it?

Helene must've seen the mortified look on her face and spoke kindly, "We will only use one room to the next in dire need or for escape."

Helene did not answer the lingering question of escape from what or whom but rather continued. "Plus, you must always be sure that there is no one on the other side of that wall save only me, or for me, you. It's not a safehold if we do not make it be so."

Kat nodded that she understood. She was agitated, embarrassed, and unsure how her words would come out so said none. And so she followed Helene, quickly making time with her in the lead and because now Kat knew what to expect in the way of turns and narrows. As if on a timer the globe lights flickered off behind her as they passed through, throwing the passageway back into shadows in their wake.

Helene paused at the entrance to Kat's bed chamber. She pressed her hands to either side of where the door should be. Kat was surprised that it wasn't visibly evident and said so.

"Just another precaution, another protection. It wouldn't do if someone were to get in here, from either side. That would be bad enough. But to lead them to the other would simply be senseless danger to us both. Our secrets need to remain ours," she whispered.

Helene placed her forehead against the wood that Kat knew must be the door back into her chamber. She closed her eyes and slowly breathed in and out, muttering something lowly under her breath. Her eyes popped open at the audible click. The door swung open, and then they were back.

Helene strode through and turned to Kat as soon as she passed, the door lightly snicking into place behind them.

"Be sure to lock your bedroom door before you attempt to pass through again. It would not do for you not to be here and then suddenly be. You can easily explain a reason for delay in opening your chamber door to the maid and such, but you will never be able to explain a sudden appearance from nowhere."

Helene moved to leave as briskly as she had come.

"So what am I to do if you are off again?"

"Practice. Find your way through and back."

"But I haven't—"

Helene cut Kathleen off before she could finish the question. "Haven't what? Learned the spell? Magic? Trick?" she paused. Kat could tell she was getting annoyed with her by her tone. "There is no trick to it—it is in you, or I wouldn't have sent for you."

"But?"

"But nothing. Much of real magic is intuitive—not set spells, recitations, formulas. Trust yourself and stretch your mind to the possibilities, and you'll find your way. Once you practice, you'll find it's not that difficult after all."

Kat stood there, feeling inadequate and a bit pathetic. It seemed to her that the more she learned the less she knew.

Helene brusquely continued, "I'll send word that you're not to be disturbed until called for tea, that you've a headache and will be taking a little lie down for respite. That should buy you some time." She swept out the door before Kat could respond, but then ducked her head back in the room. "Remember not to panic or you could get yourself locked in between, and I'll not be back until supper. Focus." She smiled and was gone.

Locked between rooms? *Great.* Now Kat had a new level of stress.

Kat locked the door behind her, determined to solve this riddle straight away. Maybe Helene was right, she needed to find out how to manage this on her own. Kat stood before where she knew the door to be and placed her hands to either side, resting them there lightly. She visualized where the lines of the frame should be, slowly breathed in and out and hoped for—something to happen. Anything. Anything at all. Nothing. Kat rapped at the door with her knuckles lightly, hesitant in case what she did in here could be heard in the hallway by a passing maid or servant. She stood flustered; she didn't know for how long. 'Just practice' Kat heard Helene say mockingly in her head. Kat purposely brushed all thought of her out of her mind. She closed her eyes, focusing on the here and now—nothing else, centered her thoughts on breathing, not frustration. Kat felt a slight movement beneath her hand and opened her eyes to the door slowly opening inward.

Kat was thrilled but also cautious after Helene's ominous warnings. She quickly pulled the door firmly shut and waited the milliseconds for the lines of the door to disappear once again. This time she focused on the pattern on the wallpaper. She willed her mind to follow the dips and swirls in the pattern until it faded into a blur of motion. This time Kat didn't touch the door but could see it open ever so slightly. She again pulled it shut. But she found that concentrating on the wallpaper was disorienting, dizzying, so instead Kat tried to repeat her first attempt. She traced with her finger tips where she knew the door edges to be, cleared her mind of all other thought, and the door swung open freely.

It was easier than Kat had thought. She realized the trick, if there was one, was to hone her thoughts and believe. Clear intent, if you will. But now that she had mastered the step, she was hesitant to try the other. Kat knew the passage wound and twisted behind rooms, but without the benefit of lighting, she was loath to enter. That and the fear of being locked in were intimidating. Kat decided the first step would be taken after she figured out how to get the orbs to glow. But could she?

Kathleen was literally flailing in the dark. She tried snapping her fingers as Helene had done. She tried closing her eyes and imagining them lit, but to no avail. Kat stared into the doorway and at the first orb, willing it to glow. Nothing. She tried to reach one, tap it as one would a touch lamp, but it was disturbingly out of reach the more she tried. Kat simply couldn't manage it while remaining standing in her bedroom. Then she did what she dreaded. Kat stepped through the door and allowed it to click shut behind her. She felt her pulse race as the fear of being locked in, in the dark, for hours taunted her thoughts.

Kat stood with her eyes closed and concentrated on slowing her breathing. She cupped the pendant she wore with one hand, rubbing it absentmindedly with her thumb as she focused on one word, "Glow, glow, glow." Kat felt a slight vibration and opened her eyes to see the globes lit in a soft, hazy luminance for as far as her eyes could see before the corridor bent out of sight. She felt the pendant heat, pulse, and then heard Helene.

"Do you need me?"

Kat twisted, startled, looking about for where the voice came. Then she realized it wasn't coming from without but within. She dropped the pendant back onto her chest.

"Um, uh, no. Sorry."

Kat felt the stone go cold against her skin and realized by the shift in light that it too must have glowed, if briefly. Kat pulled the pendant up on its golden chain to peer into it. It flickered slightly, and then went dark. She suddenly felt exhausted. Kat couldn't be sure how long she'd been at it. She turned to re-enter her chamber and was met with only wall. But this time Kat didn't feel panicked but again focused on her breathing and tapped where she knew the door to be with her index finger, and it swung clear. That was it, she realized. Kat knew it to be there, and that alone made it easy. Kat gasped. She had forgotten to check if anyone was in her room first. But she relaxed when she acknowledged the wisdom of Helene's admonition to lock her chamber door, which Kat had done. She would need to remember not to skip that step—ever. Kat stood drained but proud of her progress. Her mood quickly turned to annoyance when she heard the sudden rap upon the door. She really wasn't up to company. Kat glanced back to be sure the passage doorway was again concealed and moved to the bedroom door. It couldn't be tea time already, could it?

Instead of the maidservant she had anticipated, Kat found a somewhat attractive man with dark hair and piercing blue eyes leaning in the door frame.

"I'd heard you'd taken over my room, but I wanted to check nonetheless, to see you for myself."

And so was her introduction to Caleb.

26

Awkward Conversations

Tea was served in the front parlor as it was west facing and thus could boast more sun. When Helene entered the room on the arm of Alastair, Kat noticed she looked more rested than she had in days.

Upon sighting Kathleen already seated, Helene whispered something to Alastair and hurried over to meet her.

"Kathleen, we've a visitor, I'm afraid." There was a sense of urgency in her that Kat didn't understand. "Nothing to worry about but he's—"

"He's what?" asked Caleb, who arrived at Helene's elbow.

"Quite rude, I should say," Helene replied with a smile.

"True enough. But I must admit I am still curious what you would've said to your dear cousin had I not come upon you so suddenly." He smirked.

"You'll just have to keep wondering. Ladies must have our secrets." Helene turned to Kat and stated formally, "May I introduce you to—"

"Miss Kathleen Evans, I believe?" Caleb finished.

Helene looked startled as she glanced from him to Kathleen, apparently not a sensation she was used to as she tried to cover her awkwardness with an adjustment to a wrist bangle she wore.

Kat stood and extended a hand. "We've met already as he came by to bring me my eviction notice," she said by way of explanation.

Instead of honoring the intended handshake Caleb instead took Kathleen's hand and bowed towards it as if to kiss the back of her hand.

"Eviction notice?" Helene said.

"She jokes. A simple misunderstanding, I assure you. I simply came by to see if my room was free and found it pleasingly occupied by the charming Miss Evans."

Helene quickly looked to Kathleen to confirm if this was indeed true.

"I don't know about charming, more like startled. I had, um, lost track of time, and thought the maidservant was coming to fetch me to tea and opened my door to...um, him." Kat gestured vaguely towards him.

Caleb laughed heartily. "I've been mistaken for many things in my travels but never for a woman. That's a first."

Alastair interrupted by calling Caleb over to sit with him on the cushioned, lounge chairs that flanked the large, picture window. "Leave the women to their gossip and baby plans, Caleb, and have port with me," Alastair called.

With a hasty 'by your leave,' Caleb was gone.

Helene pulled up a chair and waited for the manservant to finish serving the tea and dainties and withdraw before speaking.

"Tell all," she demanded when she and Kat were once again alone.

"There really isn't much more to tell. He came by, as I said, to inquire about his room. When I told him it was indeed occupied, he seemed gracious about it." Kat paused to recall each detail.

"But there was something...I hesitate to say anything as it was probably just my imagination."

"Go on," Helene said, leaning in.

"Well, I was standing at the door talking to him when he slipped by me to look around the room."

"Well, that was quite inappropriate."

Kat shushed her with a gesture. "No, it wasn't that. It was what he did, or I think he did, while in the room. He walked about as if looking for something, or noting changes in the arrangements. I don't know for sure. But he...he stopped in front of the wall where the door had been. I'd just come through when he knocked, but I know it was closed and hidden before I opened the door to the main hall. I know. I made sure to check before I opened the door. But he just stood there, facing the wall, deep in thought."

"And then what did he do?" Helene pressed.

"He pulled his forelock at me, as if tipping his hat, and left."

"Nothing more?"

"No, I haven't seen him until now. I feel stupid mentioning it as the door couldn't possibly be seen, but it just seemed odd."

"No, you were right to mention it."

"I swear the door was closed, the wall unremarkable when I opened the bedroom door."

Helene patted her hand. "I believe you. Let me think on it. Could very well be nothing, just a bit of paranoia. Perhaps he had a coat tree there or some such." She glanced over at where her husband and brother-in-law sat and saw Caleb watching her, intently. She smiled in return and turned to Kathleen.

"Let's talk of simpler things. It seems we are being watched. Let me tell you about the nursery progress today."

Tea seemed interminable with Alastair at home. All those romanticized BBC specials on TV never prepared Kat for the tedium of a full tea. The formality of the afternoon break made it feel awkward and orchestrated, like a dance of manners. Kat felt like she was bursting with more questions than she could possibly hold by the end of it.

Once back in her room, Kat paced. The restrained energy of listening to inane chatter made her frantic to move, if only in her room. Outside was in a downpour, so the grounds were off limits. Or were they? Kat hastily threw over her head a cloak and hood of deep garnet, so red it looked black, and hustled out of the family wing, hoping to escape detection. She raced down the servants' back staircase hoping, too, that the clean up duties from tea would suffice to keep Patrice and any other maidservant away long enough to afford Kat time out of the house. She needed now, more than ever, to get away. This corseted and constricted world was frustrating at times. Kat just needed a moment to be herself, and with Alastair taking up Helene's time, she had no ally to speak with, no one who understood, or at least tried to understand, what she felt. It was more than a fish out of water sensation. Rationally she knew that what she felt was simply the loss of common freedoms. Kat would need time to make the adjustment. But inwardly she screamed to be free, to run, and to hide.

Kat's first idea was to hide in the gardener's cottage, but then she thought better of it. Helene would know to seek her there, and if others pursued, it would not do to give away their little secret. Helene had appeared more upset than she said at Kat mentioning Caleb in her room and his attention to the wall secreting the hidden door. She'd not make a similar mistake so soon after. Kat couldn't risk exposing their workroom. No, instead she headed to a copse of trees that edged the small pond at the far side of the garden and encased an arbor and bench. She hoped to find respite from the rain there. It was beginning to drive sideways now, making all efforts with her woolen cloak futile. In her haste, Kat slid on a bit in the sodden grass and barely kept herself upright, but she made it to the bower without further incident.

Once there, she saw the woven branches of the wisteria vine and the trees, did, as she hoped, afford some privacy and kept the bench nearly dry. Kat sighed in relief as she sat on the bench, shaking back the hood and freeing her hair from the tangle of combs and pins that bound it. If she could've reached her corset stays, she would've yanked them free as well.

With eyes fixed on the pond and patterns the water made as the rain water tattooed upon it, Kathleen sat deep in thought. She wondered at her folly in coming here and what she hoped to gain, when she heard a step close at hand. Caleb came around the enclave to join her in the bower. He shook out his sodden hair, having neglected to cover himself in more than an afternoon jacket.

"I am sorry to disturb," he said. "Or rather, to be honest, no, I am not, as I followed you here. However, I do acknowledge I might indeed be disturbing you."

At Kathleen's obviously annoyed look he continued, "I know it can be unbearable to be so intruded upon, and twice in one day, but you see, I couldn't resist. I saw you fleeing across the grounds with such haste that curiosity got the better of me, and I simply had to follow. Like Red Riding Hood chased by the wolf himself." He smiled with what Kat knew must be his attempt at charming her.

"You sure are something else."

"I thank you. I think."

"You would take it as a compliment," Kat said and laughed. The laughter felt good after all the controlled and politely constrained conversation of the last hour or so.

"You are really quite pretty when you laugh."

Kat startled and stilled. She placed a hand upon her cheek where she knew Helene had marked her. But did he see it as well? She searched his face for a clue, but Caleb made no indication either way. She made a note to herself to check with Helene later. Not that it mattered, but it just seemed so frustrating to have all these secrets on top of already being so awkward here. And to not even know what she looked like in public—well, was simply silly.

Perhaps seeing her discomfort, Caleb turned to face the pond and spoke not another word for several minutes. Kat turned away to do the same but did occasionally cast a quick glance to observe his profile. From all appearances, he seemed to have quite forgotten she was there, so intently did he focus his gaze elsewhere. Kat boldly turned to watch him directly. With a short nod, he acknowledged that he knew she did so, but made no move to speak or shift his focus.

Kat scrutinized him freely. He had a strong but not intimidating jaw, a small scar over his top lip, and the longest lashes she had ever seen on a man. Otherwise he wasn't overly handsome, but more ruggedly appealing, although young. She would venture several years younger than she. Kat's eyes followed the lines of his torso and noticed his right hand where it protruded from the ruffled cuff, nimbly rolled a coin from finger to finger, flipping it over and over, weaving it between his fingers absently. A nervous habit or focal point, she wondered?

"Are you done?" Caleb spoke, breaking the silence and startling her.

"Excuse me?"

"Are you done looking me over? Do I seem the safe sort to talk to now?" He turned to face Kathleen fully, again shaking out and finger combing the dark waves of his hair back in place.

"I didn't mean to—"

"Yes, yes, you did." Caleb retorted, and before Kat could get overly offended continued, "But all is well as I allowed you to do so."

Kat shifted quickly as if to make her escape, but Caleb held her with but a touch to her forearm.

"No need to flee. Just being honest. And to prove it, I will admit I'd been watching you, and I rudely chased you here. If the servants had looked out the casement and watched I would've looked quite the fool. But I must admit," he continued in a low, sober tone, "I find you quite intriguing." Caleb looked deeply in Kathleen's eyes, and she sensed sincerity. Or he was very good at getting what he wanted, she chided herself.

"Have you anything to say?"

"Nope, I came here to not have to talk anymore." Kat firmly turned to face the pond as though that was the most entertaining thing she had ever seen.

"Fair enough."

Kat could see from the corner of her eye that Caleb had turned to do the same.

They sat there in silence for the better part of twenty minutes or more before Caleb rose, pulled his forelock in salute, and sauntered away back to the house.

27

Lowered Façades

Kathleen didn't see either Alastair or Caleb for the next couple of days, which was fine as it gave her time with Helene.

On the first morning without the men in residence, Helene popped in bright and chipper to share the breakfast she, for privacy, had brought up to Kathleen's room. Once the maidservant left and the door shut behind her, Kat could see Helene's face and eyes visibly droop. Helene had been wearing a magically enhanced façade, and the wish to forgo the "mask" was likely the reason for breakfast in Kat's room rather than in the front parlor. But the change was disturbing to see as she looked both drained and aged.

When Kathleen asked about it and her health Helene waved her off, stating it was nothing, just the normal progression of pregnancy, she assured her. But Kat wasn't buying it. She pushed, and Helene snapped.

"Do you think it's bloody easy catering to such a man's whims? Pretending to care about his business acumen and the endless boasting? I have nary a second alone to think, rest, or simply be!"

Kat had barely seen Helene except at tea and dinner. She seemed always off somewhere with Alastair. Kat hadn't, however, thought Helene would be as frustrated as she herself had been. She'd thought her agitation was due to still adjusting from the modern world that made the polite conversations and untold social expectations unbearable—apparently she was wrong.

"What if I said something to the effect that the doctor—"

"Don't you dare! I'd be confined. You've no idea how interminable that can seem. Stuck only in my room, in bed, with naught but the comings and goings of meals to indicate the passage of time. No books, no sewing, nothing. I'd go mad."

"What about your plan to use the side rooms?"

Kat could see Helene follow her reasoning. "No, no, we've got to find time for that in the here and now. We'd be so closely watched when confined. I'd not be able to stretch farther than the privy."

Kat hadn't realized.

"So, I will keep a brave face on for as long as I can manage it although this little beast within denies me sleep with all the thrashing at night and back pain by day. And when I can stand it no longer, I will let my facade fade enough to get the rest I need. Satisfied?"

Kat nodded. There was no arguing with her in this mood. She would have to assume that Helene knew best.

"Besides," Helene continued, "we've got some lessons for you to begin. So show me," Helene hoisted herself to her feet, "did you at least get the door to open?"

"That and more. I made it to your room, lit the lights, everything."

Helene looked startled. "Truly? On your own?"

Kat nodded proudly.

"Show me."

Kat had been practicing in Helene's absence and was confident that she could do all with more grace than she had at the start. Some nights when she couldn't sleep she had gone over and over what she knew until it became so simple Kat couldn't see how anyone else couldn't do it as well.

Kat stood at the as yet invisible door, raised both arms above her head, quickly pointed both index fingers at each other, and then flicked them out to indicate the lintel and width of the door, before dropping both hands to her sides, index fingers at each side drawing the lines of the door's frame. The door's outline appeared in a thin line of golden light. Kat turned to see Helene nod approvingly, impressed. Stepping through the doorway, Kat placed one hand in front of her, face up like a plate and with the other hand, facedown and crosshatch, made a swift brush across the surface as if wiping crumbs off a table and all the lights throughout the portal glowed in sequence, toppling like dominoes, one after the other, lighting in succession.

"Hmm. No snapping of fingers. Very nice, simple but nice."

She wasn't sure if the "simple" comment was a compliment or criticism, but Kat explained nonetheless, "I was worried about what could be heard by others as you said we must be wary."

"That I did, 'tis true." Helene seemed pleased at Kat's consideration as she nodded. She wandered in the passage, obviously mulling something over. "How many days until you were able to accomplish this?"

"Oh, I did it the first afternoon. Not exactly like this, the movements evolved a bit. You were quite right—it is simple really. But that first day it took at least twenty minutes to get all the way through."

Helene sputtered and turned. "Twenty minutes! Well, it seems there is more here than I first thought. Hmm." She turned back, calling Kathleen out into her room once again, and then watched as the door faded from sight.

"And you said that when Caleb came in to the room he stood and stared thusly?" Helene indicated the spot she stood facing where the door had been.

Kat nodded.

"Curious, as we both can see that there is nothing to be seen here. I have heard of some that can sense the energy… But for now, just be extra cautious. And for God's sake do not allow him to enter your room. It is not fitting for a single woman to let one such as him into her chamber." Helene waved Kathleen off before she could interrupt. "Yes, yes, it had been his room, but he vacated it months past. He's no claim to it at the moment as he gave us no notice of his arrival; he could not expect it to remain so."

"Oh, that reminds me. You had done something to my face, a mark and an eye thing. Does everyone see that or just Alastair?"

"Why do you ask?"

"It just seems silly not knowing what I look like."

Helene scrutinized Kathleen, making her squirm.

"Caleb said I was pretty. I didn't know if…"

"Ah, if he saw the mark, too?"

Kat nodded.

"Alastair 'perceives' flaws, not necessarily sees them. His perception of you is shifted, not your face. Caleb, and the others see you as you are. Remember, you have been here before. It would be more unusual to have you change than not. As for telling you you are attractive, I would think you already knew that and that his saying so might be a ploy to get in your favor or to test your vanity. Men say and do such things most often not for the recipient but for their own gain. Beware of the guile of a handsome face."

"Oh, and as for Caleb I don't truly think him handsome, not in the true sense. Just interesting and a bit aggravating."

Helene laughed. "Those are the most dangerous of men because they can worm themselves under your skin as they aim for the heart."

"Trust me, I am in no mood, nor in the market, for a man."

Helene looked at Kathleen and saw she meant what she said. "Good, keeps things simpler if that stays true."

"I couldn't agree more."

28

Heated Questions

They spent the better part of an hour in Helene's hidden alcove compiling basic healing packets for nausea, aches, rashes, sores, sleepiness, and sleeplessness. It was what Helene called "hedge magic." She'd insisted that Suzy must've had it too as she treated Kat's nausea, but Kat wasn't convinced this wasn't just stuff one could've learned in a medicinal herbology class. However, in Helene's current mood she wasn't about to argue the point. She told Kat that all magic needed to start small and build upon what they knew about nature. To honor the herbs, to create the healing properties, was the beginning of harmony.

"Okay, now you try."

"Try what?" Kat was perplexed. Up until this point they were assembling basic recipes for healing that Helene had perfected over the years.

"Use your intuition, your inner sight to create a cure or poultice."

"For what exactly?"

"That is for you to decide. Determine the need and then puzzle out the solution."

Kat looked at the bits of this twig and that herb, recalling most of their names and properties but could think of nothing. This was beyond her, and frankly, she didn't see it as magic at all.

Helene's patience broke. "You aren't even trying."

"I'm sorry but this, this just isn't me."

"Weren't you paying attention?"

"Of course I was." Kat rattled off name after name of plant cuttings and uses. She'd repeated them enough over the past hour that it almost became a tune in her head.

"Then why not?"

"Well, maybe because I know the wrong combination could kill someone. Where and when I am from this is done by pharmacists. I don't see how this is teaching me what I need to know about magic. Is this why you brought me here, to learn healing? Come to think of it, I still don't know why you brought me back at all."

Helene brushed off the question and, obviously frustrated, began to pack up and put away the samples in assorted bags and bottles to be stored for another day. Kat could see that she was exhausted. She stopped to hold the small of her back frequently but would not allow Kat to help with the clean up.

Kat didn't know what made her think of it, but she clapped her hands together, rubbed them briskly against each other, and then placed the heated palms to the small of Helene's back. Helene stopped what she was doing and sighed.

"There, how did you learn to do that magic?" Helene turned to Kathleen quickly, eyes scouring hers for answers.

"It's not magic; it's just...hands."

"But the heat?"

How could Kat tell her that she'd seen Mr. Miyagi do this in a '80s film? "It's just hand warmth, I assure you." Even as she said it, it ceased to be true. Helene leaned over the work table so Kat's hands could better reach where she ached. Kat's hands affected a vibrating glow of heat. All she knew was that she thought of the heat, thought of it focused on the small of Helene's back, and it coursed through her. Kat could feel it now warming in her veins and then centering in her palms to act as heating pads. Kat spread her fingers to spread the area of warmth, and then drew her hands slowly apart until they were off Helene's back but the glow remained, softly humming where Kat had previously placed her hands.

Helene eased into the chair, sighing. "That is indeed magic. Tell me of it."

Kat explained as best she could what her thought process was and the inspiration as clearly as possible. But Helene was right, there was no denying that the result was more than a hand clap and friction.

"It seems you have a latent talent for the arts or perhaps it feeds off of the proximity of two of the same blood. We will have to tread carefully as we progress. You've no talent for healing in the traditional way, but with your hands you affected a very palatable cure."

Kat stood looking at her fingertips, her oh-so-ordinary hands, and wondered. Had she something that had been ignored all along? Was it indeed "in her" begging to be let out? And how could she control what she did not understand in the slightest? Kat would mull these questions over the next few days. She found it hard to believe it came from within her but more through Helene. Otherwise what did it say about who she was?

"Tomorrow we will work with crystals," Helene explained. "I want to test you with different forms of magic to better learn what type of witch you are."

Apparently there were categories. Who knew?

29

Confounded

Weeks passed and Kathleen grew anxious and irritable. Helene was in full confinement, her health having depreciated to a state that she could no longer hide the toll it was taking. Alastair, fearing for the child and mother, would entertain no compromise. Shut up in her rooms, with nursemaids constantly at Helene's elbow, made it impossible to speak freely, and the expected entertainment for 'ladies' made Kat want to scream out of sheer boredom. Horrid serial novels, puzzles, letter writing, and needlework were what was expected of them both. As Helene's companion cousin, Kat was seldom given the freedom of fresh air, and so she paced.

Helene's back ached with no respite so she was bedridden as a precaution. Nothing Kat could say or do would be listened to as how could she explain what she knew of modern childbirth? The fact that Kat's aunt had had similar symptoms indicative of a breech birth could not be explained with any credulity. It was in the few moments alone with Helene that Kat broached the subject.

"You mean the child will have to be turned while still inside me?"

"I'm afraid so, or at least that is what I suspect. I've heard it is quite a common occurrence."

"And 'hula hooping' movements might ease my pain?"

"So Carol was told—although I am not sure of the reasoning of that. But they were adamant that walking helps the birthing process," Kat shrugged.

"I don't know that I am comforted by having someone from the modern world telling me these things or not as it all seems quite incredible."

"Really? Someone who figured out how to move between times thinks these methods incredible? Isn't that ironic?"

Helene laughed weakly. "I concede. But what can we do? No one here would believe such advice. They'd undoubtedly sedate me, thinking me delusional to conjecture such."

Helene made good points. Kat nodded and paced.

"Sometimes it helps to watch you pace. I can imagine myself walking. I wonder if my legs would hold me at all these days."

Kat stopped, chasing a thought. She must've stood there, lost in her thoughts, for several minutes because abruptly Helene called to her quite urgently.

"What is it? Speak quickly before they return."

"I'm still working it out, but I was wondering, if when you travel through time you return but moments later here, could we transport you to my time to have the baby?"

"I'd thought of that. I'm not sure what would happen to the child. Would the child belong to then rather than now? I can't risk it."

Kat paced some more, increasingly frustrated with each step.

"Perhaps we could stall the others on some such task I would devise and you could…?"

"Ah, hell no! I passed bio class by writing the lab reports. After that grasshopper's eye burst open, squirting me in the face while I dissected it, I was done. I cannot do it. Capital CAN. Capital NOT. There is no way I'm reaching in and... and..." Kat shook her head heartily for emphasis.

"You must."

"I'll throw up. Or pass out. Or throw up and then pass out. I'm telling you, I can't do it. And if anything were to happen to you or the baby..."

Helene sighed a deep sigh of resignation. "Well then what good is it knowing what should be done if it cannot be done?"

Kat threw herself into a chair near the empty hearth. Her head rested in her hands.

A maid walked in, busied herself, straightening the room, freshening the ever present flowers, and gathering what needed to be laundered. When she asked if Helene needed anything, Kat popped her head up quickly and stated, "She craves cool water. Fetch it from the deep well by the gardens—it's cooler there and tastes sweeter, she'd said."

"There is cool water right there on the bedside."

Helene caught Kat's meaning to stall the maid and piped in, "Nay, 'tis tepid. I crave the cold. Please heed me, or shall I ask my lord Alastair?"

At the mention of her husband's name the maid curtsied and hurried from the room.

Helene pushed herself up on the pillows. "Have you an idea?"

"A question first. Is it possible to bring someone else back, not of your blood?"

She thought. "I don't see why not, but whom? You cannot expect to abduct a physician?"

"No, better—Suzy. She already knows about you, me, the situation. And you said she is a natural witch with her healing. I know that when she was in the Peace Corps she delivered babies many times." Kat beamed.

"Peace Corps?"

"Never mind, not important. What matters is she's delivered

babies before in very..." Kat paused to choose her words carefully so as not to offend, "very, rustic circumstances."

"Would she come?"

"I think she wanted to come with me before. The questions now would be how to do it and how to keep the doctor Alastair hired away long enough for Suzy to help?"

"The doctor will be easy. He's more advisory than hands on. There would be a midwife on hand, anyway. But if your Suzy were to agree, she could be that midwife. Let me work out the logistics. I should think one thing would be needed—you would need to bring her to be sure she arrives safely. Yes, that must be done. I'll work out the rest."

Helene's lady's maid soon arrived with the cold water and quite out of breath. Kat asked Helene's leave to go back to her chamber as she now had something else to occupy her time and thoughts.

They had gone through it over and over again, trying to figure out all the angles of bringing a second person back, a person who was not blood relation. There was no way to know if it would work, but they both agreed it was worth a try. Helene's aches and discomfort grew; however, it was far too early to indicate labor, nor was it congruent with the symptoms—therefore more disconcerting. Kat knew all new mothers feared for their child's safety, but this fear was real, not imagined. They both knew a breech birth in this day and age could mean death to both mother and child. There was no doubt something had to be done.

Another nagging question tugged at the periphery of Kat's thoughts. How would they be sure to return before Helene gave birth? They'd managed to devise a type of synchronized spell to draw both Kat and Suzy back to Helene in three days time, synchronized in both worlds, now and future...but that was assuming that Helene would be able to focus, or indeed have alone time, at that hour. As long as her health held, it might be possible. They consulted star charts and books that Helene had held secret from Kathleen until this time. She never revealed the source of these documents, tsking Kat away at any inquiry. It was finally determined that Kat would leave in a day's time and, three days after, return at the hour Helene normally scheduled to bathe. That seemed safest as that was when being alone would not seem so awkward. Kat had to chuckle inwardly as this was how the whole thing started—with a bath tub. But the irony and humor was lost on Helene. Kat could see she truly feared the outcome of their venture and that sobered her mood.

Kat skipped lunch the next day, only partaking in a bit of bread and cheese at tea to settle her stomach before time travel. She knew that waiting on the other side, Suzy would be ready with her herbs to combat the nausea that haunted her, but she wanted to do her part in preventing it.

Tea seemed interminable. Alastair and Caleb, both being back in residence, seemed intent on detaining Kathleen and demanded her full attention as Helene was not allowed to depart her confinement even for tea. Any other day she would've been fascinated to partake, or at least overhear, the conversation about industrialization knowing what she knew of the future, their future. But today, Kat knew time was fleeting, and her mind was on her imminent departure.

While Alastair seemed content to engage Caleb with his ideas regarding the latest stock report, Caleb seemed determined to keep Kathleen under his sharp scrutiny. Silent, or not, Kat seemed to draw his full attention. She found it quite unsettling to be the focus of such consideration. At times, it appeared he was trying to read her very thoughts, as if he saw something unknown to others, herself included.

Finally, when Kat was once again back in her room, she felt relieved of the burden of trying to stay focused on the here and now when in fact she was already mentally on her way home. Kat shook off any thoughts of Caleb and what his behavior could mean. He was more of a nuisance than anything else. She needed to center her thoughts on the task at hand.

Kat had barely closed her door when Helene slid into her room from the hidden, adjoining passage.

"Is the door bolted?"

Kat nodded. "How about yours?"

"Alastair thinks I mean to rest now. We should have enough time." Helene pulled from her pockets the charmed medallion they had fashioned that contained a stone much like Kat's with matching ear bobs. "Make sure these are on her. They will serve as a homing beacon—or at least I believe they will. The worst that can happen is nothing."

Kat bent to tie her low boots and then pulled a satchel from under her bed. Inside it was a complete outfit for Suzy to return in should she agree to come. Kat tucked the earrings and pendant inside a side pocket. Helene had also insisted on crystals for clarity and balance, so these, too, she dropped in pockets. Going to the bedside table, Kat picked up her own pendant and slid it over her head, moving it to rest within the bodice of the gown, nestling it against her chest. Kat could feel it heat against her skin slightly. She adjusted the miniature of herself and Sky hidden in her sash, feeling reassured with its presence. Suzy promised it would bring her home. Kat only hoped that she would still be there waiting.

"Well then, are you ready?"

"Yes, I have everything."

"The crystals?"

"Yes," Kat patted the side of her bag. "Wait!" She hesitated,

"We've been so focused on going and coming back, but how will you explain when they find me gone for a few days?"

"I've got it sorted. The coach from town is due within the hour. Patrice's younger sister, Elba, will don one of your cloaks and go into town, supposedly to tend to some errands for me. She's scheduled to return about when you do."

"How is anyone going to believe that? Do we look anything alike?" Kat challenged.

"I've come to know that people believe what they want to believe. They see what they want to see. And with the hood up, who's to say who is under it? I doubt many will notice you are gone as you won't be away long at all."

30

A Wrong Turn

When Kat arrived back in her shop, she found Suzy asleep in the King Louis reproduction chaise Kat had bought, not to sell as an antique, but as a staging piece. She didn't have to wake Suzy as she'd always been a paranoid sleeper, always with an eye open it seemed. Suzy yawned and stretched.

"How was it?"

"Good, actually really good, mostly."

"Well you'll have to tell me all about it once you get some rest." Suzy paused and looked Kat over. "You were gone a long time, weren't you?"

Kat shifted uncomfortably. "Why? What's happened?"

Suzy laughed, "No, no. It hasn't been long here—you'd barely left. It's your hair. It's longer."

Kat couldn't help the automatic reflex to touch it. "Well, I'll be damned. I never thought of that. That's one way to get past a bad hair cut." She laughed.

"How long were you there?"

"I'm not sure—weeks. Possibly as much as two months. I forgot to keep track."

She nodded. "Well, let's get you some of my special tea and get you in to bed. We'll have plenty of time to catch up in a few days when you are up to it." Suzy started to drag Kat behind her to head up to the rooms she kept above the shop. She planned to tuck Kat into bed like she did when Kat used to sleep over as a kid.

Kat hesitated, pulling Suzy to a stop.

"What's wrong, dear? Are you feeling sick already?"

"No, that's not it." But Kat paused, noticing the lack of disorientation. Perhaps, she thought, she was getting used to time travel. "There's a lot I need to tell you."

"Yes, I am sure dear, but we've plenty of time for that."

"No," Kat said, insisting. She waited until Suzy turned back to face her directly. "Helene needs me to bring you back."

"Back? Back...then?"

Kat nodded.

"Well, how is that supposed to work?"

"Make me some tea and a sandwich, and I'll fill you in."

It was very late by the time Kat had answered all her questions. Suzy sat pondering, undoubtedly thinking of more.

"It'll make so much more sense once you're there."

"I don't doubt it. But that isn't what I am worried about." Suzy paused and drew a deep breath. "I am not worried for me."

"Then what? I always come back."

"Yes, dear, you always come back...and part of me wonders if you always come back because I am waiting for you. I know it sounds foolish even as I said it. But I wonder, if no one here was waiting for you, purposely waiting for you, could you slip away? It's probably a stupid question, but I can't help wondering it."

"It's not like that."

"Can you promise me that no matter what happens that you'll be able to come back here, to this time, to your Gran? To me?

"I promise." Kat reached down to the sash that encircled her waist and revealed the miniature she had pinned there so many days earlier. "This anchors me. I won't forget who I am or where I belong. I promise."

Suzy and Kat spent countless hours the next afternoon at the library scanning medical journals on childbirth. But while Suzy was right, Kat needed sleep, and although she was still tired, time was passing quickly. Kat felt pressured to depart in two days time. They had to use what time they had to learn as much as possible that could be used to help Helene.

Kat didn't bother opening the shop, placing a *Closed due to flu* sign in the window. Since Kat's mother was away with her Christian Book Club on the annual casino trip, she needn't worry anyone would be overly concerned. Shipments came from online auctions, but other than cataloging and storing, Kat left the shop business alone. It bothered her at times to think of how much of her life, too, was on a shelf, but it couldn't be helped. Kat made a silent vow that after she got Helene set to rights that she would return and focus on the here and now for a while. A nagging thought at the back of her mind feared some intangible, unspoken doubt, but she brushed it away in haste to get back lest they be late for the birth of Helene's first child.

Kat was surprised at how quickly Suzy agreed to come back with her. Maybe she shouldn't have been—she'd always known Suzy to be fearless. After her initial concern for Kat, she hadn't looked back or doubted. Suzy instead focused on refreshing her knowledge of midwifery.

"Think I'd be able to smuggle back some obstetrical tools?"

"I don't know if we should."

"Well then, I'll just have to research what I can expect to be there in that time and figure out how to use it for our needs. I sincerely hope it is a simple case of turning the child and nothing more. I doubt the doctor will step aside long enough to let me do more."

When they'd done what they could do from here, Suzy stood by Kat's side, wearing the ear bobs and pendant. The two were dressed as if they were going to tea on a PBS show. They'd gone over everything, every step, every plan Helene made. They now stood in a circle of crystals as Helene had assured Kat they would amplify the energy. And yet as she stood there, satchel draped across her back, Kat just knew something was off.

"Suzy, you don't have to do this," she began.

"Nonsense. I want to. Who knows, maybe I already have." She winked.

"Excuse me?"

"I've watched the time travel movies. Maybe I already went back. Think about it. If you are her great, great, great grandchild she couldn't have died back then. Maybe I was already there, and that's why you are here."

Kat stood speechless, blinking at the logic. It was either genius or the dumbest load of crap she had heard all week. "Yeah, I don't know about that..."

"Well," Suzy continued cheerfully, "that's how I am thinking of it. You see, if I already did it, then I have nothing to fear, do I, as I've already succeeded? I am just following through with destiny." She smiled brightly.

There was nothing Kat could say so she just returned her smile. "You ready?"

"Yup! Let 'er rip!" Suzy pulled down antique driving goggles over her eyes although Kat had told her she looked damn silly and wouldn't need them. Suzy insisted; she was worried about the wind in her eyes. Sometimes Suzy was the most grounded person Kat knew, and other times there was no reasoning with her "Suzy-logic." And that was one of the reasons why Kat loved her so much.

Kat rubbed her pendant with both of her hands before dropping it to rest upon her chest. She slowly whispered the words she'd practiced each day since she left the past.

"Hand in hand, your hand in mine.
Across land, sea, space, and time,
Back to the start, future meet past,
Bring me to thee, and with thee mine,
Where we will, let us both go,
As you will, make it be so."

Suzy squeezed Kat's hand tightly as the air shifted and swelled, colors melded and then faded into a blur. The pendant pulsed, slowly heating, glowing. It felt as if it grew and swelled on Kat's chest. Kat focused only on her breathing and Suzy's hand in her own. She again felt the sensation of shifting, the floor being removed from below her feet, a gradual nothingness—but it was slower this time, hesitant, awkward. Then Kat felt Suzy scrabbling at her hand, clutching at her, clawing at her skirts as Kat was whisked out of Suzy's grasp in a silent wave of what seemed unending screams—whether her own or Suzy's, Kat didn't know.

Kat landed with a thud on the carpet in front of the hearth in Helene's rooms. She looked about, wildly.

"It's okay, you're back safe and sound."

"Where? Where is she? Where is Suzy? I felt her being pulled from me!"

Helene slowly rose from her settee, stiff in her movements.

She paused before speaking. "'Twas not to be, I guess. Ah well, but at least you are here to help. That is a relief." She outstretched her arms to take Kat into a hug.

Kat shook her off, walked past her, looking around the room frantically.

"She's not here, clearly. It didn't work. Let's move on."

"Move on?" Kat was incredulous. "What do you mean move on?" Her voice became shrill. "The woman I trust most in my life, damn it...the woman who is more family to me than my own family, is lost and you say 'move on'? What is wrong with you?"

Helene's anger flared, a truly disturbing sight until she quickly banked her feelings. She cooed, tried to soothe Kathleen, "She'll be fine, dear. She obviously didn't come here. She is most likely safe at home, glad she is excused from the task at hand. I shouldn't worry. Besides it's me that is truly in danger. If anyone is going to rage it should be me. There's no need for you to be so selfish."

Kat felt like she would burst a metaphorical aneurysm in her head as her blood pulsed wildly. She was both furious and terrified. To be "shushed" so was insulting and infuriating. Kat was scared and wanted to cry. Worse yet, she felt so helpless that she wanted to beat something to a pulp. The dichotomy tore at her. A sick feeling formed in her chest as she feared the worst.

All these emotions must've played across Kat's face as Helene chose her words more carefully. "I believe her to be where you left her—no harm done. Truly. She might be disappointed but naught more. We knew it was a long shot at best, no guarantees. Well, now we know, blood calls to blood, no more."

Kat whipped about to face her. "Can you guarantee she is safe?"

Helene stood silently, watching.

"Can you?"

Helene took a deep breath before beginning. "You know I can't, but," she quickly continued, "it makes sense that she was simply left behind. No reason to let our imaginations get away with us."

"Send me back."

"Now you know I can't send you back right after. It's too dangerous."

"Send me back!" Kat demanded.

"It was never guaranteed, and you knew that. You knew that there was a risk. She knew it, too. You just have to wait to see. She should be fine."

"Should! Are you serious? How can I wait around for 'should'? She's all alone. This is all my fault. I should've never gone back for her. It was too risky. Why did I even think I could? You should have told me." Kat looked accusingly at her, anger and fear battling for control.

Helene said nothing. Her face turned red, but she said not a word, instead waiting for Kathleen to make the next move.

Kat could see Helene fumed at her accusations, but to Helene's credit she neither defended herself nor challenged Kat. That worked better than a pan of water thrown in Kat's face to cool her down. "Please, send me back," she begged.

"I can't. You know I can't." Helene paused, watching the misery wash over her. "You'll just have to wait a few days, and then you can slip away and check on her. But remember," she said putting a cheerful face on, "we can send you to any time. She won't be alone long. She'll be just fine."

"I pray that you're right." Kat, not normally a religious person, prayed more that day than any other day in her life until that point. She knew not, and could not know, what happened to Suzy just yet, but she reassured herself she would, and soon.

31

Foul Moods

The "travel" sickness hit Kathleen hard that evening. She'd neglected to take her normal precautions. And with the energy expenditure of her angry outburst, it weighed on her, but she wouldn't allow Helene to tend to her, preferring instead to wallow in her foul mood alone. Kat sipped some herb-infused tea, ate some bread and cheese, and hoped to sleep it off.

Kat didn't sleep well, tormented in her dreams of having lost Suzy somewhere "in between" here and there. It was her biggest fear. She hadn't realized before just how much she counted Suzy as family. And, aside from Gran, she was the "home" she thought of most.

Hopeless and dejected, and a bit dead inside, Kat finally went to Helene's sitting room at midday. Formerly just another bedroom, it was used now as her personal parlor temporarily as Helene had begged some relief from her confined spaces. Kat hadn't seen her earlier for she had been unfit company and had breakfasted alone in her room. Kat was relieved to see that Alastair's place had not been set as that indicated he was away.

Helene looked up from her seat by the window and merely nodded a greeting. When Kat made movement to join her she called to the parlor maid and indicated she'd finished and would like to return to her bed to rest. Kat hurried over to assist her, but Helene waved her off. She swept by Kat as gracefully as she could in her late stage of pregnancy, with a polite nod, the only acknowledgment.

Kat realized Helene was still smarting from her accusations and temper. Forced with no other option, Kathleen descended to the day room to eat with the others. She chose seating near the window so that she could look out across the grounds with a glimpse of the pond. There Kat was deep in thought, mindless of the girl who set out servings of this and that before her when she heard a familiar voice.

"I'll just join her there. No need to seat me at another table."

Kat quickly looked up and saw Caleb gesturing to her small table. She'd purposely chosen it so she could be alone as the table could barely hold more than her luncheon plates and pot of tea.

Caleb smiled broadly, noting Kat's discomfort and was all the more animated, she thought, because of it.

"We'll be quite economical over here. I'm sure she won't mind sharing her tea and sundries." As Caleb spoke, he picked up most of Kathleen's dishes, merged their contents, until he had reduced all onto one crowded dish, and gestured to a servant that the now emptied plates be removed and thus made space for himself.

Kat glared at what now looked to be an overloaded, buffet plate from the 21st century. He, too, suddenly seemed to notice how terribly crowded it looked, and relieved her plate of a few of its contents, popping them into his mouth. Kat didn't know whether to laugh at him or slap his hand away.

And while Caleb busied himself, touching and rearranging her lunch, Kat couldn't help but reach up to feel if her hair was in place...and then hated herself for such a feminine move. She brought her hands down to her sides and scowled.

"Oh, you're a cheerful lot this fine day," Caleb said, and then looked Kathleen over critically. "I'd say the hair is fine, if you ask me."

"I didn't—"

Caleb cut her off. "But there is something in the eyes. Not sleeping well, are we?"

Kat would've growled had she thought she'd get away with it, but she didn't want to give him something new to criticize.

"'We' wouldn't know how you slept, but I slept fine. Just fine."

He laughed. "Truly? You intend to lie when it is so obvious by the circles beneath your eyes that what you say is untrue. Why is that?"

Kat sat mute, fuming at him and her own ineptitude as the servant brought another setting and lunch fixings for him. Caleb made deliberate, graceful movements as he set about settling in with his lunch, placing a cloth napkin across his lap and organizing his forks and spoons. He nodded to indicate tea and motioned with but a hand flick for two lumps of sugar and cream. Everything about him was the well-mannered gentleman if you ignored his rudeness. When the servant finished, Caleb again turned his attention to Kathleen.

"Well, what have you to say? How can I be of assistance?"

Kat was speechless, something that seldom happened to her in her real life, but was an all too common occurrence when Caleb was around.

Caleb languidly took a bite of a cucumber sandwich and then placed it aside in favor of egg salad. Pleased, he again turned his attention to her.

"I don't know what to say, honestly," Kat said.

"Well, that is a good start, and an honest one, too. I don't know why I seem to draw the worst out of you, but I do." Caleb waved Kathleen off as she started to deny it. "We both know that it is true so let's leave that alone. But what is it, I'd like to know, that makes me so disdainful to you?"

Kat sat, unblinking for a moment. She wasn't going to deny "disdainful" either, as to be fair it was true. But for the first time she pondered that point as well. Why did he rub her wrong and so quickly?

"I can't exactly say. But to be frank, I don't really know you at all and yet you push and...cajole as if we've know each other for ages." Once started, she couldn't stop. "You're rude, proud, and so sure of yourself. It's...it's..." searching for a word that wasn't slang from her day, "it's off-putting."

Caleb laughed again, heartily.

"And that!" Kat stood, pointed at him accusingly. "I say something horrible to you, and you laugh. How can you be so arrogant?" She sat back down with an exasperated sigh.

"I am sorry." Caleb did his best to stifle the chortle, smothering a smile. "I just find you so refreshingly real. After all my travels these past few years it is one thing I'd begun to believe was lost in the world, honesty. Brutal, vulgar, glorious honesty. It makes me want to hug you out of the sheer joy of it and wonder. Where are you truly from as you are not of this earth?" He smiled the broadest, most charming smile—and it made Kat want to slap him for it.

"Well, I don't know where you've been that you can talk to a lady like this!" Kat rose again in protest. To what exactly she was protesting, she wasn't sure. He'd said nothing false, and yet she felt nakedly insulted.

"Oh, you are no lady, to be sure. A lady would've batted an eye, raised a fan and hidden behind it, or stormed off long before now. I am not quite sure what you are, or who you are, but to be sure, it is not a lady."

Infuriated, Kat stormed off, but Caleb's laughter chased her far longer in her head than could be accounted for by basic physics.

✤

It'd been a couple of days, and Kat was more than ready to return to Suzy. She nervously put clothes away and tidied toiletries, needing something to do while she waited to be sent back. Kat didn't know for how long she'd be needed there or if Suzy had remained back at home. Too many things were up in the air that needed resolving. She was still so angry at Helene for risking her friend, and more so her part in the plan. Until Kat knew Suzy was safe, she couldn't even begin to forgive Helene…or herself. Not yet anyway. It might not be fair, but that was how she felt.

Kat heard a light tap on the door and ignored it. If it were Patrice, she couldn't be bothered. If it were Helene, Kat knew she'd eventually just walk in anyway, welcomed or not, and she certainly was not ready to be gracious yet.

Sure enough, in swept Helene. "I know you are readying to leave, but I must ask you one last favor." When Kathleen continued to ignore her, not even turning to acknowledge her presence but still affecting a need to tidy, she followed up with, "Please."

Kat turned to face her. Helene appeared more haggard than she'd ever seen her, but Kat also knew how she could manipulate her looks. She no longer trusted Helene so Kat doubted what she saw, but it worked on her emotions regardless.

When Kat remained silent, Helene simply continued. "I haven't much time—I had to sneak out of my own rooms to speak with you, so please listen. I know you will leave shortly, but we still have the problem of the breech. I only ask of you that you get someone who can help."

"Get someone?" Kat sarcastically asked. That was the issue that started this mess in the first place!

Appearing nonplussed Helene continued, "I know someone who will come, well, might come, if she knows how much I need her."

Kat looked at her skeptically.

"It's just a few hours ride by coach. I can have Patrice lead you. You'll still leave as soon as is possible, I promise."

"If you already knew someone, why did you need me to get Suzy? You make no sense."

"You'll understand my hesitancy when you go there. Alastair must not know. But she'll not deny me, I am sure of it. I cannot be left alone. It'd be risking the babe. My life, I am not worried about, for 'tis not my time. But the child. Surely you will give me that?"

Kat didn't know what it was in her that made her agree to help. But before she knew it she was in a coach, headed to god-knows-where with Patrice to bring back a midwife who must stay hidden from Helene's husband. It seemed nothing was easy when it came to Helene.

They rode past the nearest town, and then further into the late afternoon. Slowly, houses became fewer and farther between until Kat couldn't remember the last homestead. They wound through a heavily treed glen for some time until Patrice announced they had gone far enough. They were to go on foot from here. Kat looked out of the carriage window and saw nothing except woods and realized that if they didn't hurry the sun would be going down before they returned. Patrice assured her that their destination was not far at all, that it was just hidden.

Kat stepped down out of the carriage to stand beside her.

"Okay, so where are we off to?"

"Shush." Patrice pulled out a stone much like the one Kat wore about her neck and held it out like a dowser stick. She slowly turned this way and that until they both saw the stone make a brief but unmistakable flicker. They began to walk in the direction to which it pointed. Patrice led, making twists and turns, walking where there was no path, but with confidence that they were going true. Approximately ten minutes from the carriage, Kat was ready to call a stop to this nonsense and demand they return to the manor when Patrice declared they were there.

32

It's All Relative

But where exactly was "here"? Kat looked about but saw no dwelling, no path, only more of the same, dense woods. Patrice tapped Kathleen's shoulder to get her attention and pointed. From what Kat had thought was merely more undergrowth and shrubbery rose a small waft of smoke. She squinted and could make out the outline of a small, low hut ensconced in bramble and bracken to better blend into the wood. Kat was both relieved that they had arrived and frightened at where they'd come. She couldn't fathom who Helene might know out here that could be of help. Or was it even safe? If it was safe, wouldn't they have visited before?

Before Kathleen could voice any of her concerns, a woman stood before her as if out of thin air. She was wiry and tall, or would've been had she not been so hunched over. She looked ageless, ancient. She had clear, blue-gray eyes that seemed to pierce Kat's thoughts. Most disturbing of all were the lash marks that cut across her face, long healed but clearly indicated by the raised and scarred skin surrounding the cuts. One such mark crossed an eye but left the eye intact.

If she noticed Kat's stare she ignored it. She was probably used to the attention the scarring brought.

"Why are you here? Are you here for help or to make an offering?" The woman paused impatiently, twitching and moving some part of her at all times. It was somehow familiar, but Kat couldn't recall from where or how at the moment.

"Both, I think."

"Both is it?" She laughed. Kat could see that several of her teeth were missing, although the rest looked well-tended. "How about you start with the offering before I decide if I will help?" She held out her hand. Patrice placed several large bills and a strand of alternating garnets and pearls.

She looked up quickly when she saw the strand of gems. "This is no ordinary offering. Whom do you serve?"

While Kathleen attempted to stammer a response, she persisted. "Who? Who? WHO!"

"Helene."

"Ah, I thought the pearls and garnets be a bit dramatic for you common lot, no offense intended. What has she done now?" She motioned to Kat to follow her into the cottage. She turned and went inside before Kat could say a word.

Patrice stayed rooted in her spot and refused to follow. Kat, however, wanted privacy in discussing such a private matter so she followed, but not before she threatened Patrice with death by her hands should she abandon her here. When Kat took Patrice's guiding stone as insurance, the girl began to tremble. Kat told her not to worry, that she'd return momentarily with an answer as she was just as eager to head back to the manor as Patrice.

Kat found she had to bend significantly to enter the cottage, and then could not fully straighten once inside—no mystery about the hunchback, she thought to herself. The woman offered Kat a tree stump as a stool as she took another, drawing a pipe from within her cloak.

"Do you smoke?"

"Not since high school," was Kat's unguarded response. She clapped a hand over her mouth.

The woman laughed heartily. "Not to be worried, lassie. 'Tis nice to meet an honest person these days."

Kat found it ironic that she was having a similar conversation to the one she'd had with Caleb not so long ago. She would have to work on not being so transparent—seemed to be a problem almost anywhere she went.

"Tell me about my girl. What has she done?"

"Excuse me? Your girl?"

"Ah, she didn't tell you. That's interesting. My you are a trusting sort to come out here with only that halfwit as companion," she gestured with her thumb pointing back towards where Kat had left Patrice, "and without a proper reason or explanation."

"Oh, I have a reason. The child she carries is breech, and she'll need a midwife that can turn the baby."

The woman shook her head, slowly and widely, from side to side. "I told her not to marry him, that he'd be the ruin of her. I foretold untold troubles to counter the good, but she thought it worth the risk, so desperate she was." She took a long drag on her pipe and paused to exhale, drawing it out as long as possible. "She was so desperate to leave what she was for who she thought she needed to be. Foolish girl. You can run but you can never outrun who you are down deep to the core."

The woman continued her slow, contemplative smoking, as if she forgot Kat were there, so focused was she on her thoughts and the patterns the smoke made before they wafted away.

Kat took a moment to look around and was startled to realize that it all looked very familiar. This was quite nearly a reproduction of both the cottage room and the hidden room behind Helene's sleeping quarters—work table, jars, and small sacks of this and that, a hearth banked low, while glowing, floating lights lit all but the deepest corners. At one side of the room was a small bed covered in what looked to be a pile of rags with a fur draped over the end post. At the hearthside table stood a small collection of earthenware dishes and bowls. The poverty was evident, but there was no feeling of want that Kat could detect.

"She's always been ashamed of whence she came. Always wanted more, that one. No, she wanted to be a lady, not a witch, although it be good business at times. She wanted stability, no more moving, no question of where her next meal would come from. She had pride, vanity, and it pained her when a lot would take to taunting the likes of me. No, she did what she needed to do for her. I just wish she'd chosen better. But wealth and status are alluring masters."

"Will you come, when it's time?"

"Aye, I will, although I doubt I'd be welcome by the master. Tell her to do a sending through the stone." She tapped an amulet much like the pendant Helene wore about her own neck. "I'll be there." She pocketed the bills Kat had given her and returned the strand of garnets and pearls. "I've no use for that lot. People would think I stole it, and that's not a burden I dare risk. Now, off with you. Your task is done."

She fairly shooed Kat off, which she minded not a bit. She couldn't wait to head back. Kat found Patrice standing where she left her, shivering although it was not cold. It seemed that without the stone Patrice didn't even know how to get back to the carriage to wait. Kat couldn't understand it as she could clearly hear the horses whinny from where she stood, but since stranger things had happened in the last several months, Kat dropped the thought and led Patrice to the carriage and home.

They made all haste back to the manor. Now that Helene would be provided for, Kat saw no reason in delaying her departure. She must get back to check on Suzy. God, how she hoped Suzy would be there, waiting, as usual. Her only comfort was that to Suzy it would be but moments, while to Kat it had been agonizing days of worry and guilt.

Kat climbed the stairs, two at a time, in her glee at the thought of returning home, ignoring all lessons to the contrary as to how a lady should comport herself. *Screw that!* she thought. She was going home and might never return. Kat didn't give a fig—to use their term—who saw what. She didn't plan to be here to deal with any repercussions or rebuke.

Kat was bursting with energy and excitement when she rounded the corner of the hall and walked right into Alastair, waiting there, just outside Helene's door.

"Ah, so here you are, you who were to be her companion now chooses to arrive to check on her mistress. I've a mind to flog you for your negligence—especially since your one task, the whole reason we tolerate you, is to comfort my lady. If it hadn't been for one of the upstairs maids checking in on Helene we might not know her labor had begun."

It couldn't be worse timing—but it couldn't be helped. *Or could it?* Kat couldn't help wondering. She knew it was selfish, but she'd waited so very long already to go home.

Caleb stepped out from behind Alastair's massive form, "Nay, Al, she'd not been gone long and undoubtedly on some task for the missus, isn't that so?" He peered at Kathleen, willing her to agree.

"Yes, my lord Alastair, I was on my mistress' errand. If you'd let me through it might bring some comfort to her." Kathleen curtsied and bowed her head, if only to avoid his glare.

Once allowed, Kat slid into Helene's room, the energy and mirth she had entering the manor now much deflated by the thought that she'd be delayed at least several hours, if not days—if Kat could even get away at all now that the baby was near.

The doctor stood at the head of Helene's bed, a hand at her brow and another at her wrist.

They both turned when they heard someone enter.

"There now, your cousin has returned and can minister to you while I go down with the men. It's like to be many hours before you have need of me. She can undoubtedly keep you company while you wait."

Helene rose, bucking and rocking out of the bed covers in the throes of a contraction, eyes spewing metaphorical venom at the doctor as he saw her pain but turned to leave nevertheless. Her wild eyes caught Kat's, and she could see the fear there. Even though Kat desperately wanted to, she did not turn away. Kat focused on every soothing thought or mantra she could recall and mentally projected those towards Helene. Kat had no idea if her efforts did anything, but she held her gaze until she saw Helene ease as the pain slacked.

Kat scurried to the head of Helene's bed, wiped her brow, and offered her water, which she refused.

Helene licked her lips to speak and rasped, "What did she say?"

"She'll come. You've only got to call her, 'doing a sending,' she said."

Helene nodded, exhausted.

"I don't understand. When did this start? Your labor shouldn't be this bad at the onset but only toward the end."

Helene didn't answer Kat's question but motioned her to the side table where she found the doctor or maid had undoubtedly relieved her of her jewelry for the birthing. There, albeit more ornate than Kat's, sat the pendant on a chain whose stone was almost identical to hers, with ribbons of red running through it.

"Bring it to me. Let me call her while I still can. Watch the door so that I am not disturbed as I do so."

Kathleen stood by the door, nervously blocking the entrance should anyone choose to enter. She could see from her vantage point that the stone glowed boldly in Helene's cupped hands as she muttered something Kat could not make out as it was in no language she knew. The stone went dark for a moment, and then pulsed, the same intonation of words recited in response. She watched as Helene slumped back into her pillows with a sigh of relief.

"She comes. Watch for her from the far side of the garden. She should be at the cottage shed in moments. Go!"

Helene gave Kat no time to ask questions. She quickly made her way through the manor and out the kitchen's back door. Kat couldn't be sure when it began, but she found she really didn't need to ask questions as much once she sorted out her own thoughts. Undoubtedly, however Kat traveled through time, Helene's mother could do so here, in this place and time. Kat had just arrived at the gardener's cottage door when out stepped the crone.

The woman said nothing but only nodded in recognition and gestured that Kat lead the way.

"I knew it'd be the back door and hidden passages for the likes of me. She'll not change, not even for need." She sighed beneath her breath. "Although, I must ask your help to keep me away from that mad husband of hers. It'd do her no good if he saw me here. He'd not let me near her, to tell the truth."

"Doesn't he know...?" Kat whispered.

"He knows that I am not the sort he wants near his like. Heed my warning." She gave Kat a dark glare.

Since Helene had given Kat a similar warning, she grew cold with fear. What if she was wrong and the child was not breech? Would this risk be worth it?

Upon seeing the hallway clear, Kat slipped into her bedchamber, beckoned the woman to follow, and latched the door behind them. The woman looked unsurprised at this sidestep. Kat went to the wall and called forth the door that would lead them to Helene's room. She looked back to explain when the woman only nodded, somehow intimating that she knew all along.

Within moments they were in Helene's bedchamber, at her side, as another pain ripped through her.

The crone placed her hands on Helene's distended abdomen and chanted as her hands spread and moved over the contracting muscles, easing and releasing them.

"The child is indeed turned. That is why you pain so." She turned to Kat as if anticipating her thoughts, an uncanny trait she shared with her daughter. "You did right to call me." She turned back to Helene. "Your body wants to wrestle the child out, but the child's body fights you."

"Will you turn the baby?"

"Aye, she must be turned or risk losing all. Although I wonder at the speed of your labor." She glared at Helene, accusingly. "I wonder at the timing." She nodded towards Kat, to which Helene turned her head away in disgust.

"Well, Miss Kathleen, are you ready to get your hands dirty? Seems that one here wasn't ready to let you go just yet."

The line from Miss Prissy from *Gone with the Wind* of "I don't know nothing about birthing no babies" ran through Kat's mind and seemed appropriate at the moment. Kathleen shook her head vigorously that she had no intention of being on the receiving end of the baby.

The crone laughed at her obvious fear. "Go to Helene's head and place your fingertips to each side of her temple." At Kat's confused look she snapped, "Heed me, girl! We've no time for dawdling."

Kat did as she bid and waited. "Now think calming thoughts, no matter what you hear or sense, stay focused on a peaceful scene, soothing and calm. Your job is to concentrate on that while I do what must be done here."

Kathleen tried to conjure an image that was particularly peaceful and latched on to a memory of a hammock at the side of the sea. Granted she had been there with the idiot, Wayne, but she focused on the hammock, the waves gently rolling in at mid-day and the sea breeze. Kat slowed her breathing to match the rhythm of the waves and felt a healing relief wash over her as she perceived Helene's tension melt under her hands and release.

She was still deep in her reverie when Kat felt a hand at her shoulder.

"Well done, girl. Good to know the talent will continue."

Kat's eyes popped wide as it finally sunk in—this was more than Helene's mother; she was another one of Kat's grand-mothers!

"Kathleen, let me properly introduce you to Isabelle, your great grandmother five times removed."

Speechless, Kat could only nod. How could she have been so stupid to not make the connection? Perhaps it was because she had a hard time believing who Helene was as well. She still felt like such an idiot just the same.

"You did well, kid." Kat almost jumped out of her skin when Isabelle used a phrase so often used by Suzy. Kat had almost forgotten her in the panic of the moment. "She should have no trouble birthing now that the child has been turned." Kat had trouble shifting her attention back to Helene mid-thought. "That fool of a doctor should be just fine as I've done the hard part. Nothing to fear now, so I'll be off lest I be discovered."

Kat rose to lead her out.

"No need, girl. I'll find my way. I know my way about the shadows." She gently patted Kat on one shoulder as she moved past her.

And without another word to her daughter, nor a word from Helene either, Isabelle was gone.

33

Curious Reprieve

The birthing went smoothly from this point forward. Helene's contractions increased, and Patrice was sent to bring the doctor. In the wee hours of the morning, Adele Evangeline was born.

Once mother and baby were settled in for the night, Kat trudged to her room, spent, with only the thought of the surrender to sweet sleep. She was emotionally and physically drained, and while Kat would've loved a bath, she hadn't the energy to draw one nor the heart to ask any of the other maidservants to do so either—all of them had been called into service for their mistress. Even the cook had been put to task with keeping the men fed and the kettles full.

So when Kat entered her room she was shocked to find both Caleb and a steaming tub placed before the hearth. She didn't know what it was about the man that flustered her so, but she both wanted to weep with joy at the thought of a bath and wanted to rail against him at his presumption to be in her room. Kat knew it had been his room prior, but it was hers for the duration—a fact he was well aware of.

Caleb quickly relieved Kat of any need to speak. "I knew that this is what I would want at the end of a day as long as yours has been. If you don't want it, it can be ignored and taken away in the morning. None will be the wiser. I bid you goodnight."

As he rose to leave Kathleen sought for words, but only "Thank you" came out. It was hard to argue with a man who asked for nothing. She was too tired to think on it further. Kat started to walk back across the room to slide the door's bolt closed when Caleb popped his head in, just his head. "I'd latch the door tight if I were you." His mouth formed a wicked grin, and he slipped away, narrowly missing the boot she'd thrown at the door.

No, Kat would think no more of him, she decided as she slid in to the gloriously deep tub. She hadn't been in the tub long when she realized she was both starving and thirsty. Kat reached to the side table to grab a towel and saw a carafe of wine waiting upon the table. She sighed with pleasure. Kat continued to soak until she thought all her skin would wrinkle. As the water cooled, she quickly scrubbed and lathered, finally popping out of the tub and slipping into the robe she had seen laid out earlier—probably his. Kat blushed to think of it, and shoved that idea aside. It was thick and warm, having been laid over the quilt rack near the hearth.

Kat's stomach did a quick flip and growled, reminding her that she hadn't eaten since before riding out to Isabelle's cottage ages ago. The wine had warmed her, and dulled her senses a bit more than she'd liked, but her stomach would have to be appeased before she would be able to get some sleep. Impulsively, she decided she'd slip down the back stairs to the kitchen, grab a sandwich and some fruit, and be back in the room before anyone was the wiser. All were most likely abed. It must be half past three or closer to four AM by now.

Tying the robe closed with its sash, Kat decided to forgo shoes in favor of the quiet bare feet would provide. She darted down the back servant's stairs with only a candle. A few gas sconces still lit the way, so it was easy going. Kat soon found herself in the larder. She grabbed a heel of bread, some softened cheese, and was slicing through some left over ham when she heard someone clear his throat behind her.

Kat clutched the knife in a fighting stance and pivoted. Caleb was likewise in similar undress, flannel robe of the same strong colors covered him from neck to ankle, but he was likewise barefoot, and appraising her of her attire.

She couldn't help but laugh. "Okay, I give up. Am I in the Witness Protection Program, or what?"

"Pardon? The what?"

"Never mind." Kat gestured with the knife, laughing.

"Uh, please point that elsewhere, or for the love of God will you make me a sandwich, too?"

"Sure. It's the least I can do. I owe you for the bath."

"Nonsense. Was right I did so—I think you saved her today."

Kat froze mid-slice. "Excuse me?"

"I won't tell, but I know you got help as the fool doctor didn't seem to be attending to her. You may have saved the day. My brother would be grateful if he knew of it, but my guess is it better we not talk of such things."

Kat swallowed the lump in her throat and continued slicing, avoiding his gaze. "Yes, I think that best."

"Very well then, not another word on it other than thank you."

She hurriedly finished making Caleb's sandwich and hastened to her room. Kat's stomach still growled, but her appetite was spoiled. Caleb was both charming and exceptionally sharp—a dangerous mix if she was to stay anonymous, and Helene's talents kept a secret.

34

Hopeful Beginnings

While not a son, Adele was shown no shortage of doting from her father. Alastair guarded both Helene and Adele as if sent as a sentry, he was so devoted. Kat couldn't get a moment alone with Helene as he'd ordered maids and nurses around the clock. And while she was eager to get home, Kat warmed at the thought of his pleasure in his little family.

It became quite clear that Kat was truly unnecessary and at the earliest convenience spoke to Helene hastily.

"Helene, you've no real need of me. Let me leave, I beg of you...Suzy."

"But of course." Helene beamed. The nervous, intense woman was gone and in her place, a doting mother and beloved wife. "Do you see how he loves her? She's wrapped him around her little finger already—nothing is good enough, no maid quick enough, no expense spared." Helene sighed.

"I am glad for you all, truly. It's good to see."

"Of course in a year or so we'll hope for a son, but for now all is well."

"Was it much on your mind?"

Helene looked at Kat incredulously, "Women have been put aside for less!"

"Seriously? What a load of...Alastair! Hello."

Alastair swept into the nursery with Caleb in tow. "Ah, there are my girls!" He bent to place a kiss on his wife's cheek. "How are you, my love?"

"Well. Happy."

"As well you should be. A fairer angel was ne'r birthed."

Helene laughed, "I'd say not as she favors you!"

Kat gathered up the bits of sewing that she'd taken to carrying to feign some sort of activity—a ruse, as well as many others, she tired of assuming. Kat had almost made it to her room when Caleb stayed her with a word once out in the hallway.

"Kathleen?" He paused, waited for acknowledgment that she'd heard him. "Will you leave now?"

"Excuse me?"

"Now that the baby is here safely," he gave her a knowing glance, "will you be leaving our company?"

"I hope to soon. Uh, not that I meant..."

"No offense taken. Helene had said your stay was temporary, although I know she will miss you."

"That's kind to say."

"Not kind, but rather true. Will you be back?"

Kat paused, unsure how to proceed. She knew better than to prevaricate and tried not to lie as a general principal anyway—lies, she'd found, were too hard to keep up with. "I honestly don't know. It will depend on what I find when I return home. I fear I am needed there at the moment."

"Well, then, I guess you'd better not delay."

"My thoughts exactly."

Kat left that night, ever fearful of what she'd find upon her return.

35

Perspective

True to Helene's words Kat returned home with far too many days spent on her end but within moments of leaving Suzy. This thought alone helped her begin to forgive Helene. Kat hadn't fully realized just how scared she was for Suzy—and mostly selfishly for herself, until she saw her.

Suzy lay sprawled on the shop floor, a bump forming on the side of her head where she'd hit something on her way down. She was out cold and shivering.

Kat sat there crying, holding Suzy partially on her lap, swaying and blubbering, the like of which she hadn't since Sky died. She knew Suzy was alive—her heart beat, her blood pulsed, and she breathed, but all the emotions of the last several days overwhelmed Kat now, most of which were the result of fear. How could she have risked Suzy? How could she have been so stupid? The thought of getting through life without her—unfathomable.

Since Suzy had come back into Kat's life she realized how much she had lost when she'd hid from her. Kat had stayed away so as to not feel the guilt and loss of Sky. Kat thought that by staying away she helped both of them heal, and maybe forget. But she realized now that that had been a mistake. With Suzy back in her life, Kat had more of her life to live. She had love, acceptance, and yes, parts of Sky—in her mannerisms, slang, and gestures. To run from death doesn't heal death—it delays it. Kat vowed there and then to never to take for granted those she loved. Sadly, the list wasn't very long.

Suzy woke up sometime during Kat's wailing. Likely she had nearly drowned her in her tears. Suzy was alert and watching Kat, looking a bit frightened at her sobbing.

"What's wrong? Are you hurt? Who do I need to punch?"

Kat laughed and kept crying. She didn't know how to stop the tears now that they'd begun, but the purpose changed. Leave it to Suzy to worry about her!

"Seriously, who do I need to pound?"

Kat shook her head vigorously, laughing—and crying. "No, no, Suzy, I'm fine." She wiped her eyes with the back of her sleeve, sniffling a bit in the process. "We're fine. I was just so worried about you."

"Why me?"

"Don't you remember?" Kat peered at her closely. She still hadn't let Suzy go but hugged her close, albeit awkwardly.

"Well, we were, um...oh!" Suzy eyes popped wide. "What happened? Did she tell you to bugger off?"

Kat laughed hard and heartily. "No, I got there and have been there the better part of a week. You didn't get through, and I thought you were lost...between."

"Between what?"

"That's what scared me. I didn't know if you were here, safe, or in 'limbo' or something. I don't know how this works other than you scared the crap out of me. I came back and found you passed out on the floor with a huge bump on the side of your head. I thought, I thought..."

"Shhh, shhh. It's fine, dear."

Kat didn't know how, but the cradler became the one cradled. "Then I guess you're buying the beer and telling the tale." Suzy smiled widely and then, and only then, Kat let herself believe all was okay.

Later, Suzy sat listening to Kat's tale with a bag of mini frozen peas on the side of her face, sipping a Guinness.

After she'd told all, Kat found she'd replaced fear with anger. Anger at herself for being reckless with someone she loved, but even more anger at Helene who used her when she had another option so near by.

Suzy listened, nodded at the appropriate times, and let Kat vent for a while.

"Are you done?"

"What?"

"Are you done beating yourself up for what you didn't know, what you couldn't know, and what you can't change?"

"But Suz—"

"No, you had your say, now I will have mine. I'm guessing she had her reasons not to call on her mother. Don't judge her until you know all the reasons, that'd not be fair."

Kat moved to interrupt, but Suzy waved her off.

"Don't forget I could've said no. I chose to try. I risked myself. No one makes me do anything anymore, not since that bastard ex-husband of mine has anyone made me do anything."

"But I am so angry at her. She knew. That's what gets me, she knew there was another option."

"Yes, kiddo, she did. You've a right to feel hurt, lied to, even used, but you cannot let anger chew you up. It's dangerous. It gets in you, deep, where you don't even recognize it, makes you paranoid, suspicious, bitter. It takes time away that could be spent on simple pleasure and turns it to dust."

36

Awkward Questions

Kat wondered sometimes if the anger she felt was because she'd been stressed for so long worrying about Suzy. How was Suzy able to forgive her so freely, so quickly? Kat couldn't let it go for a long time. It startled her from her sleep, manifested itself in nervous ticks when she had time in the shop with nothing pressing to do, which was often in this slow season of frosty mud and icy rain. Kat was frequently sad for no clear reason, and her nails looked like they'd been gnawed off by ravenous mice.

To be honest with herself, Kat missed it—the excitement about learning of things she'd only read about. Experiencing another world, time period, and yes, even slowing down. Kat realized she liked being treated like a lady. And part of her fear was that she'd never go back—that all of this would fade into a memory. So Kat took to wearing long, boho skirts almost daily. She experimented with her hair that curled mercilessly but made lovely tendrils when bits escaped while the rest was in a twist. Plus it kept her nervous habit at bay—if Kat kept twirling and breaking off hair she'd have a bald spot soon.

And she missed Helene. Being with Helene answered a lot of questions Kat had about herself. She now understood her empathic moments in the shop and learned to control them. Kat practiced the basic spells and manipulations she'd learned but had no real joy in it. She felt more alone than she had in ages. There's something in having someone know you, the real you, and merely accept it. While Helene wasn't exactly what Kat would call a friend, she appreciated her.

Kat mulled on these thoughts and mucked about for weeks like this when she decided to do something about it. She headed to the local library nestled in a converted stone church. Kat decided to hit the stacks and learn all she could about witchcraft and its lore. Suzy had asked her once if she would go back, and Kat had told her honestly that she didn't know if she would. She'd meant that, and still didn't know what she'd do if asked. Things had gotten far too tense at the end. But Kat did know she wanted to know more about what and who she was.

She was checking out a few titles on witchcraft when a familiar voice called her name.

"Kathleen? I thought that was you!" It was Tara. Kat hadn't seen her in ages. "Oh," she said perusing the titles, "you taking that class at the community college? I was thinking about it."

"What class?"

"Oh, sorry, I assumed. They have this mini-mester thing, in their special topics series, something like 'Women and Witchcraft in Literature.'"

"Really? When does it start?"

"I think soon. I was going to check into it, too. Sounds like fun. I need to get out of the house. After the twins were born I swear I haven't had many moments to myself. Marcy's become even more unbearable, if you can believe that. So I am avoiding the theater, and I need another excuse to escape the house a couple of nights. Plus, it will give me a taste of what going back to school would be like. I'd love to finish my nursing degree. It's expensive, but with the pay raise I'd get having it, it would pay for itself, or at least that's my pitch for selling it to Eddie." She giggled awkwardly—perhaps realizing she may have said too much. "But think about it. It'd be fun to take it with someone I know." She paused, thinking, "Hey? If this isn't for the class, what's up? This still can't be for Econ—that ended ages ago."

"Oh, just research. Econ got me thinking," Kat said, ad libbing. "New Age has been a growing business, was wondering what it's about. You know. Just research. Maybe a way to expand the shop?" She shrugged. *God, Kat, you really are such a terrible liar,* she thought.

Kat doubted she bought it. It made no sense to her, so why would it make sense to Tara? *Research witchcraft for an antique shop? What, am I selling cauldron's and shrunken heads? What was I thinking?* Kat's thoughts raced within her head. But somehow it was enough to move Tara on her way. Kat promised she'd call if she signed up for the class, and she was seriously thinking about it.

Kat thought about the class all the way home and decided by the time she'd entered the shop that she would register. Why the hell not?

She'd just gotten off the phone with the college bursar, paying for the class with her credit card, when Kat's mother walked into the shop with her friend, Irving.

"Ah, there she is, alive and well."

"Yes, Mother, I know I should've called. Hello, Irving, how are you?"

"Never mind about him. Let me look at you. What have you been up to?"

With a wary eye, Deirdre eyed the titles of Kat's library books that lay on the counter. The titles were provocative—*Everyday Spells, Mother-Maiden-Crone, Animal Lore, A Witch's Coven,* and *Wic-*

can Sexuality. She had to clear her throat and fake a cough to look away after that one.

"What's all this?"

Kat was relieved she could both lie and tell the truth at the same time as she had always been a terrible liar. Just getting accused made Kat blush as a kid, her freckles glowing traitorously, so she was always getting in trouble with no real reason. "I'm taking a class."

"Hmm, weird topic for a class. It makes me wonder with all your years of going to school, are you a college student or a shop keeper?"

"Can't I do both?"

"I suppose, but I doubt well. You'll short-change one or the other. When are you going to settle down and make grandbabies for me to spoil?"

"Candace and Tim—"

"Bah, that may never happen for either of them. Plus with Tim, I'd probably have to go on the road with him to see the kids. He's aways on the move. Couldn't send him mail if I wanted to."

"Well, Mother, as I am not married, nor dating at the moment, I'm afraid you are out of luck. Three strikes." Kat shrugged and grimaced, but Deirdre was not amused.

"Irving has a cousin that has some boys about your age, we could maybe...?"

"Ah, hell no!"

"Watch your mouth, young lady! I see you are dressing like a girl these days, but you talk like a sailor."

"And where would I have learned that?"

"Ah, fuck off!"

It was their first sincere laugh in each other's company in ages.

The mini-mester started, and Kat was eager to learn—something, anything. "Women and Witchcraft in Literature" sounded like a fascinating class. She realized that it actually was a stall tactic. Kat hadn't decided what she would do if Helene sent for her again. Kat was both curious and fearful of going back while also scared that if she didn't she'd regret it the rest of her life.

It seemed that each time Kat returned from Helene's she had more questions than when she left. The more she learned, the more she yearned to learn. Why? Kat couldn't even answer that simple question. What was she hoping to gain by learning any of this?

Kat remembered that as a teen she had watched the vampire and witch movies, dabbled with the Goth look, and dreamed of being more than average with every viewing of the X-Men and Xavier's school of special students—who didn't? When Hogwarts was the rage, she wished she'd been able to go away to school, away from her brother and sister, her overbearing mom, to be with people who were like her. But isn't that the dream of every teen?

Now to know that she had roots among the women depicted in the stories they now studied in class was surreal. Kat found that she read the stories with a double eye—one for the tale itself, one looking for clues. She'd always loved books for the escapism. But now she read with knowledge—at least her small corner of knowledge of what a witch could indeed do. It seemed the tales were divided into two camps—the fantastical, romanticized, magical stories, and those a bit more raw and based somewhat in reality. Kat discarded the first batch as creative fiction and delved into the latter, seeking for more truth. It seemed to be a jagged and dangerous history in those, filled with fear, hate, witch hunts, and suspicion. It seemed to her the suspicion of the witch was the real danger as the true witch might not even be the one pursued. Food for thought.

She was walking home from the library, a new habit Kat'd started since she last returned from Helene's—at least when it wasn't a downpour—when she saw Suzy hurrying towards her.

"Finally decided to save the planet and walk?"

"Um, not really." Kat hadn't thought about it, but when she returned to the here and now she suddenly realized how foolish it was to drive the several blocks into the town center when she could walk. In Helene's day she had walked—everywhere. One didn't harness a horse and carriage for such a small distance. Kat hadn't thought about the changes she was making, she'd just changed. Hopefully for the better.

"I wish more people walked or biked. Damned selfish planet if you ask me, using resources we don't need to use except for our own lazy demands. Good for you. Glad I got you thinking."

Kat didn't want to correct her as Suzy had been a tree-hugging, environmentalist long before it was cool to be so. She figured she'd let her have this "win."

"Yup, realized you were right. Plus, between the spring re-stocking, prep at the shop for the eventual summer tourists, and this night class, I really needed to get out and stretch my legs."

"Well, good for you."

"So what's up?"

"What do you mean?"

"You were the one chasing me down Second Avenue. What's the word?"

"Ah shit! I almost forgot—I was taken on a green tangent. I was at your shop dropping off some oatmeal cookies."

"Really? Thanks, you know—"

"Never mind that." Suzy cut her off, hands waving. "That's not important. Anyway," she caught her breath, "I went upstairs to drop the cookies off on your table with a note when I noticed you'd left your pendant out." She paused for dramatic effect. "It was pulsing, and words, if that's what you can call them, were... droning. Seemed important so I came looking for you."

Kat stopped walking, frozen in her spot, thinking about what it must inevitably mean. She was being called back. But would she heed the call?

37

The Return Call

They hurried back to Kat's rooms above the store. She pulled the matching ring from the store safe and placed it next to the pendant where it sat in its velvet-lined box. Kat watched and thought, slowly sipping English Breakfast tea while her mind raced. She mindlessly munched a still warm cookie but didn't really taste it. Every past moment spent with Helene flooded her mind. Suzy and Kat sat wordlessly, watching the pendant and ring pulse and hum in sync, in a repeating pattern. It was like the pieces were working as a beacon, cycling through the same message for a minute, and then going dark for five, and then repeating. As minutes passed Kat felt her pulse begin to echo in response. Her mind screamed for action, any action, while simultaneously frozen in fear. Somehow she began to register words rather than beats in the pattern. Kat looked up, startled, and she could see from Suzy's unchanged mannerisms that she was alone in the discovery. *Great, just great*, Kat inwardly moaned. *God, I hope I'm not simply going mad.*

The words that hummed in a monotone weren't in English, but oddly enough, after hearing them repeat in replay after replay, Kat found she could make out the meaning. She realized that once she'd stopped trying to rationalize everything when it came to Helene it became clearer. Her head ached from trying to sort it all out, trying to make a decision she wouldn't regret. It was a relief when she finally gave in and heard its message as clearly as if someone whispered it in her ear. It translated to "Help. Please come, quickly. I've need of you."

Eventually the cycled message stopped, and the pendant went cold, the red thread dimming to its normal color.

After a moment it abruptly broke her gaze. Kat had been staring at the stone intently for so long, zoned out, that its inaction startled her to alertness.

Suzy broke the silence. "Well, damn."

"Yeah." Kat resumed her tea, now sipping the cooled and forgotten cup.

"Do you have any idea what the noise meant?"

"Oddly enough, yes. I don't know how I do, but it sorted itself out after a time."

"Well?"

"Well what?"

"What'd it say?"

"She needs me back. Now."

"What are you going to do?"

"I'm not sure yet. Not sure I can really refuse. I'd feel guilty if something bad happened, but then again, I really don't want to go back. I felt trapped the last time, and I resented that. But she is my grandmother—of sorts."

"Not of sorts. She is."

Kat snorted at that and glared back at the stone, daring it to say anything more that would make the decision clear or at least easier.

"Well, while you think on it some more I'm making something for you to eat."

Kat moved to get up to help.

"No, no, you just take your time and think. Never short-change yourself moments to simply think." Suzy rustled through the cabinets, muttered something about Kat not stocking the basics and was out the door before Kat could register she'd left.

Suzy found Kat in the same spot she'd left her when she returned. Kat sat motionless, her tea cold, forgotten again in her hand.

"Did it spout its mumbo jumbo again?"

Kat nodded. "Revised message, but same intent. Seems urgent."

"Did you come to a decision?"

"I have to go." Kat shrugged, stretching her shoulders.

"I thought you'd say that. Grabbed some groceries to get your kitchen up to snuff, too. I couldn't even make a roux with what you have in your cupboards, but I brought back Chinese food from that new place on the corner in case we needed to hurry."

"You rock!"

"Yes. Yes, I do."

"You get the steamed dumplings?"

"What do you take me for?"

Kat rummaged in the closet until she found a small, silk bag to drape across her body for when she traveled. It held Suzy's herbs, although Kat needed them less and less now, and a few modern conveniences like feminine products—she shuddered to think she could live without them again, and Kat didn't know how long she'd be gone—a tube of antibiotic cream, a pack of gauze bandages, and a pen to use with the journal Helene had given her. Kat didn't know what Helene would say when and if she saw these things, but she didn't care. Helene had been calling the shots thus far, but Kat figured she needed her help so she'd have to take her as she was. The bag was small and mostly flat, so it should be unnoticeable beneath the voluminous skirts, petticoats, and the shift Kat had grown used to wearing. Only Patrice, if anyone, would ever get a chance to see these articles, and frankly, based upon what she already knew, Kat doubted she'd take a second glance, and so she'd risk it.

Kat pulled from the closet a simple cotton overdress she'd dug out of the theater closet. It was simpler than most she wore when with Helene and therefore more truly *her*. Kat used to wish for pants, but now she enjoyed the freedom skirts provided—just some of the fabrics were a bit too stiff and formal for comfort. And the lace! Thank God, her status didn't warrant much, if any, of that. It was positively cruel how badly that stuff itched.

She stopped to laugh at herself. Here she was getting ready to travel through time to meet with the family witch, and she stressed over fabric. What a life she led! Kat hesitated to bring out the last item at all. She slid the box from under her bed from where she'd stored it. While she had said, when she last returned, that she wouldn't leave home again, a side of her must've known better. She'd found a reproduction company online that made stage-ready boots to suit the period but made with modern ergonomics and soles. Kat hadn't been able to resist and told herself they were for use in the theater, when in reality she craved the comfort her modern hikers and walking shoes provided should she ever go back. She guessed a part of her already knew she would return someday. Kat scrutinized the shoes, now confident that at a glance they were passable for the period, but she also knew if someone looked at the sole, she'd be outed. Kat sat on the edge of her bed and handled the mid-calf boots, caressing the supple leather. It took her only a moment before she decided. Kat stripped off the modern laces and replaced them with those from the shoes Helene had outfitted her in last. That helped the overall appearance. As long as she kept her feet firmly beneath her, and with the help of the skirts, no one need know Kat stepped a bit more comfortably than others. She thought, *Really, what's the point of being from the future if you can't add a bit of advantage from it?*

Kat paced as she remembered that she never knew where, or for that matter, when she would arrive when Helene sent for her. As Kat slid the pendant over her head and the ring back on her finger, what she wondered most was where she'd land this time. It seemed that Helene controlled or willed her where she chose; Kat had no say in that matter. The uncertainty worried her, but she was determined to resolve and answer this part of the many questions she still had on the matter. Kat had to stay more alert to learn how this was indeed done. She was confident that as she grew more comfortable and accustomed to this mode of travel that she would unravel the mystery, much like Kat had with the secret doors. Once Helene's needs were seen to, that would be her focus of this next journey.

Kat arrived at the manor farm just in the tree line behind the farthest field most immediate to the road behind the house. Patrice was there waiting with a coach and four.

"Hello, Patrice." Kat noticed she wore Helene's pendant about her neck. Could that be some sort of beacon to draw her to where she willed? Kat had to find out this time around.

When Patrice didn't answer her, Kat probed. "Where to Patrice?"

"To the manor farm."

"We hardly need a ride. We could just cut across that field just there." Kat pointed.

"The missus thought it best you not do so but rather appear 'long-traveled.'"

Kat cocked an eyebrow. "You've no idea."

Patrice smirked. Then Kat noticed that the horses appeared tired—very much so, and in need of a rub down.

"The horses?"

"They've been worked to make it all the more true."

"But surely Mrs. Brown—"

"She suspects much, that is true, but to give her more would give her too much power over her ladyship. She thought it best to limit Mrs. Brown's thoughts on the matter. Take care you do the same, she said to advise you."

Kathleen heard the tone and wondered at it but briefly before she continued.

"Things are not as they were, Miss Kathleen. You'll soon see."

They arrived at the manor farm but moments later. Mrs. Brown did not seem pleased to see Kathleen. But according to Patrice she'd been apprised of her impending arrival.

"I found it odd that you left so soon after the birth," Mrs. Brown began.

Kat saw Patrice wince and wait for her response.

"Especially since you'd come to help with the bairn, or so you said," Mrs. Brown continued.

"It couldn't be helped." Kat mentally reminded herself to stick as close to the truth as possible—easier to maintain the story that way and fewer trip ups later. "I had to rush back as there was family that needed me most urgently. Couldn't be helped. But now that that is settled I am back to do what I can for her ladyship. Where might I find her?" Kat took on a brisk tone she thought Mrs. Brown would most respect as it was clear she resented her.

"She's in her rooms. I've prepared the room most adjacent for you. It's not so big as hers, nor so fine, as when last you stayed you stayed in her ladyship's own rooms. But I doubt you should mind much." Her eyes shifted. Kat could feel the dismissal and judgement. She should know, her own mother was a master at that look.

Kat wouldn't let Mrs. Brown know that she riled her. "I'm sure whatever you've prepared should be fine as I am not here for my comfort but hers." A glance from Patrice confirmed she had handled it just right.

"Shall I take you to the room now, Miss?"

"No," Patrice intervened, "I shall take her to her kin first and will show her to her room after. Her ladyship's been asking after her. Please see to her bag." She motioned to the small trunk in the carriage.

Bag? Kathleen made a quick adjustment to her skirts as if shaking them out after a long ride to cover her surprise at arriving with luggage. She couldn't be too careful with the sharp-eyed Mrs. Brown. Undoubtedly, Helene had ordered one packed for her. It made Kat even more anxious as it looked like they were to stay here rather than at the main estate. The question was why?

38

Legal Rights

It seemed Patrice had not only become more vocal since Kathleen last left but was handling Mrs. Brown as well. Kat found that to be an interesting and intriguing development. She was dying to ask how long she'd been gone but thought it best to deal with that when she was alone with Helene. Patrice led Kathleen up the main stairs although they both knew she could find her way—even in the cover of darkness, if need be. As Kat walked up the stairs following Patrice's slow pace, she couldn't help but remember how interminable her previous stay at the farm had felt. Doubts began to settle in her chest, but Kat reminded herself that then she had been left alone for most of her stay, quite unfamiliar with Helene and all the rest that accompanied her. Kat brushed off a brief shudder. Surely this would not be the same. She both hoped for and feared the answer to that.

Patrice held open the door. Kat stepped into the room and found Helene propped into a reclining position upon the bed.

Helene's lip was split on one side and badly swollen, blood purple. On her left temple was a knot that was the yellowed-green of a partially healed wound. Her wrists were rubbed a raw, angry red, and where her sleeve gaped Kat could see the blue-black purple of a deep bruise on her upper arm. *What the hell had happened here?* Kathleen wasn't always Helene's biggest fan but seeing her like this...she wanted to scream and punch someone. Shaking, Kat clenched and unclenched her hands at her sides as she moved closer to Helene's bedside.

Helene's eyes remained closed and her breathing rhythmic. Thinking her asleep, Kat spun around to demand an explanation from Patrice when she heard Helene's voice faintly rasp.

"I think you already know, don't you?"

Kat squared to face her. Helene grimaced, which her distorted mouth made look even more grotesque; it was a mockery of a smile.

"I have a suspicion. But why?" Kat leaned in.

"I got too happy. I got careless."

"What the devil does that mean?"

"It means I risked everything and damned myself." Clutching her side, Helene winced, took a deep breath, and struggled upright. "It means I'll have to be repentant and take care I do not cross him again."

"Helene, seriously, what is going on here?"

"He knows, Kathleen. He knows what I am and that which I come from. If it wouldn't have embarrassed him to explain my absence later, he might have killed me."

"But how? You were always so careful."

"Someone saw my mother in the house the night Adele was born. Someone who knew what she was made the connection and told him. I'd embarrassed him and risked his name. And this is the result. A warning he made quite clear with each blow so I could contemplate my path to redemption."

Furious, Kat panted and struggled to regain control of her breathing. "Redemption! But you'd done nothing wrong! You needed help that that fool doctor would've neglected. Maybe if I explain; I could say that—"

"He has Adele."

The words were like a slap of cold water, an insurmountable wall. Kathleen stood silently, letting the truth of the situation sink in. She shook her head with sadness, and tears welled in her eyes as she thought of how happy Helene had been when she had last seen her. Kat felt weak, helpless. She couldn't imagine how Helene felt.

"How long has it been since you've seen her?"

"Nine days."

"Nine? But the lip?"

"A refreshing reminder when he came to see me yesterday. Nothing more."

Internally, Kat shuddered to think how men in this time could so beat a woman—and it be his right, his due. It dawned on her that to read about this in a textbook was far different than to see the law exercised firsthand, with someone you cared about. She took a deep breath and sighed. Kat felt helpless.

"What can we do?"

"We wait in hopes of earning his forgiveness. Thankfully, Adele has a bit of me that should serve to remind him of his wife. Meanwhile, I need your help in healing."

"But I know little to nothing about healing... Your mother."

"She can never come here ever again if I am to live through this and see Adele again!"

"You can't be serious! She's the most skilled healer. Surely he would allow her to—"

"He said I was tainted by the very devil himself. He said that a wife of his cannot be connected to a common hedge witch. He's had her removed, paid the servant for her silence in doing such a duty, and sent her away where her words will matter to none."

"Removed?"

"His words, not mine." Helene's eyes took on a far away look, gazing but unseeing. "I believe she has left the county and wanders." Her voice trailed off.

Kat wondered if Helene's thoughts followed the steps of her mother.

The next several days were largely spent at Helene's bedside. Since she was lucid, albeit weak, she led Kat through her knowledge of poultices and herbal remedies. She'd send her out to the gardens and green house; together those had most of the ingredients needed to suit her needs. Patrice went with Kathleen sometimes to help her locate some of the more elusive ingredients or those more difficult to identify. Kat felt a bit guilty during that time in the sun as those moments away from Helene's sickbed were something she looked forward to. The time with the plants was the only reprieve Kat had from her bedside and the stale smells of the room.

But largely the main healers were time and hearty broths. As Helene's bruises faded she grew hopeful of being restored to the estate and her daughter. She became unnaturally chipper, like the syrupy cheerful demeanor of a stage performer. She preened in front of the mirror, attempted to camouflage with both her physical and magical arts the damage Alastair had wrought. When she was not satisfied, she became frustrated, and threw her brushes and pots of creams aside in despair. Kat would retreat into her own room or the garden. She'd learned to let Helene have her fits alone. There was no containing her anger—it was best to let it run its course. Helene developed a nervous energy, one that Kat couldn't always predict how it would be relieved. Oftentimes it was not pleasant. The broken pottery and tossed coverlets could be easily forgiven. But the vulgar epithets and unwarranted accusations, while understood to be a product of her feelings of helplessness and frustration, were ultimately shards of venom that were sometimes hard to not take personally.

And so Kathleen read to her. She would do anything to take Helene's mind off of Adele. It was most often after these times that Kat thought it odd that Helene never asked about what her life or the world became. It seemed to Kat that Helene fervently denied anything existed other than this moment, this time. Occasionally, Kat would begin to tell her stories, albeit unasked, and Helene pointedly refused to hear any of it, even of the most mundane details about Kathleen's friends and family; she wanted none of it. It were as if Helene willed Kat's previous life to be non-existent. It was only Kathleen Evans who existed in the here and now. Kat couldn't put her finger on it, but it worried her.

Kathleen had learned a lot already during her current stay in the past. The farmhouse no longer seemed an outpost while she had the company of Helene and Patrice. And while she knew she couldn't consider returning home until Helene was safely restored to her own home, Kat began to miss her routine, her things, her bed, her life. So Kat took to taking walks, long walks where she could think. Helene's dilemma frustrated and angered her, but there was nothing she could do—especially when Helene seemed resigned to 'amend' her ways to be restored to Alastair's favor.

Kat had just returned from a short walk to gather some blue bells and daffodils to brighten Helene's room when she heard voices and followed them to the front parlor. She was surprised to see Helene and Caleb having tea and what looked to be a lively conversation.

Both looked up as Kathleen awkwardly stepped in. She was speechless at the scene that presented itself before her. Her mouth hung open a moment too long to have been unobserved.

Helene looked up at Kat and smiled her slow, languorous smile, and with an elegant sweep of her arm, offered Kathleen the empty seat by her side.

Kat stood a moment transfixed, processing what she saw, and eyeing Helene closely. More in tune with Helene now, Kat could detect the tiniest winces of pain through the slightest of flickers in Helene's eyes but nothing else betrayed her. She had seen to all else, using her power and magical skills to affect a glow of health. As she hesitated longer, Kat saw Helene's eye flash heat in warning, and she quickly took the offered seat.

"There you are." Helene began brightly.

Kat knew Helene's carefully controlled tone did not reveal what the effort took of her.

"I was just telling Caleb that you'd returned for a visit, and I was familiarizing you as to the workings of the farm should you decide to stay and help with the overseeing of the domestic staff. Alastair's expansions will, of course, demand more travel on my part as my place is at his side, and your assistance can help fill the void I would leave—at least temporarily at times."

All of this was news to Kat, but a flicker of Helene's warning glare told her otherwise, and Kat went along with the ruse.

"There is so much to learn. It seems my cousin does the work of five women with all she's responsible for both here and at the manor." Kat fluttered her eyelashes—a mockery she knew Helene would later tell her was not appreciated, but Caleb either didn't notice it or was too polite to say otherwise.

Caleb seemed quietly reflective for a moment, cleared his throat, and then smiled warmly at Helene. "Ah, but surely I have taken too much of your time already. I only meant to stop in for a quarter hour as I seemed to have missed you each time I inquired at the house. I must let you go about your business. How Alastair can stand to have you away even but a moment I cannot fathom." He winked and again smiled at Helene. Kat realized he was giving her an excuse to leave and return to rest—and it was smoothly done. Caleb rose to acknowledge her leaving with a bow but did not turn to watch her go. When Kat, too, rose to join her, Caleb stayed her with a hand at her wrist.

Kat strained to watch as Helene made her way to the base of the stairs before Patrice was at her side to half carry her back to bed. Her efforts to appear well exhausted her. She'd pushed her limits. Kat's eyes followed her until she rounded the corner. Kat turned to look at Caleb, who had in turn been watching her the whole time. She felt a moment of panic, wondering if any emotion had played across her face, giving her away.

"Did you need to speak with me?"

Caleb looked intently into her eyes. Awkwardly, moments passed before he spoke. He shifted the hand he used to stop her departure until his fingers gently intertwined with her own. "Is she hurt badly?"

"I don't know what you—"

"Dammit! We both know what happened and by whom. Will she heal fully?" Kat saw concern replace the anger in his eyes.

"Yes, I believe so," she muttered with downcast gaze. Caleb gently touched her chin and lifted it, making her face him.

"You needn't fear me. I do not take after my brother or his ways. If I could fix things for her, I would. But for now, I will trust you have matters in hand. Please let me know if you have need of me or if I may assist in any way. Do not hesitate to contact me. I am at the big house at the moment, assisting Alastair in his expansion process. I should be staying quite some time...as I hope you will, as well." Caleb gave Kat's hand a quick squeeze before releasing it with a short bow. He hastily gathered his things to leave. "But for now, do what you can and trust in me. I'll be back to check on matters from time to time as well as to work on loosening my brother's heart."

Caleb gently ran two fingers down the side of Kathleen's face as he spoke and now, with the absence of his touch, Kat felt a chill. She pulled her wrap about closer, and as much as Kat really didn't want to, she rose to follow Helene back to her sick room.

39

Deadly Secrets

As the days passed, Helene steadily grew better, and Alastair began to come around to visit from time to time. It nauseated Kat to see her bow and coo as if nothing had happened, nothing mattered, save pleasing him. She couldn't understand how Helene, a witch of some power, could cower and bend to a man's will like that. Kat vacated Helene's rooms when he arrived as she knew she wouldn't be able to keep the disdain she felt off her face nor lie convincingly of his welcome. Helene knew it, too, and so let Kat be—for both their sakes.

One such afternoon Kat wandered the grounds aimlessly and found herself at the edge of the wood she had discovered so long ago. It seemed a world of time ago. She'd almost forgotten her prior interest in the abbey. Ironically, the same desire to return home and get away from Helene drove her here. That much Kat could recall quite clearly.

With ease, Kat returned to the abbey churchyard she'd promised herself all that time ago to explore, brushing away the wind and storm as one would a gnat. With Helene's help, although she was largely bedridden, Kathleen had developed in the Craft. The result being improved confidence in her skills. It appeared confidence bred success. Kat wanted to laugh when she realized it was much like that motivational poster from the '70s—if she could "see it" she could "be it." The protection charm that had seemed a challenge prior was now but a mist of lies.

Kat wandered around the abbey grounds, enjoying the peace and privacy that the safeguards to keep intruders out were sure to afford her. For a few moments, she hummed along to an Aerosmith song that played only in her head when she heard a familiar growl—she'd forgotten the dogs.

She turned slowly to face the sound. At full attention and standing stock still, were three of the biggest hounds Kat had ever encountered in her life. They seemed even bigger than when last she remembered. Black with brindled fur, the beasts snarled and snapped in warning. When Kathleen stepped toward the graveyard, they squared up, formed a line, and growled all the more loudly. Kat stopped where she stood. She thought about making a run for the tree line as she knew from prior experience that that was where their boundary lay but then realized something. Why would they stop at the tree line? Why not pursue? With their speed and hunting capability, undoubtedly no one could outpace them. Then why give up so easily? Part of Kat was screaming at her subconscious to shut up, let blessings lie and make it to the tree line, but another side of her wondered. If the wind, rain, and storm were to keep her from the church, what did they protect?

Kat turned to face them. They slowly advanced. Her knees quaked, but she stood her ground while mentally being thankful she had worn her modern boots; they might afford more traction if she'd guessed wrong and needed to bolt for the trees. Kat took a small step forward. The dogs seemed to swell in size and ferocity. Another step and more of the same.

It was clearly an elaborate illusion but why? Kat threw back her capelet across her back and closed her eyes. It took all the courage she had not look at the threat directly and ignore the low growls that rumbled from their chests. With eyes closed Kat centered her thoughts within like Helene had taught her for basic healing spells. She drew deep, slow breathes and raised her arms slowly, directly overhead. And then, with a huge, expelled breath, Kat's eyes snapped open. She dropped her arms quickly down to her sides in a slashing movement to see the hounds blow apart like dried leaves in a storm. Triumphant, Kat dusted off her skirts, stood a bit taller, righted her shoulder covering, and entered the small churchyard cemetery.

"Just what were you protecting? Or hiding?" Kat muttered out loud. She moved slowly through the gravestones, catching a name here and there in the carvings, but most were so weather-worn that not much more than a partial date or name could be read. Time had been an unkind caretaker. Kat felt drawn deeper and deeper within the hallowed grounds, almost to the wall of the church itself, to a stone of pink marble. An obelisk, it appeared recently erected, undisturbed by time. But as Kat paced around it, she could find no markings anywhere on its surface. That couldn't be right. Another lie, she was sure of it. As she stared, the stone flickered, in and out of sight, in and out of existence. It was both here and not. Kat concentrated on the ground upon which she saw it last and willed it to appear, muttering the words of a spell unknown to her consciousness. When it blinked back into being she let her hands slide up the face. Later, if asked, she wouldn't be able to recount what she said but rather that she felt the ancient words rumble from somewhere deep, words that while unknown to her, echoed with the emotion she imparted them with.

Kat called to the stone much like she had that hidden doorway in Caleb's former room. She entreated it to reveal its message. Slowly Kat felt a shift and crack. The stone began to age, and weather marks pitted its smooth facade. The pink surface dulled to common stone, and the markings revealed themselves as if carved before her that very moment. First the date was unearthed, a mere five months hence. When the name became clear so did so much more. Kat hoisted her skirts and dashed to return to Helene—Helene would know how to explain the things she had seen, or at least Kat prayed she would.

When Kathleen returned to the manor farm she was met by the scowling Mrs. Brown.

"If you are looking for the missus, you've missed her."

"Missed her? I didn't know she was going anywhere today. She would've told me."

"She might've told you had you been about, but you were nowhere to be found. A message and a carriage arrived from the big house. She was wanted at home. I'm to tell you to pack her things and meet her there as soon as can be managed. Although I don't know why she trusts you to do it when you are always off hither and yon."

Kat paid her no mind but set off up the steps, bounding several at a time. By Kat's estimate no more than a quarter hour had passed before all was ready and waiting in the back larder for the carriage to return for her. If it were just herself Kat would've taken the time to walk the fields. It would've given her both action and the time to think through what she would say to Helene when she did get to her. However, with all the boxes and bags Patrice had squirreled away over the last few weeks, there was no way Kat could carry it all without the help of the carriage. Just getting it all down the stairs had been a task in itself, Mrs. Brown being notably absent, as were the kitchen help, regardless of her calls for assistance. It annoyed Kat to no end that they'd stoop to such petty games. She realized who Mrs. Brown reminded her of—Wayne's mother. Some things never change.

When the carriage finally arrived, the ride itself was frustratingly slow. And as there was no emergency, Kat couldn't justify asking the driver to bring the horse to a trot. Each plodding step beat tension in her breast. No matter how she thought about it there simply was not a good way to broach the topic of Helene's impending death. It would be a shock for her to hear to be sure. Kat wondered, *just how does one begin such a conversation?*

40

The Wrong Foot

Kathleen jumped down from the carriage almost before it stopped. She left the bags to the driver and housemaids and set out to find Helene. In all her thinking during the interminable ride the only thing she had determined with certainty was that she must tell Helene immediately, come what may of it.

Her rooms were empty. Kat dared not check the room between the walls physically but knew them to be empty nonetheless when she placed her hand upon the wall and sought mentally within. Kat looked out from her windows where she could see a large expanse of the gardens and those, too, were empty. She made her way to the morning room, knowing, if anything, Helene would return here for afternoon tea. Instead, she came across Caleb.

His back was to Kathleen. He seemed to be contemplating his cigar. Before Kat could sneak away unnoticed, Caleb called to her although he stayed turned away.

"I've realized you are the key to what has been troubling me lately."

"Excuse me?"

"Come and sit. It's rude to speak to someone's back."

Kat resisted the temptation to say that it was he that had put himself in that situation, not she.

"I need to find Helene."

"She's with Alastair. She will have no need of you at the moment."

As it seemed she would have to wait a bit longer, Kat chose a seat directly opposite him, but Caleb still avoided her gaze.

"Well?" Kat prodded.

"It was the other day when things began to make a bit more sense, you see." Caleb looked up at her expectantly but at her blank gaze continued. "Finally, I had some proof that what I felt to be true was indeed so."

"What on earth are you talking about?" Kat had no time for his nonsense and made a move as if to rise to go.

"What on earth indeed?" Caleb paused. "Let me explain. For some time now I've had a feeling...oh, it is difficult to explain." He held his hands out as if trying to grasp or grapple with something. "I've known that things here are not as they should be."

"Alastair."

"No, not just Alastair and that situation, but long before that. It's just that...it's been," Caleb sought for the right words, "it's been a ridiculously long year. Extended. Stretched thin." Seeing Kathleen wasn't grasping his thoughts, he continued. "It's like déjà vu. Have you ever had déjà vu?"

Kat nodded, "Yes."

"Well, I have it all the time. Everything seems as if it has happened already, recycled itself, and happened again. A new incarnation if you will."

"I have no idea what you are talking about."

"Yes, yes, I think you do. You see it was you that proved I wasn't going mad."

"I don't see how that is possible. I have no idea what you mean."

"You see, since I am always in a feeling of perpetual déjà vu, I have time to be observant. Things I would've noticed no longer interest me as I have seen them at some time, somehow, already. It's as if time has been stretched like toffee—spread thin and elongated. It's made me cannily observant. I only now notice what is novel or new. Like that pendant you wear—I've seen that before."

"Well of course you have. It's Helene's."

"No, no, it was on someone else, and the ring, too. But weren't there ear bobs that went with the lot?" Caleb scratched the side of his head.

"Who? What are you talking about?'

"I would think you know. It's all hazy in my head. I know it to be so, but it's been muddled as if in a dream. But I know it to be true...and I think you do as well. I can see it in your face. A niggling of truth, an unanswered question. I feel mad, but I know I am not. This is where you come in to the story, literally." Caleb paused, eagerly, as if leading Kathleen to an astonishing discovery. "Where are you from, truly?"

"Excuse me?" When Kat saw that he was serious in his questioning she grew frightened. "You know where, a few counties to the south where my mother has a—"

"No, no, you misunderstand me. I don't mean what you have told the others. I am asking for the truth."

Kat rose brusquely, arranging her skirts and turned to leave.

He said it so lowly, so softly she barely heard. "It's in your step, your footstep."

Kat whipped about. "Are you nuts? Truly? What is wrong with you?"

Caleb laughed and came to stand near her. "The day I visited you at the manor farm with Helene, you came in a bit muddied from scrabbling about the weeds and hedges in search of flowers or some such.

"I don't scrabble," Kat muttered.

"Yes, yes, you do. I've seen you, but that aside, that's not important. That day you left very distinct footprints outside the back door—the likes of which I have never seen before. So I ask you again, where are you from truly? Or should I say *when*?"

Visibly startled, Kat gave herself a quick shake, and fought the urge to look down at the offending boots. She stood mute, an arm's span away from him, and simply looked Caleb in the face while she could feel her heart quicken. It beat as if it would burst out of her chest. What would happen to Helene if he knew the truth? Kat's mind fought for a plausible explanation. She feared she might pass out. Caleb stood unfazed although Kat knew she was a terrible liar and was sure her face, and the emotions that raced across it, betrayed her.

After a few uncomfortable moments, Caleb spoke. "I've known for quite some time that Helene is 'special.' However, when you arrived things seemed even more out of joint. And then the footprint confirmed what I already knew." He paused, and looked entreatingly into Kathleen's eyes. "You're smart, and witty, and loud. You say what you mean and feel at all times. You know things you shouldn't and don't know things you should. In short, you don't belong here because you never have."

Kat blinked but said not a word. She had no idea what she could say that wouldn't make it all worse.

"For God's sake, put me out of my misery and tell me I am not imagining things." Caleb reached for and took Kat's hand and covered it with his other.

Part of Kat wanted to, part of her wanted to trust him and in turn have someone on her side who knew the truth of it all. But there was another side that feared for Helene, and likewise, her own safety. Kat didn't know what to say or do to protect Helene.

She'd been clear about Alistair's thoughts on the matter. But he looked so sad and pathetic, Kat had to say something.

"I would like to speak with you, honestly, but I simply can't. Helene..."

"Ah, Helene," Caleb dropped her hand, "but of course. I understand your hesitancy. But rest assured—"

"No, that I cannot do until I speak with her. I've news to bring her of the utmost import, and you are scaring me."

"Well then, let's get you to her and continue this at a later time...I am sure I have nothing but," Caleb said and sighed heavily.

41

Finally Some Honesty

She found Helene in what was to be the future schoolroom by day and playroom to the children born in to this house. Alastair held Adele high on his shoulder while Helene clung to the crook in his arm, smiling broadly. They were following the architect as he led about the upper rooms of the house, talking of dormers and window seats and the like.

Kat tried to get Helene's attention, making awkward hand and facial gestures, but she got the sneaking suspicion that she was being pointedly ignored.

Caleb, who had followed behind, witnessed Kathleen's frustration. He intervened, calling Alastair aside on some feigned matter of importance regarding a venture. With a quick wink at Kat, he drew Alastair away, succeeded in getting him to step to the far side of the room to discuss business. Alistair still carried the sleeping Adele.

Kat took her chance at a quick moment and came to stand at Helene's side.

"Please, I must speak with you immediately."

Helene continued to watch her husband walk away, their daughter on his shoulder. Her eyes glowed with love, a fixed smile upon her lips. Once she saw Alastair was deeply engrossed by whatever Caleb had to say, she turned to face Kat with a low growl. Her face contorted into a sneer.

"What? What is it that you should interrupt what we are doing here? Unbelievable, Kathleen, you are so daft! I have only just come home and back into his graces. Do not risk my fall again, I warn you."

Taken aback to be treated so, Kat's face must have shown her shock even as she watched Helene's temper cool. Kat worked to control her emotions, her eyes narrowed as she forced herself to mirror the cold she felt.

"I assure you it is of the utmost importance that I speak to you at your earliest convenience, my lady." Kat proudly enunciated her wording and punctuated it with a curtsy. Kat could see Helene's face soften, perhaps with the pangs of regret, but she couldn't be sure. She didn't wait to find out, but rather turned heel and returned to her chamber to fume.

"He doesn't let me hold her. Ever. Alastair always has her with him or with the nurse. It's a subtle but continued threat. She carries my very heart and soul, and he keeps her from me in warning that should I step out of line, I shan't see her. It's torment, truly, and it's driving me mad. I just need time to win him back until he trusts me again."

Helene had come to Kathleen's room long after everyone was asleep. She tugged Kat awake with her tale. And while Kat sympathized with her, truly, she found it all revolting nonetheless. Sure, she'd read of these dark ages of marriage but to see it first hand was an abomination Kat found hard to stomach.

"Just give me time. It won't be long, I am sure. Few men can resist adoration and a gracious curve for long." Helene attempted to joke as a small smile crooked the side of her face.

Kat decided not to sugar-coat her words as time was short. "It's you, Helene. You are in danger. How and why I do not know, but I saw..." She drew in a deep breath before rushing on, "I saw your tombstone carved with a date not long from now. It's..." She paused to see Helene's reaction. Kat knew it would be tough news to take—if at all believed.

Helene appeared to shrink, as if drawing herself in from within. Her eyes looked vacant, uncomprehending for a moment or two. It was as if she were a candle that was about to be blown out but wavering. Kat continued to watch when suddenly her eyes brightened like a flame renewed, fiercely glowing until they pierced Kat's.

"Of course I know of the marker's existence. I placed it there myself. I put the shields around the site. It is funny that you, of such natural talents, do not recognize my handiwork so readily. I have always known. It was long foretold. And repeatedly." Her eyes cooled and dimmed momentarily as if she were elsewhere, remembering.

"But it makes no sense. How can the stone exist if you are here and now and it hasn't happened yet. I don't understand. Surely it can't be real? Just a warning, maybe?"

"Always can't..." Helene sighed. "I will try to explain, but I will be brief, enough to quell your curiosity so you'll let me be. You meddle and question too much already." She ignored Kat's look of insult and continued quickly. "You exist, so time has, in reality, moved forward, and so, too, the stone exists.

Helene waved Kat off when it looked like she would interrupt. "I will someday die, as we all will," Helene began to pace, gesturing with her hands. She sought her words carefully. "Caleb speaks of feeling *stretched*, yes?" She turned to search Kat's face for the truth in it.

Kat stayed mute and only nodded.

"I've heard him mutter so from time to time. No pun intended. In this place, this time, the clock has been replayed, extended. Untampered with, the stone would become reality. I first saw its manifestation when your grandmother was here. A pesky side effect of calling her back...you see, I had seen what was to come. No time to bother about the details of that now, but in my haste to draw Edy back to avoid my destiny, it, that offensive bit of marble followed her through somehow."

Helene drew herself up, straightening her back and squaring her shoulders as if ready to battle. "And in my fear of things to come, things I previously only suspected *might* became *would*, and I was too rough with her. Simply put, the stone will exist—in your time most assuredly, the question is when in my time."

"But why? The date. How?" Kat sputtered.

Helene laughed a hard, cold laugh. "I think you know the answer to that as well as you've been witness to the results of his handiwork. You should know that men of great power demand their right. It is their best and worst trait combined—successfully wrought, it will yield great wealth and influence for years to come."

"Then leave him now and live!"

"Foolish girl. How? Return to whatever hovel or shanty my mother has retreated to? Find a cave to hide in from the angry mobs? No!" She shook her head. "I'll not go backwards when I have risen so far. This time I will not lose—I will not succumb. This time I will be the victor. I can almost taste it."

Kat shivered as Helene's voice lowered, calm and purposeful now as she continued, "I must be patient and play my hand carefully, and then nothing will stand in the way of my making." Kat let Helene's words roll over her, absorbing them, finally understanding as the puzzle pieces began to shift into place.

"Caleb said he felt as if time recycled..."

"Yes, yes, Caleb is astute. Couldn't be helped. Each time as the date of my predicted demise would near I'd check the signs and the stone. And so far, I haven't been able to divert the date by more than a few weeks. It's funny. I used to resent the grave marker as the omen of doom, but its date is not a fixed point. Leave it to Caleb to notice the subtleties of everyday life. Too bad he was the younger brother or I might have made a go of it with him. He is far more evolved than his powerful brother. Too bad."

Kat ignored that remark. It was too cold and calculating to respond to. "He notices things… he recognized the pendant and ring from somewhere else. Said there had been ear bobs, too."

Helene smiled the languorous smile of a cat with its cream. "Leave it to Caleb to remember that detail in spite of everything…" She drifted off dreamily for a moment. "Yes, there had been ear bobs. Helped with the balance—that's why you are so nauseated each time you travel. The bobs fixed that little problem, but they are gone now, somewhere, I know not."

"But didn't Suzy…?"

"No, no, not those. For bobs to work they have to be of the same set, the same forming. It's in the creation that…never mind. They are gone."

"Who, then who wore—"

"Who wore them last? Truly? You know the answer to that. Your grandmother wore them last, just a bit ago."

"But that was ages ago! Decades. Caleb certainly couldn't—"

"Don't you remember? I told you it was months ago in my time, decades in yours."

Kat stood as if struck. Oh my God, it was all too clear now. She berated herself, how hadn't she seen, understood it all? "Then why? Why me? Why now?"

"I guess I owe you that much explanation," Helene sighed. "With you here, my power is redoubled, magnified, if you will. Your blood is my blood; power draws to power like me to Alastair."

"And with me here you hope to overcome Alastair? Is that it? You'd use me to beat him?"

"'Use' is such an ugly word. I mean to get past this hump with your help, and then the world is open to all sorts of opportunity. I mean to lead and build with my husband. I mean to fashion a fortune that will rival the likes no one has seen. I mean to grow and build and succeed as no woman has."

"But the stone, your name, the date?"

"Merely what was to be but not what is—not now. I've learned where I failed and am correcting it all. It shall not be a truth but only a possibility soon erased. I am so close."

"So you would cheat Fate?"

"Fate!" Helene swelled and grew, filling the room with her presence. She was both glorious and terrifying. "I defy Fate! Since when do you, from your modern world, acknowledge Fate? You would demand her place, her choices, and not be dictated to? And yet you ask me to accept Fate?"

"No, no, that's not what I meant. I only—"

"You know nothing! What you know I have provided you with, nothing more. You shall help me get past this ripple in time, and you shall see for yourself that I have not fought, scratched, and cajoled my way this far to slide into nothingness. My daughter will know me, and I shall beget others. I have seen that future unfold as well, and it is a good one."

Kat shook. This was far more than she ever imagined—Helene was pulsing with rage. Kat had never seen her so angry. It was like Helene's mask had fallen and, revealed behind it, had been a beast all along. Kat wanted out—and now.

"I want no part of this. I want to go home."

"Well too bad, little girl, you're not to leave—not until this bit is done, and I have no more use of you. You shall stay and await my need of you."

Kat felt as if she had been slapped for indeed she was. Helene made it clear she had put Kat in her place. She was trapped, broken, and so, so alone. That was the worst of it—knowing she was helpless, with no way home, and at Helene's mercy. Kat felt beaten, much like an abused dog, left to creep into the corner to lick her wounds. Thankfully, Helene swept out of the room, closing the door with a final flourish. Kat was left to her thoughts and her fears of being trapped here for good. Kat crawled back into her bed and pulled the covers up under her chin. She shivered, but now not from the cold, as she imagined the worst.

42

Feeling Ill

Kat spent most of that evening and the night staring into the darkness, letting the shadows playing off of her one lantern feed her despair and fears. She soon knew she hadn't been far from the truth. It quickly became apparent that she was indeed trapped here.

At some point Kat must have succumbed to sleep for a bit. When she finally got out of bed several hours later she found a cold breakfast by the hearth. Much later, Patrice returned, bringing her her supper on a tray. Kat'd been so upset she'd worn herself out between the pacing in the morning, the frustrated pillow punching, and then the unavoidable jag of tears as she cowered under her covers. At some point she must've fallen asleep and missed the midday meal.

When Kathleen asked about the room service, Patrice gave her a tight-lipped, wan smile and said the missus said she was ill and to be left to rest. Kat snorted in response. She wasn't overly surprised. Seemed to be Helene's style—to confront, and then push aside. Kat was used to her moods swings by now—or at least observant enough to acknowledge this to be one. She told herself not to worry just yet. It was sure to blow over. It had to, didn't it?

However, the following morning when Kat tried to go down for breakfast, she found the door sealed shut. Not bolted, no key, but sealed. *Dammit!* Kat racked her brain for what magic she knew to try to remove the blockage and nothing worked. She was stymied. Her heart fluttered—she could feel it beat within her chest. Kat slowly exhaled to control her breathing. And then she got angry. She'd rather be pissed than scared anyway. This was all Helene's fault! This was taking it too far. Kat strode over to where she knew the secret passage to be and went through her routine to release the door and reveal it to her. Nothing worked. It was as if nothing were there. Kat's anger simmered. She eyed the concealed door that she knew stood on the other side and cursed up a blue-streak. She'd used every foul word she knew and invented some creative obscenities when Kat heard the main chamber door slide open. She whipped about, ready to blast Helene for her selfishness and bad behavior but was faced with Patrice.

Kat quickly tried to contain her anger with a deep breath. "Ah, Patrice, thank God. The door was stuck and I..."

Patrice gave Kat a knowing glance. Her one eyebrow cocked like Kat had seen Helene do so many times before. She felt nauseated and swallowed the bile that rose in her throat upon seeing the same mannerism repeated. It was enough to silence her.

"I've brought your breakfast...as you've been taken so ill."

"Seriously, Patrice, we both know that I am not ill. What is going on?"

She came closer, and spoke lowly, in almost a whisper, "And we both know she can make you ill if she chooses to."

Kat's eyes popped wide. Oh my God, she was right. Kat kept giving Helene the benefit of the doubt when she'd shown herself time and time again to be a vindictive, power-hungry witch. Kat should've known not to trust her.

"What do I do, Patrice?" Kat struggled to control her voice so that she wouldn't detect her desperation. She knew it was a fine line before she cried, and she hated criers. Kat would be damned if she became one now!

"I'd stay put. At least that is the worst of it as I see it. Wait it out."

"How long do you think I'll be stuck here?"

"A few days, maybe a week. You are family so I would think she'll get over it soon."

Kat took the tray, nodded thanks. She gave Patrice no trouble but rather hurried her off as best she could while trying not to seem to do so. Something Patrice said had her thinking... Kat was family. And that is exactly why Helene wanted her kept here. Kat had no idea what Helene had in mind or how she could augment her power, but Patrice's efforts to reassure Kat actually served to remind her as to who she was dealing with. For the first time since Kat arrived to this time she felt truly afraid, deep in her bones afraid. She shivered. If Helene concocted all this to stall Fate, if she feared Alastair as it seemed she truly did, then what was Kat but a means to an end for her? Kat knew for certain she was trapped now. Helene would never let her go. Kat was on her own. She had to find a way to get away, and soon. But how? She had always been the one serving as a beacon, calling or allowing Kat to come. How would she get back home without her? Kat, who could always muster an appetite, was no longer hungry as this worked upon her mind.

Days went by and Kathleen began to make Helene's story true—she felt ill and weak. The mental stress and lack of appetite finally caught up with her. She seldom ate and slept often—partially to pass the time and partially, Kat suspected, because she was being drugged into sleep. Kat couldn't fight it; she was hopeless and helpless. Her energy waned and depression set in, but beneath it all her anger simmered. How dare Helene use her so? Kat couldn't think of a way out of her predicament.

Kat sat before the window in the wingback chair, staring blindly out when Patrice, her only contact from the outside, came in bearing a tea tray. Kat grunted in acknowledgment, nothing more. She expected no words as days ago there ceased being a reason to speak at all, each day the same as the last. Patrice wouldn't or couldn't help. She disgusted Kat. She was her only link to the outside world, and she might as well have been a stone wall. Kat couldn't move her.

Patrice went about the room straightening this and that, gathering items to launder, and stopped to pull back the curtains wider to let the breeze circulate the room when she heard voices below. Kat rose to stand in the shadow of the curtain and leaned just far enough to see but not be seen, and there was Helene. She was laughing and smiling in greeting to Alastair and his brother who had apparently been away as evidenced by the bags that the servants were unloading. Kat saw Caleb glance at her window, and Helene nodded her head slowly and soberly—undoubtedly continuing the story of Kat's unrelenting illness. She watched them all turn to enter the house, save Caleb, who stopped once more to look up sadly at her window.

Kat was tempted to reveal herself, but she knew she was being watched as Patrice gathered the dishes. She dared not risk it. And for what? Would Caleb rescue her? Sure, he claimed to be observant, but that meant nothing against the likes of Helene. Even Patrice, while somewhat sympathetic to Kat's plight, was her mistress's creature. No, it was quite clear that Kat was on her own, and if anything were to be done, she would need to do it soon. Kat had little fire left in her, and that scared her the most.

When Patrice had finished and shut the door behind her, Kat went though the tiresome and hopeless routine of checking to see if she was indeed again locked in, sealed tight, and she was. She checked more now out of habit than any deluded hope. But the voices had given Kat an idea. She went to the window where sat a few remaining blooms in a vase. Kat stood near the window and cast the petals loose through the opening. To her surprise, the petals wafted away freely with no restraint. She had surely thought that when Helene sealed the doorways from her escape that the window would of course follow. Kat kicked herself for wasting all this time! Why, oh why, hadn't she tried the window earlier? She felt so stupid.

Careful to remain unnoticed, Kat peered over the ledge. Two stories down below her window was a well-established hedge of roses. That, and only that, stood between her and the ground. That must've been what had made Helene feel secure in her trap. She'd never thought that Kat would attempt leaving in such a manner. There was no vine, no branch, no ledge—nothing that might serve as a toehold. Climbing down was not an option. Nope, Kat would have to free-fall it or nothing. She tried not to worry overmuch over that. And, furthermore, once she jumped, should she bound farther and miss the hedge, the stones of the shale and gravel pathway would be likewise painful, if not bone-breaking. Kat gulped at the thought.

But then Kat had to smile. Helene had used logic when it came to the only outlet from the room she could see. But Helene had not grown up in Kat's house, with her family, and didn't know that a lady could and should behave like a nine-year-old boy if the provocation was tempting enough.

Kat had to try it out right away. Partially, she was afraid she'd chicken out and change her mind out of fear of the thorns or the fall. She'd had her share of scrapes and falls, and she was not eager to repeat the agony. But Kat soon decided she would wait until twilight, when they all would be at the back of the house in the lounge with their after dinner brandy and, undoubtedly, tales of Alastair's latest business conquests. Kat would have the best chance of slipping out then, even if she ended up having to hobble away. Either way it was action, and she needed that.

43

Leap of Faith

The dinner dishes were cleared away. She'd only picked at the offerings, instead moving the food about her plate to make it appear she'd eaten. Kat had also skipped the wine as that was most likely the carrier of the sleeping potion she'd been drugged with nightly. As per routine, Kat knew she wouldn't be disturbed until breakfast the next day. The door had barely closed when she dropped the sketch book she'd affected to look busy and bounded across the room. The thought of action, even an ill-conceived plan like she had, pumped her full of energy. Kat flung open the wardrobe and pulled all the outerwear she could find, rolled everything out, one atop the other on the floor, creating layers of wool. She placed the cottons on top of that, and finally, her thickest cloak.

Kat stopped a moment to think. She hadn't thought much past getting away. And then what? She had no real ideas after escaping the house. Surely that in itself should be an improvement? Her mind raced, searching for an idea, any idea. Maybe she could simply hide away until after the date of Helene's demise and then see what would be? Kat shuddered at the thought of staying here that long in the past. What if she couldn't leave without Helene? *Oh my God!* Kat groaned within. She'd be stuck until the end of her days—that would be a true trap. Kat panted now, panicked. Then what? *Think, Kathleen, think!* Maybe she'd find Helene's mother. Maybe she'd help her return home? And what about Caleb? What was it about Caleb that always had her thoughts turning back to him? No, she mentally shook herself. It would be best not to wake him from whatever kind of dream this extended year was for him. He was too close to Helene, anyway, to be of real help.

She sighed, deflated, and looked out the window at the waning light. Kat would only get one chance at this. *Damn it, I'm going!* Kat tossed down the pillows first. She tried not to look at the feathery masses as they were impaled on the thick spikes of the timeless hedge. She'd tried tugging the mattress off the platform but the weight made it unmanageable. Kat had swayed and buckled under the weight of one corner of the massive pallet. She drew a deep breath, vowing not to think on it, and tossed the bedding next in one mass, hoping the bulk would provide a protective landing for her to follow. The majority stayed together as she'd planned, forming a barrier of sorts, or so she hoped. The last to go were the rolled piles of cloaks and clothing.

It was now or never. Kat hoisted herself up onto the window casement, took a deep breath, and leapt.

"Ow! Damn it!" Kat held her head. Something had given her a good whack at the back of the head. She was afraid to look, but she knew she had to assess the damage. Kat hurt in weird places. Her legs had become trapped beneath her at odd angles for so short a fall.

A quick peek was all she had the courage for. Kat opened one eye slowly. Peering almost directly over her face were Gran and

Suzy, smiling like they'd won the lottery. Kat squeezed her eyes shut, held her head, and groaned, "Ah shit, now I'm delusional."

"No, honey, you're back."

"Huh?"

"You'd been gone too long—a week on our end. We knew we had to do something."

"What?" Kat's eyes popped open, and she sat up. "Truly? I'm back? But how?"

Suzy pointed at Kat's grandmother who beamed. "Seems your gran is full of secrets."

Kat looked from one to the other. Grandma held out her arms and uncurled her fingers that revealed clasped in each hand the matching ear bobs Caleb had mentioned. Kat couldn't stop laughing and crying. She was back.

Suzy arranged to take Gran home with them for the weekend. Obviously, there was a lot to talk about, and under the watchful eye of the nursing home staff, they wouldn't be able to count on more than a half hour without interruption.

Sneaking Kat out of the nursing home in "costume" was something else entirely. Kat worried she would have to go through the scene she had been in in that play ages ago to cover for her odd attire, but it turned out that in a place filled with as much drama as a nursing home, Kat's wasn't even noticed.

And she was dying to ask questions—oh, so many questions, but once they hit the highway home Gran fell asleep, and Kat followed suit shortly thereafter. When Suzy roused her a few hours later she was terrified that coming home had been a dream. Kat was never so happy to see the antique shop as she was this evening.

While the others slept Suzy had stopped along the way back at the local Greek restaurant and gotten them all kale soup and pastitsio. Kat was barely through the door, hadn't taken her shoes off yet, when Suzy took over. She insisted they sit down and eat some food before they got "knotted up" over the Helene issue. Kat really couldn't argue. She hadn't had an appetite while being held at the house, and she'd lost a few pounds. But with the smells coming from the bags and containers, Kat didn't think she'd have a problem. From the worried glances from the two of them and the tag-team "eat more" mantra, Kat knew she must look worse than she thought. She couldn't argue with the food. But Kat paused to fling the ring to one side of the apartment and rip the pendant off her neck and do likewise with it.

Gran watched and nodded. "Wise move, honey." Gran dropped the ear bobs into the bowl in the center of the coffee table where they gathered to eat, Kat on the floor and the others on the sofa facing her.

It didn't even bother Kat that they seemed to be watching her while she ate. She was just glad to be home. Between bites she told them of her adventure. Suzy and Grandma alternated with obscenities when things turned bleak in her story.

Kat was working on another helping of pasta when she recognized Gran's I-have-something-important-to-say stance. Gran's shoulders were proudly pushed back, and she looked a full three-inches taller.

"Well, kid, you ready for a story?" Gran recounted much of what Kat had already learned from her stowed journal but now it made so much more sense having seen and done all that she had in this past trip. Plus, it was a bit surreal to hear Gran tell it firsthand. It was scarier somehow this way. When she got to the part where the journal pages ended Kat's ears picked up.

"I decided that those last few pages were too dangerous to keep in print, and you'll understand why after I explain. I tore those pages up and burned them—cast a little spell of my own, too, so that they would not be found or undone. I hoped I need never tell you this part, but I feared the power she had, feared it could turn her. That's also why I hid the bobs." She nodded to the earrings on the table.

"Where? How did you...?"

"Fish tank."

"Gran, what?"

"Bottom of the fish tank."

Kat looked at Suzy for help.

"Yep, kiddo, right there mixed in with the shiny rocks."

Gran laughed. "I still have a few tricks up my sleeve." She winked. "Never count an old lady out. That'd be a dumb move. Anyway, I had to. You see, I saw something that no one would believe had I told them. You both know they didn't believe the simpler bits of my story—denied even the parts I could prove. They sure would've locked me away forever had I told them what I am about to tell you."

They both leaned in closer, willing Gran to continue. But Kat also knew that if they rushed her she might lose her place in the story.

"I saw something most unholy—I shudder to think on it. Helene was at the hearth, and I smelled something really quite odd. I couldn't place it. It was sweet and pine-like, but not. Turns out it was the amber. She was heating it in oil, just enough to start to burn and make it malleable. I watched as she reached in with the iron ladle and set the glowing mass on a cast iron form." She paused a moment and sipped her tea. "This is where it got really strange. I saw her draw a knife to open a small vein in her wrist—not enough to be dangerous but to get a steady stream of blood flowing which she gathered into a small glass. She said some words I did not understand, other than they were some sort of spell, and then I saw her etch into the heated amber a rivulet pattern with only her fingertip and air. Into this she poured the gathered blood. That's the pattern you see there in the ear-bobs." She pointed.

Kat nodded. She recognized that pattern clearly as belonging to the set. "Gran, and the writing on the setting of the pendant?"

"I couldn't tell you. I know she had the pieces set but the etching may very well have been added by her after. I think that likely. Some spell or charm, to be sure. Here, let's test this out. You take one ear-bob in your open hand, and I'll take the other one."

They each looked at an earring and watched the red within begin to pulse and contort.

"Now, bring our hands closer together slowly, blood to blood."

As they did so, the glow got stronger, deeper, and almost frantic when nearing each other.

"I think that is why you were held. You made her stronger, blood doubling blood. It looks like she'd hoped to use you to block whatever it is Fate has chosen to bestow. I am so sorry, I hadn't any idea. But now, after your story, I see what I saw was so very much more than I feared."

It all made sense. Helene was calling blood to blood through the amber. That's how she got Kat there in the first place. Now the question was what to do about it.

Suzy echoed her thoughts. "So, kiddo, what do you do with them now?"

The thought of going back after what she'd endured was unfathomable. But then there was her curiosity...and a level of family loyalty tossed in to boot. Would Helene survive? What would happen to Adele? And Caleb? Could she walk away from it all? From him?

"I think, for now, we store the pieces separately but securely. Now that I know about this blood calling to blood thing, could I be drawn back without willing it with only one piece?"

"I don't know. Helene did it before. But to be safe, I wouldn't wear any of it unless you are willing to go back."

"Oh, believe me I am not wearing any of this—maybe ever. Actually, right now I'd like to burn the lot of it. In fact, in the morning I am getting rid of any amber in the shop as well. I'll donate it...somewhere, for God's sake. No, after what I saw, I am not taking any risks."

Suzy nodded. "Might be extreme but wise."

Kat's emotions overwhelmed her. She felt everything at once. She felt furious and sorry for Helene in the same breath. She hated Helene for how she'd used her. Kat wanted to burn all traces of her and erase all knowledge of her. She couldn't even begin to think about forgiving her. Kat would never trust Helene again. Kat wanted to scream at her, shake her, and she couldn't. And then she remembered that there had been good things, too. Kat hated that even now, after all she had done, she had a softness for her. Hating her was easier.

"In fact," Kat suddenly had an idea, "How about each of you take a piece with you? Gran can store the bobs again and Suzy the ring. That way I can be sure—"

"Sure to have a way back home." Suzy finished her thought, nodding. "I like that. And I have a gun safe that should store this little time-bomb just fine."

Kat cocked an eyebrow. "Some pacifist."

"Hey, it's great dry storage for my weed. Had to get something out of that first marriage that was worth keeping."

Kat looked over at Gran. "Well, no one noticed the ear bobs where I hid them before so no reason to fix what ain't broke." She smiled. "Plus, I made sure to put the fish tank and contents in The Will, to go to you." She winked.

"Creepy, Gran, but okay. I get it."

"Why yes, yes, you do."

"Wise ass."

"What was that?"

"I love you, Gran."

"Aw, I love you too, dip shit."

And they laughed. It was so good to be home.

44

Decisions

Over the next several weeks the pendant glowed, calling to Kat. She left it out in the glass dish on the center of the coffee table where she could easily check on it with a glance. Kat didn't plan on touching it anytime soon. Occasionally, she'd come in from the shop and see the neighbor's cat poking at it, nudging it with his nose while a low hum could be heard. Kat made a mental note to remember to keep the bedroom window closed from here on to keep him out. Last thing she'd need was the cat running off with the damn thing.

Kat, if asked, wasn't totally sure why she left it out like that—part of her told herself to keep an eye on it. Part of her knew better, knew that she was feeling guilty, worried. After all Helene'd done to her—and done for her, to be fair, Kat felt guilty about abandoning her. She knew the logic was flawed, but she couldn't help it.

Kat was at the sink rinsing pasta shells to prep for stuffing with a cheese mixture when Suzy came in.

"You look distracted, kiddo."

"Hmm. What?"

"Exactly. And cooking? Looks enough to feed an army. You expecting company?" Suzy poked her nose under a pot lid and sniffed deeply.

"Just you."

"Bullshit. What's up?" Suzy put her hands on her hips.

"Nothing."

"God, you're a bad liar. I know that pendant has been lighting up like crazy and doing that creepy chanting thing. Remember I have the matching ring. Fairly kept me up last night."

"I thought you'd locked it away?"

"Yeah." Suzy gestured toward the table. "Like you." She pulled out a velvet pouch. Kat could see the ring pulsing through the thick fabric.

Kat stood there, wooden spoon in hand, motionless for a moment, and then softly said, "What should I do?"

"What do you think you should do?"

"Seriously, Suzy, none of that Yoda crap. Tell me what to do."

"Honey, you know I can't. I'll tell you what..." Suzy took the spoon from her hand and turned the stove and the warming oven off. "How about you talk your way though it? I've found that if I say what I'm thinking out loud it often reveals what I need to do."

Kat made a face, scrunching her nose and pursing her lips with doubt.

Suzy huffed out a breath and continued, "I don't know exactly why it works, but maybe it has to do with the choosing of the words. When I choose how to frame my problem, I tend to 'lean' in a direction. Sometimes I knew the answer all along, and sometimes I surprise myself. Subconscious Freud stuff—man's famous for a reason. It couldn't hurt to try." She gave Kat a soft shove.

"Well, it's like this..." Kat paced an aggravated march throughout the small kitchen. "I can't stop thinking about her situation."

"Kiddo, you want to sit down? I could make some tea."

"No. No, I think the pacing helps, feels like I am doing something."

Suzy nodded and hoisted herself up on the countertop to get out of her way. At Kat's surprised pause, Suzy laughed. "It ain't Cirque du Soleil. When I get too old to lift my ass then move me into the home with your gran. Such a cynic." She shook her head side to side.

"Okay then...back to the situation at hand," Kat drew a deep breath. "I know Helene's feeling trapped, but what she did to me was so many layers of wrong. And what exactly did she think I could do to help? I haven't been any help so far. Was she going to try to hurt me?" Kat stopped and turned, thinking it through. "No, that doesn't make any sense as my 'being' is part of her legacy, isn't it?" Kat didn't wait for an answer but kept pacing. "Okay, so let's recap—so far she's stalled time. That's the best I can sum it up. But that tombstone exists... So is it her fate to die no matter what she does? Could I actually protect her? Do I even want to? Should I? How can I help anyway? Time continuum crap—ah, damn it! God, this is frustrating!"

Kat's pacing matched her frantic reasoning until she stopped and flung her arms out in frustration. She drew in another deep breath as Suzy motioned for her to continue. "So, let's see. Helene is family, and she did teach me things about myself and magic. She did treat me well—well, until that last bit. But that was also after Alastair nearly killed her. Caleb seemed okay, and he's clued in to something being wrong. Maybe he could step in? But then again Alastair is his brother; that'd be a tough spot. Then again she lied and manipulated us all—including Gran. Although you have to love that Gran outwitted her in the end. Fish tank. Positively brilliant. "

Kat stopped pacing, and faced Suzy. "Wait a minute! That's it! If she can call to me through time then I should be able to call to you and Gran. I need to go back and at least try to help, or I'd feel like a horrible person the rest of my life. And I won't get stuck there as I'll have you and Gran anchoring me here! You did it before with me on the other end. We should be fine. I bet I can travel with just the pendant. I've done it before with just one piece, and the pendant obviously has more power. You hang on to the ring and Gran to her bobs."

"That's my girl."

"You knew that is what I'd say?"

"Not exactly, but I thought you might. You take things on that you couldn't have changed and carry such guilt."

Something in her face made Kat realize that at that moment they were both thinking about Sky.

"I believe that if you think you might be able to help, that's what you'd do." Suzy hugged Kat tightly. "And you got that damn straight that no one is going to take you from me. Now, let's go pick up your Gran. We've got work to do."

45

Blood Debt

Kat was greeted with open arms by a frantic Helene. Her hair mussed, it was apparent she had been crying for some time, her eyes rimmed a raw red. Her nightgown was unkempt and unwashed for what looked to be several days. She clutched Kat to her tightly, shaking while telling her of her untold joy at having Kathleen come to her aid.

As soon as Helene loosened her grasp, Kat looked about to see where she had landed. She was in the hidden room between what had been her bedroom and Helene's. The worktable was on its side, its legs removed, to make room for a small bed in the corner.

Before Kat could ask she responded. "I know it's not ideal, but it will be temporary, I promise you. You'd left so hastily last time and to return in like manner would cause too many questions. I'll put you up here for the night, and then make better arrangements on the morrow."

"I left for good reason, as you well know." Kat cocked an eyebrow.

"Well, we'll not dwell on that right now. Let's get you settled into bed. Patrice will bring you some tea to help you sleep, and we'll sort this all in the morning."

At Kat's raised eyebrow, Helene continued, "Just tea. Camomile."

Patrice moved from where she had been standing in the shadows and set about making a pot of tea on the small hearth's blue flame.

Kat hadn't realized it was night here as there were no windows and no source of light in the room save what was brought in or summoned. It was only early afternoon the day she left so she wasn't really tired but saw no way around it. She resigned herself to going to bed early.

Some time later, Kat didn't know how long had passed, she awoke in a cold sweat. The same odd, blue flame burned in the hearth although it threw no heat. Helene sat beside her, mopping her brow.

"Hush, dear, and go back to sleep. You've nothing to fear." Helene soothed Kat back to sleep with her words and gentle ministrations.

The next time she awoke Kat felt dry, parched beyond all belief, ridiculously sluggish, and muddle-headed. She couldn't seem to focus her eyes. Her head felt thick, her thoughts slow as if in a fog. Patrice now sat beside her while Helene busied herself among the fireplace ashes.

Kat turned her head to get a better look and tried to shift her body to do the same when she realized she was tethered, hand and foot, to the bed. Kat panicked and strained against the restraints. She violently pulled and tugged, making the small bedstead shake and knock against the floorboards. In her attempt to break free she realized the true danger—she was being drained. Kat could see from the many lacerations on her forearms that she was being bloodlet. A pan stood at the side of the bed slowly being filled with her blood.

"Helene, damn it! What are you doing?"

Without turning around to face her, Helene continued with whatever she was doing. "Patrice, please make sure her stays are secure."

"Helene! You can't do this! What the hell are you doing?"

Now she turned, her eyes slanted in a cold glare, Helene's face firmly set in a grimace. "I am doing what must be done. And don't worry, you'll live. You are no use to me dead. I just need your help for a few more days and then I will send you away or back as you choose."

Kat watched as Helene strode to the side of the bed, staunched the flow of blood momentarily with a cloth, and poured what had just been in her veins into a small pot that hung from the hearth. In front of the hearth Kat saw a tray of what looked to be softened honey.

"Wait, wait! What is that?"

"You mean to tell me you don't recognize amber, such as you are wearing?" Helene laughed softly.

Kat tried to push herself up on an elbow but failed as she was tied tightly. "But amber doesn't melt, it just burns away, like incense. I should know as I've sold enough of the stuff."

Helene turned to face Kathleen, fire reflected in her eyes, furious, and set with anger. "You silly girl!" She shouted. "This is why you will never have the power I have. It melts because I make it do so!" She made a sweeping gesture with her arm. "Do you seriously doubt that a witch who can bring you back in time cannot make a bit of amber melt? It is because you say 'can't' that you will always be small! I have defied Time and will overcome Fate.

A bit of petrified tree sap is nothing to my powers." She leaned in to growl in her thinly controlled rage. "You see only the natural laws and not how to shape them to your will, and that is why you will always be weak, puny, and insignificant." She paused, struggled to calm and center herself.

"Watch as I 'can't,'" Helene said, and then laughed.

Kat could only watch in horror as Helene took a short stick, waving it over the amber. Her actions were mirrored when the designs she formed in the air created matching runnels in the face of the stones. While still making no direct contact, Helene poked and scraped the amber as she saw fit, into patterns of unknown meaning to Kat. On top of this she poured some of the contents of the smaller pot, steeped with Kathleen's congealing blood. Kat fully understood now what Suzy had researched so long ago and how the pulsing pattern of red came to be in the pendant she had worn. It made Kat shake with fear and disgust. She felt nauseated. The reality was far more horrifying than one could imagine...and the smell of heated blood tinny and putrid.

Helene turned to face Kathleen directly. "On some level you had to already know so don't act so surprised. How else do you think that blood can draw to blood? But this time we are creating amulets to strengthen and protect me. A far more admirable cause than mere time travel, don't you think?"

Kat gave up straining against her restraints when she realized Helene was right. She had accepted it on some level. But it made Kat sad nonetheless for who she'd become, innocence lost, thanks to her tutelage.

"Patrice, let's free her arms and sit her up. She must needs be thirsty and starved. We mustn't take too much, or I won't be able to keep my promise."

In a rush, Kat shoved up, attempting to bolt upright once freed, but instead found herself dizzy and light-headed. Her

head spun, and the floor appeared to lurch below her. She was far weaker than she had suspected when lying down.

"How long have I...?"

"Just a few days, and we took breaks so there is nothing to worry about."

Kat was indignant, and oh, how she hated her now. She needed out, and she needed out now. Kat flailed pathetically. This was worse than when she had been tied up! She couldn't muster any energy. Kat was helpless. Her whole body shook in frustration.

Patrice helped Kathleen into a sitting position, propped her up with pillows. She then brought forward a tray of food Kat hadn't observed before. The tray held a kidney and steak pie that was more gravy than anything else. Patrice served a similar pie to Helene in front of the hearth. Kat's blood chilled in her chest when she saw that Helene dipped the dipper into the pot that she knew carried her blood and covered the pie on her plate with the wine-colored, sticky mass. The bile in Kat's stomach roiled. It was all she could do to fight the feeling.

Kat knew she had to get out of here—this was madness! She needed her strength back. She was a sitting duck in the state she was now. Her hand shook wildly as if palsied when she reached for the bowl. Kat was forced to allow Patrice to feed her when she realized she couldn't even control a spoon to her own mouth. Days of inactivity and the rubber band sensations in her arms made her helpless to do anything to help herself. It was terrifying. In that moment Kat thought of Gran. She tasted her own tears as they rolled down her face openly. Kat was at her own personal bottom. And that's all she remembered. Kat hadn't figured on the food being drugged, as well as the tea, and she nodded off again.

She awoke not knowing how much time had passed, alone, unfettered, and wrists bound in bandages. Kat was somewhat relieved but knew until she got home she wasn't truly safe. She dragged and pulled herself into a sitting position. Her head spun, and her skull felt split open. Her body ached everywhere, and she felt so very weak. But she had to try to get away. Kat pulled herself up and promptly fell to the floor. She lay still, panicked, worried someone had heard, but then realized someone noticing might not be such a bad thing. Kat pulled herself up again only to stumble and fall. She decided to stay down and began to crawl through the passage that wound between the walls. Slowly she made her way towards her old room.

Kat hoped beyond hope that she could muster the power to summon the door and escape. She reached for the reassurance of the pendant, the pendant that would take her home. *Shit! Oh shit!* It dawned on her that Helene must've taken it. Of course she had! "God, I am so stupid sometimes. Get a grip, Kat," she whispered to herself. *Sarah Connor up!* Kat channeled her favorite heroine—Sarah Connor from the *Terminator* movies—her go-to badass. *Okay*, she thought, *I lost my ticket home, but that couldn't be helped. But I'll be damned if I quit.* Kat only needed to get away from Helene. She'd figure out the next step later. Breathe and move. That was all she could do.

Helene was mad—mad with fear and mad with power—and would do whatever she needed to get her way to safety. Kat had made a mistake in having compassion—a mistake she vowed not to repeat as she crawled and slowly dragged her body across the floor boards.

When Kat got to where she knew the secret door had been, she mustered all the strength she had to pull herself up by the boards and wall framing, scrabbling against the wood. She wondered if she sounded much like a rat would trying to chew his way in. Kat used anything she had, nails, elbows, and even her shoulder to shove and wedge herself upright. She fought the nausea and pushed away the doubt.

Finally there, Kat stood in the spot she had opened so many times before. Dizzy but determined, she panted and willed her breath to calm and sync with her heartbeat. Her head pounded, and she could swear she could hear the blood, what was left of it, pulsing through her veins in throbbing waves. Kat focused on centering her thoughts, slowed everything until one thought was supreme, opening that door. Kat said the words she'd said time and again as she spread her hands against where the doorframe should be and willed it open.

It refused her. Kat wouldn't panic yet but drew in a breath, slowed her thoughts, and concentrated. Nothing. It would not let her pass. At first she was bewildered, disoriented. Kat looked about frantically, making sure that she did in fact stand within the right panel, the correct recess in the wall. Had she somehow miscalculated? No. She was trapped.

A low sob slipped out before Kat forced herself to resist succumbing. She banged her forehead in frustration against the plaster twice, desperately scratching at the wall.

And then Kat heard a returning knock.

Kat stood silently, listening, straining, willing it to occur again. It did. She rested her cheek against the cool plaster, this time joyful tears fell. And then she heard a voice.

"Are you in there?" Caleb paused so long Kat wasn't sure if she had imagined his voice calling from the other side. But then she heard, "Kathleen, I beg of you, if you are in there, give me a sign."

It was Caleb! Kat gasped, found she couldn't form a word in response, her throat parched mute. Instead she rapped on the wall three times in response. Three raps were returned.

Kat swallowed deeply, willed herself to horsely croak, "Caleb, help me."

"All right. I don't know exactly how to get you out. I believe there is magic afoot. Let's counter it with willpower. Do me this favor—rap to either side of where the wall is thinnest, to let me know where there is only plaster, not beams, and then stand back."

Kat nodded.

"Kathleen, did you hear me?"

"Yes, yes." Kat knocked to either side of her body across the span of plaster and lathe and then wrenched and shifted her body behind the nearest post.

Kat heard crashing and pounding from the other side of the wall, followed by cursing. After a momentary pause she heard a deep thud. Kat peered around the post and saw the wall punctured with the iron, fireplace poker. Caleb jabbed, poked, and tore at the plaster until a section fell out, lathes splintered and fell around her bare feet. There was an opening not much bigger than the size of a pie plate when she saw his head pop through the hole. Kat could see him clearly, but he couldn't see her as his eyes were unfocused and unaccustomed to the darkness within the wall.

"I'll get you out. I swear it."

But before Kat could respond she heard Helene's voice and a chill ran through her body. Helene stood on the other side of the wall with Caleb!

46

Biding Time

"So, you'd wreck my home to get to the girl?" Sarcasm dripped from every syllable, her voice eerily low and controlled.

"Helene, what have you done?" Caleb demanded.

"Oh, don't you speak to me that way. I've done no real harm. I just needed her for a spell." She chuckled at the pun.

"I demand that you release her!"

"Do not dare speak to me in that manner. I am your brother's wife and deserve respect as such. However, as I have no further need of her at the moment, let's get this over with before you further mar my home."

With a quick flick of a hand the doorway reappeared. Helene released the counter spell with an almost imperceptible movement. Kat peered around the doorframe and into the room.

"Just keep her close but hidden from your brother, and I'll leave her to you." Helene turned to walk away, but paused to glare at Caleb directly for emphasis. "But cross me and you'll never see her again."

With a curt nod, Caleb quickly stepped through the door that had manifested in the wall and led Kat into the daylight, supporting her with one arm around her torso. His other hand held the hand closest.

"I want to take her from here."

"You may take her as far as the rooms at the end of your hall but no farther until I am sure I have no more need of her assistance. But I warn you again, keep her out of Alastair's sight. I finally got him to forget her disappearance. Her return would cause undue…complications."

Caleb's eyes traveled over Kathleen's form, taking in the bandages, the blood stains, the unkempt hair. He couldn't help his nose involuntarily wrinkling at the unwashed smell. Kat flushed and looked down in shame.

Helene laughed. "Even now she is proud."

Kat looked up in feeble defiance that was quelled when she noticed that about Helene's neck lay a choker of amber, blood stones, evenly spaced with garnets, making the threads of red from within the stones stand out more brilliantly, and all edged and framed in fine gold.

Helene saw where Kathleen's eyes lit, so Helene, with a smug smile, stroked the choker lovingly before she whisked her skirts about and left the room.

Caleb turned to Kat and softly began, "If it's too much for you, you could rest here in your old room until you are better."

"No!" Kat shivered but not from the cold air. "I wouldn't and couldn't feel safe here anymore knowing what is behind that wall."

"What is behind that wall?" Caleb shifted as if to peer in but Kat stayed him with panicked hands on his sleeve.

"Ask me another time and I might tell you." Kat was too exhausted, too angry, and too weak to begin the tale. And she didn't know where to begin to explain to Caleb all she knew.

Seemingly heedless of her embarrassment, Caleb called down the hall to the nearest maid to assist in getting Kathleen down to the East Wing where he'd taken residence in a suite of rooms long abandoned. Kat made a feeble attempt to maintain some semblance of decency and composure but quickly dropped any effort to do so. Her head spun, beating madly in pain. Her legs ached from long disuse, and she was painfully aware that she was standing in a long-soiled, nightdress. With every movement her muscles screamed in protest, but she was determined to get as far away from that room as possible.

Best intentions aside, Kat didn't protest when Caleb swiftly drew her off her feet to carry her the rest of the way to his rooms. Their progress had been slow as she stumbled often, taking a misstep or from leaning heavily upon him for balance. Somewhere along the way Kat passed out from the dehydration, the loss of blood, or the endless potions Helene had used to keep her sedated as she robbed her literally of her life's blood.

When Kat came to sometime later, she pushed herself up on elbows from the bed upon which she lay to better see her surroundings and realized she wasn't alone. Caleb sat in a chair on the opposite side of the room, watching her struggle to sit upright. He watched without saying a word, fidgeting with something in his lap. Kat quickly realized, to her horror, that he held in his hands her undergarments, a Nike sports bra and boy-short underpants. Kat nervously patted herself down and realized she was wearing others under her shift.

Caleb observed Kathleen's rising color. He awkwardly cleared his throat and looked away, avoiding eye contact, as he spoke. "They've been laundered but a bit worse for the wear I'm afraid." His eyes turned back to Kat as he held the bra out to show her. The straps were hanging unattached, the bra cut through as if by a knife or rough scissors. He pointed to the Nike swoosh symbol.

"A crest?"

"No, a maker's mark."

"Curious." Caleb again cleared his throat, "Sorry about the..." He pointed at the obvious cuts in the garment. "It was simply impossible to remove otherwise."

Embarrassment alone carried Kat out of bed and across the floor to retrieve the garments. She snatched the bra from him and deftly unhooked the hidden fasteners.

"Oh, I guess not." Caleb smirked, attempting but failing to look ashamed.

Kat slid in the chair opposite of him with a sigh and winced at the sharp pain behind her eyes. Adrenaline boost gone, she felt disoriented, unbalanced.

"2017."

"What?"

"You asked me once where I was from."

"Is that a street address?"

"No, a date. More specifically a year."

"A year! Surely not?"

"What can I tell you? You have the proof in your hands."

Caleb stood and awkwardly returned the underpants to Kat. "I'm sorry I ruined the other," pointing to the bra. "If it's any consolation, the maid helped with this." He gestured vaguely. "I only looked to be sure I only cut the garment and not you."

Kat nodded. She couldn't care less what he saw as he had gotten her free of that monster, Helene.

"Well, you've given me something to think on—2017." He shook his head, processing it. "I shall leave you now to dress or rest as you see fit. I'll send Aida up to assist you."

"But Alastair mustn't—"

"Aida works for me, and me alone. Your secret is safe."

She passed the time slowly moving about the small room, walking tentatively by grasping pieces of furniture along the way for support. Kat took in her surroundings as she moved. The bed was covered with a coverlet of ivory, embroidered with flowers. The rest of the room, starting at the foot of the bed, had the same dark tartan weaves Kat remembered that Caleb favored. Other than the two chairs opposite, there was nothing much to see. The room was spare and tiny. It was too small a chamber to be a guest room or one of the family rooms. She was undoubtedly in a dressing room, a maid's or manservant's chamber, probably off of his suite of rooms.

Kathleen was fingering the bed covering, tracing along the intricate stitching, when Aida came into the chamber.

"He thought you might need a bit of a woman's touch in here. I hope it suits."

"Yes, thank you, Aida. I could see a woman's hand in this." Kat ran a hand across the spread.

"He's a kind one, that one is. He's been watching over you night and day."

"How long have I been here?"

"Just a day and a half. Fretful sleeper though, so I'm surprised you are up already after what you've been though." Aida nodded, pointedly looking at the clean bandages Kathleen wore about her wrists.

"Do I have you to thank for this as well?"

"Aye, miss. He didn't want the rest of the household to know your business. I don't think I need to tell you the other, the elder, is not an understanding sort." At that she looked nervously about her. "I shouldn't speak thus. They say the walls have ears."

If she only knew, Kat thought.

Kat spent a few more days in the maid's quarters, as she learned she'd correctly guessed earlier. Aida came at regular intervals and saw to her every need, although she wasn't as chatty as on her first day awake. She kept Kathleen fed with thick broths, sweet wine, and rich meats which quickly built her energy up. But Kat couldn't leave the room—that was one of the conditions she had to keep for Helene to allow Caleb to take Kat from her. Kat was still trapped but in a much better cell. So she made it a point to take daily strolls through Caleb's suite of rooms to strengthen her muscles and to fight the fatigue that was always threatening to drag her under. Undoubtedly, time would be required to dispel the effects of whatever she had been drugged with.

Caleb was often gone before Kat awoke and seldom spent time in his rooms at all. She wondered about it and asked him once when he came to have tea with her, but all he'd say was that he was weighing and measuring an idea. What idea, he wouldn't divulge, so it nagged Kat's thoughts from time to time when she wasn't already being paranoid about Helene.

Kat knew the date had to be fast approaching when Helene's fated demise was to occur. She couldn't help but wonder if Helene had solved her problem. Kat took to watching the gardens from the window seat in Caleb's room. She made sure to conceal herself behind the curtains, leaving only the smallest opening by which she could peer out. Kat was rewarded twice with the view of Helene, Alastair, and the baby out for a walk. Helene now pushed the pram proudly while Alastair kept a hand protectively on her lower back. They seemed the picture of happiness. At one point Kat saw Helene pause, look up to where she sat. And while Kat knew she couldn't see her, she also knew Helene could sense her. Helene feigned interest in a bloom to cover the brief stop, threw a glare at the window, and moved along. Kat shuddered and pulled her shawl closer around her shoulders.

47

Cheating Fate

Finally, the evening of Helene's fated death was upon them. Kat paced the room, absentmindedly thumping her right thigh with a closed fist until Caleb's raised eyebrow cued her in to the nervous gesture. Caleb knew something was amiss, and while Kat didn't dare tell him exactly what was wrong, she could tell by how he watched her that he knew, nonetheless, that she feared something imminent. Caleb dined with her in his rooms that evening. He told her that he thought he'd need to feign an excuse from dinner, but it was Helene who'd excused herself earlier, claiming a headache. Kat, who knew her better, knew she was undoubtedly protecting herself somehow with the dark magic she'd been progressing in with the help of Kat's stolen blood.

Jumpy throughout dinner, Kat knew she was not much company for Caleb although he tried to steer her to lighthearted topics. At every noise, she started. Kat developed minute shakes in her hands, and the more she tried to stop the twitch, the worse it got. She gave up on the soup altogether as she spilled more than she ate. And, frankly, she wasn't tasting any of it as her mind was elsewhere. Kat strained to hear a sound, any sound, to tell her how this night would progress. Her pulse hammered in her ears, pounding in anticipation of—something, anything. At every footfall in the corridor, she was convinced Helene came for her, to do who knows what, but she feared it nonetheless. Kat hoped that when this night was done her nightmare might be over, and perhaps she could finally go home. Mentally Kat screamed that this needed to end, and yet she knew she was powerless to do anything but wait. So she stood to take another agitated walk about the room, anxious to be doing something, as the meal was already ruined and ignored.

"It's today, isn't it?"

"Hmm. What?"

"Whatever it was that Helene needed you for is here, now, isn't it?"

Kat stopped and turned to face Caleb. The time for lies was over—tonight whatever would be, would be. "I believe so." Kat choked out softly as she looked him directly in the eyes.

"So it'll be over soon then?"

"I hope so."

"And then?" Caleb stood and moved closer to her.

She paused to think. Kat had only thought of this night, nothing further. "I guess it depends on how it works out for her."

"Cryptic." Caleb nodded to himself. "She's a troubled woman, Helene. And dangerous, I think. Possibly mad?"

"Yes," Kat whispered. A tear leaked out before she could brush it away.

"I'm here. I'll not let anything happen to you." Caleb closed the distance between them. He brushed the tear away with the gentle swipe of a finger before taking her hands within his own.

"No, if she comes for me, I'll be the one who'll handle it—I may be the only one who can." Kat sighed, straightened her shoulders, and lifted her chin. Whether she was trying to convince Caleb or herself that she was up for the task was unclear. "I just wish the hours would slip by faster tonight."

Kat didn't attempt to go to sleep. She was too jumpy, tense, unsettled, and was doing little to hide it. They had said nothing to each other, but almost as a tacit agreement Caleb stayed. They sat up all night before the hearth, silent in their own thoughts for the most part.

It was nearing dawn when a bleary-eyed Caleb spoke, "I have to know...if this, whatever this is, is over, will you go back?"

"Back?"

"To where, er...when, you are from?"

"Yes, I hope so."

Caleb nodded, said not a word more, and waited out the rest of the night with her. At dawn, Kat, exhausted, crawled into her bed still fully dressed, stopping only to pull off her boots. She knew she would need sleep to be ready to face whatever came next. Kat stretched and breathed a sigh of relief, rolling her head across her shoulders. It was over! It had to be. Kat felt Caleb pull up the bedding to cover her shoulders before she nodded off.

Early the next afternoon, fully refreshed and cheerful like she hadn't been in ages, Kathleen asked Aida for Helene's whereabouts. Aida told her she was in the small library and quite alone, the master having left on a trip that morning. Surely, Kat thought, it was safe to leave Caleb's room now.

Kat made her mind up to confront Helene and be done with

it. She should be in a fine mood having passed the danger.

But Kat was wrong. If she had been agitated and jumpy last night, Helene was more so this afternoon. She looked like she hadn't slept in days—her eyes were bloodshot, her hair in disarray, and her hands nervously twitched from time to time as if in a spasm. When she saw Kat she became enraged. Color rose in her cheeks, and her eyes narrowed.

"You dare come to me without invitation!"

"Helene," Kat entreated, "It's over. You're safe. You've won."

"No, no, no!" Helene shook her head wildly. She looked mad, convulsively shifting, her gaze darting about the room. "You never can cheat death—ever. It's a tease. Death is taunting me, lurking behind the curtains, whispering he's come for me!"

"Helene, no, you're safe." Kat felt a tightness in her chest and mentally pushed down the bile that rose in her throat at the thought of this not being finished.

"I'll never be safe so long as Alastair lives. I know that now. I may have escaped this time, but it's not over. Can't be over."

"Helene," Kat said firmly, "it's over, and it's time to send me home. You've no need of me now, and you said you didn't want Alastair to see me, so send me home. Now's your chance."

"No, I might need you again." Helene shook her head wildly. Then her tone shifted, softened, "We're good together, you and I. We need to stay together, help each other as family."

Her stomach flipped and rolled, anxiety threatened to take over, but Kat straightened her back and willed it to pass. "I don't belong here, Helene. You have everything you need right here. You don't need me anymore." When Kat saw her unmoved, she tried a different tack. "You'd be safer without me. No one for him to question you about and wonder."

Kat could see Helene thinking it over, mulling the idea in her head. "Maybe."

Helene's eyes became vacant, unaware of anything or anyone. It sent a chill down Kat's spine. She left Helene in the small library muttering to herself, undoubtedly having a battle with reason.

Alastair returned three evenings later, and the screams could be heard everywhere as they echoed throughout the house. Kat's heart stopped for a beat in terror. She gasped, gulping air, as she ran towards Helene's voice, but Caleb beat her to their rooms.

They found Alastair astride Helene, strangling her upon their bed while she laughed madly even as her face purpled. Kat froze, unsure of what to do, watching the scene as if it were in a horrible late night movie. Caleb grabbed Alastair from behind, tried to pull him off of her. He succeeded briefly, releasing Helene from Alistair's grip. His action broke Kat out of her helpless daze.

Helene reared up, fire in her eyes as she glared around the room wildly, meeting each of them with piercing scrutiny. Kat could feel Helene's hatred permeate her bones with a searing intensity. Her palpable energy knocked Kat breathless and slammed the center of her chest, pushing her back a pace. Kat watched, horrified, as Helene's head swung from side to side as if unhinged. Venomous words, too rapid to recall, spilled from her tongue, some in English and others in an ancient tongue, dark and forbidding with its heavy consonants and droning intonation. Helene paused a moment and gasped for air, tentatively touching the imprints Alastair's fingers had made upon her throat. Kat could feel heat swell with her anger, slapping at her like the gust from the proximity to a volcano. Helene's eyes slipped back into her head, only white now showing, as she reverted fully into the ancient tongue Kat knew she used to create spells. Kat trembled and grew light-headed, and felt helpless in the face of this maelstrom. She was powerless to do anything but observe Helene's hands as they purposely stroked the blood stones about her neck as one might stroke a favored pet. The low drone of chanting could be heard echoing in the stones, magnifying the words upon Helene's lips.

Kat jumped back a few steps as she watched Helene grow and swell as a heavy, hazy, purple smoke filled the room. It swirled about, engulfing each of them, threatening suffocation. She was simultaneously awe-inspiring and terrifying. Helene no longer looked human but monstrous with her feral anger and daunting size. Kat had grossly underestimated her powers and stood as helpless as a lamb before the slaughter. She bit her lip, and so desperately wanted to look away but couldn't. Fear kept Kat riveted to Helene's face and her fate.

Alastair's eyes widened, and he screamed, "Witch! Whore! Demon!"

With his words, Kat was released from her fear-induced trance. From the doorway where she stood, she urgently called to Helene and begged her to retreat, but she was ignored. Kat took a deep breath and then released it. She closed her eyes, focused inward, and tried calling to her mentally, but Helene easily brushed her attempts off. Kat was as helpless as the others against her rage. Kat felt damned regardless, so she did the only thing she could think to do—Kat ran towards her and tugged at her sleeve to get her attention.

The face Helene turned to her was one Kat had never seen on a human. She seemed possessed of hate—cold, evil, calculating hate. Veins pulsed in her temples, her skin appeared to wrinkle before her, grayed, and mottled. Her eyes glowed eerily orange from an unnatural internal light, her gaze painful. Kat could feel Helene measure her, and then she laughed. Her laughter buffeted Kat with waves of force. But Kat would be damned before she went down without a fight! She lunged for Helene's necklace just as Alastair took the fire poker and hit her soundly on the side of her head. The necklace pulled free, breaking apart, scattering stones across the floor as Helene turned to battle her husband.

Instinctively, Kat reached to grab one of the stones as it skittered across the floor. Her gaze landed on Caleb, and she paused. Kat held his glance for but a moment, and in that moment a thousand words and thoughts flooded her. But when she bent to retrieve an amber she felt the pull of the stone pulse in her hand. Kat quickly lifted her eyes to Caleb as he lunged toward her, arms outstretched. He yelled a pained, "Kathleen, nooooo!" Then he and the room dimmed, and were gone.

48

What If?

"Oh, thank God!" Suzy hugged Kat tightly to her. She cried and rocked, and Kat couldn't help but cry as well. "We'd tried for days and couldn't find you. I thought I'd lost you."

"Never again, Suzy, never again. I am putting my time traveling days away for good, starting with this."

Kat took off her shoe and smashed the recently-formed, blood stone from Helene's necklace until it shattered. "I'm never going to be this vulnerable again." Kat paused, looked at the crushed bits, and slid to the floor and on to her knees, overtaken by racking sobs.

It was fall again. Kat looked forward to the colors of the leaves turning and the following snow. Life seemed blessedly simple now, and she was content to be a shopkeeper and Gran's legacy. Gran had passed a few weeks earlier, and Kat buried her with the amber bobs on her ears. Some of the aunts had muttered at them, wondering where they'd been hidden. When asked, Kat told them they were a gift—she still stayed as much to the truth as possible. After all they'd been through it seemed a fitting end. Kat knew it was what Gran would've wished. She'd had the last word, and that was important to Gran.

Kat tugged her sweater closer around her and felt a sort of peace from the shop now. It were as if she had a part of Gran with her every day. And the time in the past made Kat appreciate the furniture and baubles so much more. Some of it reminded her of Caleb, too, and Kat found that comforting as well, although bittersweet.

Suzy and Kat eventually took a trip abroad to England. There were things Kat still had to know, and they couldn't find the answers in the States. Suzy spent some time researching the family and church registers, and they traced the churchyard where Helene was buried. Most of the abbey was in almost unrecognizable ruins, but enough remained to cause Kat to shiver in the memory of it all. But their trip confirmed Helene had died that last night Kat had been there. To be fair, Helene couldn't blame anyone but herself for that one. The house was gone—long ago burned down by some freak lightening strike. Kat found that somewhat fitting as so much power had once been contained there. Of Caleb, Kat found no news in the old papers and records, but maybe that was a good thing, too. Gran had always said that "no news was good news."

She'd lost the pendant—or rather Helene had taken it from her, so that was long gone and lost forever. But the ring she found she couldn't part with—partially because Gran gave it to her. Kat thought she might sell the metal for scrap and destroy the stone like she had the other. But being undecided, she locked it in the store safe, tucked in that small, leather box she'd asked Gran about so long ago. However, after seeing Helene's grave, Kat knew for sure that she was gone. There'd been no other contact and enough time had passed—literally and figuratively. She no longer feared the ring and wore it again on her finger.

Kat leaned against the front counter and sipped some of Suzy's seasonal, mulled cider, and couldn't help but reflect on all that had passed as she tended to do when business was slow. Kat asked Suzy once why it seemed Gran got better with her memory so close to the end so that they'd never needed the code word. Suzy believed that talking about the past, both hers and Helene's past, probably freed her. Kat liked to think it helped in some way.

And now it was the season for family again, and Kat had new ideas for the shop on that account—especially since her adventures in the past. She would fill the window display with hope and warmth, warm golds and rich, jewel tones. Although there was a crisp nip in the air, Kat kept the window cracked open to let the air circulate. She drew a deep breath. She could admit to being melancholy at times—especially when she thought of Caleb.

Kat had taken to the odd habit of rubbing the stone in her ring as if to polish it against the sleeve at her wrist—an absent-minded habit. Today, as she did so, Kat couldn't help thinking of Caleb and wondering *what if*. She was so deep in her thoughts that she didn't hear the tinkle of the shop's door chimes until the door snapped shut.

And there, in the doorway, stood Caleb, smiling broadly and holding out, one in each hand, Helene's remaining blood stones.

R. S. Beck

Born Rebecca Sánchez, Beck was raised in the Hudson Valley of upstate New York. Beck often reflects on the people and places of her youth in her writing. Of the first generation on both sides of her family to speak English as a first language, Beck was taught early on the importance of words—the right words. However, like many, Beck had to leave home to realize what she needed in a college was in her (metaphorical) backyard at her beloved SUNY New Paltz. There, Beck continued her education and received both her Bachelors and Masters degrees in English. Beck later traded the Shawangunk Mountains of New York for those surrounding Asheville, North Carolina where she spends her day largely in the past—teaching about dead British writers. On weekends, she likes to treasure hunt with her husband, rummaging through estate sales, and collecting pottery and blown glass from local artists. She is enslaved by two cats that frequently let her know her services are lacking. However, her grown children seem to tolerate her better as she makes a mean cheesecake.

CPSIA information can be obtained
at www.ICGtesting.com
Printed in the USA
FFHW011321091019
55440384-61232FF

9 781943 419777